GOLD FOR THE CAESARS

by

Florence A. Seward

Prentice-Hall, Inc.
Englewood Cliffs, N.J.

© 1961 by Prentice-Hall, Inc.

Copyright under International and Pan-American
Copyright Conventions.

Library of Congress Catalog Card Number 61-5519

Printed in the United States of America

35770-T

For
 My Husband, Ralph W. Barris, M. D.,
 and My Son, Richard L. Barris.

Nations and empires flourish and decay;
by turns command and in their turns, obey.
Ovid

GOLD FOR THE CAESARS

Gaius Julius Lacer was battling depression brought on by the still April heat, by concern over the fate of his chained laborers, and by suppressed fury against the imperial *praefectus* and his trio of freedmen. Back on the finished south sections of the bridge, whips were lashing human backs, although here on center-bridge not a knout was in sight. Gaius never used whip-hand methods. Lightly, his long ashwood pole touched the glistening naked back of a Negro in ankle-gyves, helping shackled Britons lay decking on the tremendous midchannel pier of the structure destined to span the turbulent Tagus River in west central Roman Spain. During the summer the treacherous Tagus dwindled to a meek stream cattle stood in, and a man could wade across in narrow places. But not now. Melting snow and rains of spring had made the river deep and bold.

"Caution, Syphax and Cifgli, caution, all of you," Gaius warned over the creak of pulleys and cranes and rasp of rocks. "You're too close to the dropoff. Rest a while."

Thus far, in the two years he had been supervising the building of the spans so ambitiously designed, Gaius had not lost a worker by accident (he tried not to remember the men dead from disease, flogging, and slow starvation) and he was responsible for nine hundred workers, including three hundred recent replacements from prisons in western Farther Spain. The task of laying the wood decks, operating stationary hoists and revolving winches, pulling wagons of squared gray granite blocks and tools and lifting dressed stones by ropes into the maw of the vast unmortared masonry was a complex job of supervision; even the rockwork—the Tagus was to be the ideal bridge of stark and classic lines rivalling the sublime simplicity of old Greek temples—was still far from completion. And it might never cross to the north bank of the Tagus if Ferox Piso, the overseer, kept scourging the slaves.

Looking south, Gaius let his eyes roam over the three hundred and more feet of finished arches where men in waist and ankle-irons pushed barrows of chisels, iron wedges, mallets, picks and levers along the surface, and others dragged hewn granite in squat wooden carts, all trying to avoid the straps of Ferox Piso and his three assistants.

Beyond the floggers on a terrace stood the legion tents and food-sheds. In the steep humped land could be seen the shallow caves where Ferox Piso occasionally let ailing laborers recuperate—and dying men die, with Gaius trying to ease their agonies and offer what comfort he could. The lesser of the slaves were dumped in the river by the legionaries of Ferox Piso.

For a while Gaius studied the red and green and white flags hanging limp above the army tents. The air seemed to have stopped breathing. The heat was suffocating. Soldiers in flashing armor and brown cloaks were shouting at slaves on land, prodding laggers lightly with spears. A man could endure that. But the laborers were dragging and pushing granite slabs down a long, shallow ramp to the stone-cutting area at the approachway of the bridge where giant man-operated hoists lifted the rocks into wagons. Other creatures could have done the work more easily.

Gaius remembered the majestic caravans of two years ago: eight pampered elephants coming and going, coming and going, dragging enormous chunks of raw granite from the quarry ten miles away. Expecting that placid and willing pachyderms would perform the heaviest work on land and in the river, Gaius had been courteously informed otherwise by the Roman freedman owner of the tusked giants and cheerful African mahouts. The Roman proprietor of beasts and Africans would count himself blessed by Vulcan if Rome ever paid him for the hauling alone, and a wise man never petitioned the emperor for large or small sums owing. In Caesar's Town to the southeast, the townspeople had promised in writing to pay him *before* his ponderous pets performed, so he and his quadrupeds had dragged the rocks to the site and were off for a festival honoring the Goddess Demeter, where he hoped to scrape together enough money to buy new harnesses and—more importantly—new parade-crowns for his beloved big friends. He was acutely embarrassed that his lead bull's silverplated headgear and gold tassels were tarnished and bedraggled, even though the times *were* bad . . .

Gaius wondered if he would ever get the great beasts back.

A rich voice behind Gaius spoke and he turned to Syphax the

Negro, squatting on his chains. "Our lord architect is a man of mercy."

"The lord architect is one of us," said Cifgli, a slender young Briton. Clanking to a barrel, he scooped water in his hands and drank, while several other slaves, their coarse black loincloths filthy and every man bearing the scars of flogging, urinated over the brink of the board deck.

Cifgli began tossing handfuls of drinking water at his comrades. They shouted for more. Gaius, also dipping in his cupped hands, showered the nearest workers stretched out on the boards. Their lot was hopeless, but water to cool perspiring bodies could give a few moments' uplift to the human spirit.

"Lord architect, so strange a sky," called a sad young bearded Jew from another crew resting near a winch on which was coiled the heavy rope. "I fear God is coming in wrath. See you the brown clouds far in the southwest, gallant Roman?"

Gaius had already noticed the yellow-brown mass, but had concealed his apprehension. "Wind and dust," he replied. "Far away. It may not strike here. But if it does, remember storm-rules: fall flat, find cover if you can." Men and bridge had been buffeted and drenched before by violent storms sweeping the tortuous course of the Tagus, but never had any storm harmed the slaves or the arches. Only the superstitious had suffered during the tempests.

But this time the dull clouds in the southwest looked as if a huge puffball was forming; Gaius had never seen its like before. The hot air was motionless, the very atmosphere seemed enslaved. But as he watched, the eerie mushroom cloud-mass seemed to recede to the south. Evidently the storm had other plans for its future.

Which reminded Gaius of his future. He reflected wryly that if placed on the slave block, his price would be too excessive for any potential purchaser. A nugget of consolation in that. Who could afford to buy Gaius Julius Lacer? Not only did he consider himself the most dedicated bridge-builder in the Roman Empire, but also the most knowledgeable in the rock history of the earth. Yet as a slave he could never be acclaimed as the creator of public works for the glory of Rome.

Rome. The City. He imagined himself placed on a block in a slave mart with Syrian jugglers, Thracian dancing girls, Greek philosophers, Gallic lacemakers and Cappadocian confectioners . . . The auctioneer might cry: "Attention! Look here! Ho, what am I bid, what am I bid, for this splendid specimen of slave flesh? He is

an architect! A rare fellow, never have I sold one like this before!
Never flogged or branded. Never in chains. A creature of culture
who can also serve as tutor for your noble sons! And not for ba-
silicas and domes alone do his dark eyes flash, domina . . . ah . . .
his breadth of shoulders, note you his handsome smooth-shaven face
and bristling straight black hair . . . His price? Ah, noble senator,
great *patricius* of the Curia, cast your patriotic orbs on this bridge-
builder, sold only once before, and that when he was a tender newborn! No bad habits, no rebellion . . ."

No rebellion—

With a glance of hatred over his shoulder in the direction of
Ferox Piso and his aides swinging leather straps at the slaves, Gaius
walked to the edge of the wood decking of the center-pier and
looked down.

Almost two hundred feet below and one hundred to the north,
legionaries and unfettered slaves on rafts and scaffolds were erecting
the next upright of unmortared granite blocks. A bleak victory to
Gaius was that the most difficult triumph of the mass would never
be seen again, except by fish. But he saw it in mind: the submerged
feet of the great granite leg duplicating that of the pillar he stood
on.

Immovably based on the hard rockbed now deep in the current
stood the four huge cribs, the boots of the feet. The inner walls
were constructed of thick timbers bolted together, the space between the two wood facings filled with twelve-inch-thick hemlock,
then lined with oakum fibers and pitch, to calk the seams. The
hemlock triangles exerted tension or compression only longitu-
dinally, thus barring the danger of bending. The cavity of each
crib was filled with solid asphalt-concrete. The four outer walls of
the joined boxes angled inward, forming a truncated triangle, but
the combined foundation was square because inverted triangles on
the rockbed, reinforced the core structure with downward diagonals
of asphalt layered between thick planks, and outer straight walls of
calked logs, brickwork and stone blocks. A true foundation, able to
meet force from any direction and withstand it. Gaius' master had
claimed that perfect triangulation was an achievement only bestowed by the gods in languid gestures of beneficence toward human
architects, but Gaius knew he had succeeded through his own careful planning and minute inspection.

On the north shore of the Tagus stood blocks of gray granite
that had been ferried across the river on pontoon barrel-floats.

Each had to be dragged and pushed to the nearest revolving wood crane anchored in its mortared caisson in the gravelly shallows of the water. Gaius reflected how all the slaves pleaded for river-duty, for then they could work without gyves or cudgeling. And the few favored by the gods had the comparatively easy task of depositing loose stone *riprap* around the bases of the two great piers to prevent undermining by the Tagus.

When the river shrunk in summer, towering wooden scaffolds would rise in the stream between the two tallest piers; durable hemlock, oak, and chestnut timbers securely bolted and laterally braced with logs secured in the two masonry masses confronting each other. Up the ladders would go unchained workers to begin the great semicircular masonry of the granite arch. When the last keystone was fitted and the timber supports taken away, it would be the granite marriage of the two tallest verticals of the bridge.

—Why think of marriage? This bridge was his life, but his wife and baby son had gone where all dead go, wherever that was. And never again would *he* marry until he was emancipated—

"Lord architect," said Syphax, quietly, and Gaius turned to the Negro and his co-workers on the timber deck, "when we finish your bridge may you walk on it some day in freedom."

Gaius had no illusions about that. Freedom? Freedom and peace anywhere in Roman Europe, Roman Britain and the provinces of Rome sweeping from east to west, embracing all the habitable northern lands of the African continent? Freedom and peace in the Roman provinces of Asia Minor? The Arabians and their desert were not in the emperor's grasp, nor was the powerful nation of Parthia in the Euphrates-Tigris region and eastward in Middle Asia—but all the rest: Syria, Bithynia, Cappadocia, Judea, Cilicia—all bowed to the monster in the Purple Toga, the Emperor Domitian . . . In Europe the Eagle Standards and forts began at the North Sea, on the Rhine, on its western banks; continued all along that river and controlled the land between it and the Danube, on, on, to the Black Sea . . . Rome engaged in sporadic warfare now and then with the Dacians across the Danube to the east, and against the wily Parthians in Asia Minor, but all lands, seas and islands west of the Rhine-Danube frontier and the confused boundary of Asia Minor—all was part of the glory that was Rome.

Here in Hither Spain, this farthest western province of Rome, all was supposedly peaceful, with its conglomerate population of Roman colonists, Spanish natives, civilized Celtiberians of ancient ancestry who were thought to have originated long ago somewhere in the Indo-European region, and the Celt guerrilla tribes. One did not count the long-gone or absorbed Phoenicians, Greeks and Carthaginians . . . Peace in Roman Spain?

The dark Celt blackcloak horsemen frequently attacked Roman cavalry patrols and road-builders, and the weather was always an enemy. Freedom and peace for Gaius Julius Lacer? He was not in chains; he walked and looked free. And he could escape, but what escape would not end in irons or in death?

A harsh voice from the finished southern part of the bridge bellowed:

"Get to work, you black spiders, Jewish rats, British scum, Gallic idlers, Egyptian beanpods! You—Gaius the Julius! Who do you think you are? The Sacred Julius Caesar in buckskins? Turn your face this way, Gaius, so I can give my eyes a banquet on that big nose of yours! Crack your pole on those slaves, or heave them overside if they won't work!"

So far Gaius had answered Ferox Piso, *praefectus* of the bridge, tersely, but respectfully, but now his dammed-up fury burst at last.

"I do not and never will lash my men," he thundered, over the creak of winches, scrape of granite and grinding of iron wheels. "And my bridge cannot be built by dead men!"

Syphax and the Britons and nearby crews scrambled upright in a rattle of chains to return in haste to work. "Oh, gods, gods," cried the black, "protect our man of the bridge!"

"The lord architect can protect himself from Ferox Piso, don't worry about that," soothed Cifgli. "Help me with this board, Syphax."

The Negro, unable to foresee a peaceful solution for the oncoming clash between Architect Gaius and Overseer Ferox, said shakily, "We have our good days when the god is in centerbridge. Then we keep our blood to ourselves. My back's about healed. How is your rump, Cifgli?"

The Briton replied dubiously, "Convalescing, my friend, convalescing."

But Gaius heard none of this. He strode past the terrified slaves, walking south on the paving of the finished piers and arches. Now at last he was close to Ferox Piso, who was lashing a fallen Negro slave and did not see Gaius come forward.

Without a word Gaius wrenched the whip away. Then he marched to the manager's three freedmen and snatched their straps.

Stupefied, the trio turned expectantly towards Ferox Piso. The lordly one still had his right fist upraised as if grasping a knout.

"No more flogging," said Gaius, without raising his voice.

Handsome in a heavy Roman way, his curly black hair glistening with fragrant rose salve, Ferox stared incredulously. Then his smooth-shaven jowels quivered and he took the stance of a commanding general. His brown linen tunic was delicately flecked with blood of the lashed. A sheer scarlet cloak of fine-weave cotton hung carelessly over his shoulders from a gold medallion brooch at his throat.

"Give back my whip." Ferox spoke as softly as Gaius.

Gaius stared.

"My three freedmen will likewise appreciate the return of their leathers," continued Ferox. "At your convenience, Gaius the Julius. Pray do not hurry. My troops tell me you are a lover of . . . poetry. Spout some, dirty slave!"

Gaius threw the whips into the Tagus.

Ferox's voice cracked like a lash: "I should remind dainty Gaius the J. that I have two hundred soldiers close by." He kicked the prone Negro he had been bastinading, but moved away when Gaius came two steps closer.

His eyes on Ferox and the stunned freedmen assistants, Gaius pulled the bleeding black upright. "Go north to centerbridge," Gaius ordered the weeping slave. "The others will wash your wounds." The beaten man was not a man, but a Negro boy of less than fifteen. Weakly the child tried to kiss Gaius on the hands, then he trudged away, dragging his iron links between his feet.

"God architect, I remind you that I give the orders," Ferox chuckled, adding a polite afterthought: "How would the slave of rocks like to feel the kiss of a whip?"

Gaius instantly replied, "I remind the noble Ferox Piso that I am a bondsman of Apollodorus, the empire's renowned architect. I remind the noble Ferox Piso that I am patrician by birth and have rights under the laws. I remind Ferox Piso the patrician that he is neither architect nor humanitarian, that his reputation preceded him to this bridge. I remind him that it is whispered he served with great lack of distinction for two years in *Legio XI* until its *Dux* lost a wager to Piso and thus the commanding general arranged an honorable discharge for Piso on the grounds that he had lung inflammation and but a few months to live." He had said too much, he was looking death in the face, but wrath and pride drove him.

Ferox gazed as if entranced. All over the bridge, slaves were making a great deal of noise with rocks and cranes, but absolutely no work was being done. On the south shore troops still shouted and urged the workers roped to rocks.

Then in despair Gaius looked at the sky. Immediately he shouted, "The noble Ferox Piso must order the men off the works at once! Look—that brown cloud! Sir, my apologies, I humble myself—order the men off the arches at once! Look over your shoulder, sir! It may be a *turbo!* A *turbo!*"

His face a dull red, Ferox Piso roared with laughter. "Only the first slave of the rotten Lacer heritage and a coward, too. I give you permission to command Jupiter the Best and Greatest to take his tornado elsewhere." Suddenly he stooped and grasped Gaius by the ankles and jerked.

Down went Gaius, caught by three slaves cowering behind. All three sprawled in a tangle of chains near a rock-wagon. Unhurt, Gaius was spat on by Ferox, but he did not notice, he was transfixed by the giant brown cloud churning out of the southwest, its long stem reaching down to land.

There was a curious humming in the motionless air and slaves started screaming, but Gaius could not move, a strange pressure holding him flat on the men under him.

"Danger! Danger!" blasted a soldier on shore. "TROOPS—INTO THE CAVES—"

Ferox and his three freedmen started racing to the south bank where slaves still harnessed to rocks stared idiotically at the oncoming whirlwind, the great *turbo* of Olympus.

Gaius tried to get up and fell on two layers of slaves. Then an avalanche of rocks seemed to thunder overhead and early afternoon dimmed to pale brown chaos.

A helmet flew past his head, then a whole oak tree, a moist rootlet tickling his forehead for a flash of time. He was already dead, but he still breathed in gasps and squinted into the horror around him . . . A gilded sandal whirling, frail leather lacings still neatly tied around the bloodied ankle of a woman's dainty white foot, the toenails brown with henna—tall iron hoist, and revolving drums coiled with ropes, huge block granite slabs tossed up and disappearing in the unearthly vortex above.

He heard the foolish sound of his laughter, for the end of the world was too horrible for grief or love or hope. Men were motes, stones were feathers, gravity was dead, and man and his works would all be sucked up into the supernatural vacuum of the colossal *turbo*. Had he already died and awakened in the Underworld? Torn memories stormed him.

That pimpled youth in the chariot with two Arabian horses that had almost trampled small Gaius, the first rock he had split with a wedge and mallet, the immortal Horace had written: *"You while in life are honored as divine, and vows and oaths are taken at your shrine"*—the palsied *flamen* in the Temple of Jupiter had a tic in his right eyelid, stop the tic—the black cypresses are mourning, Golden Milestone blinds me, not gold, but fool's gold, lead floats to the top in smelting silver ore if—blow the bellows, I know how it must be done, jig the sieves, don't open those floodgates—Empedocles and Plato and Pythagoras taught reincarnation, a single pine cone is the answer to it all . . .

The noise was so deafening that it seemed to create a vast silence and Gaius realized he still lived. He would try and observe as long as he could breathe and see . . .

He saw prodigies of the unearthly power of the tornado. A purple wig of tiered curls bobbed gently nearby until pulled upward . . . a necklace of amethysts, bronze balance with armatures and pannikans solemnly motionless— Gold comb, red rooster, silver mirror, all vanishing.

Then he saw a length of papyrus outspread, so near that he read two words: *CARISSIMA MEA:* until it disappeared along with a big stone corn-mill spraying grainlets upward. Then new horror loomed almost directly overhead, high, but too low: an enormous embossed bronze door with a slender length of timber driven through the metal. The menacing portal vanished to his left as he dazedly watched an earthen ampulla spouting red wine on a peacock fan, yellow marble table with bronze lion legs, small wooden hoop, and a newborn lamb curled peacefully around a big painted bust of Emperor Domitian. The baby animal's head was bloody.

"An easy death," Gaius whispered as image and dead lamb whirled up and away.

Suddenly the *turbo* was churning north with its awful debris. Gaius was sprayed with grit and mud and sand as the hideous clamor began lessening. . . . He closed his eyes.

A few warm raindrops struck his neck. Then tiny hailstones began pelting his thick hair.

He must count the icy pellets. One, two, three, four, five, six, seven, eight, nine— Nine. No tenth stone? Only nine . . .

He began hearing the cries and moans of slaves and distant shouts of soldiers. Somehow he found himself on the wooden floor of the midchanel pier, looking down.

Terrified faces of slaves and soldiers stared up at him, workers still grasping mallets and wedges, hands frozen to granite suspended in rope slings. Even the rafts were motionless. Not a man moved. Then the log floats began swinging languidly against anchor chains.

"Speak!" Gaius called. Were the men below dead standing up? To his relief, the river crews began sluggish movement.

"It was a *turbo*," Gaius shouted to them. "Make a count. Any men lost? Did it hit down there?"

At last a thin voice of a soldier below hailed, "All safe. Not a man even scratched."

Workers behind Gaius on the bridge were jabbering in their various tongues. Some were laughing hysterically.

"What special orders from Lacer the architect?" snapped a military voice and Gaius saw a gray-haired adjutant standing at stoical attention beside a block and pulley. His was the face of a fiend, and the lips were pulled down in a twisted grimace.

Gaius wet his parched lips. "Orders?"

"Saw worse at Pompeii fifteen years ago," barked the soldier. "When Pluto blew up Vesuvius, that was the end of the world. I'm not superstitious, but people said then that the burial of Pompeii and Herculaneum was a sign the gods had doomed Emperor Titus."

Behind the soldier Gaius saw a water-barrel perched on top of a winch, neatly balanced . . . a squashed beehive glued by its own crushed wax and honey to a square of granite . . . two blue-winged magpies fluttering unhurt around the honeyed stone . . . a dead brown bear and corpse of a deer flung on a rock-wagon . . . meat from Jupiter's *turbo*.

"We lost the centurion and his two aides. Officer had his neck broken, aides were cracked against trees," continued the soldier, matter-of-factly. "Piso's gone with his three aides. All smashed against rocks and tossed in the river. I am Quadratus, acting centurion."

The triumph that was Rome . . . even in disaster Rome rose again . . . in the shape of the eternal Roman soldier. Paradoxically it gave Gaius new hope. "I understand," he said, thinking the ugly face of Quadratus looked good, in spite of the seamed scars pulling down the soldier's bumpy cheeks.

The young Negro boy Gaius had sent to centerbridge sank to his bony knees and kissed Gaius' hands. "Lord, lord," sobbed the young one, "the brave Syphax held me down, he, the big brave Cifgli saved many before—before."

At last came the tragic announcement from a youthful Jew:

"Lord Architect, I saw Syphax and Cifgli thrown over the brink. They were men of mercy. Jehovah, Jehovah. . . ."

In a fatherly way Quadratus touched Gaius' shoulders. "It's better than dying in chains," said the soldier. Gaius wiped his eyes with the back of his hands and embraced the stoical man in armor.

Far to the north and east, the brown destroyer of the sky was dissolving in haze while overhead low gray clouds poured rain as if the gods in atonement were bathing the men and the bridge, washing away the dirt and gravel and the blood. To the south and west, the afternoon sun shone on near green humped hills. The rain stopped at last. The air smelled of wet earth and cinnamon.

Gaius, Quadratus and ten soldiers inspected the bridge and the workers. Except for Syphax and Cifgli, not a man in chains was missing. Injuries to the others were minor: gravel-burns, sore eyes, and one slave with a copper nail driven through his left thumb. On the south shore, the slaves roped to rocks had been showered with trout and were ravenously eating the raw fish.

Save for the centurion's tent that had been sucked up by the *turbo,* not an army shelter was so much as dusty. The foodsheds were gone, but dead sheep lay all around, as did palm-fronds, lemons, a woman's green silk stola and a column of crates that slowly collapsed as Gaius and the soldiers drew near. The boxes were filled with dried figs, dates, bolts of silver-shot blue silk gauze and white plaster figurines of Juno and Minerva, the small images unscathed.

The bridge reared proudly out of the wreckage.

Men had died, but the foundations and finished buttresses, piers, arches, paving and coping lived for the centuries to come.

The new bridge *praefectus* was Pomponius, an impoverished patrician in voluntary exile from southern Spain. The first sight of the grim aristocrat in white struck terror in the slaves, for they saw the long face of Roman ruthlessness, stiff graying hair, and big fists that seemed made to grasp knouts.

The men waited in fear for a battle to loom between the bridge architect and the new bridge manager. Would the god architect win this one?

Pomponius made it clear from the start that he loathed the stink of sweating slaveflesh, the bridge, and humanity in general. If Lacer kept impassioning for elephants, Pomponius would loose a few wild camels to tame the young tiger of a bridge engineer. This was followed by the arrival of twenty burros the next day. As to whether the men were flogged or unflogged were trivia of sublime unconcern to Pomponius, a former *legatus* of *Legio XX*. He suggested that Lacer become Lacer the Lasher—with his tongue. What were tongues for? The overseer demanded privacy. He got it. He spent most of the time in his tent conning scrolls of philosophy and poetry; cursing the authors; and secretly composing and correcting a letter he intended to send by couriers to the emperor when the Tagus bridge was finished.

As time passed, the slaves dared exchange shaky grins each time Pomponius stormed out of his tent to shout at the god architect, for amazing new concessions might be forthcoming. Their hopes were met.

Lacer's written requests infuriated Pomponius. So the young tiger wanted more gruel, nuts, roots and berries for his men? He dared ask that they have *meat*? Let the architect stop staring at his useless stone piers and solve a few real problems. Make the slaves sluice off their stench at sundown in the Tagus, so as to sweeten the air Pomponius breathed. At the same time make the shackled ones fish, if Lacer had enough brains to teach them how to rig poles and dig worms. Did Lacer think Pomponius was running a banquet service? The thunderbolt of Pomponic wrath next cracked on the two hundred legionaries at the site. Hunting parties began riding out and back each day, bringing wagons of wild plums, apricots, blackberries, and slain boars, deer, partridge, rabbits, pheasants and squirrels. Then to the amazement of the men, cartloads of castoff tunics, boots, felt caps and cloaks began arriving from Caesar's Town.

The great center arch was completed ten days ahead of schedule in September. Foundations of the land piers on the south bank were well advanced before the first snow fell. The awed laborers, warmly if raggedly clothed, and adequately fed, discussed the situation in reverence. Surely the merciful fury of lord Pomponius and the wry smiles and twinkling eyes of the great architect were gifts from the gods. Had there ever existed two Roman patricians as invincible in fury and in stones as the noble Pomponius and the noble Lacer?

No more catastrophic storms assailed the stonework. A few elderly slaves died of natural causes and age; so did the Negro boy the bridge builder had saved from Ferox Piso. The soldier, Quadratus, bade farewell to the architect in January and set out for his next legion post on the island of Malta. Almost a year had elapsed since the cataclysmic *turbo*.

In mid March when the bridge was close to completion, Pomponius finished the final draft of his letter to Emperor Domitian and sent the sealed scroll off by military couriers bound direct for Rome.

A month later when the noble Tagus Bridge had finally risen as an affirmation in stone of the divinity in all moral men and a tribute to the glory of Rome, the stunned Gaius Lacer stood in centerbridge surrounded by sorrowing slaves, idle machinery and bridled burrows.

Soldiers had just brought the tidings that Pomponius lay dead in his tent—a dagger in his bloody breast and his harsh face majestic in death. Under the body the troops had found crumpled copies of a letter Pomponius had sent to Rome the month before, excoriating Emperor Domitian's crimes, and a scroll which had evidently arrived with courier horsemen from Italy last night, which read:

DOMITIAN, MASTER AND LORD, TO POMPONIUS THE LIAR, COWARD, SLANDERER, ANARCHIST, AND ATHEIST. THE INFAMOUS FEMALE YOU MOURN SHOULD HAVE JOYFULLY COME TO OUR SACRED COUCH WHEN INVITED FIVE YEARS AGO. INSTEAD YOUR VICIOUS WIFE STABBED YOUR YOUNG SONS AND DAUGHTER AND ENDED HER VILE EXISTENCE WHILE YOU WERE PRIVILEGED TO BE ABSENT FROM ROME FIGHTING FOR OUR IMMORTAL GLORY. COMMIT SUICIDE.

Gaius read both documents and mutely returned them to the expressionless legionary who had shown them. Later the architect silently dedicated the Tagus Bridge not only to the man he had built it for—his idol, General Marcus Ulpius Trajan—but for Pomponius.

At its highest paved level between the precipitous terrain of both sides of the river, the splendor of granite towered over one hundred and eighty feet above the stream.

From north to south the magnificence of the Tagus Bridge measured six hundred and seventeen feet long. It was a triumph for

Gaius Julius Lacer, although it would not be officially declared complete until a Triumphal Arch was reared in centerbridge.

It came to the attention of Proconsul Cornelius Classicus, procurator of eastern Hither Spain that a slave architect and geologist named Gaius Lacer was a man of great skills and integrity; and the Proconsul, who had pressing need for a bondsman who understood the materials of construction, as well as the meaning of various aspects of the land and rocks—specifically one who would know gold when he saw it—ordered Lacer to eastern Spain.

⊓⊓⊓ 96 A.D. ⊔⊔⊓

II

The bronze chariot of Proconsul Cornelius Caecilius Classicus roared upland through an evergreen valley in eastern Hither Spain, with the Proconsul braced upright next to his charioteer in this two-wheeled horror. Yet if he valued the respect of his few cavalrymen thundering at the rear, he must carry out the tradition of open-to-wind war car travel of other Roman governors, clutching the elliptical metal shield of the jolting carrier with one hand and waving godly greetings to fearful Spanish natives in vineyards and olive groves with the other. He was the symbol of Rome, second only to Emperor Domitian as supreme authority in this eastern zone of Roman Spain. And he had to hold this power until he got the gold.

Gold.

Rich Spanish gold deposits to be mined for the Caesar, yet never to arrive in Rome. The gleaming yellow metal would vanish when blackcloak guerrillas attacked the Roman miners (the very audaciousness of Classicus' secret plans seemed favored by the deities) and preliminaries were meshing smoothly. Now he was to interview Gaius Julius Lacer, the slave architect-geologist who would be chief engineer of the old ore territory in northwest Spain—and eventually murdered as his predecessor, Publius, had been. How else was Governor Classicus to obtain the gold and settle accounts with the voracious moneylenders in distant Rome—while Enna, his wife, insisted on economy, knowing nothing of her husband's debts? Unfortunately Enna was of purple ancestry with solid ranks of influential friends as patrician as herself; otherwise Classicus would months ago have ordered her money-vault guards to step aside so he could take her fortune—even if this meant leaving the lady herself wrapped in a shroud.

Enna still at times had a maddening fascination, past forty though she was. Hazel eyes tinged with blue . . . and if her maids artificially maintained the glossy chestnut brown color of Enna's curls, no one would ever guess. As to her passionate admiration of General Myron Frontinus (which Classicus was not supposed to detect) that fitted in with his own determination to seize the Spanish gold. Her interest in Frontinus, now Classicus' treasurer, would prevent her aquiline nose from sniffing out the secret plans of her spouse. Towards her husband she was so cold and upright as to be monotonous, yet since Classicus might still lay his hands on the thousands of gold and silver coins in her vault he must continue his role, for a time longer, as an affectionate mate.

His gubernatorial smile on duty, Classicus glanced at the man holding the reins, General Myron Frontinus. A little banter with the treasurer of Hither Spain might help one endure this shattering ride and ease his hidden concerns.

"My noble Frontinus, why do you yet wear the uniform and gear?" This had to be shouted over the grinding iron wheels and pounding hooves. "Once out of the legions, surely a Roman patrician ought to don the toga? Not that I recommend the garment in vehicles such as this; the wind is an enemy of pleated togas. And may I jest about that slender sword at your belt? What is its purpose? To stab butterflies?"

The maimed but muscular left hand of General Frontinus gripped the carrier rim while his strong and normal right clenched the reins of the galloping grays. Brown eyes mild, he glanced at the proconsul. "Habit," called Frontinus. "The blade is flexible Spanish steel." With that he turned his attention back to the horses.

Feeling rebuffed, Proconsul Classicus meditated in derision that a retired paymaster-general trying to pose as a charioteer made himself look ridiculous.

"Frontinus, what is there to know about the slave rock-expert?" Classicus inquired through the blustery but warming March wind ballooning the folds of his fine brown hooded cloak.

The reply came clearly: "Gaius Julius Lacer is completing the bridge that Publius was building, until Rufus' black mastiff knocked Publius off the spans to his death in the gorge. You know that, of course."

Did the treasurer suspect, Classicus wondered, that the death of Publius had been an assisted one? Yet what could Frontinus prove? What could any man but dead Publius prove? In gratitude the proconsul silently lauded the gods for the unexpected lunge of the big black dog of Commander Rufus Liscus. . . .

Then, suddenly and without warning, the governor was suffused with such weird phantasmagoria that the embossed harness of one chariot gray seemed loaded with brass bells clapping metallic music, and his forehead felt elongated to a noble white Corinthian column, his blue eyes metamorphosed into priceless rubies . . . The odd hallucinations fled almost instantly, but Classicus gripped the shield of the carrier harder to test its solid bronze reality. No one knew of those frightening aberrations at times seizing his senses, and as usual, after a moment, his customary aplomb returned and with it a surge of euphoria, his brain again keenly capable of dealing with important plans. He would escape the monetary vise he was in (although he dared not send a request to Emperor Domitian for earned salary—the thought sent shudders through him); not for Cornelius Caecilius Classicus a black future of imprisonment or possible slavery for debt.

Now they drove through a eucalyptus park that enchanted Classicus. Juvenile Romans in purple-bordered white tunics and gray capes sat on benches with waxed tablets and *stylii,* watched by a Greek in gray pacing before his small male pupils. Shouting friendly salutes, Classicus waved and the students forgot lessons and cheered lustily until the Greek pedagogue raised his ferule. Then the chariot increased speed, thundering and swaying past small farms.

At this moment Classicus glanced back, startled, at a herd of black cattle behind a pink stone wall. Had he really seen a two-headed cow with a nuzzling calf and heard a concert of lyre-music bubbling from the animal's horns? Absurd. Merely another bizarre deception enacted by his eyes and ears. Yet he pushed aside his brown cowl in order to see better, breathe deeply of the piney air and gather courage from inspirational vistas of far snowy peaks wrapped in togas of lavender and gold mist. In those mountains lived his powerful, secret ally, Chieftain Luna Malendi, leader of the Arvacan Celt Blackcloak nation, and exultation flooded the proconsul briefly, thinking of the support he could count on there.

Never had there been, nor would there be, a public reversal of Proconsul Classicus' reputation as an honest, loyal, and merciful governor; he had been a scapegoat long enough for thefts by others. Bitterly he contemplated that gold ingots from both provinces of Spain mined by aristocratic favorites of Domitian did not go to the Emperor, even though the aristocrats claimed to have put these in the holds of ore-vessels bound for Italy. He had tried to inspect these shipments at first, and been so sharply rebuked that he never asked to go into the ship-holds again. Nor did he dare refuse to sign cargo invoices the emperor's friends carelessly presented for his signature as a sop to his authority in Hither Spain. He had been their dupe.

That he himself had thus far escaped imperial wrath was due to the emperor's fretful amity towards Enna and himself, coupled with the brave intervention of his senator friends in Rome. They had called the August One's attention to chaotic conditions in Spain, urged Domitian not to blame Classicus, the honest and popular proconsul, for vanished Spanish gold, and had persuaded the Master and God to let Cornelius Classicus start a mining venture of his own to open the abandoned mines of antiquity in northeast Spain. In this way, Emperor Domitian would be sure of at least one dependable source of precious metals coming into Rome.

Yet Classicus realized that the good will of Domitian Caesar depended principally on other things. If the Holy One's current charmer (or charmers) were artists in love making, Domitian spent days emptying prisons, cancelling scheduled executions, and giving baskets of meat and bread to rich and poor alike. During such halcyon intervals, Emperor Domitian tried to surpass his dead brother, the Divine Titus, and his spectacular sire, the Divine Vespasian, who people still remembered with awed gratitude. When Domitian's mood was gracious, his mercy and generosity were majestic. He spared fallen gladiators whether the Vestal Virgins signified mercy or death; he even went so far as to free Christians bound for the Flavian Amphitheatre, and it was reported he had several times stated that the followers of Christ were truly moral and understood the truth about love.

It was the constant dread of a black reversal of the imperial temper, plus the burden of his debts and Enna's prim refusal to give him her fortune that now sped Classicus in a jangle of wheels and clatter of horses towards Gaius, the slave architect and geologist. Unlike dead Publius who had been a patrician and free, Gaius Lacer was a bondsman. Slaves did as they were ordered, or were garroted.

"Good crops will help the natives and colonists pay taxes," said Frontinus, and Classicus turned to the treasurer with a show of pretended interest. "Corkoak harvests should be favorable this year. The same for olives and first-press oil."

"Commendable," said Classicus. "Frontinus, what wisdom was brought by the newest delegation from Rome?"

The measured smile of Frontinus appeared and disappeared. "They pounded your best marble tables and blamed you for an ore bireme that sank off Gaul two days before the Nones. I called their attention to the absurdity of blaming you for a shipwreck; or of accusing you of tricking gold from independent patrician prospectors."

Classicus felt a spark of gratitude, but before he could say so, a rabbit racing ahead of the chariot caught his attention. It was growing . . . growing . . . into a lion! . . .

"The perfume of the spruce and pines is salubrious," he said, quickly. "Observe the far northern mountains capped in helmets of golden snow." And the lion vanished.

"Poetic," replied Frontinus, "if those distant heights were not full of Celt guerrillas."

A dangerous topic, to be handled carefully. "Why not accompany me when I make my next diplomatic journey to Chieftain Luna Malendi's domain?"

"Not for me, Classicus," responded Frontinus. "Celts are Celts, be they blackcloaks who hate us, or whitecloak *Togati* who out-Roman us."

"Chieftain Malendi is a man of culture. He speaks Latin and Greek to perfection; his voice has the music of the mythical Aeolian Harp. He may wear a silver cuirass and gold helmet with two long ibex horns, but warriors worship him."

"Does the chieftain still hate Emperor Domitian?"

"No," Classicus lied, and began a convincing distortion of the truth by which he based his desperate hope to seize the Spanish gold. "The great Celt prince is peaceable. Now and then he lets his tribesmen challenge whitecloak Celts to brotherly demonstrations of skill. Which side can leap highest over campfires, juggle the most daggers, down the most mead or buttermilk. They are primitive like —children."

The chariot thundered into a long canyon where talk was impossible, giving Classicus leisure for recollections of how he had accidentally established the necessary confidential relationship with Chieftain Luna Malendi. It had began on a golden November afternoon the preceding autumn. . . .

Having received a dispatch from the Senate that he must make a diplomatic journey north and try to heal a feud between the Black-cloak prince and Emperor Domitian, the proconsul dutifully travelled north in his luxurious bed-carriage, escorted by his heavily-armed cavalrymen. He had no fear, for pro-Roman whitecloaks also escorted him, but he secretly resented having to donate gifts to Chieftain Malendi. The Senate had commanded it, but the offerings must come from Classicus' coffers.

He was welcomed with glacial courtesy by the sinister Celt in black tunic, silver breastplate and ibex-horned gold helmet. In the guerrilla chief's tent later, Classicus suavely extended the good wishes of the *Patres Conscripti*, also a small casket of jewelry (from Enna's dower collection).

Enigmatically amused, Malendi studied the filigree gold bracelets set with tourmalines; a pin studded with pearls; the gold link necklace with a carved amethyst locket, and a small ruby ring. The last, Malendi gave to a guerrilla aide with instructions that unwed Celt women draw lots for it. Then he sat down next to Classicus on a bench against one camel's hair cloth wall of the tent. After a lengthy silence, the blackcloak began speaking in flawless and melodious Latin:

"The monstrous Caesar threatens to send *legios* against me because I have excoriated his violence and vileness. Aye, he threatens, the debauched one does. Then of late have I heard the strange tidings that the Roman Senate is ordering you, Roman procurator of Hither Spain, to mine gold and silver in territory that has belonged to my tribe for centuries. Know you about that, Roman?"

Honestly dumbfounded, Classicus exclaimed, "Honorable chieftain, I know of the emperor's animosity towards you, but this is the first I have heard about being ordered to dig gold in your domain!" His amazement concealed a sudden flash of an idea: if he could win the friendship of this canny Celt chieftain, he would also win the support of Malendi's army of guerrilla horsemen. Right then had sprang to mind the perilous plan to get the Spanish gold, but of course he did not mention it.

"Gold means little to me," Malendi mused, his strange, dusky-opal eyes resting with considerable warmth on the proconsul. "Yet before I would allow Romans to mine in my domain, I would first have to learn the opinion of Governor Classicus about the beast of the sword in Rome. Speak, Roman proconsul."

Classicus abandoned caution. "Chieftain, endangered are both of us by the bloody Principate of Domitian. I speak truly. I trust you. I wish to win your friendship. Let us aid each other, for moral fraternity knows no boundaries."

Malendi looked with frank approval at Classicus. "How many

Roman legions are in western Farther Spain then, brother excellency?"

"Three, most valiant brother Malendi. Counting foreign auxiliaries, approximately sixteen thousand."

The saturnine face of Malendi softened, and a gentle smile lifted his thin lips. "I command ninety thousand cavalry warriors, including fighters of blackcloaks swearing allegiance to me . . . Malendi can spread a band of anti-Roman cavalry troops from the rim of eastern Spain to the western edge of this peninsula bounded by the Atlantic."

They exchanged guarded glances blended with looks of mutual accord.

"Brother excellency," Classicus said in undertones, "if and when I hear of any treacherous moves against you, I shall send warning." Considering the sudden good shape of affairs building in his favor, Classicus dared speak a complete falsehood: "Noble Malendi, Governor Maturus of Western Spain is ambitious to become emperor. He commands the three legions. Say he were to obtain more legions . . . ?"

The chieftain appeared quietly amused. "Your colleague in Farther Spain sends me lengthy scrolls of good will so filled with legal terms that Malendi can not determine whether his words be screened threats or merely the outpourings of a wordy man.

"I shall have no further dealings with Maturus out in his white city of Gades. You and I will work out a system of diagrams for use in our letters, honest brother Classicus. And some day Malendi may be of use to his trusted *frater Romanus,* the noble Classicus?"

Classicus sighed wearily. "Gallant chieftain, should I need your great assistance, I will put my need before you frankly."

"So be it," said Malendi.

Classicus was inwardly so elated he could even endure a blackcloak banquet with equanimity: acorn bread that tested the strength of jaws and teeth, slabs of beef *fried* in hoglard instead of delicately-browned in olive oil, or roasted, the Roman way. Then he must extol the merits of buttermilk which he detested, and try to dispose of the lingering sting on his tongue with dried figs and dates, a sound Roman conclusion to the repast in Malendi's tent. Afterward the Celt leader drolly observed, "This is the season when my warriors begin to seek their pleasure behind the cowhide portals of their domed sod huts you admire so much, brother Classicus. I trust your strong claim for interior joy will be satisfied this moonlit night."

"My 'strong claim,' chieftain?" asked the puzzled proconsul.

"It will be explained," replied Malendi, smilingly.

Having noticed Celt women in long black robes, wearing high horned headgear thickly draped with dark veils, Classicus' pulses began to throb, thinking of the beauty those coarse gauze draperies might conceal.

But in his secluded domed hut that night, Classicus waited so long by lamplight that he at last decided Malendi had forgotten to send a Celtic beauty to make the night blissful. Resigned, he blew out the flames of three oil lamps and settled down in his floor-bed of furs. From the distance came the hum of Celt gibberish, hoots of owls in the mountain forest, and the boisterous laughs of his Roman cavalry in a mead-drinking bout with hilarious blackcloaks around a far campfire.

Suddenly callused hands touched his face in the darkness of his hut and he let out a muffled cry.

"Roman god, your servant comes in reverence," whispered a low female voice in halting Latin. "Not until your lamps went out dared I humbly come to your shrine, Lord. Your servant won the boon of the ruby ring."

But he had already pulled the supple form down to his bed of pelts and was wrenching off her rough veils and long coarse garments. His fingers made out the girl's saddle nose, thick, soft lips, and mane of tangled hair. This could be distasteful if her face mattered, which it did not. Avidly his hands moved over her smooth and rounded body . . .

Desire flamed in him. And in her. Soon the fire of lust united and ignited them in a blaze of passion mounting to a violent climax that left him dazed.

Hercules! These Celt females are wild animals . . . must teach this she-cougar a few refined Roman variations . . . He had no chance. She was a huntress with a thousand savage enticements that soon roused him again, and brought him to another glorious conclusion. She was insatiable, but he pushed her away and slept dreamily.

When the sun awakened him, he saw Enna's ruby ring flashing redly in the elkskins where his Celt girl had writhed. Later he learned from Malendi that to Arvacan Blackcloaks the ruby signified uncontrollable desire . . . and had brother Classicus found the Celt woman sufficient unto his needs? Nor would Malendi retain the ring; in itself it meant nothing to the Celt girl he had deigned to honor, but she was henceforth exalted and forever nameless. . . .

His lips twitched in amusement as he thought about the Celt woman and the ruby ornament, while the chariot rumbled into the steep hills. Through the deepening abyss at his left poured a tumbling mountain stream. On roared his chariot and the paved way began ascending in a gentle gradient, and the long canyon was left behind.

Then Frontinus called, "Do you think Lacer will find gold in those northwest mines? From all we can learn of that region, the Phoenicians took out all of the gold and silver fifteen hundred years ago. I have to arrange financing for the gold expedition. I think it's a waste of tax funds."

The proconsul was delighted to pull a righteous long face and emphatically concur. His one hidden hope was that Gaius the slave would stumble on virgin lodes in mountains some miles from the ancient Phoenician tunnels and rock galleries; in wildlands that could not support human life and had never been fully explored to the best of Classicus' knowledge; but he did not say this.

"Here we are," announced Frontinus. They jolted to a halt in a forest clearing off the road that led down to the wide approachway of a limestone bridge. The spans were familiar to Classicus, except that now the parapet walls on each side of the structure were completed, leaving the wide center area for the passage of pedestrians and pack animals. When he had conferred not long ago with Publius, there had been no retaining fences on the bridge. His expression affable, the governor tried to forget the disastrous private talk with Publius in this very clearing shortly after serving the patrician architect the poisoned wine—and before Publius walked back out on his bridge and began to stagger. Thank the gods that black dogs cannot talk.

While his tent was being erected, Classicus displayed his knowledge to attentive Frontinus. "Observe, my noble friend, the soldiers down on the arches. See the smoking cauldron? That contains molten lead. The workmen first put the iron cramps into position and then pour in molten lead. Watch, my friend." After a tense wait, Classicus remarked, "Perfect. The soldiers and their foreman work together splendidly. Frontinus, I am going to my tent. Listen to the larks or pick a few daffodils or pet the chariot horses."

The treasurer's slow smile appeared and ebbed as he turned and walked to the brink of the cliff to watch the men on the bridge over a thrash of white water deep in the gorge below.

In his tent Classicus glanced in a silver mirror and smoothed his rumpled gray curls with a gold comb. After an admiring appraisal of his dimpled chin and perfect Roman profile, he put the hand mirror and comb in a box and sat down in his ebony armchair. It was a relief to relax in the sponge cushion covered in tufted yellow velvet. He arranged the wine jug, goblets, and water vessel on the small white marble table. Opposite was a stark iron X-legged camp chair to be occupied by Gaius the slave architect.

An orderly marched in, followed by a man in worn buckskins and dusty legion boots.

"Your excellency," barked the soldier, "this is Gaius Julius Lacer, bridge architect, mineral expert, and road builder." A salute, and the legionary tramped out.

By Pollux, the trooper need not have introduced Gaius as if he were Romulus, thought the governor, at last turning his affable attention to the man. Classicus was startled.

He was looking at a sunburned young man of powerful visage, features almost too rugged to be handsome in the classical sense. Was the slave architect tall, or did he seem tall because he stood so straight? And what a head of straight black hair that Gaius had . . . women must fight over him. What color his crinkled eyes? Black? Slate blue? He reminded Classicus of legendary patriots he had read about, in ancient republican days when Romans killed quickly and lived simply. Bestirring himself, he said,

"You look like a man braced to throw a spear. Be seated."

In the muted greenish light of the white tent, Gaius' eyes seemed to turn to flint. Silently he sat down.

Gods, the fellow's nose is better than mine, ran the thoughts of the proconsul as he immediately rearranged his plans and decided to treat the slave with genial courtesy implying equality. "Gaius," he said, "are you by chance kinsman to Consul Julius Lacer, the great patrician high in councils of emperors a quarter of a century ago?"

The bondsman replied, "Twenty-seven years ago when I was an infant, my father, Consul Lacer, sold me at birth. He was in debt, your excellency."

To hide his surprise, and ease the gathering tension, Classicus poured white wine into the two silver goblets, added dopples of cold spring water from the crystal ewer, and slid one cup across the marble tabletop to Gaius.

The slave ignored the hospitable offering.

"No refreshment, my young friend?"

"Only after the day's work is done, governor." He spoke with a quiet authority Classicus envied.

Thoughtfully the governor sampled his tangy cold drink, rather nettled that the talk was not proceeding as he had planned. "Your mother? Relations?"

Gaius answered tersely: "She died giving birth to me. No relations, excellency."

His lordly host sat intrigued and smiling. There sat no common slave or average young male. And just what had Classicus expected? A pervert with gold hoops piercing his ears and reeking of perfume? Unfortunates such as that were not confined to the slave caste, of course. But Gaius was a class in himself. Worse, he made the governor feel like a goatherd.

"Gaius, tell me about your life and work," said Classicus.

The sire of Gaius had sold him two days after birth to Apollodorus, the renowned architect from Damascus. Raised in his patron's villa in Rome, the education of Gaius began when he was three. Tutors taught him rhetoric, reading, and writing. Later he was drilled in Latin and Greek. When he was seven, his master began instructing him in minerals, geometry, and rudimentary principles of architecture, starting with the use of the square, rule, and plummet line, and the practical usefulness and beauty of the arch.

"I worked as an apprentice on my first bridge when I was eleven. Ten hours a day. Two hours each night Greek bondsmen of my master schooled me in the arts."

Classicus interrupted: "Commendable . . . er . . . commendable. Pray continue." Was the young thug inwardly laughing, wondered Classicus, deciding to handle his slave architect with skill.

"And the humanities," said Gaius, ironically. "Philosophy, the historians, Greek and Roman poets. The education of a patrician, your excellency."

Leaning back in his cushioned armchair Classicus reassembled his thoughts. There was some vital connection between this impressive slave-brawn and Commander Rufus Liscus, who would be chief of the gold mines. Classicus got part of the explanation before his mind lost the rest . . . If Gaius and the legion officer were enemies their mutual loathing was destined to rebound to the golden good fortunes of Classicus himself. With a sense of the bizarre fitness of things pleasing to the gods, he recalled that he had the solution to the enigma in his wall safe back in his New Carthage legation on the Mediterranean coast. It was an innocuous document which indirectly supplied the key to the relationship and coming hostility between this slave architect and the bearded legion officer, Rufus Liscus.

"My young friend," the proconsul said, cordially, "you have no forehead or face brands, so your master has not imprisoned you for insubordination or attempted escape. Nor are your ears notched. But you wear the bronze armlets bearing your master's name?" A timely and delicate reminder to Gaius that he must not consider himself an equal of Proconsul Cornelius Caecilius Classicus.

Gaius looked steadfastly at his host. "That is correct, your excellency," he said, bleakly.

"Any insignia burned in your body, Gaius?"

The bridge builder crossed his muscular brown arms. "There are none, governor."

"Then you are fortunate that your master is more of a kindly patron and father than a master."

Silence.

The proconsul changed tactics. "My young genius, do you ever smile?"

Reluctantly the tightly-closed lips of Gaius parted, revealing a hasty glimpse of clean teeth. Then his mouth closed.

Did Gaius have a wife and children and any money of his own, the proconsul inquired, courteously? Gaius had neither family nor money. He was fed and clothed by the legions; the noble Apollodorus was paid five thousand in gold annually by the imperial *Fiscus* for Gaius' work building bridges, roads, and mining. His name was listed in the slave civil-service rosters of both Spanish provinces.

For a startled moment it seemed to Classicus that the spring water in the crystal bottle had turned to solid silver. The container would be too heavy to lift. Then the governor furtively lifted the small jug and saw to his relief that there was still liquid within. He turned his attention to Gaius. Did the young stalwart know that should he be allowed to earn and keep fifteen thousand in gold he might be granted the right to buy his freedom and birthright as a patrician?

The quiet in the tent became so pronounced that the governor heard the tweeting of birds and neighing of horses out in the pines. At last came the rejoinder of Gaius:

"As the poet Horace wrote: *'I search and search, and where I find, I lay the wisdom up against a rainy day.'* "

Classicus stared vacantly for a while. Having expected an outburst of profanity or a babble of frustrated ambitions that would reveal the true nature of Gaius the slave, he had instead been treated to a dose of poetry that kept the portals closed, concealing the real character of the slave builder. *This slave is wary . . . but he is also vain, rebellious, aspiring, quietly arrogant; probably a sleeping volcano. But this mass of slave power will be indispensable for the next year or so, ergo, keep matters on a friendly footing. I will find some way to bribe him if I have to.*

Suddenly Gaius said, "Your excellency, I hear that Publius the architect plunged to the rocks from the spans outside not long ago. Fatal accidents will occur unless safety precautions are observed at all times." A blend of grief and anger crossed his now expressive features.

Instantly alert, Classicus replied, "A great architect, splendid character, close personal friend of mine. I delivered his funeral oration."

Now the face of Gaius was interested and sympathetic. Leaning over the marble table, he said, "Governor, have you ever witnessed the awful destruction of a *turbo?*"

Baffled and relieved, Classicus replied, "I have not. I heard of a big tornado, however, that caused a little havoc in western Spain two years ago." He was bewildered by Gaius's sudden cold glance. The slave was more and more of an enigma. . . .

"That whirlwind killed some of my friends," said Gaius, shortly. "I survived. My friends died."

Classicus rallied to say, *"Dolendum est quod."*

"My apologies, excellency," said Gaius, his face flushing, "but there was a mining disaster I wish to speak of." And he proceeded to describe a tragedy of five years ago in an estuary mine in southwestern Farther Spain. He had directed his chained men in the building of a medium-sized earth dam to block a mainstream flowing west from the confluence of three small rivers. A large lake was soon formed behind the earth barrier and watergates, leaving the drained rockbed ready for digging.

His hands doubled up, Gaius continued, "My men dug without success for days, excellency, and the channel was littered with tailings. Then I discovered the protruding head of a great lode of gold. What did I do?"

Classicus was fascinated. "I know not, young genius."

"Sir, I reacted like a fool," muttered Gaius. "I climbed the embankment and told the patrician prospector of the big strike. I explained the men would need a day or two to clear the site of heavy stones, weeds and mud before we could begin extracting the rich ore. I was still talking as the smiling prospector signalled to men at the watergates."

Guessing the end of the tale, Classicus waited in sympathetic silence.

"Before I could stop his men," breathed Gaius, "up went the floodgates! We call it the boom-off. The force of water impounded, tons of it, the lake foaming death, down it roared on my chained, screaming, trapped men. Rocks, logs—and my men—all swept away." His face white, Gaius whispered, "Soon the gates went down. The channel had been cleared of debris and living *men*."

"Tragic," sighed Classicus, hiding his boredom.

"After that I remained in the pit with the new slave force," continued Gaius. "I made more strikes. I shouted the tidings up to the patrician and warned him not to open the gates because I was too valuable to be washed away. He never did. He was angry, but he never crossed me. He had to wait a little longer for his gold. The second two hundred slaves survived, excellency. I wonder if any are alive today."

Classicus had lost control of the interiew and must re-establish his authority. "Gaius," he said, firmly, "you are to be chief engineer of mines in the Sil River basin in northwest Farther Spain. I pray all goes well with your rock-gangs. Never must it be said that Cornelius Caecilius Classicus allowed slave workers to drown in gold fields." There was an artistic truth that startled and pleased the proconsul. "I will allow you wide latitude in handling your men, subject to Commander Rufus Liscus, of course, who will be acting brigadier in charge of troops and slaves. Appoint safety-monitors—whatever. Strive to find gold, for the emperor is pressing me mercilessly. I am counting on you." He arose then, wishing to end the interview.

The architect gazed obliquely as if weighing an offer, not a command. Then he replied, "Governor, I accept the challenge."

Blinking away his astonishment, Classicus genially left the tent with Gaius, going out into the shifting green and sunny light of the pine forest. Then Frontinus came forward from the approachway of the bridge and the governor presented Gaius—as Gaius the slave.

"It is an honor to meet Gaius Julius Lacer, the patrician," said Frontinus, admiringly.

Reddening with pleasure, Gaius said, "The general is very kind."

"Let me congratulate the man who did the undoable," went on the treasurer. "You, the patrician architect who designed the Tagus spans many architects said could never be built, or if they were, would collapse."

"My Tagus Bridge will never fall," said Gaius, quickly.

"Come, come," Classicus jested, "a bridge is only a bridge. Spain will soon be criss-crossed with roads, aqueducts and charming stone spans. Gaius, complete these arches. You will be summoned to my capitol of New Carthage shortly." He started toward the chariot and tethered grays, beckoning Frontinus to follow.

Frontinus did not leave at once. "Again, my compliments to you, Lacer, on the erection of your great Tagus bridge," he said to Gaius, and a look of respect passed between the slave and the general.

Frontinus seemed quietly amused as he again took the reins of the chariot horses while Classicus seethed in silence. But as the carrier ground into shaking motion, the proconsul said, loudly, "We must be back at the legation by lamplighting time. I yearn to spend the night with my dove of an Enna."

Since his treasurer was hopelessly in love with Enna, Classicus sensed that Frontinus' slight smile gave way to grimness, but the man kept his eyes on the horses and said nothing.

The journey back to the Mediterranean coast was a masterpiece of clatter without conversation.

III

That evening, after a bath and anointing and light supper alone, Classicus entered his wife's sitting room to catch up with her day's events in the legation. She sat on the gold brocade couch in the marble chamber, unringed white hands twisted together in the lap of her green silk gown. She seemed to be listening to the cries of tropical birds outside in the legation gardens of New Carthage, or the muted rumble from the Mediterranean wharves far below. But one quick look at her hands and the proconsul knew her thoughts. Enna's interlocked fingers always signified a day of charity: money and baskets of fresh loaves, shellfish and garments for needy Roman colonists and Spaniards alike. He approved. As the Lady Excellency, her steadfast generosity enhanced his spotless reputation as a humane and honest ambassador of the emperor. But since her principal obsession was merciful government, he decided she must, at the moment, be pondering administrative matters.

"Well, my love," he said, seating himself on a gray velvet sofa across from her, "aside from helping petitioners this fine day, have you let your mind dwell on affairs of state, both provincial and imperial?"

Her fingers began pleating the green flounces of her skirt before she answered.

"I have received a letter," she said finally, "from Pompeia Plotina Planta."

Relaxed and interested, he commented, "Every time you hear from the wise woman, I expect repercussions through the empire. How is Domina Plotina? Still giving her husband military advice? Not that General Trajan needs it. I continue to get glowing reports of his popularity among our guerrilla friends up north. What news? Fashion tidings, for example?" he joked. "Has she broken down and taken to wearing silk instead of cotton and linen? If the dawn ever comes when Plotina wears a single jewel, even a simple cameo—"

"Rome has promoted Marcus Trajan to General of the Rhine legions," said Enna, quietly. "He and Plotina are at present the guests of Verus Maturus out in Gades. They will be here in a few days on their way to Germany."

Long ago Cornelius Classicus had trained himself to hear good or evil tidings impassively if he chose, but this news was magnificent. The departure of General Marcus Trajan from Spain was another sign that the Divine Ones on Olympus looked with favor on his gold-for-Rome activities; and he resolved to be truly devout the next time he offered oblations to the deities.

But since Enna was watching, he began to jest about entertaining the distinguished soldier and his plain wife, Plotina. Hail, austerity; no dining couches, only chairs. And give Trajan what he wants: ungarnished food, with radishes and lettuce for the luxury touch. Yet did gracious Enna believe the promotion might stimulate the General to try Turbot Domitian, Lobster Livia Imperial, Partridge Pies in Butter Pastry Cages, and Filbert-Date Tarts *Hispania?*

"Be serious," Enna said, frowning. "Are you pleased that Marcus Trajan is leaving Spain?"

Classicus carefully selected a salted almond from a green glass bowl. "He's been promoted to Field Marshal. Of course, let us hail his fair fortune. But who replaces Trajan in Farther Spain?" It had suddenly occurred to him how important this might be to his plans.

"General Lucius Antonius. Sent direct from Rome."

"Antonius," said the governor. "Who is he?"

His wife's hazel-blue eyes—beautiful, passionate eyes in a cold and spartan face—seemed appraising. "According to Plotina, an able and loyal officer. Cornelius, why do you ask?"

His glance roved over her aquiline profile and high-held tiers of chestnut curls. "My dear domina, the hackles of our northern guerrilla wolf-tribes rise quickly, even though the whitecloak *Togati* seem submissive and peaceful; we cannot afford an antagonizing replacement for Trajan."

Anxiously she whispered, "And how about the Arvacan Blackcloaks? Chieftain Luna Malendi? Isn't his the largest guerrilla nation?"

"In all of Spain," he agreed. "Enna, your fumbling spouse conferred amicably with the fabulous Malendi last November. He is now my brother. I am his. As to his future intentions let us pray all proceeds harmoniously—as I am sure it will." That prevarication was necessary, should Enna confide in Frontinus.

Her narrow white hands relaxed. "I am relieved. Marcus Trajan did so much to help Malendi's people. They worship Trajan."

"As they should," come the proconsul's hearty assent. "He is a great man; practical idealists and humble intellectuals always are."

Enna said: "I think it may be auspicious that Trajan has been transferred to Germany. On the eastern frontier he will command thousands of troops, far more than the three legions he had in western Spain under Governor Maturus." She glanced cautiously at her husband. "Each morning when you offer wine and salt and cakes to the Genius of Domitian . . . but you know what I think and hope."

She had startled him, which rarely happened, and momentarily he was frightened. "My love, indiscretion is not one of your faults. Emperor Domitian will never abdicate. He will reign until he rots or the empire rots. And Trajan of Spain will never seize the Curule Chair by force. Could it be, my fairest, that you place confidence in the astrologers?"

Enna did; she thought of the prophecies constantly. Therefore, should Emperor Domitian die by violence next September—

"You are aware," her husband stated, "that the Emperor is still alive and only forty-five. He claims he's immortal; maybe he is. But if he is assassinated as predicted, our Conscript Fathers will fight it out for the Dictatorship; and from my experience in the *Curia,* and knowing how senators can mangle the government, I would forecast that my friends in Rome will compromise on an innocuous old advocate such as Senator Cocceius Nerva from Crete. Big-nosed Nerva will hold power, his asthma allowing, if the Legions and Praetorian Guards receive big enough donations from the Treasury, if there is any money left in the imperial vaults."

"So many if's," said Enna, shaking her head and giving Classicus a thoughtful glance. "Cornelius, what is wrong? For the past year you have been so irritable, without reason. I know you worry about money, but . . ."

"But what—?"

Her maternal look nettled him: she was sympathetic but unyielding. "Cornelius, I've given you my jewels and the last of my dower money. If I let you have my legacy fortune, you would squander it in a month. One of us must be practical and plan for the future."

He arose and began pacing to give his temper time to cool, remembering that his treasurer, Frontinus, faced no looming danger of bankruptcy and imprisonment. While not wealthy, the ex-general was in comfortable circumstances—and Emperor Domitian doted on his legionaries. It was rumored that the madman in Rome actually shed tears over casualty lists from eastern battlefields, and never did he touch property or money of his soldiers and retired officers, such as Myron Frontinus. Thus it was necessary to remain in the good esteem of Frontinus as long as possible.

"Enna," he said, returning to his couch, "since you have such excellent theories about government, kindly enlighten me about my colleague in Farther Spain. Is Governor Verus Maturus a planted spy from Rome?"

Like Juno in glistening green silk she sat on her gold-cushioned sofa, as though waiting for something. "Of course not, Cornelius. In the emergency ballot-box drawing last October, Verus drew Farther Spain. Remember?"

Classicus' laugh was not pleasant. "It must have been managed so Maturus would win western Spain. Why else would he be sent to the end of the world? The only light reading I have these days arrives in letters from Rome that lampoon our bald and outjawed Maturus. The emperor must sob nightly at his absence," chuckled the governor. "Maturus' loud orations on the sanctity of the laws always lulled Domitian to sleep."

Enna looked mildly irritated. She picked up a hooped circle of linen and began stitching with a gold needle threaded in crimson floss. "Verus Maturus may be somewhat pompous, but he is an honest man and a brilliant jurist."

Yawning, the proconsul remarked, "I'm honest, too, but pinched by poverty. I'd feel much safer if I had some legions under my control; a few foot guards and cavalry are not enough. After all, according to Rome, I should have two or three legions under my authority also."

She sighed. "Everything is so chaotic these days, Cornelius. But all of Spain is peaceful now. What worries you?"

He would confide moderately that he was infuriated over a letterscroll from Governor Verus Maturus requesting permission to come to New Carthage to survey the *lex* archives and district courts of Hither Spain. Not that Classicus cared, but what right had that legal vulture to pry into the affairs of eastern Spain? Maturus should stay home in Gades on the Atlantic coast.

"But each Spanish province is entitled to a pair of Proconsuls," Enna reminded him, "one to collect taxes and administer the public works and military, and the other to serve as Chief Magistrate." She bit off the red silk thread of her embroidery and laid the round of silken white fabric on a table. "And since Rome has not yet sent you a judicial co-worker, Verus Maturus is only trying to assist you by offering to come here and survey the working of the laws and courts."

That was true and Classicus felt better. Invite the governor of Farther Spain to study the march of justice in Hither Spain, on the stipulation that Classicus be forced by the Senate to reopen abandoned mines which were in Maturus' region, and that the noble Maturus would lodge no objection? A case of both governors patriotically easing mutual burdens. He looked with approval at his wife and started a new subject. "Enna, today I interviewed the slave engineer who built the Tagus Bridge. I'd forgotten the bridge until know-all Frontinus looked ready to fall on his knees when I introduced him to the young geologist—a patrician sold at birth by his spendthrift sire."

"Frontinus showed me the secret intelligence reports on Gaius Julius Lacer," she said. "Cornelius, why put this bridge architect to work mining gold?"

"My cherished domina," he retorted, "the Emperor demands gold and more gold to pay peace-tribute to those barbarians across the Danube. The Holy One in Rome undoubtedly thinks Spain is a solid gold peninsula. Very well. Who knows minerals as well as Gaius Julius Lacer? I'd guess that young Lacer is even superior to our late lamented Publius. And may I remind my love that the sooner I launch a mining venture under my own control, as the Senate orders, the sooner those contentious inspectors from Rome will stop coming here to accuse *me* of gold thefts. Let them expose the real culprits: the men who mine for their own profits and overlook sending one-half the gold ore they dig to the emperor!"

For a moment Enna's wonderful eyes rested upon him. "Dear husband," she said, quietly, "you are exhausted. Why not a swim in your plunge, and then . . ." There was a faint flush on her cheeks. "Why not spend the night with me?"

Briefly conscience battled a strange and sick revulsion complicated by the fleeting illusion that his wife was a harpy with the body of a bird and the head of a maiden. Nauseated by the unreal image, he seized on a throbbing suspicion. "I see your scheme," he said accusingly. "You wish to keep me from my new Greek slave girl!"

Enna arose and tried to lay peaceful hands on him, but her hyacinth perfume smelled like burning feathers and he wrenched away and started for the white pilastered portals. Ashamed, he let her touch his arms; now the fragrance she used was wistfully delicate and flowery.

"Cornelius," she said, calmly, "I have talked with the slave girl today. Penelope is a good girl, a maiden, and has survived terrible tragedy in Greece. Her father was killed and every male villager except the children—all slain. Penelope was taken by Roman troops who cast lots for her. She begged them to kill her. Curiously, they did not molest her. Then the centurion decided to send her to Emperor Domitian; again she pleaded for the dignity of death. At last the soldiers took her to a seaport and sold her to an old Egyptian who promised his protection. She is a strong, lovely, deserving girl, and gentle as a breath of spring."

His apathy gave way to euphoria. "Some of those insurgent Greek provincials are the breath of death to Roman tax-collectors," he replied, humorously. "And for every Roman slain, an entire Greek village is put to the torch and the sword. Keep that in mind, my love."

Enna became coldly insistent. "Cornelius, a girl like Penelope is not to blame. Please let me find a husband for the poor child?"

"I'll bargain. Give me the keys to your money vaults and you can have the golden-haired goddess from Greece."

Enna's thin red lips quivered.

He had lost again. "I am not going to flog Penelope," he said, angrily. "I treat my concubines with respect. Why do you drive me into scenes like this? You didn't free Penelope, did you, woman? Where is she now?"

Enna watched in aloof despair.

"Where is Penelope?"

"Under guard in your suite."

He lingered at the fragrant dark sandarac doors between the white pilasters while Enna watched. At length he bowed elaborately, opened the doors and looked back. "Try and understand your barbarous husband, my love. *Vale.*"

IV

On the Ides of March, couriers escorted Gaius Lacer on horseback from the bridge to the New Carthage legation. Late that afternoon he had Governor Classicus' pink marble pool to himself. Since opportunities to swim had been few the past year, he decided to test the crawl-stroke, which soldiers had recently told him was the fastest, most powerful method for human propulsion through water. Inhaling through his mouth, he began the alternate arm-strokes and leg-kicks, ploughing through the water of the plunge so fast that he almost rammed his head against a pink marble dolphin at the opposite end. He was exhilarated; here was the stroke of all strokes. He swam back and forth seven times.

When ready to dress he was astounded by the sartorial array held out by admiring Moorish slaves. Gone were his battered old boots and gravel-caked buckskins; in their place was an assortment of fine-weave undershirts and drawstring short *bracae* of best quality Egyptian cotton; kidskin tunics of various lengths; a short cloak of velvety doeskin and four pairs of new brown leather high boots in various sizes. The shoes were even lined with white padded cotton insoles. Dressed in the well-fitting clothes and footwear the exact size, Gaius buckled on a polished oxhide belt studded with copper nailheads. Looking in a bronze mirror, he ran an ivory comb through his thick, straight black hair and decided he was now a civilized Roman.

On the main floor of the legation he was directed to a yellow marble anteroom where a burly soldier stood on guard. The legionary gave him an appraising squint. "You must be Gaius Julius Lacer, the architect," he said in an ocean-breaker voice. "Heard big things about you." The soldier shifted his spear from right to left and again to his right fist.

Years ago Gaius had evolved the philosophy that reticence was a shield for his dignity. "I am a bondsman," he reminded the soldier.

"Blistering hades, what of it?" the guard replied. "My father was a soldier, so I've never been a slave. But no citizenship for me until my eighteen-year stretch is up. Some troops are yoked to a twenty-year pull, so I guess I owe Mercury a goose for my lot. One more year and I get my pension and land. I'm paid and receive bounty money now and then, but no soldier's free. Ever carry a sixty-pound pack?"

The heartiness of the legionary somewhat thawed Gaius' customary wariness. "No," he said, politely.

The soldier's garrulous thick lips extended cordially. "My name is Flavian. No relation to our Flavian emperor. I'm with the first cohort of the First Cilician, came here from Egypt last year. Before we shipped out of Alexandria we were treated to a scroll of love from the emperor." A smile sweetened his craggy face. "Some happy tale: after we get honorable discharges, we're legally married to our wives. If we marry after our service, our women get citizenship, too. As for myself, I found Beryl the first month I got to Spain, married her before my comrades saw her! My wife's father was a soldier, too, of course. Beryl lives in Ioza, now a cave village."

In spite of the man's loquacity, Gaius sensed his sincerity. "I wish you and your domina happy years."

"Same to you and your lady."

Gaius smiled. "I'm not married." He had quickly identified Flavian as an adjutant, by the brass-tipped leather tabs of his breastplate and ringed helmet ready for the horsehair crest of commissioned rank. Only the bravest became *optios;* occasionally one such as Flavian rose above tradition to become an officer, a rarefied military realm customarily reserved for aristocrats.

Flavian suddenly stiffened to salute and thrust out his lance.

Two ladies had strolled into the room. One was of medium height, had eloquent topaz eyes, high layer after layer of lustrous brown curls and wore blue silk. Her companion was older, heavy of nose, slightly freckled and stately. Her pale auburn hair was confined by a chaplet of brown wool threads braided on wires and her ordinary gray linen robes resembled those worn by freedwomen. At once Gaius noticed that she smiled and frowned at the same time, and when her sagacious eyes studied him, he felt as if he were being judged. And despite the gray linen, he recognized her high rank and that of the lady in blue silk. He bowed and caught a waft of hyacinth and pine fragrance.

"You are Gaius Julius Lacer?" inquired the aristocrat in gleaming blue.

"I am, my lady."

Enna glanced at her Junoesque companion in gray and again at Gaius. "This is the Domina Plotina, wife of General Marcus Trajan. I am Enna, wife of Proconsul Classicus."

How control his astonishment at meeting the magnetic Plotina, wife of the great Trajan? And the Lady Excellency of Hither Spain? What should a bondsman do in this situation? Fall to his knees? Kiss their hands? Or freeze to a military stance? He chose the last.

Plotina scrutinized him solemnly. Plotina, the austere and yet utterly feminine woman, the wife and confidante of General Trajan. "When I was a young girl," she said in low, deliberate tones, "my parents and your sire often entertained each other in Rome. I recall that your father was a Consul the year you were born."

Inflamed by resentment of the father he had never known, Gaius spoke of something else. "My lady, I built a bridge for General Trajan. I built two bridges for him. I'm ashamed of the first."

"And which bridge fails to please you?" Her searching eyes were the color of emeralds.

"The one near the General's home village of Italica," he replied, eager to win her approval. "In western Spain," he added, unnecessarily. "It is a permanent bridge, but it is homely. Three arches unequal in length." He could not stop the outpouring. "It looks off-balance, but it's safe and it will endure. The old wooden spans collapsed after a flood. I picked a new site upstream with a natural causeway of granite reaching out into the water."

He glanced at Flavian, but the soldier stood motionless in leather shirt, shoulder and body metal and steel helmet, his spear straight at his side.

"And the other bridge you built for the General?" asked Plotina.

"My lady, it is the Tagus Bridge north of Caesar's Town." He looked away in acute embarrassment. He had stopped in time before he launched into a description of brick walls coated with stucco, rammed earth cottages in rural Spain . . . An excitable tongue was a foe if he hoped to gain his freedom and patrician rank.

Better hold to his determination to ward off all but superficial associations.

Plotina at last observed, "You resemble your sire, Consul Julius Lacer. It was in those sad days he was trying so hard to borrow money to buy you back from Apollodorus." She frowned and smiled. "I was only a young girl then, scandalizing my noble parents by studying histories of military campaigns, but I remember it was said your father's ceaseless activities in your behalf caused his premature demise." Her green eyes were kind. "Did your patron, Apollodorus, ever tell you of your parent's last request?"

Gaius tried to control himself. "No, my lady."

Her hands touched his. "Consul Julius Lacer's dying appeal to Apollodorus and a few friends and slaves at his bedside were, *"Raise my son Gaius Julius Lacer to be a noble patrician, but teach him an occupation. Tell him it was luxury and idleness that ruined me. Tell him my ghost will try to guard him."*

Gaius looked his gratitude. The load of hate against his dead father lightened a few degrees.

"Come," said Enna, lightly taking him by the arm.

Soon he and the ladies entered a lamplit marble room where two men stood conversing near a long table covered in white damask, piled with red roses surrounding a small plaster bust of Emperor Domitian crowned with a wreath of green laurel. Instantly Gaius recognized the toga-clad man as Governor Cornelius Classicus. And the other one?—the lean, tall soldier of majestic mien? One quick look and Gaius lowered his head, unprepared to meet his idol, General Marcus Ulpius Trajan of Italica, Spain.

". . . and since the emperor's friends cannot mine sufficient gold in Britain and other provinces to meet the imperial quotas, we in Spain must assuage our Caesar's worries by the ore we hope to dig in Governor Maturus' western Spanish domain. Ah, the ladies! And our mining genius!" came the voice of Proconsul Classicus.

Gaius looked at the red and blue floor as the men drew close.

"Our architect is modest," Classicus jested. "Marcus, allow me to present Gaius Julius Lacer, master of limestone, granite, sandstone and flint; artisan of alluvials and all such magic arts."

Gaius heard the assured bass voice of General Trajan addressing him: "Look up, man. Always hold yourself in high regard."

Raising his head, Gaius looked into the black eyes of Marcus Trajan. *"Gratiae,* sir," said Gaius, his heart beating faster over the pleasant realization that he and the General were the same height.

"Tell me about your bridges," said Trajan, as though he really wanted to know. "How many? Where?"

Feeling at ease, Gaius answered, "Sir, I have supervised six under the guidance of my patron, Apollodorus. I was an engineer for the long Emerita Augusta spans, sir. Chief engineer for two others. I also finished a small work that a patrician architect had almost completed before his death, sir."

Trajan's eyes crinkled cordially. "Your age?"

"Sir, I will be twenty-eight on the Ides of April." It was like talking to a friend he had known for years . . . or a father.

"Lacer, have you ever designed aqueducts?" Trajan asked.

Gaius was thrilled afresh, for he had been addressed by his surname, as an aristocrat customarily was. "No, sir, but I could, General."

The officer's dark eyes seemed to bore into Gaius, then Trajan glanced quickly at Enna.

"Gaius, we would like you to have dinner with us," said Enna, smiling at Gaius and Plotina.

Worship of the gods meant so little to Gaius that he almost sat down in the carved cypress chair indicated by Enna before Classicus began intoning a religious rite in Greek. The proconsul offered small silver dishes of salt and barley bread to the sightless white bust of Domitian, lapsed into Latin and raced through an invocation to Jupiter and all the gods of Rome. Gaius could not understand a word until the governor chanted, ". . . under the benign protection of the *Lares* and *Penates* of this Domicile." Gaius recollected in time that the Divine Ones must sip wine before human beings, so he, too, tilted a silver goblet and a few drops of purple wine spattered on the blue and crimson mosaic floor. Then they sat down.

Gaius now became overwhelmed by a sense of not belonging. Gleaming black hands of Negro slavegirls held out blue enamelled platters of baked lamb sprigged with parsley; whole lobsters in yellow dill jelly; silver baskets of ruffly lettuce; radishes impaled on ivory skewers; boat dishes of steaming asparagus and a huge bronze casserole of roast chickens pushed forward on a wheeled trolley. Then he caught sight of a black in a red loincloth balancing on his head a massive silver tray supporting an elaborate superstructure that gave off the aroma of baked pastry; it reminded him of the wooden scaffolding of a bridge. So many foods were offered that he was unable to choose any and gestured away the smiling servants.

They listened to Governor Classicus discourse with authority about iron, silver, quicksilver, cobalt, lead, tin, and gold. Then Gaius became aware of the voice of General Trajan who was seated across the table at the right of Classicus.

"Would Lacer the builder like a radish?" The officer handed one on its ivory stick to Gaius.

"*Gratiae, gratiae,*" said Gaius and his tension subsided.

"We have a starting point for friendship," said Trajan. "Your patron, Apollodorus, is a close friend of mine—a brilliant man." Taking two lettuce leafs from a silver basket proffered by a Negro girl, Trajan handed one to Gaius and before the architect could thank him again, the General went on, "I have been searching my memory. Now I recall that Apollodorus mentioned your name to me some years ago. He called you his most capable and promising young man."

"Thank you, sir," said Gaius, happy that Trajan had not used the word, *slave,* and wondering with amusement if his evening's conversation was to be restricted to words of gratitude . . . He ate his radish and lettuce with contentment.

"Apollodorus is meeting me in southern Gaul," Trajan continued, his keen black eyes twinkling in approval as he watched Gaius. "Your patron will accompany Lady Plotina and me to our home in Colonia Agrippina at the Rhine. Your noble protector goes to build border garrisons. Hardly architectural and artistic monuments, but without such strongholds, the barbarians from across the Danube might destroy the cities, roads and bridges we have."

"General Trajan," said Gaius, "my patron, Apollodorus, is as patriotic as he is artistic. An illustrious teacher." Gaius searched for the right phrase and a simple statement leaped to mind: "General, sir, my patron Apollodorus has the humility of ability." His conscience was pleased.

So was Trajan who made no comment, but his dark eyes inspected Gaius as if he were a new recruit for the legions and had met the rigorous tests of the commanding general. At length Trajan said,

"You finished the Tagus Bridge ahead of schedule, Lacer, and I regret my Gemina legion had no chance to give it the test. How enduring will your Tagus Bridge be? How safe? How about flood crests? The legions always march in broken steps across any bridge, of course, for vibration of steps in hard rhythm could knock down arches. How about vibration?" The quick queries resembled a series of hammer-strokes.

Gaius wet his lips and again was standing on the bridge, watching an ominous cloud roaring out of the southwest—"General, sir," he replied, "I do not mean to be blasphemous, but my Tagus Bridge survived a terrible tornado. Men died—but the Tagus Bridge . . . not a single unmortared granite block was shaken. The great *turbo* of Jupiter did not harm my bridge, sir."

"Ye gods," said Classicus, jovially, but made no further attempt to enter the conversation between General Trajan and Gaius.

The general commented, "Lacer is not guilty of blasphemy. Shall we say Jupiter tested your bridge and found it worthy? I say aye."

Gaius reddened. Then he blurted, "My Tagus Bridge will stand throughout eternity, sir. I mean—forgive me—sir, I build for the future."

"What will the future do for you?" asked Marcus Trajan.

Feeling on trial, Gaius caught a reassuring smile and frown from Lady Plotina. In a chastened voice he answered, "General Trajan, sir, I am trying to say that I build honest bridges."

"The only kind worth building," said the officer, quickly. Gallantly he turned to Enna at his right. They began discussing the need for farm subsidies to aid hard-pressed Roman colonists and native farmers of Spain. Every thoughtful comment of Trajan showed genuine concern over the economic distress and declining birthrate of the empire's agricultural population. Soon the proconsul added his observations, showing a humanitarian concern for the plight of the poor classes and Plotina, too, joined in the talk.

Relaxing, Gaius smiled in his winecup, conscious of straining his ears in order not to miss one word from the tongue of his idol. Happening to glance across the laurel-crowned bust of the emperor, Gaius saw Governor Classicus staring at him dreamily. It was so strange a look that Gaius was puzzled. Plotina, sitting to the left of her host, seemed also aware of the handsome governor's rapt preoccupation, while Enna looked tense.

Then the governor rubbed his eyes and chuckled, "Our young architect needs sustenance." Jovially he raised his goblet toward Plotina, then interrupted Trajan who was telling Enna about his respect for the intelligence of women.

"Trajan, you have our mining genius in a trance," Classicus bantered. "Pray insist that he partake of more than a lettuce and a radish. His big frame needs sustenance!"

The General began passing small platters and bowls across to Gaius: a whole roast chicken, black olives, white shrimp meat swimming in sweet red vinegar, and wedges of cheese. Soon Gaius was eating heartily. Sampling some partridge and flaky butter crust, Trajan pronounced it elaborate but tasty, then he ordered Plotina to regale her palate with roast duck and honeyed red apples. Conversation became light and gay, and Gaius was swept into it. Trajan asked shrewd questions about architecture and geology and Gaius heard himself describing the different building stones—granites, marble, sandstone, slate and limestone. Humorously he described the damage sometimes done to great earth-dams by muskrats, beavers, shrimp and other animal life.

"Our animal foes," Trajan remarked with a smile. "What other factors threaten a massive work such as a dam, Lacer?"

"Water running over the crest, sir," said Gaius, "is one grave menace. Any considerable leaks, of course, are fatal. If the foundations are not driven into impervious subsoil, or if there is any shifting of the earth, the construction is doomed."

Classicus joked, "The emperor should levy legions of beavers to build empire dams, my noble friends. Think of the saving of money and human labor, gods, that would be something!" He arose, strikingly handsome in a purple-chevroned toga and his guests stood also. All extended goblets towards the image of Emperor Domitian surrounded by red roses.

"Let us drink to the health of our Master and God," said the proconsul.

Everybody drank in silence.

"Intermission," said the governor and clapped his hands. A slave orchestra hidden in bowers of potted palms and ferns at once began plucking harpstrings, blowing flutes and small trumpets, and launched into the stirring overture, *Roma Aeterna*.

Gaius watched the pretty Negro slavegirls bear out the roses from the table and return with garlands of yellow rosebuds for each place at the table. One shy Negress signed for Gaius to let her place a flowery chaplet on his head, but he grinned and backed away. Another girl in gray washed his hands in a silver bowl, but he balked when she knelt and tried to unbuckle his boots so she could bathe his feet. The orchestra played on, the fragrance of the flowers was alluring, and Gaius' spirits rose. He wished he had coins to give to the delightful dark girls who treated him like a great aristocrat.

Genially the governor insisted on placing a blossom circlet on Plotina's head-dress, got it on rather askew and was proud of the result. Enna put on her own garland and looked smilingly at the General. Trajan, with a burst of laughter, bestowed his chaplet on the frizzled black hair of a beautiful Negress servant who broke into tears of delight and prostrated herself at his boots. He lifted her up, gave her a piece of cheese and a copper coin. Out she scurried, her face glorified and gleeful. Then the proconsul laughingly put a flowered circlet on his own silvery curls, took Enna's arm and began strolling around. Plotina and Trajan paced in the opposite direction. Meanwhile a fresh parade of Negro men slaves bore in a wheeled float decorated in pink geraniums and white carnations, carrying a magnificent peacock imprisoned in a wicker cage. Squawking raucously the bird tried to spread its tail. Around the enclosure of the peacock were piles of fruit nested in ivy leaves: forced-ripened yellow pears, ruddy pomegranates, white grapes, red grapes, hothouse persimmons, clusters of currants and quartered lemons embedded in honeycomb.

Staring at the profusion of fruit and the imprisoned bird, Gaius could not analyze his instinctive reaction of sudden distaste. At last he returned to his cypress chair.

At the other end of the room Plotina talked in undertones to her husband. "Marcus, my dear, I have a ridiculous question: is it contrary to legion regulations for a bondsman to wear the uniform?"

"In my experience the question has never come up. Why do you ask, Plotina?"

Soberly she said, "I really don't know whether it is my idea or Enna's. But I sense that she is interested in Gaius Lacer, perhaps concerned over his safety, since mining is almost as hazardous as fighting. I wonder: when Lacer becomes chief miner up north, would it not be well for him to wear the uniform and armor? He will be directing a small army of surly prisoners—condemned murderers, arsonists, rapists, thieves. And a few legionaries. Even men in chains take orders better from a man in uniform. So if Lacer had an unofficial officer's rank—"

Trajan glanced sharply at his wife. "How would that insure the young patrician's safety?"

"The cuirass and helmet would help. So would the authority."

Deliberating with himself, the General finally said, "It could be done. Courtesy rating. A specialist of sorts. No pay, no weapons. But recognition, in a way, of his achievements and lineage, his dignity."

Her smile and frown gave charm to her freckled face. "Now it's your idea. I like it."

Trajan chose a small cluster of grapes from the peacock float and gave them to his wife. "I'll recommend the plan to General Antonius; ask him to send my request to Governor Maturus. Since Maturus is entirely agreeable about mining in Farther Spain, most likely he will approve an officer's commission, special—for young Lacer."

"It is too bad that Gaius Lacer cannot be a Tribune," sighed Plotina, and ate a few sweet white grapes.

"That high?" asked Trajan. "Only patricians hold the *tribunus militum* rank. Of course Lacer's father *was* a Consul."

Plotina's high forehead wrinkled in approval of her husband's decision.

Over dessert Trajan announced the plan to make Gaius Julius Lacer a detached legion officer with the rating of military tribune under the orders of Commander Rufus Liscus.

Gaius was agreeably stunned, not so much by this surprising good fortune coming from General Trajan, but because his hero had measured up to his ideal. There was nothing of the dissembler nor the effeminate about Marcus Trajan; he was a man, a clean shaft of steel. Now, more than ever, Gaius understood why Spaniards and Roman colonists lived in the hope that Trajan would be emperor some day, why many soldiers believed that the revered Marcus Trajan was on his way to the Purple Toga.

When Enna signaled that the party had ended, Classicus affably informed Gaius that Flavian the *optio* would show him to his quarters in the courtyard barracks. Deep in the ferns and palms the slave orchestra poured out the rousing music of *Hail The Eagles* while Gaius stood watching his superiors leave the room.

V

Outside the banquet chamber, Gaius started toward the anteroom, lost his way, and found himself walking through a wide porphyry corridor, at intervals passing palace guards with out-thrust lances standing at stiff attention. Eventually the marble passage opened into a white colonnade giving access to a loggia and the legation gardens. He stopped to look out into the torchlit darkness and to breathe the blended fragrance of the flowers. Gaius resumed walking, too proud to ask a guard for the way to the anteroom. Soon he stopped near a white staircase to examine an alabaster statue of Diana in a secluded niche.

He saw a girl gliding noiselessly towards the loggia, a girl of tawny golden hair, gowned in silver-embroidered white silk and wearing glittering diamonds at her throat and wrists. Not having seen Gaius, she peered furtively to the rear, drew her sheer white silk mantle more closely around herself and then stole towards the outdoors.

Gaius had never seen such a peerlessly lovely woman. Instantly attracted to her, he moved behind the statue pedestal, wondering if he dared speak, or ask if she needed help? Could *he* help her?

Hobnailed boots sounded on the floor; two guards appeared from the gardens to thrust their lances crosswise, barring the mysterious beauty's advance.

She shrank back, turned, and ran to another space between two Corinthian columns. Another pair of guards marched forward to block her. Then a centurion entered from outside and the terrified girl shrank back against a pillar.

The centurion gave a courtesy salute. "His excellency's orders are that you remain in your apartment after sunset."

"But I implore you to help me," she pleaded.

"You are allowed in the gardens only in the daytime," the officer answered, but his eyes were kind.

"Lord, help me get away!"

The officer shook his head. "I am sorry, domina."

She fumbled at the diamond necklace; it failed to unclasp in her trembling fingers. "Take the jewels," she begged. "Help me escape, lord centurion."

"I cannot. Allow me to escort you to your suite."

She darted into the red marble corridor, but retreated as soldiers marched toward her. At last she was surrounded by ten guards and the centurion. They did not touch her, but flight was now impossible.

Even in tearful despair her face was hauntingly lovely to Gaius, watching from behind the Diana statue, as she and her courteous military escort began ascending the stairs. Then she looked down, saw Gaius, and her eyes widened in child-like surprise and helpless appeal. His glance was mystified, uncertain, and wondering. All too soon she and the officer disappeared at the top of the marble flight.

Now where was his optimism of a half hour ago? Gone. Ruined by his chance observation of a young woman—a captive—who lived under guard in this vast legation. A woman. This was no time to lose his head, and over a girl who in all probability was the slave siren of another man. Love and marriage were of vital importance to Gaius, but long ago he had decided to wait for the right woman and the right time: the time of freedom. The present and future were too precarious for him to indulge in any passing affair; secretly he was proud that he had never stooped to sexual diversions.

He still remembered his indignation of years ago when he had found himself locked in a rose-bedecked suite by Apollodorus with a wistfully pretty Syrian slave girl of thirteen, a total stranger. His master had forced marriage with the slave, and in time Gaius had stopped treating her like a sister and the intimacy had been satisfying. After two years as his wife, she had died with her unborn child and Gaius had grieved for months—blaming and hating himself and loathing Apollodorus. Two months after his wife's ashes were respectfully interred in his master's ancestral mausoleum, Gaius was summoned to the great man's study in the villa in Rome.

"Gaius," said Apollodorus, "I have purchased a new bride for you, a lovely German girl of fifteen, healthy and buxom, well-bred and of good education."

"No, sir," Gaius had said, firmly. "No more locked bedrooms and sudden brides!"

The gray-haired Apollodorus sniffed acidly. "May I remind my Lacer that it is abnormal for a vigorous young male to live as a celibate. Why your hatred of woman?"

"I don't hate women!"

"Why the wrath? The Lacer pride?"

"Sir, sex urges are creative urges. There are many ways in which the creative energy can be spent. A man does not have to prove his masculinity by the sex act alone."

Apollodorus looked as if he had bitten into a green quince. "Gaius, we could debate the philosophic ramifications of sex for hours—but philosophy is one thing and physiology another. Let me remind you that my time is valuable and so is your time—which is also my time. Listen to reason. You could shorten your bondage to me by siring healthy children of the Lacer blood which I could sell for big prices."

Gaius nearly struck his master. "No child of mine will ever be sold!"

"Your temper matches your talents, Gaius," said the architect, pushing aside a pile of architectural drawings for a temple. "But there could be freedom for you in procreation. Early freedom. Why prolong your term of indebtedness to me? The healthy German maiden—"

"No child of mine will ever be sold!"

Apollodorus leaned on his muscular arms and waved a long forefinger at Gaius. "I paid over fifty thousand in gold to your sire, which in turn paid off some of his debts. I did that, not out of any burning desire to own a lusty red infant, but purely because your grandfather saved my life during the siege of Jerusalem. When I purchased you I gambled, for you might not have survived infancy. You did. Now I am faithfully following Consul Lacer's deathbed instructions—and I do not have to."

"A helpless infant, sold like a lion cub for the arena—" Gaius picked up an architectural drawing and caustically remarked, "Master, you used my suggestion about groined vaults after all."

"Who taught you about vaults and arches, how to split and cut stone, the effect of weather on substances, the stresses, the strains?"

"Life," Gaius snapped, and felt foolish.

"The first wise comment you've made today," said the elder architect, with a smile. "Gaius, if I and my wife were as wealthy as we were years ago, I should not feel forced to have you earn for me the investment I made in you. And if I die before you, my sons will be your new masters. They might not allow your wrath, nor respect the nobility of the Lacer *gens*. But, never again will I surprise you with a blushing virgin to wife. Live your celibate existence; be sure it is celibate. Now, I entreat my fifteen-year-old Lacer to grace that chair with his noble presence."

"Fifteen I am, sir." Gaius remained standing. "But I have the knowledge and skills of a man of fifty."

"Suffering gods," breathed the master architect and master of Gaius, "before I send you to Gaul, we will spend an intensive four weeks first reviewing bridge construction—then canal building. Did you study the scrolls and diagrams on the latter subject?"

Gaius ripped off a proud commentary: "Canals serve for navigation by ships. Irrigation. And drainage of marshy lowlands. The ancient Assyrians, Egyptians, and other old races built simple artificial waterways, sir. Roman methods are far superior."

"You humble me," said the older man, acidly. "Can a bireme go uphill? What do we do with ships in countries of varying land elevations?"

Speaking with restraint he did not feel, Gaius answered, "Sir, the ancients towed their barges on rollers between canal sections where the physical features of the earth rendered level water passages impossible." Proudly he continued, "We Romans cut tunnels and erect short ship aqueducts, where necessary, to equalize geographical irregularities. In its simplest form, sir, a canal is simply a waterway between two land masses resembling dams. The depth and width of the water-passage must accommodate the displacement of the largest vessel which is to pass through. If a navigable river is in the locality, it may be used in its natural state, or deepened and widened, if necessary. As to artificial embankments of earth and rubble and clay, and retaining piers—"

"Oh powers of heaven," moaned Apollodorus, his penetrating blue eyes staring beyond Gaius. Craftily he inquired, "In building a canal, how do we grapple with gradients?"

The answer came instantly: "Sir—master—your question is ridiculous. I will not be trapped. There are no ascents or descents in a canal. Uniform water level is maintained by a series of level water sections—."

"Enough—adequate—more than adequate—sufficient," sighed Apollodorus. "I am a boy of fifteen myself. If the lordly one will sit down and allow *me* to expound?"

Gaius had sat down.

Gaius shook his head to clear away the memory of that clash with his owner. No doubt the vigorous sixty-year-old Apollodorus had several spies keeping watch on Gaius Lacer in Roman Spain. Let them spy and pry into his life and affairs; his heavy work more than used his energy. And he was no longer fifteen—he was twenty-seven. If he never saw Rome and his master again, there would be no outcry from Gaius Lacer. And some day he would be emancipated—and then would he search and find the ideal woman.

She would be a shy, untouched maiden of patrician family. Educated, of course; able to do more than spin and weave and embroider, and toy with a lute or lyre. Beauty, too, was a requisite, but secondary to high moral character and good health. She was keeping herself for him—as he was keeping himself for her.

Not for him the conquest of woman after woman. Too many men damaged their health and characters with female chattels like the girl of glorious tawny-gold hair, . . . beauty with the false lure of chastity. He must put all thoughts of her out of mind. . . . Did she symbolize his own galling subjugation, as enslaved in her way as he was in his? Why waste thoughts on her? Such bejewelled charmers passed from man to man, sunk lower and lower, and ended as raddled females of the wineshops. By tomorrow he would have forgotten her pleading blue eyes.

He stamped away from the Diana statue, asked a guard how to reach the yellow marble anteroom and finally arrived. Flavian, the guard, was still standing at attention.

"I hear, sir," said Flavian, "that soon you'll be in uniform." He added, "Congratulations."

Gaius stared casually over Flavian's helmet. "Could you tell me, Flavian, who is the golden-haired girl in white silk?"

Flavian leaned on his lance and a remarkable smile adorned his seamed face. "Sir, we call her 'the goddess.' Every night a different dress, different jewels. Her name is Penelope. Slave captive from Greece, she came in not long ago on a rich old Egyptian's trireme from Ostia. When they brought her out to the wharf, I and some of my comrades happened to be helping load an ore ship. We looked at her—then we started passing a helmet to collect money to buy her freedom. But Governor Classicus was there, too, and he took a longer look." Watching Gaius shrewdly, the guard frowned. "Sir, I could name at least ten officers and thirty men who would go down on their knees to help 'the goddess' and never touch her."

"Go on," Gaius urged.

"Go on? His excellency Classicus always picked untouched fruit. Healthy virgins. So the goddess is in good hands."

Gaius felt a rush of detestation of Proconsul Cornelius Classicus. As for Penelope, she was temptation he had already conquered. He was disgusted and disillusioned. He would forget her, starting now. Sad blue eyes she had . . .

VI

March and most of April passed. In the New Carthage legation all seemed calm, but slaves and subordinate provincial officials constantly whispered their relief at being in Hither Spain under the beneficent protection of Governor Cornelius Classicus, instead of in Italy where executions throughout the domain of the Caesars were reported daily. The dispatches also brought Classicus orders to speed his mining expedition in Spain as quickly as possible. The proconsul bore the demands equably, but the man whose concern mounted was Frontinus, fiscal administrator of Hither Spain. After a lengthy exchange of letters with the Senate, he had received permission to use certain Spanish tax funds to finance the forthcoming gold search in northwest Spain. But there was another matter, a concealed affair.

One sunny April morning the treasurer was admitted to Enna's suite by a guard at the door. Once inside her sitting room, Frontinus made sure Enna was alone. "Do sit down," she said, warmly. "Frontinus, you must be weary. I should be, but I'm not. I've talked to fifty-two people since the first hour of appeals."

He took a citruswood chair beside her gold brocade couch. "Generosity replenishes beauty and energy, Enna."

"I like that better than a compliment." Her rose silk gown gave a touch of color to her ivory-tinted face.

"It is a compliment, Enna."

"Dear friend . . . what am I going to do about you?"

Frontinus poured red wine into a goblet, holding the stem in his gnarled but strong left hand, and gave the cup to her. She took it but did not drink. "I can see that you bring grave tidings." She placed the winecup on a polished fruitwood table.

Frontinus watched the sunlight through a casement explore her sensitive face. "Enna, I could handle this matter without telling you," he said in a low voice.

"No. I insist that you keep me informed. How much money is it this time, Frontinus?"

Slowly he replied, "I need five thousand gold coins before the revenue ship sails for Italy tomorrow. Enna—everything I have is yours to command. I could sell my abacus slaves. I own two sheep farms, four small villas, and I have considerable assets in gold and silver coins. I want to liquidate my holdings."

"Never, good friend," she breathed. "Is my husband involved again? Oh, I talk like a child."

The treasurer got up and stood looking at her. "Since your husband continues to steal tax monies, and falsify the reports, it is clear that he believes neither of us know it, and Rome does not suspect him. Enna, Enna. When will you tell him he must cease robbing the imperial tax coffers?"

She shook her head. "I don't know. I must protect him. You know he needs me."

"I must protect *you*," he answered quickly. "If I loan Cornelius money . . ."

"Frontinus, this is my burden! I will not let you become involved."

The treasurer stared. "Then I must warn your husband myself."

She became aghast. "Never do that! Cornelius might . . . might kill you."

Frontinus saw her looking at the slender sword hooked to the belt of his gray uniform, and wondered what she would do if some day he had to use the blade to protect her or himself against Classicus.

Hastily she said, "Cornelius has not yet sold my jewels. Poor Penelope—the child tried to give me my own diamonds and sapphires yesterday. She is only nineteen. I cling to the hope that a new *Imperium* will come to power and straighten everything out." Her narrow face became sad. "Frontinus, you must understand that my husband needs me. Lately, too, I have the fearful feeling that he is not a well man."

"Enna, face the situation," said the treasurer, keeping his intense hatred of Classicus to himself. "Why does Cornelius need large sums of money? Where does the money go?"

She tried to defend the proconsul with wifely indulgence. "He did pay five thousand in gold to buy Penelope from that aged Egyptian. He works so hard . . . his pleasures . . . But let's talk about *you*. Frontinus, you so resemble a thoughtful philosopher without a beard," she said with forced gaiety, "that sometimes I forget your heroic career in the legions."

"Enna—"

"We are talking about you," she insisted. "You are a hero."

"Paymasters are not heroes, my fair—" he caught himself and went on, "my fair-minded woman of integrity."

She gazed in concern at his maimed left hand and arm. "You were in action a year ago when the Parthians raided Middle Asia and Armenia."

"All I did was throw my payroll accounts at them," he said, trying to meet her mood. "The sight of those staggering sums reduced my attackers to insensibility."

She smiled dubiously. "The commanding general did award you a citation."

"He and my fighting comrades felt sorry for me."

Enna laughed softly. "Sir, you are dreadfully unconvincing." Her light mood changed to concern. "Frontinus—what can we do about Gaius Julius Lacer? When he goes north, he will face difficulties . . ."

"What difficulties, Enna?"

"I—Frontinus, the rumors must be true. That ferocious big black dog of Commander Rufus Liscus. The dog must have forced Publius off the unrailed bridge, but how? If Gaius knew how unprincipled Commander Liscus is—"

"Enna, Enna," the treasurer reproved. "The morals of Commander Liscus and the actions of his trained mastiff are neither proved nor disproved." He checked himself, wondering if Liscus was a hireling of Classicus. So far all Frontinus had was a tenuous suspicion that the proconsul planned, by some means, to get gold for himself. If Enna suspected, too, naturally she would remain loyally silent and thus shield her husband. So he introduced a new topic. "Enna, you and Lady Plotina succeeded in obtaining the uniform and armor for Gaius. Did you confide in the wife of Trajan?"

"Oh, no. Plotina is my best friend, but I would never discuss that matter with her. She and Marcus missed not seeing you, dear friend. Did you help the village treasurer upcoast straighten out his accounts?"

Frontinus had endless patience. "I did, Enna."

She smiled brilliantly. "Frontinus, I feel sorry for Gaius. Can we —can we help him, you and I?"

"Perhaps I can," he said, reflecting, and recalled how the adjutant, Flavian, seemed to look upon Tribune Gaius Lacer as a hero. With this in mind, Frontinus had privately investigated the adjutant's army record and found it extraordinary. The guard's bravery and honest loyalty to friends was impressive. Therefore the treasurer hoped to manipulate matters so that Flavian and some of his cohort mates of the First Cilician Legion would be assigned guard duty with the gold mining expedition.

The voice of Classicus was heard from the sandarac portals. "Still deep in fiscal conference?" Immaculate in a fresh toga, he advanced and kissed his wife's hands. "My love, how go your donations to the hinterlanders? Gods, you get up before the birds. Well, I do good works, too. If I had any real authority I'd slash taxes. But hearken to a deed or two of mercy your doting spouse has accomplished since the third hour. I halted two fights in the forum of our delightful city of New Carthage. The first had to do with a gang attack on a group of miserable Christians who would have gone down under a hail of stones had I not happened along."

Enna gazed adoringly.

"It gave me great joy to whip the stone-throwers," beamed Classicus. "Gods below," he went on, giving Frontinus a bright smile, "I'll never imprison the followers of the Jesus superstition. They pay their taxes like everybody else. I care not what god they revere; our extreme privilege is to bow down to Domitian."

"Cornelius, you are magnificent," breathed Enna. "What was your other good deed?"

"That? A Jewish fish dealer. Poor creature, some rogues had tied him and were going to shave off his beard. He still has it, and I received a Hebrew blessing which invoked Moses and Abraham." Looking vastly pleased with himself, the governor affably inquired, "Frontinus, are you keeping accurate track of my wife's legacy funds?"

The treasurer was standing. "My privilege."

Classicus hesitated and stared fixedly at the financial administrator until Frontinus began fearing the proconsul had overheard what transpired during his talk with Enna.

Then the curious rigidity left the procurator's handsome face and he sank down on the couch and poured wine for himself while Enna turned her back and hastily penned a few lines on a narrow length of papyrus. She casually gave it to Frontinus. "Will you handle this little matter for me?" she asked, lightly.

He bowed and walked out. Not until he was in the hall did he glance at the brief communication:

> To my vault guards. Give the noble Frontinus five thousand gold coins. Enna Gracchus, wife of Classicus.

He moved on, not seeing bowing slavegirls, while wondering whether the obligations of Classicus were a normal amount for a man of his class, or did Classicus owe five, ten, or fifteen thousand sesterces? Or were his private debts even higher? Did he owe several thousand or more in gold?

VII

To Gaius, normal life was best lived out of doors with forests for walls, the sky for a roof, pine boughs for a bed, and wool cloaks and pelts for warmth when he slept. Thus adjustment to life in the palatial legation on the blue Mediterranean coast was not easy. For one thing, he felt intrusive. When legionnaires saluted, he had to remember not to bow politely. When slaves prostrated themselves to hear his occasional questions as to how to find his way about the palace, he felt conspicuous and chagrined. Such tokens of respect made him savor more keenly his ambiguous position: a legion officer, a tribune, who was not an officer, armor and plumed helmet or not; an enslaved patrician deferred to as if no bronze armbands engraved with the words: APOLLODORUS OF DAMASCUS encircled in his upper arms.

True, escorted trips under guard to silver mines and gold washeries often took him from the legation. But there was always the return and Penelope, that tantalizing magnet, hidden somewhere in the vast marble building. Each day he tried to push her persistent image out of his mind. Sometimes it would dim, only to thrust back suddenly into his consciousness. He found himself peering down corridors, up at balconies and staircases, hoping for a glimpse of her. He looked in vain.

It was a relief to keep working on expedition equipment, maps, expected weather conditions, and the length of time it would take his thousands of laborers to drain the Sil river channel, build a dam, and drive shafts. He must also study yellowed old scrolls of the geographers: Theophanes, Polybius, Posidonius, and the more recent writings of Strabo; all dealt with Spanish terrain, minerals, and people. Out of this mass of information, which was a mixture of truth, superstition, and pure fancy, he was expected to forecast how much gold, silver, and other useful ores might be dug from the Phoenician mines of antiquity in northwest Spain. For the most part he sat engrossed, but often he saw Penelope's face in the unrolled parchments.

One day he stopped to read what he had just penned: "Deposits in the Sil river basin should contain gold, silver, iron, and blue eyes, and her hair is gold and diamonds." Angrily he wadded the page into a ball and dropped it in a brass waste receptacle.

To drive his thoughts from Penelope, he wrote a brief report on a grim subject: mining hazards. He had seen too many shackled men die from breathing lethal gas in underground tunnels, too many corpses with crushed skulls and bodies when support timbers collapsed under pressure of earth and rocks above. He recommended wooden helmets and heavy boots for the workers, and emphasized the need for safety monitors to give warnings at the first sign of gravel and rock avalanches. The likelihood seemed remote, despite the kindly promises of Proconsul Classicus, but up north Gaius would use any influence he had to insist on humane treatment of the manacled rockgangs. He knew what gold fever did to men.

"Gaius, my young friend, pray do not toil so hard or scowl so deeply," said a pleasant voice. "The time of gray hairs and death comes all too soon."

Instantly arising, Gaius bowed. "Your excellency."

"Let me pretend that I am the mining *auctoritas*," Classicus smiled, taking Gaius' red cushioned oak armchair. "I admire your writings. Commendable. I stopped to inform you that some Cilician infantry troops are going with the expedition. One of them, an *optio* named Flavian, will be your aide. He is requisitioning equipment which should make life comfortable for you in the wilderness. Even a tin bathtub and a small altar, should you have a favorite deity or two. My young friend, do saunter out and breathe fresh garden air for a change. The day is clear and grand. Meander up the Staircase of Fountains. Marvel at the tropical bird sanctuary. Those I heartily recommend."

The governor waved a debonair dismissal.

In the gardens Gaius walked on blue gravel paths winding between yew hedges, white statuary groups, past sculptured oaks and evergreen shrubs. Occasionally, beautiful slave girls glided past in swirls of gossamer scarlets, purples and greens.

He turned off the stairs into a clipped green lane and thought he saw a glimpse of tawny golden hair and a blur of pale blue silk. Penelope? He began to walk faster, in pursuit. Yes! There she was again, in a semicircular dell of clipped boxwood. When he rushed to the place, she was gone. He sat down on the back of a carved limestone lion in the green lair of the rock beast and tried to reason with his emotions. His were the reactions of a lovestruck boy, not a man of twenty-eight.

Something lightly brushed his left cheek. He jumped up.

There stood Penelope.

Involuntarily he stretched out one hand.

She shrank away.

He approached; at last he had her almost backed into the thick green boxwood.

Seeing her at close view, he found her lovelier than he had remembered. Sad blue eyes flecked with smoky amber; skin the color of pale ivory. Lip rouge and purple eyeshadow, too—but he had the feeling that a servant had applied the cosmetics and Penelope was ashamed of her painted face.

Subconsciously seeking flaws, he noted that her red lips were wider than his ideal. And when she opened her lips and smiled timidly, he saw that one of her small white teeth leaned against its larger center mate. Her profile? Not perfect, either, for her nose uptilted slightly. But her yearning smile was more appealing because of the slanting tooth, and what statue had a nose as beautiful as the Greek captive's?

What was he thinking about? She was the governor's mistress!

Keep your head, he warned himself, trying to fight down the wild urge to sweep her into his arms.

"Lord tribune, sir," she whispered.

Well, walk away! If you get any closer, you'll push her into the boxwood! He moved closer, bemused by the slender gold chaplet studded with amethysts crowning her coiled and wavy hair. She had a poignant appeal . . . he stared in her eyes.

Pleadingly she looked up. "Sir . . . I came to warn you." Her Latin was quaintly accented.

He dared glance at the draped blue fabric outlining her breasts —and immediately looked away.

"Listen to me, listen," she urged. "Governor Classicus is almost bankrupt. He may plan to have Commander Liscus, the cavalry officer, hide the gold you find, then accuse you, could it be that?" Fearfully she glanced around and Gaius was so bewitched by her profile and shoulders that he hardly heard what she said.

"Lord, I know who you are," she went on and her voice had a musical lilt that entranced Gaius. "After that night on the staircase, I asked the gracious Lady Enna. She does not despise me." Tremulously she went on, "Lord tribune, I think the governor hopes to bribe you—I'm almost sure." Her face reddened. "The proconsul drank too much last night and I lured him to talk about you . . ." She became abject. "He muttered about gold . . . and his debts . . . and about you, lord tribune. You and Commander Rufus Liscus. The commander is his friend. I want to help you," she said, faintly.

A new approach, thought Gaius. A clever brain behind her mask of beauty and calculated blushes. Stir up a scandal by firing me against Classicus; I'm fired against him too much already as it is. If I fall into her net I'll end up in a legation dungeon.

"You must listen," she insisted. "Do not be a pawn of the governor, I beg you, beg you—do not be trapped, do not take what he offers, no matter what it is." She tried to grasp hold of his breastplate and her nearness was too much.

He swept her into his arms and kissed into silence her muffled pleadings. Expecting the experienced response of a *concubina,* he was surprised by the eager childishness of her lips and the trembling of her body in his hard embrace. He kissed her again and again— her mouth, neck, lips, shoulders—yet fighting down the impulse to explore the tempting roundness of her body as his passion drove him. It was madness, it was sublime, and they were the only lovers in the world.

He heard endearments rushing from his tongue that he had vowed never to speak until he had found a woman worthy of them, and at length his will power gave him strength to push her away—a rough release of repudiation.

Now you've done it, he thought, hating her for having stirred the passions he had kept imprisoned through the years. Yet his physical desire for her was strangely mixed with tenderness, even knowing she would drive him insane and undermine his character if he let her. He should teach her a lesson . . . these gardens were a maze of green labyrinths of yew concealing miniature temples and secluded white pavillions with cushioned bronze couches conveniently placed for lovemaking. What was he thinking about! She was a prostitute!

His face was hot as he stared over her head. "Domina, I apologize," he said, bleakly. "You will never forgive me."

But his glance seemed trapped in her smoky blue eyes. She turned and fled out of the boxwood dell of the stone lion, leaving Gaius in a daze until the rough voice of Flavian interrupted his confused reverie.

"Sir—" the guard saluted—"Lady Enna asks you to come to the Green Atrium chamber. You are to be presented to Governor Verus

Maturus of Farther Spain." The soldier's thatchy eyebrows went up and his canny dark eyes squinted. "On your guard, tribune," he muttered. "I saw what happened here, but no one else did."

Gaius fell into stride with the legionary. "I must have lost my head," he told Flavian. "I apologized to the lady."

Flavian seemed to have forgotten it already. "I have news for you, sir. I'm going to be your orderly. I thought Governor Classicus was going to send some of the Theban Legion infantry with the gold expedition. That's what the noble Frontinus advised, anyhow. But the Proconsul makes his own decisions. I'm your aide. I hope we go near or through Ioza, so I can see my wife Beryl. Will we, sir? Ioza? Is it on your maps?"

Thinking of Penelope's face and body, Gaius at last said, "Ioza? Yes. We'll go through the cave village."

VIII

Outside a yellow pilastered doorway to the Green Atrium chamber, Gaius heard an authoritative voice pouring through the grill above the ashwood portals. He knocked, but the voice rumbled sonorously on:

"—and judging from what you have already told me, Enna, I see no way to liberate Gaius Julius Lacer by ordinary *legis actio* in *Jus Naturale,* or *Jus Civile.* If Apollodorus were willing to transfer ownership, it could be handled in *Jure Cessio.* You would appear as plaintiff before a magistrate and claim ownership of Gaius. The presiding judge would call on Apollodorus to refute your claim. He would either plead no defense or hold silence. Result? The jurist would declare Gaius to be your bondsman. It is cheering that Myron Frontinus is anxious to help you secure the young geologist's freedom. Why not let the noble Frontinus purchase Gaius?"

Gaius knocked again, loudly.

"Enter," called the restrained voice of Enna.

He opened the doors and stood in acute embarrassment, before the two people seated at an ivory-inlaid table at the far end of the room. Like walking into a forest of jade, thought Gaius, his interest mildly stirred by the tall Corinthian pillars of verdant-hued stone. He barely heard Enna:

". . . price for Gaius is too high for Frontinus."

Governor Maturus, a heavy, balding man seated next to Enna,

gestured Gaius to come forward. Then the dignitary arose. He wore a brown tunic, worn leather belt and a startling waist-length toga which (Gaius had heard from barracks-talk) was the only one in the empire. This (the soldiers had gone on) was worn not in affectation but because the traditional long garment of patrician rank had once tripped Maturus and sent him sprawling on the Senate floor in Rome. The white wool toga with diagonal purple stripe was so unusual that Gaius understood why the taste of the Proconsul of Farther Spain was a subject of jest at banquets in Rome. But Gaius at once liked the man's shrewd dark eyes, sharp beak of a nose, strong jaw and prominent lower lip.

Enna presented Gaius to her distinguished companion.

"It is an honor, young man," boomed Maturus, resuming his seat. "I have walked back and forth over your Tagus Bridge. Since the City has not yet sent orders for its dedication and undoubtedly never will, I hold to myself that right. Some day, perhaps, I will see a Triumphal Arch in centerbridge and perhaps a temple at one end. Every bridge, every mile of paved roads—tangible achievements which help unify Spain's isolated plateaus, valleys and mountains—stimulate the interchange of people, goods, and services. I can recall when my noble sire and I rode muleback on goat-paths in central Gaul." His probing dark eyes also swept over Gaius with approval.

"Your excellency is generous," Gaius said.

"Lady Enna and I were conferring in private about you; remain on your feet, young man. It is good to see a healthy man upright instead of prone on a sofa. Now I shall attempt to clarify your legal position."

Maturus attacked the subject vigorously. An old law, before the reign of Augustus Caesar, allowed slaves to own anything they were capable of purchasing, from a quinquereme to a bakeshop. Many of the empire's distinguished men of the past had once been slaves, but thanks to lenient laws had accumulated property, risen to high empire offices, high social status and to renown in the arts. But during the imperium of Octavian Augustus Caesar, so many vulgarians had ascended to wealth and prominence that the Sacred Augustus finally listened to his advisers and passed a new law. Henceforth only the finest intellects among the bondage classes were to be emancipated. Edicts passed by succeeding emperors applied further restrictive measures, until now masters were recognized as preeminent. "Today," the governor's trenchant voice went on with undiminished vigor, "if an owner lays prohibitions on his slaves, bondsmen are bound by the laws to obey. Yet if an owner is indulgent, the slave can build his own fortunes."

Already knowing the facts so cogently explained by Verus Maturus, Gaius merely nodded.

"We proceed," Maturus drove on. "Lady Enna wonders if I know any eligible woman of wealth in Farther Spain who might purchase you and take you as her husband. I know no women of such means. Yet if we found such a domina, she would have to *manumit* you before becoming your wife. I quote from a statute: 'The female citizen who cohabits with a slave herself becomes a woman in servitude.' Tribune Gaius Lacer, I do not intend to sound patronizing."

"I understand, your excellency," Gaius replied, his ears ringing from the discourse of the imperial administrator of Farther Spain, but admiring the official more than ever.

"My two sons and three daughters wed years ago; now I wish I had an unmarried daughter, that I might purchase you for her," pronounced the governor. "I hear excellent reports as to your character and health. Doubtless you could reward me with outstanding grandsons."

Gaius swallowed the angry urge to proclaim: 'No more forced marriages!' good sense insisting that Proconsul Maturus had spoken as a jurist and with full respect. The magistrate's next statement afforded Gaius hidden satisfaction:

"But I have not the funds to purchase you, estimable Lacer. I continue . . ." Actually Gaius was neither slave nor freedman, but in a station somewhere between the two extremes. His rights as a freeborn patrician son of Consul Julius Lacer had not been abrogated, only suspended until his emancipation at some future date. In the strictly legal interpretation, Gaius was not 'corporeally possessed' as were captives. Certain laws safeguarded aristocratic bondsmen. For example, Gaius was specifically exempt from the limitations of the *Lex Aelia Sentia* which prevented freed slaves from gaining citizenship if they had been branded, chained, worn armlets of slavery, or been subject to deserved punishments by their masters. On the other hand, as a bound patrician, Gaius could even file suit for damages against his owner, in case of unjust sufferings from flogging, abusive language, and—in rare cases—public humiliation. Nevertheless, all legislation upheld the absolute control of Apollodorus over the person and earnings of Gaius Julius Lacer.

"I understand, your excellency." Gaius shifted his feet slightly before they went to sleep under his weight.

"Sit down, Lacer," called Maturus, indicating a chair opposite Enna. Gaius gratefully obeyed as Enna gave him a weary smile and then turned to the governor.

"Next on the agenda is your personal tragedy of years ago," announced Maturus, softening his strident tones still more. "Your master joined you to Metanny, a Syrian slave girl. That was his right and not to be construed as public disgrace. As you doubtless know, it was not a marriage, but a condition of sanctioned sexual intercourse."

Enna hastily said, "Verus, I fear you embarrass our bridge builder."

"Tribune Lacer," the governor said, "I beg clemency. You understand that I speak as a judge, and frankly I must, in order that no misunderstanding may color what I say."

Gaius tried to return the judicial gaze calmly. But his whole life spread out for strangers to dissect and criticize—then consign him to the pit out of which his pride was forever goading him to struggle. Suddenly the yearning face of Penelope appeared to him, arousing him to further conflicting emotions of desire and disgust—and curiosity concerning the concubine of Cornelius Classicus.

Enna inquired, "Gaius, may I ask: were you in love with the Syrian?"

"My dear Enna," blustered Verus Maturus, "love has nothing to do with betrothal and consent to wed. Marriages are contracted by guardians of young people for the procreation of healthy heirs. If this estimable young man is ever in love, he has my sympathy, but not the sympathy of the laws. Now, Lacer: more leaden intelligence. Lady Enna wrote to your master. Today she received a reply from Apollodorus. He refuses to free you until your earnings for him total forty thousand goldworth. So far, your work has brought him only fifteen thousand. When you succeed in earning twenty-five thousand more, Apollodorus will waive a balance still due. Your situation is not hopeless."

Not hopeless? thought Gaius. Will I live long enough to buy my freedom? So the benevolent Apollodorus is willing to reduce my indebtedness from fifty to forty thousand—

"Maturus," said Enna, "is there no other way? A loophole in the laws?"

"My dear Enna Gracchus," expostulated the governor, "I am a man of integrity. I am a Roman! I am sneered at in Rome by the false informers. Loopholes? Not in the laws I administer, dear domina!"

"I didn't mean—" her hands moved vaguely—"Admirable," Enna hastened to say. "Tribune Lacer, you may go, now."

"Farewell, young Lacer," shouted Maturus as Gaius wheeled about and marched to the portals. "Hold to truth!"

Gaius stopped, turned about, and saluted. On his way out he wondered why his right arm had moved as if in recognition. He was stunned, stimulated—and now possessed by a quivering thread of hope.

In the corridor he saw Proconsul Classicus strolling arm-in-arm with Penelope. Sickened and jealous of Classicus, Gaius darted into a side corridor as they passed. He heard Classicus saying:

". . . such ideas in your perfect head, *dilecta*. Then occupy yourself with the sick of the legation if you choose. Commendable . . ."

Even when Penelope glanced wistfully back as she went by, Gaius glared. Classicus had referred to her as a woman beloved. . . . And the lovely Greek girl? She had been gazing provocatively at Classicus before seeing Gaius.

He marched back to his office, at war with his emotions. You're inconsistent, he accused himself. Do you care if Classicus loves her? Or if she loves him?

He turned up the hourglass on his worktable and went back to work on his mining estimates.

IX

Early in May, the day before the expedition was to leave New Carthage, Gaius sat in his office thinking about Penelope. He had kept his own counsel while trying to reason away her warning; also the rational explanation seemed to him that Penelope despised her master, Classicus, whom she wanted to ruin if she could. Should that be the situation, however, she was endangering her life, for owners had been known to kill their slaves—even beautiful ones. Then what if her admonition were the truth? Starting on that assumption, why would Governor Cornelius Classicus hope to bribe him, a slave architect?

So far in his career, no one had ever offered Gaius money to secrete gold nuggets, use fissured granite in a bridge, or construct spans that would buckle and break apart. His integrity was well-known and respected. Being a bondsman of Apollodorus set him apart, too, for which he was ironically grateful. Then could his growing presentiment rise from another root? Further, was his smoldering hatred of Classicus due to Penelope? Whatever the causes, experience had taught him to trust his intuition and during the past few nights premonitions of danger had roused him sweating from his bunk in the dark barracks out in the courtyard of the Legation.

Yet should Proconsul Classicus secretly plan gold embezzlement, Gaius was powerless to stop it. In previous mining projects he had planned and supervised construction of masonry and earth dams; slicing off cliffs; digging shafts and building sluice boxes. Once he had directed slaves who had jigged the sieves and pounded rough gold ore in abrasive mills, but had never been ordered to oversee smelting and refining. Yet up at the Sil mines he would also direct the final procedures converting crude ore into finished gold and silver bars. Would such participation be dangerous?

He and his crews would be both watched and guarded, so if gold thefts were planned, such could still take place without his knowledge. And who was Commander Rufus Liscus, cavalry officer, chosen to be acting *legatus* of the goldfields? Did the soldier have a hold over Classicus—or was it the other way? The more Gaius tried to find logical explanations and rule out his concern, the greater grew his suspicion and apprehension. So far as he could learn, Governor Classicus bore a spotless reputation, a loyal procurator who, after his first meeting with Gaius, went out of his way to treat the builder of the Tagus Bridge as an equal.

He sighed irritably; the vision of Penelope had bloomed in his mind again. Now that he tried to avoid Classicus' mistress, the Fates seemed to arrange that he see her every day. If he walked down a hall, she often appeared from the opposite direction, shyly looking down as she passed him. Each time he had to restrain himself from pulling her into his embrace. Once he saw her on the Staircase of Fountains, talking animatedly with dignified Lady Enna; before he turned to make a hasty retreat, he heard the Greek beauty begging Enna to take back a pearl necklace that belonged to the Lady Excellency, but which Penelope was wearing.

Once Gaius looked out his open casement and saw Penelope in

the peacock garden below being caressed by Proconsul Classicus. The scene had made him contemptuous of both Penelope and her handsome master. Nor was that all.

He had also watched an innocuous scene witnessed two days ago from a hall: Penelope in a nursery, helping a dour physician treat various sick infants, including a fevered Ethiopian slave baby. He could still see the tenderness on her face as she bathed the wailing child with wet warm sponges and swabbed it with sundried linen. The baby had stopped crying at last and nestled in her arms; gently urged by Penelope, the infant began sucking a medicinal mixture of some kind from a slender-spouted ampulla plugged with a tuft of sponge.

But the ugly truth that she was the governor's favorite *concubina* always stole in to rob him of attempts to evaluate Penelope justly.

Again he heard her soft, intent voice saying: 'The proconsul drank too much last night and I lured him to talk about you . . .' That wanton confession always distorted his natural inclination to consider her as a virtuous enslaved girl. Disturbed by the thought of Penelope he got up with the idea of going to the legation library for bookscrolls of Zeno and Epicurus. At the threshold of his office he almost collided with Lady Enna.

He saluted. "The lady excellency."

She came in and sat down in his chair, her pale hands nervously smoothing the skirt of her pink linen gown. Keeping her voice hushed she said, "Gaius, I regret that Governor Maturus could not help you. The noble Frontinus and I believe that an honorable young man of the illustrious Lacer blood should not remain a bondsman. So—I have happy news for you. Yesterday I sent off a letter to Apollodorus offering to purchase you and set you free."

Free! He was too surprised and dazed to respond.

"I trust your patron will accept my offer as fast as couriers can travel from the Rhine to this legation," Enna went on. "When his answer comes, I shall send the forty thousand in gold to him by special messengers. As soon as his next communication arrives that the money is in his possession, I will emancipate you. It may take a month or more. You are under no obligation to me, Gaius. The governor and I have two sons, both grown and gone quite a while back, far away—I—you remind me of my younger son, Gaius."

His thoughts whirled. Free! A freedman could keep the money he earned! A freedman could qualify for Roman citizenship!

"Gaius, my news is strictly confidential. Some day I will tell my husband. He is overworked and tired. Do not thank me, I have a large fortune."

Excitement gave way to suspicion. A rich aristocrat like Lady Enna did not toss away a fortune, and forty thousand was a fortune by any standard, without expecting—what? From his brief observations of her, he had concluded that she loved Classicus even to the extent of ignoring his affairs with other women. A loyal wife or husband often is that way, he mused. Blind to the faults and vices of those they love, willing to overlook what they did not want to see; totally consistent in everything else, but completely inconsistent when the adored ones stepped off their pedestals.

"I must go," said Enna, arising. Gaius rushed to pull the chair and assist her. At the closed door he finally came to his senses. "Noble domina," he said, humbly, "my gratitude is too great for my tongue. How can I show you . . ."

"I said there was no obligation." She put a finger to her lips, and Gaius watched her move swiftly down the corridor where Frontinus stood waiting, the scholarly treasurer's look of devotion mirrored on Gaius' own face.

Yet, back in his office, baffled doubts returned. Would Apollodorus accept the offer, or reconsider and demand the full fifty thousand? Why was Lady Enna willing to spend such a large amount to free a man she hardly knew? Did she, too, wonder if Governor Classicus planned gold embezzlement and want to stop it before it began? Whatever the facts, Gaius' jovial mood returned. He wanted to shout. Sing. He had a rousing baritone voice, sometimes off-key, but full of vigor. He would sing his new freedom to the mountains. Compose a love song to freedom, vastly different from the suggestive passion-ditties he had heard among patrician youths in Rome.

Hardly knowing what he did, Gaius marched out of his *domus* and soon found himself at the Fountain of Ceres in the rotunda of the legation. Busy soldiers went to and fro, servants darted across the green and red mosaic floor, and water like melted diamonds spouted from the cornucopia of the marble goddess into the round stone basin. He sat down on the ledge and his first coherent thought was to find Penelope and tell her, force her to listen . . . be the triumphant Roman at last . . . but be tender, for she was still a captive.

He heard a confusion of voices a moment before Governor Classicus stalked between the tall Ionic pillars, his fine features ugly with wrath. After him hastened Governor Maturus and three imposing strangers in togas thick with slanting purple stripes. Following, marched a file of soldiers, some bearing wicker hampers.

Gaius got up, but Classicus, Maturus and the other men came forward and stopped a few feet away, not seeing him but blocking his intended departure.

"My wife received no advance notification!" Classicus was shouting. "Surely there is some *perperam facta!*"

"There is no misinterpretation and no mistake, your excellency," said a man in a toga. "Your great friend, the emperor, is grief-stricken."

Verus Maturus loudly interrupted. "Cornelius, protesting will avail you nothing. The papers you read are in correct legal form. Do not remonstrate." Maturus summoned a slave and sent him to request the presence of Lady Enna in the rotunda.

Although still unnoticed, Gaius wished frantically for invisibility.

"And when, *homo nobilis,* does the imperial mandate take effect?" Classicus demanded, gaining some control of his fury.

"Immediately, your exalted excellency," replied the emissary who had spoken before. "We brought hampers for that purpose. May I again suggest that you once more peruse the letter from Domitian, our Master and God, and the budget figures for Hither Spain?"

"Hampers," muttered Classicus. He began striding around the fountain, his handsome face dangerously flushed.

"Excellency, you will be in no immediate financial stricture," the head of the visiting delegation from Rome assured him. "Most paternally has the immortal Domitian awarded you one-fourth the funds of deceased rich men in this province. The fiscal experts of our Master and God estimate that you have sufficient money to pay this embassy's upkeep *in annum semestris*—" The speaker started to follow Classicus, both passing and repassing Gaius.

"Half a year," said Classicus, while Governor Maturus hastened after Classicus, talking as he walked. The voice of Maturus boomed in the vast rotunda while frightened slaves sank to their knees.

"Cornelius," called Maturus, "you must understand that this is an example of *Constitutio Principia.* By law Emperor Domitian has the power—"

"Our Master and God," the principal emissary from Rome chided Maturus.

Ignoring the slight reproof, Maturus thundered, "The documents brought by these officials come under the heading of *principales constitutiones*. Any imperial edict, rescript—"

Classicus flung aside the soothing hands of Maturus.

"Listen to me, Cornelius," Maturus urged. "I had property confiscated, too. Losing the fruits of one's life work is a price a loyal Roman should be willing to pay for the glory of our Emperor."

Classicus protested angrily, "My wife is a descendent of the heroic Gracchi brothers and of their mother, the virtuous Cornelia!"

"Silence," whispered Maturus. "Silence, man!"

"We are most sympathetic," murmured the imperial representative from Rome. "Our Master and God wept when he signed the order, most exalted excellency Classicus. In high esteem does our Master and God hold you, estimable excellency, and your lady of distinguished ancestry."

Unnoticed and trapped, Gaius sat down again on the ledge of the fountain. He saw Lady Enna and Frontinus hurry into the rotunda.

Classicus stopped striding around Gaius and the Fountain of Ceres. "My noble domina," he said, shakily, "these commissioners from the emperor bring me—us—shocking intelligence."

The deputy from Rome swept a bow to Enna. "My noble lady," he called, "I offer for your scrutiny these official orders from our Master and God. Our immortal lord's decision was made after he studied records on file in the inheritance archives. In checking these parchments recently, our Master and God's treasury officers noted that you, Enna Gracchus, received a legacy three years ago in excess of two hundred thousand gold coins. Our Master and God deeply regrets that he must now confiscate your fortune for the prosperity of the State."

Gaius stared blankly. It was all a nightmare. The horrible dream went on. He watched the men from Rome and their legionaries start down a staircase with a ring of keys to Lady Enna's money vaults; watched Enna weeping in the arms of Maturus . . . He saw Classicus glare at Frontinus as the treasurer politely offered to loan the proconsul emergency funds when and if needed. Even after Enna and the others left the rotunda, Gaius sat motionless on the edge of the fountain, trailing one hand in the sparkling cold water. Slave girls knelt and held up trays of wine ewers and goblets, plates of figs, dates, olives.

At last he got up and blundered somehow back to his quarters and bolted the door.

Gone, gone, was freedom now. The priceless independence Lady Enna had held out to him—gone. Snatched away in baskets bound for Rome.

X

In the legation courtyard before sunrise the next day, fire tripods illuminated soldiers, neighing horses, mules harnessed to food wagons, and women bidding farewells. In two long rows stood sleek cavalry steeds; each animal was saddled, bridled and armored. At the opposite end of the vast area, near the heavy supply wains, were twenty-one ordinary brown horses and a magnificent golden thoroughbred mare equipped like the cavalry mounts. Near the mare stood Gaius and the infantrymen.

He was too dispirited to pay much attention to the activity. He had passed a sleepless night wrestling with despair, the devastating aftermath of losing his promised freedom in the misfortune that had overwhelmed Lady Enna. Wearily and cynically he waited—steeling himself for what?

The sun rose. Fires in the iron tripods were extinguished, commands shouted, and the clash of metal gear stopped. Women exchanged last embraces with soldiers and withdrew to the legation steps.

"Oh you infantry," bellowed a cavalryman standing by his horse. "How many spines does a charger have, brave comrades?"

"*Duo bini!*" blasted another horse trooper. "One for the horse, another to pinch the crotch of the foot-soldier."

Having no weapons, Gaius could not thrust out a spear in salute, so he stood straight, gauntleted hands at his sides. Here it comes, he thought. I'm going to meet Commander Rufus Liscus. Flavian tells me Liscus owns the black mastiff who pushed Publius off the small two-arched . . .

Dignitaries were approaching, so Gaius stood even straighter. By moving his eyes slightly to the left he saw advancing a lanky tall officer in armor wearing a scarlet cloak and the green crested helmet and arm blazons of the VII Illyrican Legion. Governor Maturus strode along with the man in armor.

As they drew near, Maturus announced, "Commander Liscus, if the Arvacan blackcloaks become restless, be assured that General Lucius Antonius is in control of the wilderness north and northwest. His troops constantly patrol Asturia, Gallicia, Lusitania and the towns and regions south and east in my province. Antonius will try and keep contact with you as you proceed north into Chieftain Luna Malendi's territory."

"I shall remember, Excellency," said the commander. His voice was low and quiet.

Gaius got a swift look at Liscus, seeing a man of rosy complexion, placid blue eyes, golden brown beard and mustache. Distinguished features, Gaius thought, yet Liscus smiles too much. Is he a hireling of Governor Classicus?

They stopped. Maturus introduced Tribune Gaius Lacer to Commander Rufus Liscus, acting general of the gold expedition. Gaius gave his first official salute in unison with Flavian and his infantry comrades.

"My pleasure." Liscus smiled, his blue eyes fixed on Gaius. "We of the VII Illyrican Legion cavalry are honored to have as companions some of the valiants of the First Cilician Legion infantry." The cultured voice resumed, "Tribune Gaius Julius Lacer, on ceremonial occasions we of the cavalry mount in flamboyant Spanish style. Perhaps you go astride in ordinary fashion?"

"Sir, I mount either way," said Gaius, wondering if there was a special reason for Liscus' elaborate use of his full name.

Liscus kept smiling. "Indeed."

"The auspices for this expedition are favorable if one believes in them," said Maturus. "My colleague, Classicus, was indisposed this morning, so I performed the religious rites. I found a nodule of gold in the gizzard of a dove. Tribune Lacer, this golden thoroughbred mare, Dawn, is my pride. Consider her your own for the duration of the mining venture."

"His excellency is very generous," Gaius replied, feeling less depressed. Maturus was a friend.

"The horse must fit the rider," said Maturus, showing an unexpected nervousness. "*Vale,* commander. Tribune Lacer, good fortune." Maturus turned away.

Liscus suddenly shouted, "Infantry! Mount!"

Flavian, the sergeant-adjutant, and his men used box steps to climb astride their brown horses. But Gaius made a running leap into the padded wooden saddle of the golden thoroughbred. She tossed her ivory-white mane and whuffled in pleasure as Gaius stroked her satiny neck.

Commander Liscus watched complacently. "You are athletic,"

said Liscus, his lips still uplifted. "I admire your jump. Perhaps a symbol of the independent man who rises unaided." Languidly he continued, "Tribune Gaius Julius Lacer, I hear that your education extends far beyond levelling instruments, aqueducts, gradients and dams. Therefore I anticipate conversational combat with you. As an example: let us ponder Aristotle's conclusion that human excellence is of two kinds—intellectual and moral. May I humbly inquire if Apollodorus initiated you along such exalted avenues of learning?"

Gaius kept firm check of his temper. "He did, sir. May I add, sir, that Aristotle also taught that all the human mind needed was training, teaching, and experience; that the moral perfection of a man came later."

The cavalry leader's perpetual smile held. Then he thundered, "Cavalry! Kneel your horses!"

Even to Gaius the sight was beautiful. One hundred and thirty roans, blacks, sorrels and grays went down on left front knees, right legs partially bent.

"Cavalry! Mount!" called Liscus.

The horsemen climbed astride.

"Cavalry! Stand your horses!"

The animals reared up to the creak of leather and jingle of metal. Then an aide came forward with a spirited white stallion. It knelt without command and Liscus settled into his saddle. To an adjutant he shouted, "Bring Mars."

Soon a cavalry soldier appeared, fighting to hold the leash of an enormous black mastiff. The eager beast wore scale-armor on back and belly, metal plates over its chest, and a calfskin collar. The aide unhooked the strap and the huge canine froze to a stance beside the horse of Commander Liscus.

"Tribune Gaius Julius Lacer, dismount," Liscus ordered. "Mars wants an introduction to you."

Gaius slid off his horse.

"Mars," Liscus spoke, "greet this man."

The great dog reared up and clacked his paws on Gaius' shoulder-plates. The drooling jaws came so close Gaius could feel the animal's panting hot breath. Could the beast named for the war god be won as an ally? "Good Mars," said Gaius, softly. "Friend. Brave dog."

"Down, Mars. To your haunches," said Liscus.

Instantly the creature obeyed his master. Gaius once more leaped up into the saddle of Dawn.

A lone trumpet began to sound. Commander Rufus Liscus, his mastiff springing alongside the white stallion, galloped to the head of the double cavalry columns. Behind him two guidon-bearers proudly raised the pennons of the VII Illyrican Legion: white painted thunderbolts on green. Far at the rear behind the food and supply wagons, two mounted infantrymen thrust their banners high —white flags with red painted cobras.

All day as the procession travelled through a mountain valley, Gaius imagined Penelope with him, his right arm holding her in the saddle . . . The sun glinting off coppery rock buttes evoked the color of her tawny hair, white clouds tinged with amber sunlight reminded him of her skin. And now that she was out of his grasp forever, he yearned to rein his horse around and gallop back to New Carthage.

"Sir, what's that sour stink? I just got a whiff," Flavian shouted.

"It comes from the silver mines back in that defile," Gaius replied at last. "See those furnaces with high brick chimneys? The men inside are smelting the molten silver. The vapors are deadly if inhaled full strength." He drew a deep breath. He, too, had gotten a snatch of the noxious smell, but now the balmy warm air was clean again. He glanced at his homely big aide, wondering what the veteran's thoughts were.

Flavian's heavy nose showed the effect of battles he had fought in. As Gaius looked, the orderly's thick eyebrows went up.

"Sir," said Flavian, "the commander's cantering back to pay us a call."

Liscus galloped toward them, riding magnificently, Mars loping at the rear.

"Does all proceed harmoniously, *optio?*" inquired the acting brigadier, reining in next to Flavian.

"Aye, sir," said Flavian, his angelic smile appearing.

Commander Liscus urged his white horse around by Gaius. "Hither Spain is peaceful and prosperous." The officer smiled. "The picture may or may not change when we cross the boundary into Governor Maturus' rather disturbed domain of Farther Spain." He glanced down at his armored mastiff. "Mars had a fat rabbit and a careless otter for lunch. The otter made the mistake of challenging my dog. Tribune: my compliments on the way you met Mars this morning. Perhaps you are curious about my faithful bodyguard?"

Gaius nodded politely.

"Mars was a starving puppy with a broken leg when I found him in a forest near the Danube," said Liscus, his smile as enduring as ever. "I splinted his leg. It healed. He thrived. He is intelligent. I have taught him various commands which he obeys like a fearless soldier. He sinks his fangs in the necks of my enemies . . . or attacks their groins. Such distasteful subjects. Do I bore you, Tribune Gaius Julius Lacer?"

"No, sir, you do not." The man's a fanatic, thought Gaius. Has his brain been affected by combat or wounds? Regardless of the cause, he's a far deadlier threat to me than his black mastiff. If he thinks I'm a weakling, afraid of him or his dog—

"We erect the night-camp barriers an hour before sunset," Liscus said. "I never permit molestation of good women, but visit the nearest hamlet if you choose. Your aide will pay whatever charges you are responsible for in the taverns and brothels." He lightly slapped the flanks of his white stallion and galloped effortlessly forward, Mars plunging after his master.

Flavian whistled tonelessly. "It seems," he said to the pine-forested mountains, "that the commander thinks a lot of his dog."

Gaius shrugged, enjoying the warm breezes and serene blue sky. Liscus, the cavalry, and the mounted infantry behind cursing their sore groins; the pleb drivers of the wagons; all, even shrewd Flavian, all were privileged free men. But at this moment, he, too, savored liberty.

"Sir, shall I speak freely?" asked Flavian.

"Do."

The aide's weathered forehead twisted into a complex of wrinkles. "Then—I hate to tell you, sir, but I'm your jailer. So are the twenty men I command. Governor Classicus must think you may take a notion to chase butterflies in the mountains and keep going."

Angered, Gaius felt grateful as well, for his orderly had spoken like a friend. "I could have escaped years ago," he responded. Then he decided to sound out Flavian and gain any more information the *optio* might have. "Flavian, this gold expedition must be new in your experience?"

"Blistering hades, sir, it is. I'd rather be in battle than this thing. Yet—the farther we get from Rome, the safer we are. I hope you find plenty of gold, sir."

"Governor Classicus hopes so, too," replied Gaius as the horses began thundering over a three-span stone bridge above a tremendously deep gulley thick with sweet chestnut trees and oaks. This was one of his works: he had designed the bridge and supervised its construction, and Gaius began to feel more cheerful. He had achievements behind him, and Flavian, the jailer, was a friend. . . .

XI

By early afternoon of the fourth day of travel, the expedition entered a valley of igneous rock and slate formations, high mountains, and a stream roaring along to the left of the road. The region was new to Gaius and he looked around with a stir of interest. If he and his men had been building this road, instead of being bound northwest to mine gold, and if he could shut out the tempting image of Penelope—

"Sir, my wife's village is next," said Flavian, with enthusiasm. "It is more civilized than the last cave town we went through. In Ioza you'll see elegant living places carved out of the rock pinnacles and the mountains. Some Ioza villagers live in natural caves, too, but Beryl and I have a mountain home," he said, proudly. Then he shouted, "There's Ioza, sir! See that blue door on the third ledge path up the mountain? My wife is up there waiting for me!"

Paths looped back and forth before layers of doors on the hilly landscape, where men and women in black tunics moved on different levels, entering or leaving their homes, climbing or descending to the rocky land bordering the roadway and roaring stream. Perhaps advance word had reached the settlement that the troops of Commander Liscus were respectful of wives and maidens, for the swarthy natives watched the horsemen with friendly curiosity.

While his tent was being erected, Gaius walked along the bank of the torrent for exercise. The water looked icy, but a faint mist upstream informed him that hot underground springs tempered the chill. He stopped and touched the water. Not cold. Tepid. At places the current poured into stone ditches for irrigating grapevines, melon patches, and beds of red and yellow poppies and the irrepressible geraniums. Animals were everywhere; black pigs nosing leather tubs of garbage; donkeys pulling squat two-wheeled carts. Sheep and brown goats, urged along by dignified Spanish natives. Chickens, geese, and ducks—and half-naked small children scampered among the rocks beside the roaring water.

He stopped to watch the women washing clothes in the river,

some stamping the wet garments with their bare brown feet, while others knelt with porous stones, pounding black and red and blue clothes in hollowed limestone boulders. Walking on, he stopped again where the stream widened into a turbulent pool. Upstream where the chaotic surge tumbled around huge rocks he saw men perched with fishing poles. And, on the opposite shore, peasants in black were squatting beside coarse wire sieves: gold prospectors.

Frightened shouts suddenly became audible over the noise upstream and he saw fishermen gesticulating: then he saw washerwomen stare over their shoulders, scoop up their children and scramble off. Next—to his horror—he saw a small girl nearby stiffen in terror, let out a thin scream, then fall off a boulder into the racing cataract.

He wrenched off his helmet and waded into the water. It was colder than he thought. Abruptly the stony bed of the stream gave way and he began swimming to the spot where the child had gone under. He grasped her hair and pulled her to the surface, but she thrashed wildly and he lost his grip. Stroking frantically, for now he and the drowning child were in a whirlpool, he got her hair again, grasped her neck and began side-stroking to shore. To catch his breath he trod water. The little girl shrieked, kicked him, and again was swept downstream. Gaius drew a full breath through his mouth and began crawl-stroking, the furious speed bringing him once more to the little one who was going down in a wide pool. This time he got her neck in an elbow-lock, turned on his back with her half on top of his breastplate, and back-stroked with his left arm.

The exhausted child seemed calmer, so he shouted, "Hang on, girl; I'm turning—hang on—don't choke me! I'll get us to shore—" He felt tense little fingers clutching the back of his neck as he inhaled through his mouth, buried his head in the rushing water and crawl-stroked with all the power of his muscles. His armor weighed him down; already he was tiring—but at last he felt the stone bottom beneath his boots, and strong hands were pulling them up on land.

"The black beast is still there!" screamed a village woman. "It follows you, brave Lord! Send it away!"

Gaius turned to look. There stood Mars. Mars, the mastiff in armor; Mars, the size of a small pony. Mars: the cause of the near-tragedy. Dog of war, thought Gaius, ironically. To the villagers he called, "Do not fear the big dog. He is the bodyguard of Commander Rufus Liscus! He will not harm you."

A pretty little dark-haired woman darted to Gaius. "Brave sir, you saved my baby! *Gratiae, gratiae, gratie!!*" Her hysterical gratitude gave way to concern. "Those bronze armbands . . . noble sir, are you a slave?"

"Here's your helmet, lord officer," called a village man. "What a rescue! Wait till Turdo hears of this. He's the child's father, our village strong man, sir!"

"And I am Eunice, the mother," cried Eunice, kissing Gaius' hands feverishly. "We will reward you, lord patrician. Somehow we will reward you for saving our baby!"

Gaius, leaden with exhaustion, started back toward his tent. Mars stalked him.

"Good Mars," Gaius whispered, when he was out of human earshot. "Friend. Soldier. Good dog."

The mastiff let out a worried growl and the face seemed perplexed.

Tiredly Gaius muttered, "Listen, Mars. Don't ever leap at me— or I'll break your neck!" Then he muttered, "Be my friend. Salute me, Mars."

Mars panted noisily and held up one forepaw.

"Congratulations," said the voice of Rufus Liscus from behind. "I regret that my faithful mastiff frightened the little one." The commander almost seemed to smile as he inspected drenched Gaius. "Go to your tent. Your aide will make you comfortable." Liscus walked away, Mars loping at the rear.

In his tent Gaius let Flavian pull off his soaked boots, armor, sodden gray uniform, and go to work with rough towels, all the while keeping up a cheerful run of facetious comment. The tribune was a hero of the whirlpools—and how about conquering a hot bath in the tin tub? Sun was going down, cookfires blazing up, water being heated. What the heroic tribune needed was a soak-out, soap-over, and deep massage.

The tin tub was too small to sit in, so Gaius stood while Flavian sloshed him with hot water from hair to toes, worked up a thick coating of lather over his body, and rinsed him off. Then the aide rubbed olive oil on his skin and wiped off the excess, and finally Gaius felt his strength returning. Then into a fresh uniform, new boots and new leather belt. By that time, two infantry aides of Flavian had dried the tribune's armor and aided Flavian in making Gaius presentable once more. When he was ready, Gaius felt ravenously hungry.

"Sir, if the commander approves," said Flavian, hopefully, "my domina suggests I invite you for supper in our home."

"I should be honored, Flavian. Have you seen your lady yet?"

"A quick visit, sir. I borrowed your small altar and took it up to my place. Is that all right, sir?"

"Of course. Is your wife religious?"

The orderly first dismissed his two aides before replying, "My wife and I like to pray to all the gods, since we're going to be parents in about five months, sir."

The tent flaps opened and Commander Liscus entered. Both men saluted.

"Indeed, I do not demand constant saluting," said the commanding officer. "I left Mars in my tent. Sergeant, does all still go smoothly?"

"It does, sir," said Flavian.

Liscus pulled off his green gauntlets. "Tribune, if you do not already know, Flavian and his infantry platoon are your custodians. I hope you are not unduly offended."

"Sir, I am not," said Gaius, bleakly.

"We place you in the category of precious human merchandise," said Liscus, his durable smile appearing. "You have no weapons, but a man of your intellect and muscles would doubtless have no trouble hiding in the evergreens and trapping game with stones and rushes."

Gaius sardonically eyed Rufus Liscus. "Sir, I am familiar with the vast Spanish forests, and I know enough to be cautious about the citizens of the woods; civets, lynxes, bears, boars, and wolves—sir."

Liscus yawned and sat down on an iron-legged camp stool. "Indeed. Exotic acquaintances. Who else arouses your wariness?"

So he wants conversational combat, thought Gaius. Give it to him . . . "Commander, in hot lagoons and lakes of southern Spain, there are also reptiles and lizards. Some giant snakes are fifteen feet long, sir. And I have heard that somewhere in Spain is an evil monster blessed by Pluto—the titanic god of all reptiles!"

The commander gazed pleasantly. "My blood is turning to marble," he smiled. "If you continue your oration on scaly creatures, you may start to hiss. Let us try an inanimate subject. I came to inquire: will you let me borrow your tin bathtub?"

Surprised and suspicious, Gaius answered, "Sir, I do not own any property." What is there about Liscus that seems familiar, wondered Gaius. Have I seen the man somewhere, years ago?

"Indeed." Liscus summoned a cavalry guard who carried out the tub and marched away in the dusk. Suddenly and sharply aware that under Liscus' bland exterior the commander was uncertain and tense, Gaius decided that borrowing the tub was subterfuge. I don't want the man's enmity, I don't even know this Liscus, he thought. Is he both a conspirator of Classicus and perhaps also a spy of my master Apollodorus? And is Apollodorus involved in whatever scheme there is to steal the emperor's gold? He looked curiously at Liscus.

The commander's eyes are gray-blue, not blue, Gaius decided. Do I care what the color of his eyes is? Or wonder why he affects a beard and mustache when most Romans are cleanshaven? Hiding face scars? What if he is?

"Tribune, I have interesting tidings," drawled Rufus. "While you bathed, a small group of travellers arrived in Ioza."

Gaius folded his arms. If the commander expects me to ask the reason why, he'll wait forever.

"A friend of ours has decreed a reward of sorts to you," said Liscus. "You have been ordered to have a temporary servant of your own, tribune."

"Sir," Gaius replied, "I have no use for a slave. Flavian takes care of me, my uniforms, armor, tent, and horse."

Liscus smiled mockingly. "If Governor Maturus were present, no doubt he would confound us with a legal harangue on the complicated subject of a bondsman having a slave. True, I cannot force you to accept the generous offer, but I pray that you will see this slave before reaching a decision."

Gaius wanted no bondsman in the pay of Classicus or Liscus. No servitor to eavesdrop, report all he said to Flavian.

Commander Liscus got up from the camp stool. Gaius and Flavian saluted again. "I shall see you at moonrise in the sergeant's home," Liscus said. At the tent flaps, Liscus bowed slightly. "Enjoy your dinner, tribune."

Flavian led the way along a path in the mountain, his resin torch lighting up the grotesque rocks. He stopped before a blue portal embrasured in gray concrete. Still holding the flaming stick, he pounded on the oak door. "Halloo! Juda-Rosa, halloo!"

The door jerked open and a vivid young dark-haired woman threw sunburned arms around Flavian. Gaius caught the torch and doused it in a stone trough of water, and Flavian introduced his wife, Beryl.

She is a Semitic-Roman, Gaius decided, bowing over her hands. She had a long, perfect nose, fine black eyes, and wide red lips. Brass skewers pinned up her coiled black hair and she wore her snowy smock and scarlet skirt with dignity: she could have passed for a woman of patrician rank. Flavian has good fortune, thought Gaius, with envy.

"We are honored," said Beryl, in Latin, her voice quick but restrained. "Our home is your villa, *Domine* Gaius. Pray be seated, noble lord. I will serve supper at once!"

Gaius saluted her, thinking how appropriate was Flavian's nickname for his wife: Juda-Rose. A dark rose of Judea and Rome. He sat down on a bench and looked around the cave room glowing with lamplight on its whitewashed rounded walls. The rough concave surface supported copper and iron utensils, hanks of fleece and rush baskets hung from pegs, and string bags of dried herbs suspended from hooks. Near the blue-painted door stood an iron tripod brazier with a grilled lid under a bell-shaped copper outlet to a chimney flue. Charcoal flamed in the brazier and from the covered copper cookpots on the grill wafted tantalizing odors of fish and herbs. Oak tables, benches, black felt rugs and the white altar table off by itself were the main furnishings. The spacious room had a strong feeling of home—a happy home. Something Gaius might never have. But why pity himself?

Soon they were eating delicious boned trout and tench, zestful with onions, salt, and small wheaten balls. Stewed rabbit meat in thick gravy, crusty fresh barley bread, red wine and mild white cheese. Purple figs served in red and white pottery bowls completed the appetizing meal.

Gaius ate in silence. What was there to say? But reticence might be construed by Domina Beryl as arrogance, so he cast about for a polite topic to break the quiet.

But then knocks sounded at the door.

Flavian jumped up, jolting the supper table. Dishes, flagons, iron spoons rattled, and rabbit stew slopped as Flavian unbolted the blue portal door.

In lunged Mars, straining at the leash held by Commander Liscus. Beryl screamed. She threw herself into the arms of Gaius.

"Domina, do not fear," said the officer. "Mars—salute the lady. Mars—salute the lady."

Up went the right forepaw of the mastiff.

"Well done, Mars. A new order my dog recently mastered." Liscus bowed gallantly to Beryl, but his eyes bored into Gaius who returned the glare disapprovingly while handing Beryl to the haven of Flavian's embrace.

The commander's aide entered, took the canine's strap and led away the now subdued beast and closed the door. Looking around the cave room, Liscus addressed Beryl: "Domina, this is your only chamber?"

Her dark eyes flashed with pride. "No, commander. We have this room, four bedrooms, a stone bathing chamber and a wool room back in the mountain."

"Domina, may I inquire how you breathe in this rocky villa?"

"Through the slot windows," said Beryl, lapsing into Hebrew, recovering herself and starting again in Latin. "Through the slot windows. One in each room. Shuttered. Meshed wires outside to keep out chipmunks, rats, birds, snakes—sir."

The gaze of Liscus wandered to Gaius. "Indeed, a spacious domicile. I can see that the troglodyte life has attractive attributes."

"Cool in summer, warm in winter," Beryl emphasized, as Flavian tried to quiet her with a worried glance.

"Domina, I deserve the present coolness," said Liscus, bowing. "Tribune Gaius Julius Lacer, your slave waits outside," he said, and opened the blue portal. "Men! Bring in the slave of the tribune!"

Two infantrymen entered, holding by the arms a figure shrouded in a brown cowled cloak. Gently the commander lifted the hood.

Gaius was stupefied. "Penelope," he gasped. "Penelope? *Penelope!*"

XII

With unusual solicitude the soldiers seated Penelope on a bench and rolled up a black felt rug, pushing it under her sandaled feet. The two men looked at Gaius enviously, then stiffened to attention.

"Dismissed," said Liscus. The legionaries marched out. "And now, Tribune Gaius Julius Lacer, do you accept this slave?"

"Whiskers of Jove," muttered Flavian.

"Lord commander," said Penelope, "I am at your mercy."

"Tribune, I am merely following orders," said Liscus, keeping his eyes on Gaius. "I ask again: do you accept her?"

"No!" said Gaius, tensely.

Beryl was looking with sympathy at Penelope.

"Domina," said the commander, "you have just met the tribune, yet the feminine hand might help us cut this Gordian knot. I pray you advise him. I am ordered to give the Greek captive, Penelope, to him. Yet he refuses her."

The vivid wife of Flavian looked bewildered. "If the noble tribune does not want this beautiful young woman," Beryl stammered, "I think she should then be freed!"

"Unfortunately, should our engineering expert refuse custody," said Rufus Liscus, "the young woman will be sent under armed escort to Segovia and auctioned off to the highest bid."

"No!" Gaius exploded. "No!"

"For a man of few words, tribune, you have volcanic depths. I repeat: if you refuse this worthy girl, Penelope, she must go to Segovia to be placed on the block."

When his wife gasped a protest, Flavian saluted. "Sir, could I speak?"

"By all means, sergeant."

"Sir," said the orderly, "my cohort took up a collection a few weeks ago to buy the lady's freedom. We turned the money over to the noble Frontinus. If he gives the coins to Governor Classicus, can the goddess go free?"

A prolonged pause followed while Liscus examined the brown leather pipings of his green wool gauntlets. "How much money is in the freedom fund, sergeant?"

"—Twenty gold coins, fifty-six silvers and thirty-five coppers! Sir, my wife and I will add to it! I got money before leaving New Carthage, commander—fifteen gold coins, tribute from the emperor!" He looked desperately at his wife.

Beryl had Penelope in her sunburned arms. "We'll give all fifteen, may God and the Roman deities protect us!"

Tugging his helmet strap, Liscus remarked, "Unfortunately, sergeant—and you, generous domina—Governor Classicus sets a high price on the Greek girl. He has ordered that if she is to be sold, the purchaser must pay a sum far in excess of the amount collected by the valiant troops of the First Cilician cohort." He stared icily at Gaius. "Penelope's starting price in Segovia will be five thousand gold coins."

"Five thousand," said Flavian, hopelessly.

The room settled into stillness except for the dry chant of a cricket hidden somewhere near the brazier of hissing embers. Gaius watched the glowing red fuel, his hands tightly clenched.

"Sergeant," said Liscus, "if I had five thousand in gold I too would gladly turn it over to Governor Classicus and set her free."

Liar, thought Gaius. Gold-thief, liar, coward—

"I ask for the last time," continued the officer. "Do you accept this blameless young woman, or must I send her to be sold?"

The inexorable question, the terrible dilemma. Send her to Segovia? No! Yet take what another man had cast aside? He tried not to turn his head to look at Penelope, but she was a magnet drawing his glance and desire. Finally, he stared at the white face that had dominated his consciousness, but avoided looking at her neck and shoulders. Even in a gray peasant smock and dark blue wool skirt, her beauty was irresistible.

"Tribune Gaius Julius Lacer—your decision, if you please," Liscus snapped.

Gaius turned his tortured eyes on the bearded face of Liscus.

"I accept her, sir," said Gaius, at last.

Liscus made a contemptuous little bow to Gaius and then a courteous dip of his helmeted head to Beryl and Penelope. "This young woman's arrival in Ioza surprised me also, tribune," said the commander. Then he unbolted the door and left, as though in anger. Gaius stared after him, stared at the closed door—

"Flavian, get water, wine!" cried Beryl. "The lady has fainted!"

Gaius felt paralyzed. He was a standing rock, his stone eyes fixed on a copper ladle hanging from a peg and his mind in chaos. Was Penelope a conspirator, hoping to use her charms to help Classicus? But the girl herself had taken the risk of warning him. At last the voices of Beryl and Flavian aroused him from angry introspection.

"Give her more watered wine," said Beryl. "Now, dear beauty, this little piece of bread. Eat, I beg you. Such a lovely girl!"

"Listen," said Flavian, heartily, "I'm with the First Cicilian, best legion in the army. Men of my cohort call you 'the goddess.' Eat, will you?"

"Mercy of Jehovah, you frighten her," Beryl scolded, affectionately.

"You and lord Flavian . . . so kind," murmured Penelope.

It seemed to Gaius that he was two men—the idealist fighting the primitive; the perfectionist clamoring to be heard over the opportunist, acutely conscious of Penelope now being his to possess. Take her, enjoy her for what she is, it isn't permanent. No, walk out! Go back to your tent. Wait for the right woman! Freedom first, then the right woman—a maiden.

"Sir," said Flavian. "She's all right now."

Gaius finally looked down at Penelope, who huddled against Beryl.

"What did they do to you in New Carthage?" he asked, rudely.

"That is not the way to talk," came Beryl's quick reprimand. "Tell me, Penelope? The tribune, he is so upset, he knows not what he is saying. Such a time! Tell me, Penelope?"

The simple kindness of Beryl produced results. In halting whispers Penelope talked. Three nights ago she had evaded the legation guards and slipped out into the gardens. She had gotten as far as the bird sanctuary when suddenly she was overwhelmed by unseen soldiers; gagged, tied, and a linen shroud thrown over her. When regaining consciousness she was in a cushioned carriage, held by an embarrassed young adjutant of the Theban Legion. Outside rode ten other legionaries.

"The Theban troops were merciful," she whispered. "They stopped soon after and struck camp. I had a tent all to myself, and every night I had privacy. The troops told me not to fear. They brought me wildflowers and discussed their wives and children in Asia Minor . . . They said the governor was placing me under the protection of a good man." Her blue eyes looked beseechingly at Gaius, but he turned away.

"Go on, goddess," said Flavian, with concern.

"We arrived just before sunset today," she sighed. "I was taken to Commander Liscus' tent. He was also kind, but disturbed. Not about me, but about something else. He gave me his tent, he had a tub of hot water brought—he was so thoughtful."

Gaius bent over her and she shrank against the curved rough wall. "Why did Classicus send you to me?"

Beryl looked up irately at Gaius. "Who are *you?*" she demanded. "So superior you are, tribune. Why?"

"Juda-Rose," muttered Flavian, "please, *mea voluptas,* this is deeper than you think. This is our home, not a besieged city."

Penelope arose. "I am ready to go to Segovia," she said, with dignity.

"You are going to bed," Beryl contradicted, getting up. "You need sleep." She stared defiantly at Gaius. "Well, tribune? Are you honorable?"

"I hope so," Gaius thrust back. "May the gods forgive my boorishness, Domina Beryl." A radical idea had come to mind and he was determined to carry it through.

"You are excused, tribune," announced Beryl, briskly. "You can go to your tent."

Gaius smiled at the wife of Flavian. "Asking your forgiveness, domina, but you told me this was my villa. Flavian, is this my home?"

The perplexed aide's face twisted into a vortex of wrinkles. "Our home is your home, sir."

Gaius drew a deep breath. "I need witnesses. I need help—because I'm going to marry Penelope. Now, tonight—in this house."

Flavian opened his mouth, but did not speak.

Penelope stared incredulously and in yearning until her blue eyes saddened. "No, my lord tribune. Even if you could wed me, it would be all wrong for you."

"I am the judge of that," he retorted. "The marriage will not be legal, but it will have to serve. Or, domina, do you fear to become my bride?"

She gazed gently and made no answer.

Beryl nudged her. "Penelope, do you want to become the wife of Gaius Lacer?"

Gaius checked his quick impulse to advise Domina Beryl to stay out of his private affairs. While appreciating her solicitude for Penelope, her emotional rebukes of himself stoked his hot pride and blazed it higher. But Flavian proved a tactful ally.

"I think," pondered the aide, "that the tribune has the final decision—with all respect to you, goddess."

"I am her friend," Beryl cut in. "She is not going to wed unless she wishes to!"

Penelope sank down on the bench. "Send me to Segovia, or send me back to New Carthage," she whispered.

"Do you think I'm a monster?" Gaius asked, bending over her. "I want to marry you! I want you for my wife!"

Beryl took crisp command. "Penelope, the tribune's honorable. Do agree. I shall prepare the altar. He will espouse you by Roman patrician rites, Penelope. I know how this must be done. I've seen one wedding of aristocrats. Flavian can be priest and I will be mistress of ceremonies."

Gaius turned to Beryl and Flavian. "Thank you, domina, but I'll be both priest and bridegroom," he said, his emotions mixed. He wanted to rebuke Beryl for ordaining the kind of marriage, while at the same time he respected her respect for Penelope and her recognition of his own aristocratic blood. Beryl rewarded him with a happy smile, patted Penelope's fair coiled braids, and bustled away. Flavian sighed like the north wind in relief.

When Beryl's impromptu arrangements were completed, Penelope seemed to tremble so on her bench, Gaius picked her up and carried her to the altar. Once he held her, he realized which force within him had won the battle. He stood her beside him, keeping one arm around her waist. "I will improvise the nuptials," he began. "I now announce that my bride will pass from the control of her sire to my hands and my house." He paused to ease the fast beating of his heart.

"Ask her the betrothal question," Beryl prodded.

"I ask my prospective wife the betrothal question," said Gaius. "Do you promise? You will answer: 'I promise.' "

Penelope shook her head. "Lord tribune, do not—"

"Say to me: 'I promise'!"

"Lord tribune, you do not have to marry me."

Harshly he told her, "Domina, I am trying very hard to give you some semblance of respectable matronhood, but your cooperation is needed!"

A shy look for Gaius and Penelope lowered her head. "I . . . I promise . . ."

"I dispense with the complicated ceremonies," Gaius continued. "Next: I pronounce the auspices for this wedding favorable." He glanced at Beryl. She beamed in return.

Beryl laid her hands on the shoulders of Gaius and Penelope, and all followed Flavian around the white altar three times while Beryl intoned:

"That jug of milk symbolizes the cow of sacrifice, oh bride and groom. That fleece represents the sheep. The piece of leather is the pig. The gall has been removed from the beasts, oh bride and bridegroom, and so all bitterness has departed." The four stopped and faced the altar. Beryl lifted an earthen dish from the white table and held it out. "The connubial cake, sanctified, oh bride and bridegroom," she said.

Gaius broke the salted thick wafer in half, offered Penelope her portion and hastily swallowed his own. "A ring," he muttered. "A ring."

Flavian held out a crude bronze circlet. "Sir, this might fit her finger."

Gaius slipped the metal hoop around the third finger of Penelope's right hand. She went rigid in his quick embrace.

Next, Flavian proffered a thick clay bowl of fiery charcoal. Gesturing to it, Gaius said, "My bride, I offer you fire, symbol of . . ." He stopped, searching his memory, at last glancing at Beryl. Her black eyes were becoming suspicious.

"—Symbol of eternal love," Gaius blundered on, and to his relief, Beryl smiled.

"How different," Beryl approved. "Flavian, did you hear what the patrician told his beloved?"

"I heard," sighed Flavian, holding out a copper scoop of cold water. Gaius dipped in his fingers and then drew Penelope's cold hand into the liquid. Again he must say a formula, but he had forgotten what the water meant in a Roman wedding. So he improvised again: "My bride, this is the sacred river of our two lives, now come together."

Beryl raised her smooth brown arms in happy astonishment. Then she said, "I will perform the bride's task." She draped a swatch of lamb's wool around a chair while Flavian awkwardly poured olive oil on the rungs. "We anoint and garland the doorposts of the husband's villa," Beryl went on. "Rejoice! Enter. The bridal bed awaits in the atrium!"

Gaius carried Penelope past the chair. "My bride, we cross the threshold into my house. Repeat after me the ancient vow: *'Where thou art Caius, I am Caia.'*"

"No," she whispered as he stood her beside him. "Lord tribune, you do not have to marry me."

"Repeat the wife's allegiance to her mate and his villa!"

Slowly she responded, *"Where thou art Caius, I am Caia."*

Beryl was joyfully weeping. *"Oh, Hymenaeus Hymen,"* she chanted, between sobs. *"Oh, Hymenaeus Hymen."*

"The maidens and the young men sing, *'Oh Hymenaeus Hymen,'*" said Flavian, gruffly.

"You are now husband and wife," cried Beryl, as Flavian took her in his arms. "Weddings always make me so miserable."

"Sir," said Flavian, "my wife and I wish you and your domina happy lives and easy deaths—"

Suddenly Penelope struggled out of Gaius' embrace as he started to kiss her.

"Mockery, mockery," her gentle voice cried.

Beryl hurried to the agitated bride. "It's a real marriage," the brunette girl soothed. "You need no *flamen* of Jupiter, a yellow wedding veil and slippers, the two-day rites, the choruses of young boys and virgins, Penelope. You don't need ten noble witnesses— none of that. You have no dower and your husband has no property, so you don't need parents or guardians to sign contracts—don't you see, Penelope? And some day when the tribune wins his independence and you win yours, you can get married all over again." As a helpful afterthought Beryl said, "Come Penelope, I will show you to your own bedchamber. You will feel better after we talk, just we two." She glanced at the nervous bridegroom.

He turned toward the blue door. "I'm going to my tent," he said, sullenly angry. Another forced marriage, his thoughts lashed, but this one you forced on yourself.

"Do not leave this cave house," warned Beryl, and Gaius turned angrily to her. "Come with me, Penelope, dear bride," Beryl soothed. "We women will talk. And if you wish your husband, I'll let him come to you."

A despairing grunt came from Flavian. "Juda-Rose, you and I should sit by the cookfire and talk about my campaigns while the tribune and his lady—er—"

"This is woman business," Beryl flashed. "Have you forgotten?"

"Uh," said Flavian in defeat.

After the women disappeared up a shallow flight of stone stairs and through a whitewashed passage back into the mountain, Flavian talked aimlessly about the legions while Gaius found a mop and scrubbed the stone floor . . . on his wedding night Lacer the patrician had swabbed a rock floor in a cave and while his unwilling bride shunned him . . . a night of bliss . . . why didn't he go down to his tent?

He was scouring the cookpots with sand and water when Beryl bustled down the shallow stairs from the bedroom passage.

"Such a busy bridegroom," she twinkled. "Tribune, sir, go to Penelope. The third door to your left down the corridor. Felicity!"

Alone with his bride, Gaius stood by the iron bedstead looking at Penelope almost hidden by a coarse sheet and thick brown wool blankets, her lovely profile and tawny braids shining in the dim light from two clay lamps on a bench in the whitewashed rounded little room.

"Look at me!" he demanded.

Humbly her blue eyes met his gray blue ones.

"It's as true a marriage as I could make it," he went on, defensively, then in irritation, "Years ago I was forcibly joined to a Syrian slave maid. That was no marriage either. Metanny and her son—my child—died." Why did Penelope's eyes have such a consoling, *virginal* tenderness? Virginal? Why the sympathy for *him?*

"Lord tribune, your misery is sacred," she replied. "But you loved her. You must have given her great happiness."

"Don't remind me," he interrupted. "Do you want me to sleep on the floor? Do you think I want you to suffer? Do you?" He began unbuckling his armor and Penelope again turned her face to the wall.

He pulled back the bed coverings and moved in beside her, but he did not touch her for a while. Then he had her in his arms and began pulling the loose cotton shift from her shoulders, fighting to restrain himself, but the infuriating realization that Classicus had despoiled her, that he held something already used and cast off by another man, hardened his mind and his love became savage. He would revenge himself on Proconsul Classicus by punishing Penelope.

The aftermath was shame. For a long time he was afraid to look at her. Lifting up on one elbow, he said at last, "I'm a barbarian. Worse. Forgive me for being like all other men."

"Lord tribune," she murmured, "you are not like the others. You want an untouched woman. Not me. Rest."

The rightness of her analysis nettled him. "You are my wife. Try and forgive me. I'll be more considerate for the married nights yet to come."

He went to sleep first, his head upon her breast.

XIII

Two weeks later in Gades, capital of Farther Spain, Governor Verus Maturus paced in his library. He had just arrived from a frustrating inspection tour and his mind was heavy with anxiety. Were the Arvacan blackcloak guerrillas of Chieftain Malendi massing for war?

Gloomily he watched military aides lay his leather dispatch cases on a gray marble table and march out, while Phrones, his Egyptian scribe, added to the pile with armloads of documents. Unwilling to belabor his thoughts with provincial affairs at the moment, Maturus went outdoors to the seawall promenade above the gray Atlantic. For a while he watched the blue-sailed fishing vessels far below, holding his short toga firmly, or the briny wind would have wrenched it off his body. At last he went inside and sat down. Freedmen added faggots to bronze braziers and glided out while Phrones took a chair across the governor's table. Sunlight poured through tall casements, lighting mottled yellow Corinthian pillars and striking red fires in the porphyry floor. When Maturus and his secretary were alone, the governor said,

"No dictation now, Phrones. I wonder if Farther Spain is still in the empire? My letters to Rome go unanswered. Does the monster and god ever read them? How much bad intelligence piled up while I was away? I brace myself for your report."

"Master, road bandits are becoming more active in this province," the smooth voice of the Egyptian said. "People write letters of protest, claiming no traveller is safe. I referred that matter to the chief of the munipical guards. He promised instant action."

Exasperated, the governor asked, "What else?"

"A few appeals have trickled in from Hither Spain; widows seeking to institute lawsuits, wishing redress for the deaths of their noble husbands."

"Bandits and litigation," muttered Verus Maturus. "Continue."

Phrones got up and leaned over the table and his voice became confidential. A letter had arrived three days previously from a treasury clerk of the noble Frontinus in New Carthage. Enclosed were three wadded and torn tax reports having to do with revenue shipments from Proconsul Classicus' eastern Spanish province to Italy. The treasury worker had apparently rescued the discarded documents after Frontinus had dropped them into a burning brazier; the writer wished to secretly inform His Excellency Maturus that Frontinus was an honest official and kind master, but the informant feared Frontinus might be innocently involved in a puzzling financial situation. Therefore, would His Excellency Maturus take any tactful action necessary to protect General Myron Frontinus?

Astounded, Maturus perused the letter and the crumpled, partially-destroyed parchments that showed scorching. Each bore rows of figures. Maturus caught the guarded implication: someone, the correspondent thought, was tampering with the tax coffers in New Carthage before the chests were placed on ship for Italy; and the filcher was not his master, Frontinus. There was no signature. The letter had come to Gades from New Carthage by fishing barge. Trying to free his mind of this information, Maturus laid aside the documents. "Phrones, I trust there is better word from Chieftain Malendi?"

"No tidings at all, master. Your recent three scrolls to Malendi were returned unopened," said Phrones, dismally.

"Get me milk, stir in two eggs and a pour of honey," shouted the governor.

Alone, he morosely reviewed the ominous situation in the north of his province. When Phrones returned, the proconsul sipped his healthful beverage while the secretary hovered anxiously.

"Phrones, my faithful scribe," said Maturus, "I learn from General Antonius that Malendi's tribesmen are spreading the rumor among the lesser blackcloaks that I, aspiring to become Emperor after the predicted death of Domitian, have imprisoned General Trajan and appointed Antonius to his post." His lower lip quivered. "What will Malendi think of next to stir unrest among his blackcloaks and his allies? Antonius and I try to please Malendi. We build roads and bridges, we give the blackcloaks salted codfish and moonstones our troops find, since Malendi's tribe considers such stones sacred. Yet not one diplomatic measure succeeds in bringing them into our camp."

"My governor, is Prince Malendi going to declare war?"

Maturus irascibly replied, "Not this year—I hope. Usually they start fighting the first day of Spring. But the blackcloaks attack without warning . . . I try to convince myself that the rising belligerence of Malendi and his thousands is rooted in their hatred of Emperor Domitian. Yet . . ."

The cautious Egyptian sat down. "Master, could that be what someone is fostering in the minds of the blackcloaks?"

"Sound reasoning," Maturus approved. "Yet to them I am the Rome they hate, and Malendi's elusive tribesmen consider us all land-robbers. I am supposed to covet their mountains, flocks, domed huts—and also their greasy veiled women. I am also blamed for skirmishes between our whitecloak *Togati* and Malendi's blackcloaks. I told the *Togati* chieftains to stop attacking blackcloak encampments and waylaying their hunters and herdsmen. But will our whitecloak allies obey?" Abruptly he turned his mind to the anonymous letter and tax reports from New Carthage.

"Frontinus is surely a Roman of integrity," he mused, thoughtfully. "I swear so by any god you could name." A lightning suspicion struck: could Cornelius Classicus be the one who was trying to defraud Rome? Enna's fortune was gone, and the proconsul of Hither Spain had lavish tastes. Couple that with the fact that any one with eyes could see that Frontinus was in love with Enna. A picture of what might be transpiring in New Carthage aggravated Governor Maturus, and made him feel more keenly how limited as a magistrate he was by distance.

At last he said, "If the emperor ever signs that pending investigation measure into law, I will have the right to make a sweeping inquiry of the tax departments of both Spanish provinces . . . and also to review the cases of executed men of wealth. Phrones—will that day ever come?"

The scribe blinked. "The god Osiris speed the day, master."

Sourly the governor muttered, "Yet, as the estimable Senator Tacitus bravely proclaims in Rome, *When the times are most corrupt, the laws are multiplied.*" Slumping in his armchair, Verus Maturus thought of Gaius Lacer and Rufus Liscus. He considered Liscus an honest, if cold and scarcely approachable man, and heartily approved of Gaius. A fresh idea took form: when men mine gold, greed is born. Greed. Greed—gold—guerrillas—and Gaius. A thorny bundle, he decided, and hoped that young Lacer found Dawn a good horse.

His spirits lifting, Maturus began studying the documents on his table. After a while he started dictating a diplomatic dispatch to Chieftain Luna Malendi, inviting the blackcloak prince to Gades for an amicable conference. Maturus would be pleased to resolve any problems of the tribal leader for the continued glory of the *Pax Romana* in Spain. Phrones' stylus raced over the waxed boards of three tablets as the governor's resounding sentences of good will for the Celt blackcloaks poured out.

XIV

Until the end of May, the expedition camped in Ioza, recruiting labor from district prisons for the Sil mines. The chained men were marched to the settlement, their records compiled by Gaius, and then packed into wagons and started north under escort of cavalry troops from garrisons in Farther Spain.

Now the last shackled worker had come and gone, and Gaius had little to do but sit in his tent, riffle through lists of prisoners' names, and try to stifle his fear about Penelope. On a sunny morning late in the month and at sunrise that day he had seen Governor Classicus arrive by carriage escorted by cavalry troopers.

If the proconsul had come to claim Penelope, Gaius would kill him and escape with her. Sensing the suppressed fury of Gaius, Flavian had reassured him that Classicus had come to confer with Commander Liscus; so far the governor had not even inquired about Gaius or Penelope. But should His Excellency make inquiries, or go up to the cave home, Beryl would inform Classicus that the Greek lady had fled long ago and Beryl had no idea where she had gone. As a legionary's wife, Beryl had nothing to fear from a Roman procurator, and she talked so fast Classicus would doubtless be bested and glad to escape the power of her tongue.

The loyalty of Beryl and Flavian cheered Gaius as he tried to persuade himself that Penelope would not be threatened. At last he became aware of a man standing by his table. Not looking up, he reached for a pen and strip of papyrus. "Your name. Home. Crime. Family, if any."

"I am Turdo," said a deep and sibilant voice. "I came to see you."

Looking up, Gaius saw an enormous man who seemed as wide of shoulder as he was tall, with wild yellow hair, a rosy, scarred face, and deepset blue eyes under thick golden brows. His sheepskin shirt and leather breeches were coated with whitish dust. Marble dust, thought Gaius.

Turdo darted a look through the open tent flaps. "Black dog commander down by stream with white toga governor," continued the giant. He reeked of garlic and perspiration. "You saved my little *puella* from drowning. You are a slave. How can I help you?"

Gaius warily considered the huge man; was this a trap? Instinct prompted him to trust the creature. But he did not speak.

"I too was a slave," muttered Turdo. "Then gladiator. They matched me with Thrysa the Terrible in the Flavian Amphitheatre in Rome." His mouth made chewing motions. "The stands bet against me, Thrysa was champion sword-fighter. I was his meat. But I get him clean, quick, in the neck. The Vestal Virgins ordered the emperor to set me free. Emperor Domitian, he was drunk. He threw gold coins at me. I leave Italy with my Eunice and daughter and sail to Spain, get work in marble quarries. I am German. Your friend. You saved my baby."

Curiously Gaius asked, "Turdo, do you ever go back to your homeland?"

The gladiator leaned over the table. "You want something from Germany? I get it. Muleteers, sheepherders, mountain peddlers, all friends. Long trip, but I get it."

Gaius pondered the risk of sending a letter to Apollodorus, but decided in the negative. Messages passing from hand to hand across the vast distance separating Spain from Germany . . . what if a loyal carrier was killed by bandits or soldiers . . . ? And Governor Classicus might be censoring mail to and from both Spanish provinces. Then he got a hopeful new idea.

"Turdo," he said, "Commander Liscus and Governor Classicus are—" he paused—"they are not friends of mine. I would like to know—if they plot against me."

Turdo's smile showed big yellow teeth. "I find out for you."

"How?"

The German smiled craftily. "Trust me." He walked to the tent entrance, then unexpectedly let out a screech of laughter and began bounding around Gaius. A moment later Commander Liscus and Mars came in.

"And just what have we here?" smiled Liscus. "Mars—to your haunches. A Celt from Galicia? Celtiberian from Lusitania? Briton? German?"

Turdo was whirling and leaping like a panther. "Allawallurba!" he said. "Wallaburolla!"

Liscus looked puzzled. "Who is this man?"

"Sir, he must come from the marble pits," said Gaius, concealing a smile.

"Indeed. And his smell is as strong as his brawn. Man, do you want to sign in as a miner? Are you a pleb? Freedman? I could use you as a foreman."

"Urgah," blubbered the giant. "Allawallugga!"

His small wife, Eunice, hurried in. She bobbed a bow to the commander, glanced vaguely at Gaius, then shrilled at Turdo:

"You big haunch of mutton! Gold crazy! Drunk again! Mead and cider turn you to pulp! You get paid twenty silvers a month in the quarries, but you want a whole goldfield! Up with you, bother not the noble lord commander!" She swatted his buttocks and he stopped gyrating. "Back to work or I beat you with brambles!" She hustled him out, his piercing laughter echoing back into the tent.

"The superior sex," observed Rufus Liscus. "Tribune, I came to tell you that we leave Ioza tomorrow at dawn. We will depart this pleasant vale and enter Farther Spain."

Gaius stared at Liscus, and a sudden psychic impression stirred in his subconscious, struggling for recognition. An invisible cord seemed to bind him to Rufus. A bond of antagonism? . . . "Commander, have we met somewhere before?"

Liscus made a little bow. "No. Not until that day in New Carthage." He drawled, "Any more questions?"

"Sir, I had the strongest feeling that we know each other."

"Indeed. Has the tribune by chance read the gripping tale of Xerxes crossing the Hellespont?"

Gaius replied, "I have, sir. The works of Herodotus, the Father of History."

"Interesting. I quote: *'The land will also be your enemy; for, if no one opposes your advance, as you proceed farther you will find the land more and more hostile.'* "

Gaius allowed himself a Liscus-like smile. "Sir, allow me to quote from the same authority: *'The beginning and end of the matter are not always seen at once.'* "

Liscus offered a mocking salute and glanced down at his crouching mastiff. "Mars, up. Heel." Man and dog walked out.

XV

At intervals during the day, Flavian discreetly informed Gaius as to the activities of Proconsul Classicus. The genial governor was dispensing coppers to the village children. In the afternoon he had conferred briefly with Commander Liscus in the officer's tent, and the word was that His Excellency would leave Ioza at moonrise to continue his inspection tour. But first he would sup and confer once more with Liscus.

Reasonably reassured, Gaius stayed in his tent, wondering whether Turdo would overhear any conversation between Rufus and the proconsul. The likelihood seemed remote, for the commander's tent was posted with sentries in front and protected by a cliff at the sides and back. As sunset drew on, Flavian went up to his cave home while Gaius remained to put his records in coffers. At last he, too, started up the mountain path to the home of the blue door. He was darkly depressed.

Tomorrow he was leaving Ioza. But tonight remained—tonight and Penelope. Why did thoughts of her always make him feel guilty and on the defensive? Their relationship was temporary. Penelope herself had twice insisted this was so and he had not contradicted her. And even during his passionate enjoyment of her, when reason almost deserted him, he had never lost control of his tongue. Not even when she gave him bliss beyond bliss, did he ever whisper, "Penelope, I love you. Adore you. I love you."

Surely he should have tired of her by now. An appalling thought struck: if she represented merely convenient sexual pleasure, why had he grimly decided to kill Classicus and escape with her? That realization brought a staggering new one: Penelope would be left in Ioza. She had no real friend except Beryl. Who would protect Penelope after he went north? He had constantly fought the idea that he loved more than her body, yet some nights he lay with her in bed, talking about his life, work, frustrations and ambitions— almost as if he were a loved and loving and contented husband. They even shared a small jest: both awoke at the same time each morning.

'Penelope, are we awake?'

'We are, my Gaius. But rest until Flavian calls that your bath is ready. Ah, yesterday's razor-knick is healed. Try not to gouge your chin this morning, lord. And will you take some fleece north to keep your hands soft and smooth? The village physician gave me pumice-powder for your teeth. You will take it? And the copper sulfate solution to rinse your eyes?'

Solicitude was only part of Penelope's baffling charm. And why, each sunset, was he so anxious to return to her as if she were the ideal woman and wife? Tonight would be the last homecoming.

Penelope . . . Penelope . . . 'Will my lord Gaius allow me to wash his hair tonight?'

How would he get along without her? Somehow she had entrenched herself in his life. But once on horseback again, bound north for the mines, his infatuation would surely die.

Yet he recalled his senseless jealousy the first time he watched her trying to help Flavian. "Let me untangle your helmet crest, lord Flavian. May I polish the lord tribune's cuirass?"

And Beryl, the vivacious Judean-Roman, considered Penelope a paragon of virtue and industry. 'Such firm and tender hands milking goats she has, tribune! And today she baked honey-raisin cakes, your favorites! How fortunate you are, Gaius Lacer.'

Near the door of the mountain habitation he stopped suddenly. Had he heard a muffled scream over the village sounds and the roar of water down below? He rushed to the blue door. It was ajar, a most unusual state of affairs. He kicked it open.

Inside Flavian was struggling with Penelope, while Beryl, with a basket of greens on one arm, stood transfixed by the water trough. As Gaius dashed in, a dagger flew through the air and clanged against a copper dipper hanging on a peg.

"She tried to kill herself—" Flavian cried. "One of my daggers— she cut her arm, I couldn't stop her!"

Beryl dropped her hamper, pulled Flavian's remaining weapon from his belt and threw it across the room as Gaius wrenched Penelope away from Flavian.

"Get linen and balsam, Flavian!" screamed Beryl, already examining the thin crimson wound in Penelope's left arm. "Jehovah be praised, only a skin wound." Flavian rushed forward with a roll of cloth and a pot of salve while Gaius held his rigid wife close. Deftly the wife of Flavian wound linen spread with ointment around Penelope's arm.

"Why?" Gaius whispered. "Why, Penelope?"

"Why, goddess?" Flavian pleaded. "Did you hear what Turdo said to me? Was that why? You're safe here, Penelope."

Beryl took command. "She needs to lie down. The tribune will take you to your bedchamber."

Gaius sat on their bed beside her. "Penelope, why?" The awful thought that she might have killed herself except for Flavian . . . "Penelope—tell me!"

Her pink lips quivered. "I do not want pity."

"Why did you try to take your own life? Answer me!" He could not keep the anger from his voice.

Her blue eyes sparkled with grief and exhaustion. Then she, too, became angry. "My life is mine. Send me back to New Carthage, give me back to Classicus, or send me to Segovia."

He put his hands over her mouth. "You are never going back to that beast!" He caught her arms, and she winced. He jerked his hand from her bandaged left arm—would he ever stop hurting her? Now he saw a new Penelope; no longer soft, humble, deferential. He saw more; he seemed to be detached, looking at her and himself, and a wave of self-loathing surged through him. He was no better than Classicus, not even as honest as Classicus. The proconsul had purchased her openly to be his concubine, while Gaius had recited ironic marriage vows because he needed and valued the respect of Flavian and Beryl.

Knocks sounded at the bedroom portal.

"How is she?" called Flavian from the corridor. "Anything Juda-Rose and I can do?"

Gaius leaned over and kissed Penelope's clenched hands. She looked remote, unattainable. He had lost her, lost her, she must loathe him.

"Penelope, say you hate me. Say something. Anything."

Slow tears crept down her pale cheeks. "I do not hate you, lord."

"Shall I let Flavian and Beryl come in?"

Penelope sat up and wiped her cheeks with the blanket. "As the lord tribune decides."

"Come in," called Gaius. "The door's not bolted."

"Some day I'll reward you both," said Gaius, shakily as they tiptoed in. "Thank the gods you stopped her, Flavian."

"Seeing her alive except for a sore arm . . ." said the aide in a hushed voice. "Goddess, you caught me off guard and that hasn't happened since my second campaign years back. Almost had to break your wrist. Never try that again—will you?"

Beryl was maternally smoothing Penelope's disheveled fair braids, but there was war in her black eyes as she glanced occasionally at Gaius. For once he endured her dislike without glaring in return, for he too blamed himself for Penelope's attempt at suicide. Then he was surprised to see Beryl's eyes soften.

"What am I thinking about," said Beryl. "I shall eat bitter herbs tonight to atone—ah, such a one I am! Now I see it all. Penelope couldn't stand the idea of her husband leaving tomorrow, that is it. Flavian, what was it Turdo said to you? Jehovah save us, our strong man leaped out of this house and rushed on up a path as I was coming in with my herbs."

Flavian began stalking about. "I got home to find Beryl's note that she had gone to gather thyme and parsley," he began. "I figured the goddess was back in her room. Then in lunged the gladiator, Turdo, killer of Thrysa the Terrible, who threatened to kill me if I spied on the tribune or planned to kill *him*."

"No," Penelope gasped.

"And that," muttered Flavian, "would have been a fight. I might have lost."

"Jupiter and all the gods, no," cried Beryl.

"I kept a table between us," Flavian grinned. "Turdo wanted to talk to Gaius in private. I told him I was your orderly and friend, sir—and if he'd stop trying to turn my home into an arena, we could talk things out. He asked me to prove my claims. So I told him that the goddess is the tribune's wife and Turdo is to keep that tied to his tongue. Victory at last. The German almost knocked me over with an embrace," Flavian went on, chuckling. "Like being hugged by a lion. But our burly champion was in a hurry, and said to tell you he has a secret listening place!" Flavian stopped and considered a moment. "Turdo said he'd overheard Classicus tell Commander Liscus that Tribune Gaius Lacer left papers in New Carthage that proves he plans to steal gold."

Gaius listened coldly. "Go on, Flavian."

"I shouted to our gladiator, 'Lies, Turdo! Lies!' And I got another lion-hug." Flavian shuddered humorously. "So by that time Turdo and I were old friends, comrades." The sergeant's sympathetic dark eyes rested on Penelope before he continued. "Then Turdo said Classicus will take Penelope back unless 'Gaius the gold-thief' finds ore and doesn't try to steal it."

Gaius' first thought was of Penelope, desperately wanting to tell her—tell her what? Could she believe he was an unscrupulous man, a gold-robber or worse? Was that why she had tried to stab herself? "Penelope," he said, gently, conscious of Beryl's piercing stare again, "the proconsul lies, of course."

"Of course," she said, quietly, but shuddered.

"Goddess, you're not to worry," said Flavian. "I'll look after Gaius. And you'll be safe here with Juda-Rose after we go north. If you have to disappear, Turdo will see to it. He'll do anything for the tribune." The sergeant sat down on a bench. "I want to think hard," he announced. At last a magnificent smile adorned his face and he pulled off his hobnailed boots.

"God of Moses, gods of Rome, what are you doing?" exclaimed Beryl.

"Tribune Lacer," said Flavian, "we're going to exchange boots. I'm taller than you, but we've got the same helmet-size, same foot size, and I requisitioned four pairs of boots apiece for each of us from the quartermaster before we left New Carthage. Put on my boots, sir."

Gaius was baffled, but he obeyed. The shoes fit perfectly.

"Press the inside leather patch on your left boot," said Flavian, smilingly.

Gaius did so, and what looked like a small bronze spearhead popped out of the shank of the boot. Flavian picked up the metal object.

"This," said the aide, lazily, "is an 'Aid to Victory.' He pressed it and an awl-shaped tiny blade flashed out of the bronze. "Once you're in practice," Flavian rumbled on, "you jerk out an Aid, snap out the blade—and you're in action." He pressed Gaius' right boot and a twin Aid emerged which Flavian handed to astonished Gaius. "These small but lethal weapons have saved me many a time when my big weapons are busy," Flavian laughed. "I, tribune, am a walking porcupine of an arsenal." He reached under both armpits and looked dumfounded when he opened his hands. "Where do you suppose these death-to-the-enemy came from, sir? Blistering hades . . ." He plucked at the leather lappets of his uniform and four more knives appeared like magic.

Penelope reached out trembling hands to Flavian. "Lord sergeant, you gave the lord tribune weapons," she whispered.

"Not me," said Flavian. "Against regulations for the tribune to go armed. But if we got our boots mixed—well, it's plain that we both wear the same size."

XVI

Early that rainy evening, Turdo, the strong man of Ioza, squatted at his listening post in a rock passage penetrating the mountain from his cave home to the marble quarries. Part of the tunnel led around through the crescent-shaped cliff that sheltered the tent of Rufus Liscus and insulated it against the clamor of the stream at the base of the slope. Deep fissures in the slanting limestone masses provided listening and lookout stations. The flame of a clay lamp burned dimly behind Turdo, eerily illuminating weird columns of stalactites formed of the ceaseless water-drip of centuries. Already familiar with the voices coming from the tent outside, the former arena champion recognized the speakers as Governor Cornelius Classicus and Commander Rufus Liscus.

In the tent, when the supper trenchers and goblets were removed by an orderly of the commander, Classicus began an affable monologue. Rome wanted gold and more gold. Gold not for Rome, but metal to send as tribute payments to the rapacious Dacian barbarians across the Danube. The emperor obviously preferred pacifying the savage hordes to smashing them. A dreary outlook—but live and endure and pray for better times. Hope that some day a new soldier-emperor would raise his sword and lead the legions to victory over the shaggy wildmen of eastern Europe.

"Now a more felicitous subject," continued Classicus. "Rufus, you should marry again. Or did your divorce disillusion you?"

"No."

"Rufus, you're an outstanding officer. My friend, your beard gives you presence. I observed the ladies ogling you back in New Carthage. And should not your children have a mother?"

For a while Rufus gazed blankly. "I prefer being both father and mother to my daughters, Classicus, rather than entrust them to the uncertain mercies of a stepmother. Devoted slaves in Ravenna vigilantly care for Primula and Sophronia." He smiled. "I see my girls as often as possible. They take good care of their father when he visits them."

"Nevertheless," said Classicus, "I had hoped to be matchmaker and introduce you to the charming blonde niece of Senator Mauricus. Confidentially, I had received orders from Rome for the execution of Senator Mauricus, Domina Decia, and their niece. I sped two men to warn the retired senator to hide his ladies away."

Rufus examined his clean fingernails. "Your confidences are safe with me. I wish I had been successful in saving Publius the architect last February."

"Another terrible decision of the Fates," sighed Classicus.

The commander seemed lost in contemplation as he talked. "I saw Publius walk out on the bridge he was building. Mars and I started out to greet him—then I saw the bridge builder stagger. There was no stone coping to prevent his fall. In desperation I tried a new command on my mastiff: *'Save!'* "

The crouching black dog at his master's feet pricked up his ears and let out a soft whine.

"Good Mars," said Liscus, stroking his beast's broad skull. "You did get your jaws into the left boot of Publius while I and the other men ran to help you—" The commander sighed. "For an awful moment the architect hung dangling—then his booted foot broke loose from Mars' teeth and he plunged into the gorge . . ."

"Be cheered, you tried," said Classicus. "His shade blesses you.

Mars, too." The proconsul smiled innocently at the mastiff. "Well—what intelligence from the Sil river basin?"

After a brief silence, Rufus said, "Five thousand prison laborers are building a camp under the eyes of cavalry troops from the three legions of General Antonius. All should be ready when I and my men arrive, so that digging for gold can start without delay."

"Splendid, commendable," Classicus nodded. "You'll be in comfortable circumstances when everything is settled, Rufus. Now—the warning I gave you this afternoon. I'm still trying to find another mineral expert, but until I do, guard against Gaius Lacer. A crafty, ambitious, secretive man. His haughty demeanor sickens me. He considers himself superior because his name is Lacer—but under his handsome mask is a treacherous mind."

The commander looked away.

"Rufus, there is one vital matter—let me start again. My noble friend, since you have not thus far confided in me, let me confide in you. By accident I found out who you really are."

"Who told you?"

"Be assured the information is inviolate," Classicus soothed. "Inviolate. Nobody told me, Rufus. But when that inheritance matter developed, I decided to write to the Questor's office in Rome for information about the Liscus family. I received copies of long-forgotten documents thirty-seven years old."

Rufus was standing, his expression one of disbelief. Slowly he sat down. "What was the content of those records, Classicus?"

The proconsul gently touched the rigid fists of the commander. "Rufus, you are the adopted son of the late Herrenius. Your honored mother was a British slave. When pregnant with you, she was sold by her owner to Herennius Liscus. You know that, of course?"

A taut silence followed. "I do," said Rufus.

"Forgive me," said Classicus, sincerely. "The adoption was all very secret, you understand, but such written accounts have to go to Rome eventually. Rufus, I salute *you* as the unrecognized son of the late Consul Julius Lacer. You should bear that distinguished name of a famous patrician noble, not Gaius. Bondsman though he is, however, he is the legal son and has the right to the name of his sire. Little wonder if you want to see Gaius dead, after he makes a gold strike. You have my full sympathy, Rufus, if Gaius is crushed under a rock-slide up north."

"I hate him," said Rufus, hoarsely. "I hate him. I hate him!"

Gaius was keeping vigil at the bedside of Penelope while she slept lightly, his mind seething with conflicting emotions—pride, ambition, self-hatred and tenderness for the girl, ranged against the voice of vanity clamoring that he wait until freedom and wed a chaste woman of his own rank. 'And what will happen to Penelope?' asked an inner voice defending the Greek captive. 'Are you so selfish you think only of your fate? Do you care what happens to Penelope after you go?'

He glanced down. She was awake.

"Lord tribune—"

"Don't ever call me 'lord tribune' again, Penelope. Call me Gaius. Or call me 'you.' Or call me a beast."

She smiled faintly, and murmured, "I promise, Gaius."

Ask her about her life, what happened in Greece! Listen to her for a change instead of talking about yourself. Staring at her, he almost wept, for there was a maternal solicitude in her expressive face that shamed him. "Tell me," he said. "Tell me everything. Everything."

A deep flush pinkened her face. "No," she said.

The bedroom door opened and Beryl darted in, black eyes flashing in the lamplight. "Tribune Lacer, Turdo has come. Now he wants to tell you what he heard—" she glanced at Penelope. "Everything is well, Penelope." But she pushed Gaius out into the corridor, shutting the door after him.

In the main room of the cave, Gaius listened as Turdo gave an account of the conversation he had just overheard from the tent of Commander Rufus Liscus. When the German stopped talking, Gaius was still speechless. Could it be true? Rufus Liscus, the illegitimate son of Consul Julius Lacer? Rufus and himself sons of the same father? *Brothers?* Now he understood his feeling that a mysterious bond linked him to Commander Liscus. Brothers . . . brothers . . . sons of Consul Julius Lacer . . .

"When brave Gaius goes north, I, Turdo, hide his lady in secret cavern if killers come," muttered Turdo. "She will be safe. She can see and hear what happens outside, but nobody will see her."

Gaius held out his hands. "Turdo, I will be grateful . . ." He was swept into a chest-squeezing embrace by the giant. Then the gladiator ran to the blue door and disappeared into the rainy night. Flavian shot the bolts.

"Blistering hades," grunted the orderly, "what do you do now, sir? Why is the governor trying to poison the commander against you?"

Gaius could understand Rufus' hate; the man must have nursed it for years, and since Consul Julius Lacer was not alive to be the target, Gaius was the obvious subject of his half-brother's jealousy and vengeance. He wondered if Rufus had come out to Spain to find and try to kill Gaius Julius Lacer. . . . The threat to himself he could meet with vigilance, endurance, and attempts to win the commander's trust. But the slanderous accusations of Cornelius Classicus. . . .

"Well, sir?" Flavian watched shrewdly.

"I'll watch and wait," said Gaius. "Some day I may tell the commander, but then I will never acknowledge the relationship if I am convinced that Rufus Liscus is a bribetaker."

He and Flavian turned as Penelope came in, wearing Gaius' gray military cloak over her white bedgown, her golden braids hanging down into the folds of the cape. Beryl hovered excitedly at the top of the shallow steps leading into the bedroom passage.

Avoiding the helping hands of Gaius, the Greek girl let Flavian seat her on a cushioned bench. "Lord tribune," said Penelope, gently, "I do not think Commander Liscus is evil. I do not think his mastiff slays helpless people. We must not forget he has been kind to me."

Jealousy of Liscus suddenly shot through Gaius. Was Penelope falling in love with Rufus? Was she blind?

"I don't know what to think," gloomed Flavian. "But nobody's going to drop rocks on your husband, Penelope. I'm not only his orderly, I'm his friend."

"Brave sirs," Penelope continued, meekly, "could it be that Governor Classicus plans on having the commander's cavalry troops steal gold, without the commander's knowledge? Or the lord tribune, either?"

Flavian warmed his hands over the red coals of the brazier. "I often brother it with the cavalry to learn what they think, when I go on a new campaign. I can say this: the horse troopers get double pay, that's tradition in the army. But so far as I can learn, I don't think any cavalryman of our expedition has accepted a bribe. Me and my Cilician Legion infantrymen aren't in any gold-stealing either, nor could *we* be bribed."

A sudden idea struck Gaius. "But there are the guerrillas!" he exclaimed. And he told Flavian and the women about the plateaus, forests and mountains of Farther Spain through which the cavalcade would ride sometime tomorrow. While generally peaceful and sub-servient to the Roman Eagles, the wilderness was thickly populated with warlike Arvacan blackcloaks and pro-Roman whitecloak *Togati*. "Rome never hears about these internecine skirmishes," he explained, "because all of Spain is supposed to be peaceful since the reign of Augustus Caesar. Under General Trajan, even the black-cloaks were quiet and contented. But now—"

"Sir, now, what about the guerrillas?"

"The blackcloaks sometimes attack peaceable Roman patrols and road-builders," said Gaius. They used both primitive and Roman weapons and their ponies were fast; and a guerrilla war could break out because the Romans were opening up the abandoned mines in the basin of the Sil river and its tributaries.

Back in the bedroom Gaius felt unwanted as he watched Penel-ope, in bed, her face to the wall.

"Is the lord tribune coming to his couch?" she asked, turning at last.

"The lord slave is going to sleep on the floor," he said, hoping she would beg him to rest beside her. Then he could restrain him-self no longer. "Don't treat me like this," he said. "Say you hate me, say anything—" What can a man say when his pride begins to crumble?

Her blue eyes brightened with tears. "Gaius, please come to bed."

Soon they lay side by side—separated. A long time later he slipped an arm around her and drew her head to his chest. She was trem-bling. "Sleep?" he whispered. "Will you sleep . . . ?"

"Oh, Gaius," she sobbed. "Be so careful when you reach Farther Spain. I will pray every moment; I will always remember."

Then he crushed his lips against hers, passion storming in, and this night they met as equals in love, the shyness of Penelope burn-ing away in the fire of their two bodies.

XVII

At sunrise the next morning Commander Liscus sat his white horse, facing rows of mounted troops. "Men," he called over the rush of the stream by the road, "we cross the boundary into Farther Spain an hour's ride from now. As we proceed we must be constantly vigilant, for the Arvacan blackcloaks may—or may not—be haters of the emperor." He paused. "Shields on arms—place!"

Metal clanked, leather straps creaked.

"Spears—up!"

A forest of iron-tipped javelins reared upward.

Liscus cantered to the rear through crowds of villagers, to where the supply wagons and mounted infantry awaited. Gaius and Flavian saluted.

"*Optio* Flavian, you and your troops are rear guards," said the officer. "This is the most vulnerable position; that is why you ride it. Be on constant guard against guerrilla ambush."

Flavian saluted. "A pleasure, sir."

Turning to Gaius, the commander said, "Tribune, where is Penelope? I have had a baggage wain prepared for her comfort. Have her brought at once."

All Gaius could do was stare in dismay. "No," he said at last. "I do not wish her to come."

Flavian muttered, "Commander, Penelope is the tribune's wife. He married her the night you brought her to my home. She's going with the expedition, sir?"

Grimacing, the commander said, "Tribune Lacer, walk your horse to that grove of alders."

Gaius and his half-brother exchanged stares, the muzzles of the golden mare and white stallion caressing each other.

"Why did you attempt matrimony with Penelope?" demanded Rufus. "She is a captive slave of Cornelius Classicus!"

"I do not leap from bed to bed or woman to woman, sir," Gaius replied. "She was forced upon me. Now, when I have earned my freedom, I will earn hers. After that, I will wed her legally."

"How do you expect to earn five thousand in gold to buy the hapless young woman from Classicus?" asked the commander.

"I am a bridge engineer," Gaius snapped. "In five years I hope to have paid off my indebtedness to my patron Apollodorus. A year or less after that, I will—" he smiled grimly—"pay off Classicus." He hoped the implied barb sank in. "Meanwhile, my wife remains in Ioza with Domina Beryl—"

"Your wife must come with us," Liscus interrupted.

"And be subjected to the dangers of guerrilla country?" Gaius exploded.

"I must remind the furious tribune that I am acting general and give the orders," said Liscus. "Indeed, I further remind you that unless she goes with you, Classicus may find out her whereabouts and order her sent to Segovia to be sold."

Then reining in next to Gaius, Commander Rufus unexpectedly jerked a short dagger from his gear. "Conceal this under your breastplate," he said. "That is a command."

Gaius was so surprised he nearly dropped the weapon while hiding it.

The earthy wet scent of last night's rain was in the morning air when the expedition began moving. Gaius paced his mare next to Flavian's brown stallion. Looking up, he saw Beryl waving and crying farewells, saw the sun glint off the brass skewers in her dark hair. He sensed that she was warning him to take good care of Penelope.

His lips set grimly. Now he had a new, grave concern: the safety of Penelope. His eyes roamed ahead to the looming mountains green with forests—and underneath the green, undoubtedly, the watchful blackcloak warriors.

That hot afternoon the expedition was travelling over a vast eroded plain ringed by mountains and stony bluffs. Occasionally the roadway led past oases of cork-oaks and willows fed by muddy brooks and narrow river tributaries. The scorching wind was dry and clean, odorous of mountain sage, wild thyme, evergreens and dust. Far away in the green and dun-brown landscape, wild black and brown piebald horses were on the run.

During the morning the travellers had stopped at two walled tent-settlements of friendly *Togati* Celts, situated on fortified plateaus where, centuries before, there had been Greek and Carthaginian cities. At each noisy town a Celt chieftain, in dusty white Roman toga over his sheepskin tunic, saluted the Romans in a mystifying dialect, interspersed with frantically cordial Latin salutations of loyalty to Rome. Observing diplomatic formalities, Commander Liscus dismounted and let himself be kissed on the forehead and ears by each Celt leader. Rufus extended the compliments of Rome to each host and his council of elders and to the pretty blonde Togati women who threw back their veils in honor of the Romans. Rufus tactfully refused offers of eager Celt ladies anxious to become his concubines: he was unworthy of such fair ones. Moreover, he never mixed pleasure with duty.

At the second *Togati* city, the Romans arrived in time to see the end of a bull-fight between two snorting black beasts and their screaming *Togati* goaders. One Celt was gored to death. When both bullocks were bleeding from many wounds, warriors dispatched them with arrows and the spectators cheered until the rocky wilderness echoed. And would the noble Romans stay for a beef banquet that evening of fair omen? Commander Liscus courteously refused and the expedition set out again.

When the second city of whitecloaks had been left far behind, the procession entered a more forbidding land of strange rock monoliths which were remnants of ancient Druid worship. The only visible signs of life in the rugged terrain were small flocks of sheep and gaunt black cattle far to the north, and wild ponies kicking up dirt far to the east. Then Gaius began seeing lone tribesmen in hairy dark tunics and horsehide mantles, watering their range ponies at muddy streams. They were Arvacan blackcloaks . . .

Outpost sentinels, thought Gaius, as he watched the tribesmen of the famous Chieftain Luna Malendi trying to appear peaceful and submissive. When you see a few, you know hundreds are hiding in the canyons . . . Liscus knows what we're getting into . . . but not Penelope . . .

He had watched her curtained wagon ever since they left Ioza. It rolled and bumped ahead, two side flaps of the tarpaulin open, but Penelope invisible inside. How was she faring? Gaius had gotten a quick look into the wain before they left the cave village, and Liscus admittedly had outdone himself in providing comforts for the only woman of the expedition. Fleece mattresses, blankets, pillows, lamps, table, folding chairs, baskets of food, ewers of water and wine, a portable *latrina,* everything—even a large chest of medicinal herbs, salves and bandages the Ioza physician had given her as a gift of gratitude.

Soldiers, Gaius mused, killed for a living. But women saved lives. Penelope, the giver. He forced his eyes to the forbidding landscape again.

Two hours before sunset a shaggy blackshirt warrior galloped to Commander Liscus, slid off his horse and grovelled on the stone road. Hail the immortal Chieftain Malendi, and would the brave lord officer of Domitian Caesar sell food for a moonstone, the holy gem? Rufus spoke formal greetings of friendship, and although refusing the moonstone, offered in return two casks of olive oil, four sides of bacon and a sack of rice. The warrior whistled—and six comrades on black ponies suddenly materialized out of ravines and galloped away with the bulging sacks.

Gaius had watched the transaction with keen misgivings. Guerrillas who failed to speak allegiance to Rome . . . he touched the hilt of the dagger under his breastplate, flexed his feet and felt the reassuring pressure of the small knives in his boots. Glancing at Flavian, he saw that his orderly was watching the rear. So were the mounted infantry; they were widely spread out far behind, javelins and swords on the ready.

Soon the road led into a mile-long canyon and side-defiles thick with pines and junipers and a bubbling brook. Then Gaius heard the distant voice of Liscus ahead:

"Halt in the ravine! Break out rations!"

"—No—!" said Gaius.

Flavian squinted. "Sir, you think we should push on to higher ground?"

"None within miles." Gaius' spine was tingling.

"Sir, I hear the commander's on the watch for five hundred cavalrymen of the Gemina legion. He's expecting to make contact with them any time now, sir."

Yet once the troops, horses and wagons were stopped in the long, deep gorge, they might be in a giant bottleneck.—Then he saw Penelope's wagon disappear into a side ravine.

"Sir, what's the blackshirt strength in this big plain, do you know?" asked Flavian as they dismounted and tethered their horses at the east end of the canyon.

"Hard to say, Flavian," and he refused the offer of a wineskin and slab of roast lamb as he watched the cavalrymen dismount and lead their horses to the wet grass by the brook. His fears mounting, Gaius clambered a rocky knoll where a sentry's armor flashed against the sky.

"*Audire, audire,*" came the thin voice of another monitor at the western end of the ravine. "Armor-flashes to the north. Armor-flashes to the north. Coming this way, commander, coming this way . . ."

Gaius was peering at the vast wildlands to the east: brown prairies, rock buttes and distant forests of corkoak and ghostly misted mountains. Methodically he began sectioning off the terrain, trying to see into each gulf of brown earth, into each grove of trees. The longer he gazed the surer grew his conviction that

107

hostile blackcloaks were thickly concealed in natural cover of the land the expedition had already traversed. He turned and looked at the exposed land to the west. The road leading out of the canyon at that end marched over a long stretch of fairly flat, denuded earth where everything was in clear view.

"Wild horses on the run to the east," sang out the sentry near Gaius and Flavian. "Coming this way, do you think, tribune?"

Gaius watched a mass of horses about two miles east, running west in a rough V-wedge—thundering right toward us, thought Gaius.

"Blistering hades, look at those animals run," said Flavian, "like the Furies are after them— Look—I saw fire just then! What . . . look! Those wild horses are throwing up dust. Dust? Looks more like smoke—"

Gaius shouted, "It is smoke! The renegade blackshirts have set fire to horses' tails to stampede them into our camps! Their cavalry must be riding behind, hanging on the sides of their ponies so we can't see them."

Flavian ran towards the west end, bellowing for Commander Liscus. "Blackshirt enemy coming! Blackshirt foe . . ."

Soon the far voice of Liscus rang out:

"*Audire! Audire!* Combat stations! Wagons into side ravines! Cavalry—mount! Mass behind trees at west end! Infantry—attack on foot from east end! Ambush foe from the rear!"

The long canyon looked deserted when the wild herd clattered in from the east, some of the piebald animal tails smoking and the stench of burned horseflesh tainting the air. The maddened beasts thundered on the paved road in a deafening reverberation of hooves. Even before the last of the pack roared out the west end, guerrilla war cries were heard from the east—and four hundred blackcloak warriors riding two to a horse surged in. The raiders in black had leather breastplates and shields, squat swords, dirks, and roped stone maces.

"Death to the Roman beasts! Death!" shrieked the guerrillas in Latin.

Liscus suddenly appeared a mile away at the western end of the gorge, flanked by the first line of cavalry.

"Javelins!" thundered the commander as the Celt cavalry rocketed westward. Liscus threw the first spear, impaling a guerrilla— and the fight was on.

Roman lances tore through enemy leather shields, cracked human breastbones, toppled Celt after Celt off plunging ponies. But black-shirt daggers thrust, maces swung and Romans began falling off their chargers. The outnumbered troops of Liscus were well pro-tected by their armor and the Roman cavalry maintained a solid and disciplined formation while blunting the first crashing assault of the Celts with a hail of spears.

At the east end, Gaius and the twenty-two infantrymen jumped out of tree cover and began slashing into the blackcloak ranks. Flavian and his veterans fought with fury, pulling guerrilla fighters off their mounts to run swords through their bodies. Using the dagger Rufus had given him, Gaius slew five guerrillas before the weapon flew out of his hand. Then a blackcloak leaped off his horse onto Gaius and both fell down. Gaius went limp, thrust up his knees, got a wrestling grip on his foe's right arm, twisted it back-wards and heard the bone snap. Leaping up, he stooped, jerked one small knife from his boot and stabbed a Celt who had slung his mace into an infantryman's neck. Then, struck from behind, he went down with a giant guerrilla astride him. Gaius still clutched the knife, but his hands were pinned under him. He thrashed and tried to roll over on his assailant, but the enemy dirk was descend-ing—

"Mars! Attack! Kill!" roared the voice of Liscus close by.

The armored dog leaped through the air, and killed the black-cloak on Gaius. He pushed off the body, jumped up and dove at two raiders trying to stab Flavian through his backplates. Then he saw a tribal fighter crawling toward the gallant Mars, who had just sunk his fangs in the neck of another Celt. The threat to the mastiff was real, for the Celt was going to stab Mars in his unprotected rump. Gaius leaped on the guerrilla from behind and drove his knife into the man's neck.

By now the battle was being fought mainly on foot. Freedmen wagon drovers were dragging Roman casualties out of the melee, catching the reins of riderless Roman horses and leading the animals into side-canyons for the Roman cavalry to re-mount. Then Gaius got an anguished glimpse of Penelope pulling a Roman wounded soldier by the shoulders in under a pine.

He had no chance or time to protect her, the way was barricaded by fighters in sword-to-sword combat and plunging Celt ponies. Gaius and the infantry began climbing the escarpments and jumping down on Celts below. Suddenly he heard a piercing whistle bleated from the packed Celt masses, the signal for retreat.

Carrying their wounded and leaving their dead behind, the raiders sprang on their ponies and galloped out of the canyon to the east from where they had attacked, their riderless horses thundering at the rear. At last the defiant cries and roar of horsehooves died away.

Gaius was trying to see Penelope, but his eyes were blurred, he could hardly stand. . . . Where was she? And then he saw her tawny hair and blue cloak far down the canyon—and Liscus, and Mars—all safe.

Then he heard Flavian's warm, chuckling comments from behind: "Sir, my troops say you've got steel fingernails. Ah. Fight and learn."

XVIII

After the blackshirt defeat and retreat, fifty-eight enemy dead and three horse carcasses were buried in eroded earth pits well away from the Roman road. Meanwhile, advance scouts of the Gemina legion cavalry approaching from the north arrived and reported to Commander Liscus. By nightfall the expedition and five hundred Gemina troopers were encamped on wooded crags and bluffs ten miles north. A mile to the west, funeral fires flared for the honored Roman slain: two infantrymen and four cavalrymen. Far around the perimeter of the temporary earth walls of the Roman camp, mounted legion scouts explored and found no blackshirts. By moonrise two hundred *Togati* horsemen with torches blazing thundered into camp; their sentinels had seen blackcloaks riding north by the hundreds. The whitecloak allies of Rome swore that the great plain and mountains east and south of the encampment were now clear of the enemy.

During the confusion after the conflict, Gaius had been unable to reach Penelope, but his relief that she was unharmed helped calm him. So did Flavian's reassurance: "Sir, she's riding far ahead in her wagon, picking gravel and dirt out of our wounded. You'll see her after we strike camp."

While Commander Liscus conferred in his tent with officers of the Gemina, Togati cavalry leaders and his own adjutants, Gaius seemed to walk in circles searching for Penelope. At last he found the torchlit hospital area and there was Penelope! A strip of white linen confined her braids as she moved quickly from casualty to casualty. Gaius knew that no physicians were present, but he was unprepared for the sight of Penelope serving as nurse and being obeyed by able-bodied troops as if she were general of the camp. Her face sooty and streaked with perspiration, she washed her hands frequently while aides kept cauldrons of water at a rolling boil, following her with rolls of linen and the chest of medicinals she had insisted on bringing from Ioza.

Trying to push through to Penelope, Gaius was unceremoniously shoved back, but he got close enough to see and hear her.

"Men—lay red-hot daggers on these wounds, that they may not swell and empurple. Quickly!"

When stoical comrades pressed fired blades on six prone wounded, their shrieks seemed to tear the air apart as the red-hot metal literally cooked bloody gashes in human thighs and arms. Then Penelope darted to another soldier sitting rigidly in a campchair.

"You four men, hold this soldier's body and legs. You—get a grip on his wrist, and you, hold the arm above the elbow. Ready now, I'm going to pull—" Calmly she gave directions while the screaming sufferer's dislocated arm was forcibly twisted, pulled and at last snapped back into his shoulder. "Strap the weak arm to his body, let it heal," ordered Penelope, moving to the next casualties.

Again Gaius tried to shoulder through the troops helping her, and again was rudely pushed back.

Someone thrust a basket of clean sponges into his hands.

"Get me two stout twigs," said Penelope, "we will cross-bind with cold wet compresses."

Unwanted, ignored and unnecessary, Gaius cradled his hamper of sponges while Penelope's soldiers handed her the instruments, bandages, and jars of medicinals.

"Roll your eye to the right," she ordered an embarrassed infantryman. "Men, bring torches nearer so I can see . . . give me a small twist of clean linen." She examined the bloodshot eyeball, then quickly snicked it with a conic point of linen. "A sharp splinter. Eyeball scratched, eye not harmed, the All-Power is kind. Who is next?"

Gaius wanted to shout, *"I am!"* Often he had felt unwanted, but never so much as now—

"—Sliver of metal embedded under his thumbnail," Penelope continued. "Give me those small bronze pliers . . . now . . . and out it comes. Soak your hand in hot water, soldier." She moved on, and Gaius heard her, "His ribs may be broken. We will do a tight chest-around bandaging . . ."

At last Gaius thrust his basket of sponges to the nearest soldier and elbowed through the throng, getting close to his beloved. She was leaning over a cavalryman. He was grunting, cursing, and trying to pull off his boots while sitting on the ground.

"Careful, soldier, we will cut the boots away, you may have serious foot wounds."

He got his left boot off and started wiggling his toes. "Nothing wrong with me, lady," he snorted. "The new boots I got in New Carthage are too tight. I've just got big feet. Gods—" and he yanked off his right boot with a great sigh of relief. "Aaaah . . . what a relief to pull off these leather-pinchers!"

Penelope's aides guffawed and she smiled nervously. At last, when all the wounded were cared for, she unobtrusively retreated from the hospital compound, Gaius following her. What to do now? Stalk her to her wagon and insist that she listen to his love? Would she? Morosely he wondered if she would shed a single tear if *he* tried to commit suicide. Now she was trudging towards her wagon which was hidden in a grove of tall old cork-oaks. The troops had already sawed down two of the ancient trees, for the hard inner wood made excellent charcoal. Then he saw Penelope stagger and he caught her before she fainted.

He carried her into the grove near a freshwater pond, and laid her on the ground near the wagon and campfire. Lighting a stick in the flames, he climbed the wagon-ladder. When he had three clay lamps burning inside, he got out and lifted Penelope up to the floor of the wain. Then he climbed up into the wagon again. Gently he laid Penelope on her mattresses. Was she sick? Dying—?

He put his head to her chest and was reassured by her rhythmic heartbeats. Exhaustion, he decided. She had given her skills and strength to save the injured, driven herself until the last wounded man was tended, until now her own body had given way under the strain.

At last she seemed to settle into deep sleep. He covered her with blankets and then an inspiration edged into his penitent mind.

"Penelope, beloved, rest," he murmured. "I'm going to heat water at the fire. All is well."

Later he was back in the wagon with a small iron cauldron of steaming water. He removed Penelope's headband, loosened her blood-flecked white smock and the waistband of her skirt. She sighed and awakened as he unhooked the latchets of her heavy brown sandals, and methodically and tenderly began washing her and patting her skin dry. Then gently he turned her and bathed her back, hips and legs. As the night air was becoming chilly, he hastily finished his task and wrapped her naked body snugly in two blankets and his gray military cape.

"Are you hungry?" Gaius finally asked her. "I gave you a bath, Penelope. A bath."

What's wrong with your tongue, you fool? Are such stumbling words a deathless example of the creative genius of Gaius Lacer, bridge builder and tragic poet of Spain? Who would remember Homer, Virgil, Horace, and all the other great ones after hearing the love talk of Gaius Lacer?

"You were heroic today," Penelope said, quietly. "I saw you."

"Don't torture me, Penelope. You risked your life, you might have been killed. But I understand now. Will you listen? I love you. I worship you. I always have. I always will. I gave you a bath!"

Her eyes brightened with tears, but she smiled. "A wonderful bath, my love, Gaius. Will you ask Commander Liscus to come here?"

"That bearded brute of a Liscus?" Gaius shouted. "Are you in love with that Liscus?"

From outside an amused voice called, "The bearded brute has just arrived. Mars, to your haunches. Wait here, Mars."

The pleading eyes of Penelope helped Gaius contain his fury as the commander climbed up into the wagon. His fair hair was combed, his breastplate gouged in six places and his green kilt torn and dirty. Ignoring Gaius, he leaned over Penelope.

"Lord commander, are you all right?" she asked.

Gaius almost leaped at his brother's throat.

"The commander was winded but not wounded during and after the attack," Rufus replied. "How can we honor the gallant Domina Penelope? Indeed, can admiration be put into words?" His tranquil blue eyes considered Gaius briefly as he respectfully touched Penelope's bandaged left arm.

"Keep your hands away from her," Gaius whispered.

"Calm down," Rufus smiled, withdrawing his hand. "The tribune will have to listen to Penelope. Domina, if you have not already done so, tell this furious man."

"He does not yet know," she said, struggling to sit up. Gaius helped, hurriedly wrapping his gray cloak around her bare shoulders. She lifted her head and stared over his. "Gaius, I am going to bear your child."

Gaius reacted with a vast sweep of joyful relief. His beloved was going to have a child, his beloved was going to have a baby! Shoving Liscus back, he began chafing Penelope's hands. "My darling, dear heart, love," he blurted. "You are my love, and you will be giving us a child." He glowered at Commander Liscus. Did the fellow think he could camp all night in Penelope's wagon? If he didn't have the decency to go, tell him to, or throw him out headfirst.

Rufus had no intention of departing. He mixed red wine with water in an earthen goblet and handed it to Penelope. She sipped and Gaius was incensed by the look of gratitude she gave Rufus when he at last took the cup from her.

"Penelope is all right, sir," Gaius said. "The commander has honored us. Now he may go."

"The commander is not going," Rufus cut in. "The commander has many grave responsibilities. One is the future welfare of this heroic young woman. Penelope: the valorous Flavian privately advised me a short while ago that you be secretly returned to Ioza to live in hiding with Domina Beryl."

A trick, thought Gaius in anguish. Or is it? Liscus has no knowledge of Turdo's tunnel . . . the German will guard Penelope like a lion. But *lose* Penelope? Not see her for many months?

"Does the tribune have any wise observations?" Liscus inquired.

Hades burn my brother, he's an honorable image of ice with a pale brown beard and mustache, thought Gaius. *Honorable?* Where had that thought come from? Now his mind was swarming with poetry that he longed to recite to Penelope; lines composed a century before by the immortal Horace: *'Think not that I have sworn a bootless oath; yes, we shall go, hand linked in hand, wherever thou leadest, both, the last sad road below.'*

"The tribune appears on the verge of tears," Rufus smiled.

Gaius forced back rage. "Commander, will you accept my apology for referring to you as a bearded brute?" Once he had spoken the words, a curious sensation of well-being filled him.

Rufus studied his broken fingernails. "A tremendous concession. The concession is mutual. Penelope, you are to rest. I will consider your situation." He got up and snapped a salute to her.

"Lord commander, you are kind, and good," she faltered.

Rufus smiled at Gaius and climbed down the ladder. Gaius heard him ordering Mars to heel, then the sound of bootsteps and clacking paws receding and blending with the sound of croaking frogs outside.

Now Gaius could talk to Penelope. Gravely and tenderly attentive, Penelope listened while he described his distorted conception of the ideal woman and his contrite dejection when discovering that she had been that woman, the true peerless one, all the time.

Penelope rested her cheek on his hands and the loving act made his eyes smart. Awkwardly he took her in his arms and kissed her tangled braids. "Our baby," he soothed. "Our daughter."

A look of delight made Penelope's face piquant. "But how does my dear wonderful know I will have a girl child? My baby may be a small man."

"We'll keep him," said Gaius, boyishly, to Penelope's laughing pleasure. "But our baby is going to be a girl. Her name will be Gaia Juliana, daughter of Gaius Julius Lacer and his wife, Penelope of Greece, the most peerless woman." A horrible thought came: what if she died giving birth? No, the gods had punished her too much already. She would not die as wistful, loving Metanny had died. Or what if Penelope lost the infant before it reached the term of birth? Regrets stabbed him. "Penelope," he murmured, kissing her ear, "if you lose my daughter, the blame is mine. Mine."

"But, I will not lose the little one," she said, smoothing his rumpled hair. "Oh, what a dreadful deed I almost committed when I tried to kill myself. I felt alone, lost, and I was afraid to face the thought of bearing my child."

"It is past, gone, it never happened," he soothed, and felt as strong as the god Hercules. Now he could fight the whole world for her and the baby. But first be the practical husband, the protector, the thoughtful male caring for the worshipped woman. "Penelope, you must eat. But first you will want to dress. I'll leave you alone for a while." She was in his arms and he pressed his stubbly cheek against her smooth one.

"Whiskers after the battle," he joked. "Old Roman custom."

Her gay laughter delighted him.

Then he climbed down the ladder and her loving face appeared between the tarpaulin flaps.

"I'll get food in centercamp and be back in half an hour," said

Gaius. "Your grove is all yours, beloved. Sentries posted far away all around you. Hear the frogs croaking in the pond? An assembly of batrachian senators arguing."

Her lips parted in a smile that thrilled him, and to Gaius their married life began at that moment.

When he returned with an iron tray of skewered hot lamb chunks, a warm wheat loaf, dried figs and a dish of honeycomb, Penelope's heavy tawny hair was braided around her head and she wore a gray homespun dress and blue cloak. Her cheeks were lightly tinged pink and her lips a natural rose. She smiled bashfully and he saw the appealing imperfection of her slanting little tooth. He smiled broadly.

"Dear Gaius, your teeth are so straight and white," said Penelope.

"The world's most flawless man," said Gaius, expansively. He held a spoonful of honeycomb to her lips. "Gaius Lacer, the rock-hard perfectionist. The empire has to run his way, or away with the empire. Other men are monsters, but not Lacer. He's a demigod. Sensitive fellow. Hurt his feelings and he'll spread his wings and fly away." She smiled at his mocking bluster.

Suddenly a voice out in the grove hailed:

"Sir, it's Flavian. May I come up?"

Another unwelcome intrusion, but Gaius gave permission and the orderly climbed the ladder into the wain.

"Tidings, sir," said Flavian. His breastplate was in worse condition than Rufus' and his ringed helmet was dented. He gave Penelope an admiring grin, then said, "Tribune, the commander has bartered Penelope's wagon to the *Togati* for six piebald ponies. Four of the whitecloak horses are to be hitched to this wain. Then, sir, Penelope is to be taken back to Ioza. I'm to go with her, sir."

"Liscus has gone mad," Gaius whispered. "What's the rest of his scheme?"

"Don't think it's a scheme, sir," Flavian replied, guardedly. "The commander ordered me to be Penelope's bodyguard to Ioza. The two hundred *Togati*, all picked night-fighters, will escort us. Not that the commander anticipates another blackcloak attack, because the dark Celts hate night combat, tribune."

Now that his love for Penelope had shown him to himself, Gaius tried to think with cool logic what was best for her. All he could foresee was danger. Talk it out with Flavian . . . "Has the commander considered that our whitecloak friends will spread the tale that a beautiful woman left this camp and went to Ioza? Couple that with the fact that Classicus goes on inspection tours," he said, sarcastically.

Flavian whistled softly for a few moments. "Commander's orders, sir. To make you feel better, our white Celts don't know a woman is riding in this wain. They think I'm taking a badly-wounded officer home to die in his domina's arms. Two miles outside of Ioza, I call a halt. I get out with the dying man in my arms, he's covered with cloaks. I tell our *Togati* the man wants to offer final prayers to Jupiter up the mountainside and be buried where he expires."

"Liscus has a colorful imagination," Gaius muttered. "Then what happens?"

The orderly smiled innocently. "It will so happen that I and my burden happen into a sheepfold where Ioza shepherds are watching their flocks, sir. I have to take a risk there, but the Iozans worship Penelope. When I tell them her secret return to the settlement is never to be mentioned, it'll be the same as confiding to a row of graves. Next, I sent one of the herdsmen to Ioza to bring back our friend, Turdo. And what could stop our chest-squeezing German from taking Penelope to my wife's home? Beryl will go into ecstacies and give thanks to her Hebrew Jehovah and all our Roman gods. Trust Beryl. She's got the brilliant mind of her Jewish mother hitched to the practical genius and wariness of her Roman sire, the gods rest the souls of both her parents."

Gaius grudgingly realized the plan had merit, but losing Penelope when he had only found her and when all was well between them —he looked at her. She met his eyes trustingly and with love that gave him strength.

"How much of the plan does Liscus know—or did my noble brother plan the whole thing, Flavian?"

"Ah," said Flavian, "he doesn't know about the letters, sir. That's my contribution. When we—"

"The letters," said Gaius. "What are those?"

When the expedition was up at the Sil mines, Flavian would send and receive letters by couriers with Beryl. In his communications Flavian would include bits of information about Tribune Gaius. When Beryl wrote to him she would relate village events and, now and then, casually refer to 'an old Spanish healer' as the best way to identify Penelope without naming her. And the tribune must keep in mind that Commander Liscus had no knowledge of Turdo's private tunnel from his cave home to the marble quarries. Penelope would be safely hidden in Ioza.

But new fears disturbed Gaius. "What if Classicus visits the Sil mines and does not see Penelope with me?"

"Spain's a big country, sir. What if Penelope got kidnapped in one of the walled cities here in the interior? Women disappear all the time." He winked. "She even might reappear in Caesar Augusta on the Ebro river. Then there are southern towns where women get lost. Hispalis. Corduba. Malaca. Carteia. I'm starting to feel lost myself," he grinned. "I'll be back with the expedition sometime tomorrow, tribune. Now: when I and our white Celts and the ponies come an hour from now, after we get the animals in the shafts, I'll call, 'Sir, how is our wounded officer?' You answer anything appropriate and back down the ladder. Up I go—and away goes the wagon and our whitecloaks." Abruptly the *optio* let himself down the rungs.

Gaius and Penelope were alone again.

Helplessly he turned to her, wanting to pelt her with questions, live her life, wipe out her tragedies . . . Too late. Too late.

"This is the alpha and there is no omega," she said tremulously. "We must give ourselves into the keeping of the All-God."

He drew her into his tender embrace. "Beloved, who is the 'All-God'? Are you a secret Christian?"

"No, dear wonderful, but I have heard their orators in Greece. The All-God must exist, he is love. Many of my countrymen worship the Achaian Unknown God." Dreamily she went on, "When I was a little girl, I would slip out of our cottage in the evening and my father would call, 'Daughter, where are you bound? Come in at once.' And I would say, 'Father, I want to see what the night is doing.' How can I explain what I cannot explain to myself? But looking at the stars, the night sky, seemed to me to bring me to God. Or bring God to me."

Gaius piled blankets behind her head and made her recline on the fleece mattresses while he sat beside her. "Was your sire a physician?" he asked. "Tell me . . . everything, love."

Her father had been a Greek freedman and rebellious sculptor because his sire had worked with chisel and marble, and Roman laws forced him to follow the profession of his forebear. Townsfolk laughed at his crude images, but bought them now and then as examples of the downfall of Greek art under the iron oppression of Roman rule.

Penelope's mother had died when she was six and soon she learned that, as a slave she was never to marry. So when her father

118

was carving and cursing the marble slabs in his workroom, she often gained permission to go and assist the aged village physician; besides, she earned a drachma or two that way. Had it not been for healing, which she loved, and the coins she earned, she and her father might have starved.

Penelope even began to hope that there might be some way through the maze of Roman laws whereby she could qualify as a female physician, knowing the dream was impossible of fulfillment, but feeding on it regardless.

Gaius lifted her into his arms and gently rocked her. "Months ago, the young men of our village waylaid and killed a Roman tax agent and his four soldiers," she whispered. "The women and girls and children knew nothing of this, Gaius. But one moonlit night, it was so calm and grand, a hundred Romans attacked our town. They dragged us all out, threw torches into every house—"

"And killed all the men," murmured Gaius.

"—And all the old women," she faltered. "The soldiers did not molest me or the other girls," she went on, with more composure. "Their captain told us he would try to sell us to kind masters. I begged for death, but he had singled me out. He said something about 'rights of plunder,' and said he could sell me for a large sum to Emperor Domitian. The soldier was merciful . . . he did not make me walk the miles to the port of Piraeus . . . I rode a donkey. I and the other girls were allowed to bathe behind interlocked shields— At the seaport the officer sold me to an old Egyptian cotton-grower. So weird he was, so repulsive to me at first. His bireme had the figurehead of Osiris painted in gilt and green and red."

Kissing her fingers, Gaius marvelled at the inexplicable sense of strength filling him; was it the power brought by absorbing the tragedies of his beloved? He had forgotten time, the camp, the wagon. He too was Penelope, sold to an Egyptian master. . . .

Penelope never learned the name of her owner. He had resembled a shrivelled ape in blue and yellow robes. Terrified and despairing, she had tried to jump overboard into the Aegean Sea after the vessel slipped its moorings, but had been restrained by the terrible grip of the old Egyptian. "An elder with the strength of *Heracles*," she whispered. "He carried me as if I were a feather into his cabin. It was the world of Egypt. Lotus carvings, purple silk carpets, ivory couches, tiny gold images of Isis, Bubastis, Serapis . . . scarabs . . . He sat me on a cushioned couch. Then he began talking in the most beautiful Greek I ever heard. His voice was music. His face seemed to turn into beauty as I watched and listened. It seemed as if all of time whirled around me, a great wind of life. I was comforted. I wanted to serve him. But at last he told me he had seen my future in this incarnation. He could not, much though he wished, keep me and wed me. We were on 'different planes.' He was bound by the future to take me to Roman Spain, where I would meet my 'matching soul.' I was so kindly warned that only through suffering and self-healing would I grow."

Gaius whispered against her cheek, "He brought you to me. Where is he now, love?"

She wept against his shoulder armor. "After he sold me to Governor Classicus at the New Carthage dock, his bireme sailed away with the outgoing tide. I saw him at the rail, his hands held out as if in blessing. The sun shone on his face. It looked glorified." She sighed, "Later I heard he died on his ship and was buried at sea; he had asked to rest in the *Mare Nostrum* of the Romans, instead of being mummified. Gaius, does life go out like the flame of a lamp? Or does it go out and return in a new blaze?"

Their lips met. A long tide of time carried them on its quiet crest, until distant Celt voices began chanting an incomprehensible song in minor chords. Then Gaius told her about his bridge. Then about Rome. He described the Golden Milestone in the Capitol, the glistening monument where all roads began and ended. Then he dared to talk about his hope of hopes: that Marcus Trajan, the humane, victorious defender of Rome, would some day be hailed Emperor.

He began hearing a jabber of Celtish male voices and whinny of horses approaching from outside the wagon—and the present rushed in again when he heard the voice of Flavian:

"Very good, fellow Romans. Our wounded officer may live. He may die. Your song to the one god of life may have helped him. But if he has to die, he'll die as a Roman should."

The wagon began to quiver and jolt as ponies were hitched to the shafts and unseen men climbed up into the driver's seat outside the braced tarpaulin canopy. Then the rich, melodic voices of the white Celts began singing the same mournful dirge Gaius had heard a while ago in the distance.

"Go, dear one," whispered Penelope, gathering a blue hooded cloak around herself and lowering the cowl over her face. "We are together. One soul. We are now living each other's lives. That is good."

"No, not yet—" But he dared not take her in his arms again.

Then came the call of Flavian, like the voice of doom: "Sir—how is our wounded centurion?"

Gaius stared at his wife, tried to see her features under the hood. She looked away. "Go, beloved, go," she said, so quietly he hardly heard.

On the ground Flavian sauntered up, in full battle gear, daggers at his belt and a cluster of short spears in one fist.

"How is he, sir?" asked the aide, loudly, while the nearest white-cloak Celts quieted down and gathered around to listen.

Gaius forced himself to reply, "We can always hope."

Flavian reached up into the wain and laid his lances on the floor. He saluted Gaius and climbed the ladder without further words. Then the tarpaulin flaps were closed from within.

A whitecloak astride one of the lead piebald ponies hitched to the wagon shouted:

"Abi! Abi hine! Abi hine!"

The wagon began moving out of the grove. It was preceded and followed by white Celts gesticulating and talking in their own strange tongue. The ferocious allies of Rome wore dusty white togas over their leather corselets and sheepskin breeches. They were heavily weaponed with squat swords and curved daggers and over each saddle hung a braided reed net, the whitecloak imitation of the snare used by unarmed arena fighters to entangle sword-wielding opponents.

He followed the wagon and horsemen through centercamp to the night wall, where they were joined by *Togati* torchbearers and all passed out the open temporary gates of oak-boughs and soon reached the paved roadway.

Staring wretchedly after the procession, Gaius watched it melt into the night, but he could still see the winking flames of the whitecloak torches. . . .

"An indiscreet performance," said the voice of Liscus.

Gaius wheeled about.

"Is the wounded centurion in that departed wagon a close friend of the tribune's?"

Gaius realized the commander had scored another victory and despised him for it. But he replied, "Sir, you are right. I should have remained in the grove. I do not know how to express my gratitude to you for your interest in the welfare of my wife."

The officer stared contemptuously. "Where is the dagger I gave you in Ioza?"

So he wants it returned, thought Gaius. We may have bigger battles coming, but the commander must have that weapon back. I had started to think my brother . . . what was I thinking?

Only an imbecile would trust Rufus Liscus. "Sir," he said, "I lost the dagger during the fight in the canyon."

"Indeed. How would you like another one?"

Gaius thought, no matter what he does now, I'll never trust him. His conscience prodded him to express gratitude to Liscus for sending Mars to his rescue during the battle with the blackcloaks, but pride fought the urging. Yet a reminder to Liscus might put the man on less sure footing. "Sir, how is Mars?" Perhaps Liscus would thank Gaius for saving the mastiff.

"Sleeping," replied the officer, coldly. He glanced around the vast encampment of tents and cookfires. The nearest soldier was far away, sentries outside the sod night wall pacing in the dark distance. Then he suddenly thrust a dagger into Gaius' hands. "Conceal it," muttered Liscus.

Gaius hid the blade under the flexible bands of his breastplate.

Liscus stalked away, the scarlet cloak of the acting *legatus* of the gold expedition rippling dramatically.

"Sir, wait," said Gaius. "If we could talk . . ."

Rufus halted and looked back. "We already have." He marched off.

He wants a state of war between us, Gaius decided. Very well. And if I ever have to defend myself against him and this dagger flies out of my hand, I have the aids to victory. . . .

XIX

Miles to the north Governor Classicus neared a temporary stronghold of Malendi on a forested slope of the Guadarrama mountains above a tributary of the Duero river. After bidding *vale* to Commander Liscus the preceding night in Ioza, the proconsul's luxurious bed carriage had borne him onward through the drizzling dark hours. An hour out of the cave village, his *Togati* whitecloaks turned back, leaving the procurator's Theban cavalry and torch-men to escort him into blackcloak territory. By misty sunrise his coach was attended by four hundred guerrilla riders sent by the chieftain as honor guards. Far ahead of the proconsul's vehicle, his legion horsemen drove a small herd of choice black-and-white cattle to be presented to the Arvacan Celt prince.

Equably the governor endured the rest of the journey on rutty trails. His mind busy, he was cheered that as a desperate last gamble a man could lose himself in Spain's wild inlands or wilderness of mountain chains. All one had to do was avoid native towns and cities of Roman colonists in the Pyrenee valleys to the east; the populous centers in the hot and fertile south; the westward settle-ments bordering on the Atlantic, and towns dotting the northern coast. A few fortress cities and scattered Celt villages occupied arable river areas in the central region, but the roadway system had not yet connected all towns of the emperor's Spanish provinces. There were vast sections where the Eagle standards had not been seen in years. Or never. These encouraging considerations were as-sociated in the mind of Classicus with the deaths of Senator Mauri-cus; his wife, Decia; and his skinny willow of a niece, Flora. All had been murdered by mountain bandits at their estate near Ioza almost a month ago.

Enna had been fond of the family. So had the proconsul, through different motivations. He had vaguely hoped to seduce the blonde Lady Decia, whom Mauricus had espoused in his dotage. Far more importantly, the governor had counted on trying to borrow money from the shrewd retired statesman. Then from Rome had come an imperial rescript commanding Classicus to execute the Mauricus family on heinous charges of sodomy and sedition. Angered by the latest example of imperial mercilessness, Classicus had dared speed a cryptic warning by two trusted couriers to the mountain villa of Mauricus. A few days later he learned to his shock that bandits had independently carried out the Caesar's decree of death. But the murderers had not found Mauricus' fortune. Soldiers of Classicus had accidentally discovered the underground money vault of dead Senator Mauricus.

His conscience clear, the proconsul could now hope to be awarded one quarter of the assets of Mauricus—if Emperor Domitian felt so inclined. Should that sizable sum eventually be his, Classicus could keep his neck above his debts a few more months. Nor allow pauper

Enna to wheedle one denarius from *him*. He would lovingly preach her dogma: economy. Meanwhile, the gods grant him laurels in his forthcoming confidential talk with Chieftain Malendi.

The conference began well.

"Does my honest Roman brother bring intelligence?" inquired Malendi when they were alone in the chieftain's tent.

Classicus had come armed with falsehoods. "Honorable brother," he began, "I fear that Proconsul Verus Maturus of Farther Spain plans rebellion against the emperor. The first part of Maturus' plan may be to conquer all of Spain."

The chieftain meditated in silence. "Is the Maturus a friend of the odious emperor?"

Classicus must give both truth and untruth to that question. "The emperor considers Maturus a lovable old fool," he lied. "Yet many senators loathe and suspect Maturus." This was both true and untrue, for the proconsul of Farther Spain was hated because of his rigid insistence on honest administration of the provinces and rigid application of the laws. Then a thought came to mind and Classicus added, "Consider, my noble Malendi: Maturus is proconsul of western Spain, where the gold is. Maturus—an acknowledged master of jurisprudence—is burningly ambitious to rise higher than a Proconsul or Co-Ruler Consul. Being favored by Domitian and detested by many senators, what more logical action than for the man to plan vengeance on his enemies and even against Domitian who favors him? How shall he achieve this? I am convinced that he will petition the corrupt Domitian for many more legions, giving as his reason that all of Spain is reverting to a state of internecine conflict between your noble tribesmen and the *Togati*. If such happens, and I fear it may, I shudder for the survival chances of my brother Malendi and his nation." Classicus was so frightened by his statements that he managed to look gravely dignified while his heart fluttered and finally resumed its normal beat.

The reply of Malendi came thoughtfully: "If the Maturus is a man of integrity, well might I order my thousands of horsemen to his side and hail him emperor."

Classicus was too shocked to speak. His gold plan could come crashing down. Then he was sure Enna had materialized in back of Malendi and was whispering to the Celt in the ibex-horned gold helmet. Involuntarily, the proconsul exclaimed, "She is to blame!

She and old Maturus, when those two are together, who knows what happens?" Then he realized his eyes had seen what was not there and he stared vacantly at Malendi.

The chieftain was scowling. "There must be a woman," he brooded, "who would supply the factor so far missing in the lengthy letters that Maturus has pelted me with. Who is the woman behind Maturus, my honest brother Classicus?"

The gods had saved him again and he recovered urbanely. "There is a woman," he breathed, "who handles Maturus as if he were a wild ox tamed to meekness . . . until she whispers the time is ripe for him to be away on a rampage."

Malendi drank from an earthen bowl of buttermilk. "Then I am well advised to consider the Maturus as a potential enemy commanding legions against me. Too often in the past have corrupt consorts inflamed the Caesars to reckless deeds; too often have corrupt empresses influenced men in the Curule Chair. Were a Roman with a virtuous wife to be hailed Imperator, I would consider vowing allegiance. Not since the reign of the great Vespasian, sire of the devil now holding power, has there been an emperor worthy of the name." His dark eyes considered Classicus limpidly. "And you, my brother? How fare your fortunes?"

The governor replied honestly, "Chieftain, I hang on the edge of the cliff. I know not what each dawn will bring. My wife's fortune has been confiscated by the monster in Rome. My own had no better fate."

Smilingly the Celt finished the rest of his bowl of buttermilk. "It is a simple matter. My brother Classicus needs gold."

Classicus stared wide-eyed. "There is none I can rightfully call my own," he said, shakily.

Malendi chuckled. "Forget not your gold expedition bound north which I have been pleased to approve for mining in my territory."

His mouth dry, Classicus sighed, "Chieftain, any ore they mine must go to Emperor Domitian."

"Honesty is worthless to a dead man," remarked the blackcoat, idly. "Why would I allow Romans to mine gold in my domain for the evil Domitian? Do I love the beast in Rome? My brother, the gold shall be yours."

The proconsul came close to swooning. A thread of decency urged him to expostulate, "Chieftain, if you mean war, men will die. Your gallant warriors . . ."

"My troops are skilled fighters," replied the Celt. "And they love killing Romans."

Classicus shivered, but triumph was now within reach. "Heroic brother, I am hampered on all sides," he said. "I place little faith in the acting commander of my gold expedition, a bearded man of ice named Rufus Liscus. And I break into sweat at nights when I think of the chief engineer I had no alternative but to take, the slave Gaius Lacer. I would not be surprised if either or both plan to secrete what gold they find on the spot."

Malendi looked interested. "Have you also considered that the gold expedition leader and the slave miner may be allies of Governor Maturus in his scheme to overrun Spain?"

Classicus gazed in admiration at his host.

The Celt laughed warmly. "Think you this Lacer will find gold in quantity?" inquired Malendi of the bewildered Cornelius Classicus. "Then let the proud builder of the Tagus spans take his time to dig the gold before we launch the sunrise of disaster. After—my warriors will take custody of the gold. Aye."

Feebly the governor ventured, "It seems a great risk, brave and honest Malendi." Even though knowing the chieftain was not irrevocably committed to seizing the gold, Classicus vaguely wanted to find some other way . . . what other way? There was no other way.

"Too long has Rome maligned me and threatened my people," said Malendi. "We have long memories. In my boyhood, an elder of the Arvacan tribe instructed me in the bloody history of the bestial Julius Caesar and other Roman vultures who all but annihilated my ancestors. I, Malendi, hold the survival of my nation and allies in my hands. That is all that matters; survival against the vicious one in Rome, and whoever comes after him, be he, too, an enemy of my people. Classicus, my brother, I will give the slave miner and his co-conspirators at least a year to hide the gold before my fighters claim it for you. If, however, you are hard-pressed before then, flee north and find welcome in my domain."

A fear besieged Classicus. "My brother Malendi, if by some scowl of the Fates you lose your war against the legions of Maturus and the men at the Sil mines—"

The Celt laughed deeply. "Fear not."

A blackcloak warrior burst into the tent and fell prostrate beside Malendi, muttering unintelligibly.

The chieftain clapped his hands smartly and turned to Classicus.

"It would seem that some of my allies fought late today with a Roman expedition far south of here, horsemen and wagons bound north—"

"My gold expedition!" Classicus exclaimed, stunned, for if Gaius Lacer had been slain, the proconsul must find another geologist.

"Did my fighter allies attack the Romans, or did the men of the Eagles attack my men?" Malendi demanded of the cowering Celt on the black felt rug.

"Immortal one," cried the guerrilla. "Your four observers, who took no part in the conflict, solemnly vow that your allies of the tribe in the rocklands attacked the Romans in the mile long ravine. But repulsed were your horsemen, suffering many dead and wounded."

Malendi glanced at Classicus and again to his crouching warrior. "What report on the Roman losses?"

"Only that your faithful observers, immortal one, swear that two Roman officers, men in crested helmets, are both mighty fighters and came through unhurt. Soon after the battle the victorious Romans were joined by Gemina troopers and moved out of the ravine of the fight and struck their night camp later on."

Classicus breathed in relief . . . only Rufus Liscus and the Lacer slave wore plumed helmets, therefore both were unharmed.

"I gave no orders for my troops to attack that Roman cavalcade," muttered Malendi, his eyes hard on the tribesman at his feet. "More truth, man," continued the guerrilla chief. "Did the reckless wretch who led the offensive against the Romans survive?"

The messenger whispered, "Nay, immortal one. He was the first to die when the Roman cavalry leader threw a lance."

"And well that spear struck truly," mused the blackcloak prince, and resumed to Classicus, "Sometimes I have difficulty controlling the anti-Roman emotions of my allies. But now—the gold prospectors will proceed peacefully to the Sil valley. There will be no war with them until I choose the time—and place . . . Black death to any rash ally who disobeys me!" he thundered to the guerrilla, who hastily left the tent.

Classicus felt as though he had fought in the canyon battle himself. He recovered his equanimity, however, and even jested when Malendi jested, that perhaps brother Classicus might care to exercise his use of a ruby ring and thus win a second boon of love from a Celt damsel.

No more Celt nymphomaniacs for the proconsul. "My noble

host," he said, smilingly. "I regret, many duties await me at home. I must begin my return journey this night."

Two hours later Classicus' carriage was rolling along on a Roman roadway leading south. The night was starlit, dark, and briskly cold. Steeped in dreams of his glittering future, the proconsul was borne along with a minimum of jolts, insulated as he was by fleece mattresses, sponge pillows, and quantities of purple velvet coverings. But at last he roused from sleep and glanced out to see a faint yellow-red glow lighting the blackness far to the southwest. He signalled a blackcloak riding alongside the carriage window and asked what the pale haze might be. The lamps and torches of a city?

The Celt replied, "Nay, father excellency, you see the nightcamp of the Roman gold expedition and Gemina cavalry. Distant it is, yet it seems close in the pure air of night."

His interest vaguely stirred, Classicus thought about Penelope. Had that stupid girl used her charms and brains rightly, he might have retained her indefinitely, even though she had been of use in disarming the slave architect. Sex and gold, a combination no man could resist. I bribed Gaius without his knowing it. . . . I can imagine the love battles between those two. Strapping slave Lacer wins triumphs in bed and between sessions of passion rants about his Tagus Bridge and the noble blood in his veins. Penelope is most likely in constant tears, moaning about her Greek home in flames and the burial at sea of that addled old Egyptian gorilla who sold her. That girl and her resistance of *me*. Love . . . what is it? Where is it?

A wave seemed to wash his mind, bearing away all thought in a surf of forgetfulness. He sat up, puzzled over a lingering ecstacy. Had his brain performed another ludicrous feat of mental tightrope walking? Sleepily he watched the horsemen with torches cantering along outside the carriage. He was tasting the flames and his mouth felt dry with ashes—"I need another woman," he consoled himself. "Enna is a frozen lily since Domitian snatched her fortune. And may lame-hand Frontinus bear up under his self-assumed burden of paying legation bills. Gods, I hope that fellow is not mulling plans to steal gold. I will let that ass live until Malendi's warriors seize the ore." Contentedly he snuggled in his velvet robes and pillows, soothed by the rocking of the coach and monotonous drumbeats of hooves.

XX

By early August the official burdens of Governor Verus Maturus eased as military couriers brought to Gades in western Spain reports that clashes between *Togati* and Arvacan blackcloaks had practically ended. Indirectly the governor learned that the Sil miners were building an earth-dam while small groups of shackled felons re-dug ancient Phoenician rock galleries and thus found a few worthless deposits of low grade silver and lesser metals. Privately the procurator of Farther Spain hoped that Gaius Lacer would not find much gold after his dam was finished; at least not until after the Ides of September when Emperor Domitian was destined to die, if the astrologers' forecasts were correct.

The Ides of next month—less than two months away. And the chaotic times cried for a strong military leader with the virtue and vision of Marcus Ulpius Trajan.

One bright day in mid-August the governor awoke fretting that no answers had come from Chieftain Malendi. Nor had he received replies to dispatches sent by ocean transport to the senators in Rome, nor any response to friendly communications sent weeks ago to Marcus Trajan in Germany. Aside from dull reports from city praetors throughout his province, the mail pouches contained only late copies of the daily *Acta Diurna* from Rome. Each news papyrus was filled with the usual reports on grain, merchant ships, temple festivals, innuendos concerning revels of the rich, and flattering descriptions of Emperor Domitian's glorious rewedding of Domitia, his divorced *Augusta,* and now and then a list of executions, which caused Maturus to proclaim to a small bronze bust of Domitian in a niche above a shrine:

"Judicial murderer! When the virtuous are slain or exiled, men of honor, substance, and courage impeached and condemned on fantastic charges, how can one salute you as 'Master and God of mankind'?"

But still Maturus hoped that this day would bring authorization from the Caesar allowing Maturus to enforce the pending new investigation law. Yet, his mind still on the unanswered letters, it suddenly occurred to him that it was not out of character for Cornelius Classicus to withhold mail; military relay couriers from

Italy stopped at New Carthage in eastern Spain before galloping west to Gades.

Composing his thoughts, Maturus strode into his gray marble bath chamber, with an abrupt nod for a smiling freedman, pulled off his long white nightshirt, and tossed it over the top of the portal. A moment later down poured a luxurious spray of warm water from a perforated copper tank overhead connected to pipes. Soaped and rinsed, the proconsul reluctantly departed his steamy haven for an adjoining enclosure where icy water pelted him.

"Wisdom of Minerva," he muttered between chattering teeth, "why do I torture myself this way every morning? The Greeks invented the nightgown, all reverence to the Achaians, but why at fifty-seven do I pay homage to stinging showers we Romans devised? Is this civilization?"

He floundered out and into the comforting warmth of heated towels held by his freedman. After the procurator was shaved, dressed, and in a fresh short toga he felt better and ready for breakfast on his balcony above the Atlantic.

Then his Egyptian scribe came and bowed.

"If it's bad intelligence, out with it," groaned Maturus. "Yet if the tidings are benign, save such until I have digested my food and can relish felicitous events for a change. Phrones, what's the bad news?"

The lean Egyptian looked puzzled. "My governor, a stranger in sheepskins seeks audience with you. I hazard that he has darkened his face and hands with walnut oil and tried to dye flaxen hair with a tincture. A very mottled effect. He refuses to give his name."

When the proconsul entered his library he almost collided with a giant answering the description given by Phrones.

"I am Turdo," whispered the visitor and drew the doors closed behind him. "The chief of Farther Spain will listen to me."

The governor was too enraged to speak; no petitioner ever talked that way to Verus Victrix Maturus. Then he was amused. "It is customary when addressing the imperial ambassador of a province to show respect," he said, glancing at dismayed Phrones.

Phrones arose. "My governor, shall I summon guards?" The scribe shrank down on his bench when Turdo loomed over him.

"No soldiers," ordered the German, "stick of a little man from the Nile."

Maturus became angry again. "I will not tolerate threats or violence. Phrones, take full shorthand notes!"

"No writedown," Turdo menaced. "Send the Egyptian out."

"He stays," Maturus announced, in fury. "Phrones is my confidential scribe; what I know, he knows."

Turdo unexpectedly acquiesced. "He can stay."

"I am gratified," retorted the governor. "Proceed. State your petition. Talk without hissing so I can understand you."

The German pulled up a cushioned marble bench as if it were a toy and sat down opposite Maturus. "I was a champion arena fighter in Rome." Turdo displayed his biceps. "In Rome they called me Big Lion."

"I am duly impressed, but I closed the Gades Games long ago, Big Lion. If it is employment you seek, Gades can offer you little. It still bears the imprint of ancient Greeks, who championed philosophy more than ferocity."

Turdo chuckled and his deepset blue eyes twinkled. "I, too, am a brain man."

This exchange was sheer idiocy but, leaning on his elbows, Maturus sighed and endured it.

Turdo asked, "Chief of Farther Spain, are you a friend of the brave man, Gaius Lacer?"

Now eyeing Turdo with puzzled respect, the governor remarked, "I consider Tribune Gaius Lacer an estimable man. I loaned him a horse last May."

"You are a good man," Turdo announced. "The lady is right."

"Who is right?"

Turdo leaned over the table. "A lady who thinks much of Gaius. She fears for him. She is afraid that Gaius will die." Turdo looked at Phrones, busy with stylus and tablet, then resumed: "The lady says Proconsul Classicus plans to steal the Spanish gold, brain man."

Maturus sighed gently. "Oh, gods," he said.

"Big fight coming with guerrillas. I warn you. Watch for gold-grab," said Turdo ominously.

There was a frightened gasp from Phrones. "My governor, do I take this down exactly as said?"

"Exactly as said," replied Maturus, and then caught himself flexing his pudgy arms to the huge amusement of Turdo.

"Listen," Turdo said. "Commander Liscus is half-brother of Gaius and Commander Liscus is friend of evil Classicus. All want gold."

The mind of Maturus was a hodgepodge of contradictory ideas. Classicus planning to steal gold. Commander Liscus a "friend" of Classicus. Fantastic. Gold . . . guerrillas . . . ?

"Big Lion," Phrones breathed, "kindly do not lean over me, for I will suffocate unless you move away." And Turdo gave Phrones a friendly poke on the shoulder.

Maturus arose and moved around the table, keeping well out of range of Turdo's arms. "Your information has staggered me," said the governor. "Had I any funds, gladly would I—"

"No pay," rumbled Turdo. "Gaius my friend."

Maturus nodded, strangely drawn to the gladiator. "Then allow me, sir, to send soldiers to escort you to your. . . .?"

"No troops," came the sibilant voice of Turdo. "Do not stalk me, chief of Farther Spain. Say I was not here. You and Nile man," he added, "say I am a ghost."

"I will respect your wishes. A safe journey back, Big Ghost," said Maturus.

The yellowed teeth of the German showed. "I fought bandits four times on the road to Gades . . . Now I turn into air. *Vale.*"

Turdo had evidently said all he wanted to say. He now left the room so silently that Maturus and Phrones for a while thought they had seen a phantom depart.

At last the governor sat down while the scribe held a fresh tablet and stylus ready.

"Phrones, when lightning strikes, what does one do?"

The secretary meditated. "My governor, in an attempt to make you smile, let me say that it is written the Sacred Augustus once had a temple erected on a country road where lightning struck down the Divine August's advance torchman."

"I am trying to build a syllogism," Maturus mused. "My mind is swamped in major premises, so where to begin? Try this: 'Most men are naturally avaricious, and corrupt government intensifies the often-subjugated desire of men for gain, well-gotten or ill-gotten.' I am only beginning to delve into the subject."

The scribe murmured, "Your minor premise might be: " 'A certain individual in New Carthage may be avaricious.' "

"No, that would be the conclusion," Maturus ruminated. "Phrones, kindly take this letter." The governor dictated:

VERUS VICTRIX MATURUS, GOVERNOR OF FARTHER SPAIN, TO EMPEROR DOMITIAN, MASTER AND GOD,

SEMPER AUGUSTUS, HIGH PONTIFF, FATHER OF THE COUNTRY, CONSUL AND DEFENDER, TRIBUNICIAN OF THE PEOPLE, IMPERATOR AND FIRST CITIZEN. GREETINGS. REALIZING THAT OUR IMPERIAL LORD BEARS HEAVY RESPONSIBILITIES, NEVERTHELESS MAY YOUR HUMBLE SERVANT MATURUS RESPECTFULLY BRING TO YOUR IMMORTAL EYES THE FACT THAT GUERRILLA UPRISINGS IN THIS PROVINCE OF WESTERN HISPANIA GRAVELY THREATEN YOUR AUGUST IMPERIUM. ALL ATTEMPTED MILITARY GOOD WILL VISITS TO THE CELT BLACKCLOAK TRIBES HAVE BEEN FUTILE: ALL MY LETTERS TO CHIEFTAIN LUNA MALENDI REMAIN UNANSWERED. YOUR HUMBLE SERVANT IS THUS FORCED TO THE GRAVE CONCLUSION THAT WAR MAY ERUPT IN THIS PROVINCE, IF NOT THIS YEAR, THEN NEXT SPRING OR SUMMER. SHOULD THAT OMINOUS POSSIBILITY BECOME REALITY, THE THREE LEGIONS NOW UNDER YOUR RESPECTFUL SERVANT'S COMMAND WILL BE OUTNUMBERED TEN TO ONE. THEREFORE YOUR OBEDIENT SERVANT URGENTLY REQUESTS A MINIMUM OF THREE MORE LEGIONS TO AUGMENT THE THREE GEMINA DIVISIONS NOW IN THIS TERRITORY. COMPLIMENTS. VALE.

When the scribe laid down his tablet and stylus, his green eyes were grave. "My governor, will the emperor think *you* are aspiring to become Caesar because you want more cavalry and marching regiments?"

That thought had been in the mind of Maturus before he dictated. "If the emperor ever reads this dispatch, he will undoubtedly burst into tears of rage and add my name to the list of the doomed. *If* maniacal Domitian reads it. We will time this communication to arrive in Rome *after* the Ides of September. Father Neptune allowing, this missive will cross *Mare Nostrum* and dock at Ostia in about sixteen days. We add fourteen or more days before money-mad freedmen in the imperial palace bestir themselves and open this scroll. I pray they never will; perhaps by then a new emperor will be installed and this urgent request will receive the thoughtful attention it deserves."

Phrones looked doubtful and frowned. "Master, do you believe the astrologers' prophecies that Domitian will be assassinated the day after the Ides of September?"

"I do," said the governor. "Pure intuition, no logic." And already he felt the invisible shaft of justice in his hands.

XXI

The men of the Sil were hard at work, the five thousand prisoners chained to each other in groups of fifty or more. Several elderly felons were unshackled to help the comparatively few troops prevent workers in chains from trying to hack off their irons and escape. Soon the sight of aged prisoners walking like free men began calming the criminals linked together. One or two trusties urged their groups to work well for Rome; toil at the Sil was far better than death in an arena. . . . As long as a man did his work well, he lived. As long as he lived, he could hope . . .

More than hope inspired Gaius. Each sunset brought him one day closer to the future when he would strike through to freedom for Penelope, himself, and his first living offspring who would be fair and lovely as her mother. Next would be born a son, Gaius *Secundus*. After that, sons or daughters, to fill his villa with loved young voices and boisterous romping. . . .

The impediments blocking his forward march were only so many rocks to be hauled out of the way. Most immediate were his entrapment in a possible gold conspiracy and the lesser peril of future blackcloak attacks. As to the first, he would be constantly wary. Regarding the second, the Sil mining camp was not isolated and vulnerable in the wilderness. Twenty miles southwest was the military camp of Legio, manned by a few troops of the Gemina. Directly north in the mountains were hamlets of friendly *Togati* whitecloaks. Farther north lay the Roman seaport city of Corunna. East along the northern coast of Spain were a few Roman colonies. All, then, was secure north of the Sil. As to the wildlands and mountains south. . . .

He no longer lost sleep worrying about Arvacan blackcloaks. Forgetfulness was helped by letters from Beryl to Flavian, which amused him greatly. Considering her burdens, Beryl was bearing up well.

Flavian kept his wife informed of general events at the Sil. He was father-advisor to his infantry; what his troops missed most of all were women. The amiable whitecloak Celts in the vicinity were chary about sharing their women with the Romans; everything else, gladly. *Pro Roma*. Therefore the aide was happy when several of his men at last offered to espouse pretty white Celt girls. But no marriages until after the gold was found.

Necessary tools and equipment were waiting when the prospectors arrived at the Sil, but before leaving New Carthage, the architect had obstinately decided to try again to get elephants, this time by a bizarre letter direct to Rome which might shock officialdom into sending elephants. Gaius wrote a report on the difficulties of rock and earth moving, but specifically penned that he did *not* want elephants. This dispatch Governor Classicus had graciously sped to Rome by couriers.

In early July, the builder of the Tagus Bridge received a dignified letter from a lordly stranger in Rome who was chief of imperial mines. The dignitary was impressed that the man who had achieved the triumph of the Tagus had no need for pachyderms, which the noble would have been gratified to send to the Sil. There had been six of the behemoths idling in southeastern Gaul. Since Lacer the architect wanted them not, the gallant beasts were now on their way to iron-mines in Italy. Realizing that Lacer was a man of miracles the noble was sending two handsome Archimedes Screws for water-lifting, which were used only in the emperor's favorite mines. . . .

Gaius could chuckle in defeat. At last he was shaking with helpless laughter.

"*Vale*, elephants," he gasped, between laughs.

. . . Everything depended on the massive earthwork dam to be built.

Not only would the structure form a lake to serve for boom-offs next year, but it would also expose the riverbottom and reveal bases of cliffs which might contain virgin lodes. In his computations, Gaius allowed for a maximum one-hundred-foot-high tidal burst of water if the floodgates should be opened simultaneously and the entire lake let out in a flood to wash away accumulated mine tailings. Such a tremendous wall of water would not endanger the Sil camp three miles west. All buildings on both north and south banks were over two hundred feet above the riverbed, on flat ground crowning low hills rising out of the water. As an extra precaution for the town and mines, Gaius planned his pyramid dam to measure one hundred and fifty feet in height, three hundred feet in width, and six hundred feet thick at its base. It would be a primitive conglomerate of logs, boulders, gravel and rolled asphalt layers, based on rock-and-earth-filled cofferdam foundations. The shallow, sloping sides would be made water-tight with mortar and in the dry west wall would be three small rock-lined spillways for the escape of surplus water. The fenced, truncated top of the works would allow Gaius and his crews to inspect the level of the lake forming and also give access to the watergates. It was another challenge; compared to the Tagus Bridge, the dam would be primitive and ugly. He was not building the perfect earth barrier, but a makeshift wall that would do its work.

From the start, he politely requested from Commander Liscus that no prisoner be flogged unless he refused to work, and suggested that the men would work efficiently if not exposed to undue hazards. Liscus had stared in silence. Without asking permission, Gaius ordered soldiers posted as disaster-sentinels on cliffs flanking the earthwork going up. Cave-ins and flash floods could menace the workers. He also commanded barrels of pure drinking water hauled from the deep well in camp every morning for the men in the gorge. Rufus was acting *legatus,* but in the rockbed Gaius was the general.

To his resentment he learned from an adjutant of the commander that all his requests were confirmed. Since the Tribune Lacer, said the aide, had also asked for wooden helmets and body-protectors for the rock-gangs, the commander begged to know which trees from the mountain forests should be cut down for that purpose. Spruce? Oak? Beech? Pine? Ash? Feeling the sting of ridicule and more wary than ever of his brother, Gaius sent word to Rufus that wood was wood— "And my compliments to the commander!"

One hot day before the Nones of September he stood on his high log scaffold-platform near the south cliffs, shouting orders through a brass megaphone to an army of prisoners resembling black and brown ants in the channel below. Cavalry guards kept order in the deeps, while other soldiers rode horses dragging carts filled with boxes of clay and fine gravel into position near revolving cranes, hoists, and vats of concrete. Layer by layer the dam was rising, but the rockbed was still a network of streams. Many prisoners manned hand-pumps of hollowed logs, others Egyptian necklace pumps of wooden buckets hung from circular windlasses, while a few fortunate trusties operated the handles of the glittering Archimedes

Screws, effortlessly pulling up water and dumping it into log troughs.

A vague sense of foreboding filled Gaius as he turned to look down at the men in the channel and maw of the dam; he felt his heart step up its beat, as he scanned the tremendous river gorge, making sure disaster-sentries were patrolling both north and south cliffs. Then he turned his scrutiny on the rockbed where all looked and sounded as usual. Stripped to their waists, prisoners chained together were splitting rocks with pickaxes and forming the fragments into piles. Others were in the earthwork of the dam, pushing iron rollers on layers of clay. Prisoners operated pulleys and cranes and there was a steady subdued hum of voices, horsehooves scraping on rocks and the sound of gurgling water sluicing into carryoff troughs. . . .

Then why this feeling of coming disaster? The sky was blue, a few fluffy white clouds, larks flying overhead. He stamped around his log tower, trying to stop the trembling of his legs. Heights never made him dizzy. . . . He scooped water from his cask and drank.

Had the platform moved slightly?

A lightning thought struck:

Earthquake?

"ROCKSLIDE!" came the thin hail of a sentry across the gorge, who with his comrades was already racing away from a section of cliff they had been pacing.

The cliff began to move.

Stones, lavender heather, yellow broom and gravel began breaking lose, moving sideways. At the base of the terrain were fifty men chained to each other, splitting rocks, widening the channel, oblivious of disaster from above—

"BACK AWAY!" Gaius screamed through his megaphone to the threatened men. "YOU THERE AT THE NORTH! BACK THIS WAY! SLOWLY! SLOWLY! DON'T TRY TO RUN, YOUR CHAINS WILL TRIP YOU—START THIS WAY—FOR CENTERCHANNEL!" Desperately he prayed the men shackled together like human sausages would escape the looming downcrash.

Chains clanking, the fifty men stumbled and floundered in slow, agonized retreat. Cavalrymen in the pit had slashed the ropes of their horses from the claycarts and slapped the frightened animals into flight downchannel to the west. But the troops did not flee. They looked up at Gaius . . .

"COME ON! ON! ON!" Gaius bellowed. A miracle might happen, for the northern cliff growled like a wild animal, but still had not collapsed. And his platform was immovable, but he could climb down the ladder if—

Tensely the tortured grains of time trickled out while the shackled line of prisoners moved south towards the center of the gorge.

Suddenly the doomed cliff opened like the petals of a rock flower and fell in. A boom of rocks and earth roared down, spitting up a geyser of gravel and brown dust. The thundering collapse soon stopped, a fifteen-foot jagged reef of stones, bushes, flowers and up-rooted saplings rearing where the fifty men had been a moment before.

Not a prisoner or soldier or animal was injured, even by flying fragments.

Gaius waited tensely. Aftershocks? A hard jolt coming? Should he order the men out of the gorge immediately? If Liscus protested, invite the commander to—what was he thinking—

Not a man moved below. All looked up at the tribune's log perch. Then cavalry horses began clattering back to their masters. Horses are good indexes, thought Gaius. If they scream and bolt again . . . But the chargers stood quietly as their troopers re-harnessed them to the clay wagons and once more climbed astride. Still Gaius did not signal for work to resume. Men below clanked to water barrels, watched by infantry men on horses. But far at the opposite side of the dam soldiers had ordered their prisoners back to work.

Then he saw Flavian climbing the ladder of his platform.

"Sir, we had a baby earthshaker," said the orderly.

Gaius nodded. He was drenched with perspiration under his sponge-lined helmet and steel band armor.

"The *Togati* north of here say this territory used to have big earth-smashers centuries ago. Only little shakes now. They say Pluto has stomach aches. Are you superstitious about quakes, tribune?"

Both drank cold water from the cask and sloshed some over their faces. "No," said Gaius. "Shifting of the ground is due to stresses deep in the earth—with full respect to temple priests who preach that these are due to the wrath of Jupiter." He smiled. "Or the internal distress of Pluto." He was astonished that he could treat lightly what might have been more catastrophic than a tornado.

Flavian tried to look convinced by his officer's explanation. Then he held out a lustrous little splinter of yellow white. "Sir, I'll never be the geologist you are. I can't tell whether this is fools' gold or real ore. Can you?"

Gaius examined the tiny, yet heavy fragment. "This is gold mixed with a small amount of silver. Where did you find it?"

"Way up northeast, beyond the waterside wall of your dam, sir. Should I turn this sample over to Commander Liscus?"

They traded a long look.

"Or, tribune, do you think I might keep this golden fingernail of ore as a souvenir for Beryl?"

Gaius smiled.

After the orderly climbed down the ladder, Gaius called for work to resume while he stared at the mountains east and north. He had thought about the region frequently since arriving; it was wild and uninhabited. Say it contained gold . . . say he discovered a virgin goldfield. Would he ever tell Rufus Liscus? Or, could he use such vital information as bargaining power to negotiate a loan for purchasing Penelope from Classicus? Who to tell? General Marcus Trajan? Not by letter. And if Trajan were to learn of it through some safe channel, how could the military genius help his admirer, Gaius Lacer, obtain money to buy liberty for Penelope? Nor must he forget his master, Architect Apollodorus. . . . *'My rebellious sprout of a Gaius, the virgin goldfield belongs to the emperor. You have no power to bargain as a free man simply because you made a big strike. I am paid for you to do precisely that. And even were you a moneyless freedman, there would still be that thorny matter of securing a loan with property!'*

Gaius spent the balance of the day down in the dam, testing and looking for displacements, fissures, scouring and thread-leaks. The buttresses were firm, expansion slots in place . . . He found no cracks in the concrete wall of the waterside which held back the stream. Still doubtful he queried the prisoners and soldiers who had been working in the heart of the barrier when the earthquake toppled the cliff. Not a man had felt the slightest quiver underfoot; not a timber propped against a wall had fallen. A soldier called attention to the fact that a plumb-line hanging on a bent stick had not moved all day. Gaius reasoned that the soldiers would not lie; neither would the prisoners. If the works were undermined and doomed to collapse, the laborers would be buried under buckling abutments, sand, clay, mud. At last he had to decide that the temblor had been localized in a rough line from his platform to the cliff that had fallen. Or the cliff was based on an earth-fault that moved and he had felt a faint effect of it on his platform.

'Your dam is safe,' his conscience insisted. 'Safe.'

Since he and his conscience were now inseparable friends, his concern was lifted.

That evening, feeling he had earned a reward of sorts for helping save fifty men from the falling cliff, he re-read eleven letters from Beryl to Flavian, which the aide let him borrow occasionally. Beryl was enduring. Soon her baby would be born. She felt fine, she was drinking all kinds of healthful tonics, and Flavian was not to worry.

Gaius smiled broadly. Then his eyes smarted. Yearning for Penelope swept him . . . A sudden thought struck: he did not know when their child was due. To put that new worry out of mind, he went outside his cabin to look at the stars and think about Penelope.

Troops were herding shifts of prisoners along the main cobbled street to the huge hillside mess area at the west end of town near the stone cookhouse and storage buildings. Torches flared all around and the soldiers cracked iron-tipped scourges on the paving to make the shackled men move faster.

"March it along!" shouted an adjutant. "Hep! Hep!"

Chains dragged and scraped as the prisoners tried to walk rather than trudge. Many looked at Gaius and glanced back for second looks as they moved past. To him it was a familiar scene; he seemed back on the Tagus spans again, working with all the races of humankind. Sad Negroes, slim Egyptians, blond Britons. Gaulics, Germans, Jews . . . and a few Romans, the last trying to hold their whiskered faces up and stare in contempt at the men they were shackled to. All the prisoners were bearded. Their leather loincloths and heavy boots gave off dank smells.

"Step it out!" shouted a legionary. "The banquet awaits! Boiled mutton, berries, roots and cider! The gods feel good tonight! March!"

Gaius watched the approach of a double column of men joined by chains, led by a gray haired trusty in a brown tunic. He halted his men and addressed Gaius:

"Tribune Lacer, I am Balbus, a trusty," he said in a reedy voice. "Sir, you saved my men today from the falling cliff. It was your voice that pulled us to safety, sir."

"Aaah," snorted a bass voice back in the ranks, "march us on, grandfather, I'm hungry. You hear me?"

"HUNGRY!" shouted the rest of Balbus' men. "HUNGRY!"

A soldier rushed back and saluted Gaius. "Sir, what's the trouble. Do you want any of them flogged?"

"No," said Gaius, sharply. "No trouble. The trusty stopped to thank me."

"Tribune, my men won't listen," piped Balbus. "But I—"

"MARCH US ON, GRANDFATHER!" roared the belligerent man in the rear.

"March—!" Guards snapped whips on the pavement.

Balbus began leading his men away.

"Hail Caesar, hail and hell grandfather," said the sarcastic voice and Gaius saw its owner: a tall young Roman of broken nose, fierce good looks nevertheless, chained to a Negro and a Jew ahead and behind him. All but the rebel looked with vague appreciation at Gaius as they moved on.

Two nights before the Kalends of October, hilarious couriers and torchmen clattered into camp with heavy mail pouches and tremendous tidings:

"DOMITIAN IS DEAD! DOMITIAN IS DEAD!"

"THEY ASSASSINATED THE BUTCHER! DEAD!"

"WE WANT TRAJAN!"

"*PRO ROMA!* TRAJAN!"

"*AVE OPTIMUS PRINCEPS TRAJAN!*"

"*IO TRIUMPHE!* TRAJAN! GIVE US TRAJAN!"

Even the prisoners, herded in their lean-to shelters behind stockades, broke into wavering cheers while troops began milling in the village streets. Some engaged in mock sword-play, others began impromptu boxing matches, and a few of slower blood danced decorously, arm-in-arm. Two hilarious infantrymen rigged an effigy of Domitian out of a bloody mutton carcass, crowned it with a garland of tough grass and burned it on a bonfire to the wild cheers of comrades.

From camps south and west of the Sil mines came Gemina cavalry horsemen to report to Liscus that military precautions were being observed against any belligerent tendencies of blackcloaks while the bulk of the Gemina troops celebrated. Liscus seemed unmoved. He ordered moderate quantities of wine for his soldiers. Meanwhile Gaius had joined the revellers in the camp streets.

He was hailed with roars and hoisted to the shoulders of two cavalrymen.

"The brave tribune will lead us in song!" screamed one of his bearers. "Lead us, sir!"

"I'm not a singer, but here we go," Gaius shouted. "The drinking song to Bacchus—your favorite! Are you ready?"

The troops were enthusiastically ready; Gaius could hardly hear his own voice as they all sang:

> "Oh, I'll pick me a plum in Britain
> Or a buxom grape from the Rhine,
> But the bliss without any trouble
> Is a skinfull of crimson wine!
> *Io! Io!* Father Bacchus, hear my plea!
> *Evoe! Evoe!* Brother goats, red wine loves me.
>
> Oh, the form divine is harlot wine,
> Sweet Circe of the cup;
> Climb the trellised bower at the moonlit hour
> And drink till the sun comes up.
> *Evoe! Evoe!* Father Bacchus, love is free!
> *Io! Io!* Mother Venus grapes love me!"

Flavian pushed through the ranks and thundered to Gaius, "Sir, I'm a father! A father! It's a son, Flavianus! Born two days after the Ides of September! Letter came tonight from Beryl—"

"Sing!" shouted Gaius. "Congratulations, sing!" Golden hope instead of red blood now sang in his veins, for surely the Senate in distant Rome would hail General Marcus Ulpius Trajan as the new emperor.

In Gades three nights later, Governor Verus Maturus received his official notification from Rome. Throwing the parchment up in the air, he shouted the fair tidings to Phrones, guards and servants. Then he and his Egyptian scribe hastened upstairs while the thunder of celebration began in the legation.

In his bedroom, Maturus removed the small bronze bust of Domitian from its niche above the altar. He marched out on his balcony and threw the image over the iron railing into the Atlantic. He and Phrones bowed ceremoniously to each other. They embraced. An instant later they were capering like satyrs.

142

A Senate parchment of notification for Chieftain Malendi had arrived in New Carthage, nestled next to the one for Governor Verus Maturus, both deep in a mail knapsack jammed with jubilant letters for Classicus and copies of the *Acta Diurna,* all from Rome. Fortunately for the governor, the locked senatorial pouch was handed him in haste by the chief courier who shouted the great announcement of Emperor Domitian's assassination, then handed Classicus his own official notification from the *Patres Conscripti.* The cedarwood cylinder containing the parchment dripped with golden cords and purple ribbons, and the fragrance of the wood seemed to the proconsul a happy augur that the noxious smell of Domitian's reign had ended with the refreshing and fragrant proclamation of the tyrant's death.

There was also a letter for Chieftain Malendi from the Senate. If the honorable Arvacan blackcloak leader would journey to The City at his convenience, the Fathers would tender their apologies that the Celt leader had ever fled Rome for his life to escape the wrath of the now dead and villified Domitian.

Classicus burned both documents addressed to Malendi.

He allowed the Senate scroll addressed to Governor Verus Victrix Maturus to proceed to its destination of Gades in western Farther Spain.

Weeks later, Cornelius Classicus learned that the Senate in Rome had chosen a new Emperor: *not* Field Marshal Marcus Ulpius Trajan, but the aged Senator M. Cocceius Nerva (precisely as the proconsul had forecast to Enna). Hardly able to contain his joy and relief, the governor of Hither Spain mulled (with some pity) the precarious elevation of senile Nerva, accurately gauging it as a stubborn senatorial attempt to re-establish the traditional authority of the legislative body over the military. And what would Trajan do when the unwelcome news reached him at the Rhine?

"He'll swear allegiance to bumbling old Nerva," Classicus told himself gleefully. "Trajan is the greatest fighter for Rome yet, but the man's too supine to march on The City, assassinate Nerva and seize power. Commendable. Gold for the Caesars. . . ."

Classicus was pleased to speed proclamations of Nerva's accession on to Maturus in Gades—and to Malendi. "Old baldy Maturus will belch," Classicus chuckled. "He, too, wanted Trajan to be our next leader. As for my invincible ally, brother Malendi, he will be ignored by the imperium of Emperor Nerva—hail Nerva."

XXII

During the third week in December, the empire celebrated Saturnalia with banqueting, song, dancing, and orgiastic rites. Experienced in surviving the annual lawlessness when slaves were masters and masters were slaves, Governor Maturus spent the nights on a bireme in the harbor while the gross carnival in Gades hailing King Saturn of Rome's Golden Age of antiquity clattered on to its riotous conclusion. The governor's ship-captain friend (who had once dared the terrors of the Atlantic and sailed around western Spain to Roman Britain) also craved dignity and had sent his crew and oar-slaves ashore. Refreshed each dawn after sound sleep in his private cabin on the quiet vessel bobbing at anchor, Maturus could face another day of the festival in his legation.

This he rather relished, being popular with his soldiers and slaves (who spared him indignities)—and a Roman magistrate widower in his fifties could endure philosophically when pretty slave girls occasionally burst into his library to kiss him. Too, tradition must be meticulously observed: the yearly homage to Saturn, who had ruled Italy's misty past with wise and disinterested philanthropy, when wars and money were unknown and all the earth's races shared equally the good things of life.

And so, on the fourth morning of Saturnalia, the governor and Phrones stood in the legation library talking loudly to each other over the noise of revelry out in the atrium. Suddenly he heard more commotion outside—and the doors were flung open and a veiled woman in gray appeared at the far end of the room. She closed the portals and bolted them.

"The first kiss of the day," said Maturus to his scribe, waiting for an onrush of amorous femininity. Then the visitor raised her veil.

Maturus was startled. "Enna!"

"Maturus," she said, "I want to die. Did you receive my letter?"

"I did not." Talking to gain time and organize his thoughts, Maturus continued, "If you contemplate suicide, I as a magistrate warn you that any patrician seeking exit from life must, according to law, first obtain the consent of the emperor. If the despairing one does not do so, his estate is heavily fined and in addition his heirs may be imprisoned." He led her to his armchair, noting wisps of gray in the fringe of chestnut curls under the half-thrown back veil and hood of her mantle.

Enna made no reply, turning away so that all he could see was her aquiline profile. He went around the table and leaned over, looking into her wan face.

"Enna, I can guess why you came to Gades," he began, but having no idea why she had. "I know a great deal more than you think I know, my dear lady."

"That is not true," she said, remotely. "Since you did not receive my letter, you could not know that Classicus has divorced me."

"No," he admitted. "Not that— What were the charges made by the proconsul against you?"

"He used the *morum graviorum* . . ."

"—Of the *Lex Papia Poppaea*," Maturus interrupted. "Whom did he accuse as your suspected lover? Enna, I am your friend."

She met his keen glance. "The complaint named Gaius Julius Lacer. It is—monstrous—"

Maturus frowned. "No doubt because you wrote a letter to his master, Apollodorus, months ago, offering to purchase the young architect." He paused and continued, "While your ex-husband entertains himself reading incoming and outgoing courier mail pouches. Merely a stray lamb of a thought, my dear domina."

Wincing slightly, Enna looked away.

"Proceed, Enna."

Her rigid composure broke. "I was so sure he loved me, needed me. So sure. I blinded myself to his women. Then his newest concubine arrived. I—feared her."

"Who is the newest siren of Cornelius Classicus?"

Dabbing her eyes with a crumpled white scarf, Enna answered, "She is not a slave. She is Zinga Rutilia, years younger than I. A—a disturbing sort of woman, a woman of savage appeal. One would think she were a tribal queen."

Maturus pulled a long face. "I have heard of her . . . Zinga Rutilia is the great-great granddaughter of the ill-fated Gallic chieftain Vercingetorix, who defied Rome. And lost. But, Enna, you have considerable knowledge of the laws. Tell me this: is it not a capital offense when a provincial treasurer tears up tax reports and tampers with imperial revenue monies?"

Her pale face went whiter. Hastily she said, "But my dear friend Frontinus destroyed the false documents, wrote new and correct ones, then I—" She stopped, horrified.

"Enna. Do you tell me all of it? Or do I tell you?"

Her head went up proudly. "How did you find out?"

"A friend of mine," Maturus lied. "A tax scribe in the New Carthage legation. His confidential letter came by fishing barge to my capitol months ago."

Her expressive eyes filled with tears. "That old man with the ague?"

"The very same," Maturus falsified.

She wept tiredly. "Did you know he was found strangled many days ago?"

"I did not. I grieve his passing. He might have proved a valuable witness. Do you know who killed him?"

She folded her thin white hands on the gray marble table. "Frontinus believes that his old clerk might have accused someone . . . and . . ."

"So the brave and reckless old man died," mused the governor and decided on a guesswork lance. "ENNA! How much money has Cornelius Classicus stolen from imperial tax collections bound for Italy?"

Her fingers gripped the rim of the table. "Beginning over a year ago, Cornelius stole fifteen thousand gold coins. He—he did not know that Frontinus always opens the coffers on shipboard for a final count of coins before the vessels sail for Italy. That is how the treasurer discovered the first false tax statement, and that five thousand goldworth had—vanished."

"Perhaps the noble General Myron Frontinus himself embezzled the money and blamed Classicus?" the governor probed.

"Never, no, no," she whispered. "You are toying with me, Maturus. My husband and Frontinus were the only ones with keys to the tax vaults. And we both know Frontinus is both wealthy and honorable!"

The governor sat on the edge of the table. "And he loves you . . . The natural inclination of Frontinus is to accuse Classicus, but Enna forbids it. She has a large fortune. So she replaces the missing coins while faithful Frontinus falls in with the plan and writes correct new tax reports. Thus Rome gets every coin due."

She looked in mute wonder. "You know . . . everything."

The governor began pacing while Phrones quickly picked up a fresh tablet and began racing his stylus across the waxed board.

"As long as Enna Gracchus controls large funds of her own," continued Maturus, "she can cover her spouse's supposedly undetected defalcations. Then her fortune is confiscated by men of Domitian and taken to Rome. I beg that you continue, Enna."

"Eight days ago," she said, hoarsely, "one of my maids brought me a bill of divorcement. Then Frontinus was admitted to my reception room. He urged me to write you about the divorce, and also suggest that you might care to return to New Carthage and study the revenue . . . situation. I wrote as my friend directed. Frontinus himself put that letter in the courier knapsack bound west for Gades."

Maturus sat down on the bench next to his scribe. "Did the honorable Frontinus keep eyes on that mail sack until it was taken up on horseback by the courier?"

Gazing despondently, Enna replied, "No. He feared to leave me alone in my suite. He returned immediately. Then he told me he had discovered another theft of tax coins. This time it amounted to ten thousand in gold valuation. I had no money left. Then before I realized, Cornelius and the Zinga Rutilia woman had entered my sitting room. The Zinga said to Cornelius, 'I love these rooms. Have Lady Enna move to the small apartment downstairs.' Frontinus, torn with sympathy for me, then accused Cornelius of embezzling thousands in gold coins from the imperial tax coffers. I was terrified. Most of all I was afraid of Zinga Rutilia. She has a frozen smile—and there was murder in her eyes as she stared at Frontinus."

His anger rising, Maturus inquired, "Who died this time?"

"No one." Enna let out a sigh of a breath. "Cornelius treated the accusation as the hallucination of an overworked treasurer who could not accurately tabulate coins because of specks before his eyes." She looked despairing. "Poor Frontinus, with his left hand crippled."

"I hear the man is a master swordsman with the slender Spanish blade," said Maturus. "The gods keep his right hand victorious. I deduce that Frontinus sent you to Gades?"

Enna seemed lost in thought, at last replying, "Strangely, it was my former husband who suggested it. I was too spent to know what to do, or where to go. Frontinus then ordered me to come here, knowing you would welcome me. Then he told Classicus and the Zinga woman to leave my apartment. They went out very quietly, but Classicus was smiling about something." She had supervised the packing of a few of her clothes and then freedmen fighters of Frontinus had taken over as her protectors. Since all the slaves in the New Carthage legation were devoted to Classicus, Enna decided not to bring any of her freedwomen maids. The men of Frontinus, all experts in use of the slender Spanish sword, had escorted her from New Carthage to Gades. The trip had been uneventful.

The governor sat down facing her, waiting for her to continue. He and Phrones looked at each other. Then Enna spoke,

"I'm tired, tired. Why go on living? Frontinus told me not to tell you how he and I had made good the tax thefts, but you've known all along. I want to die."

Maturus snapped, "You are not going to die and we both know it. You are my ally. More questions, dear lady. Enna, do you know anything about the death of one Publius, a bridge builder? He was rich and a man of sound moral reputation. I understand the last person to see Publius alive was Commander Rufus Liscus—and his dog. Yet your former husband had conferred briefly in his tent with Publius the architect before the bridge builder rushed out and started across his unfinished spans—" He was watching Enna closely.

"But that hideous black mastiff of Commander Rufus pushed Publius off the bridge! Surely you cannot implicate Classicus in that tragedy?"

Maturus shot back, "I do implicate him!" Then he launched another guess: *"The dog tried to save Publius from toppling into the gorge. Publius was staggering. Why? My deduction: he had swallowed drugged wine in the tent of Classicus shortly before. I fitted the parts of that puzzle together but recently, my dear and deluded Enna. Proof? None. Publius was fond of wine. But not that fond. A tasteless poison dropped into wine—"

Enna interrupted sharply, "The dog Mars killed Publius."

"Not proven. I have heard from talk of the soldiers in the New Carthage legation while I was there months ago that Mars the black dog kills in battle, but has never attacked a civilian." He rose from the bench and leaned over the table to look into Enna's staring eyes. "Enna, tell me about the private agreement between Cornelius Classicus and Rufus Liscus. Come, you know something about that."

She looked at him squarely. "All I know is that I think Cornelius advanced Commander Liscus two or three thousand *aureii* on the strength of his inheritance of shares in a silver mine in Cappadocia or Greece, I know not where. What 'private agreement'?"

Maturus straightened up. "Inheritance," he brooded, completely baffled. Putting that curious piece of information in a mental nook, he asked, "Enna, do you ever hear from Lady Plotina?"

Surprised, she said, "Why of course. She is my best friend."

Now the governor was interested. "What does she write about?"

Enna gave him a quizzical look. "For the past two or three months she has written about the Rhine vineyards and flax crops. Something about General Trajan's favorite brown mare having a colt last July. All about Trajan's niece and grandnieces boating on the Rhine."

Governor Maturus began pacing. "Remarkable topics," he said at length. "What do you write to Lady Plotina?"

"I write Plotina aimless letters about cosmetics and Christian missionaries and flamingos, tuna fish, sardines, a cuttlefish I saw when Frontinus and I strolled on the wharves one day. Nothing controversial." Her wan face pinkened. "In Plotina's recent letter she advised me to watch out for fishbones. What did I advise as a bleach for her freckles? What tincture did I use to keep my hair brown? That letter was so unlike her."

The governor was grinning triumphantly. "Our modern Ulysses in female form, the gods protect her. Was that letter in Plotina's handwriting? Were all the others, too?"

"Why, of course," said Enna, irritably.

"Then I have another ally," said Maturus, softly.

He changed the subject. "My dear woman, will you refresh my mind about Gaius Julius Lacer? I have forgotten how many sisters and brothers he has."

Enna stirred restlessly. "He has none. Why ask?"

"Is Gaius in love?"

Enna sighed resignedly. "I don't know, I don't know. Cornelius did send him a Greek slavegirl months ago."

"Who is she and where is she?"

"Her name is Penelope," said Enna. "Apparently my former husband found her so unresponsive in bed he was glad to give her away. Besides, he no doubt thought it would seem a generous gesture to make such a gift."

"I see," said Maturus, promising himself to find out more about this matter later. He drew a cushioned chair next to Enna and sat down. "Now, dear lady, we take up your ex-husband's friendship with Chieftain Luna Malendi," said Maturus. "All goes smoothly there?"

Enna arose and strolled to a casement window and looked out on the Atlantic. Maturus followed. He pitied her, but he had to wring from her every fact he could obtain.

She turned to him. "Cornelius has made two or three diplomatic visits to Malendi. He gave the blackcloak leader some cattle. Verus, believe me, my former husband did take tax funds, but he was driven to it by debt—and he has many virtues. I know he still loves me. He is kind to the poor. He even bravely tried to save the lives of several men condemned by Emperor Domitian. I myself saw one warning—to poor Senator Mauricus. I saw that scroll given to special couriers. I saw them gallop away with it."

"I didn't," said Maturus, preparing to launch his final blow at Enna. "Stop defending your ex-spouse. Some day your clinging love will turn to loathing. Some day you and Frontinus will wed and find happiness. You must believe that."

Maturus continued cross-examining Enna. "My dear woman," he said, "do you ever, or did you ever, read the letters Cornelius Classicus receives from Chieftain Malendi?"

She glanced with a trace of anger. "Once or twice I did. Cornelius wanted me kept informed. He is doing his best to weld peaceful relations with Malendi. I do defend him in that quarter."

"As Classicus would put it, 'commendable,'" returned the governor, with a grim smile. "Merely an innocuous correspondence. And those numerous letters Malendi sends to Proconsul Classicus must glisten with rubies and emeralds of sagacity and amity."

"Three or four times a month, I think." Enna returned to the armchair by the table. "Verus, how do you find out so many things? Cornelius would be amazed."

Standing away from the table, he looked through a casement at the Atlantic for a while. Then he turned quickly and pointed to her:

"Enna, Classicus must be heavily in debt. He has stolen tax monies. What must he do to disinvolve himself from a murderous load of obligations? Tell me, what must he do?"

She stared in puzzled wonder. "I do not know. I . . . do . . . not . . . know."

"Then it is my painful duty to tell you. Your former husband plans to use Malendi's armies to attack the Sil mines next Spring or Summer and get the gold. And the price? How many Romans will die so Classicus can blandly go his way free of debt?"

Enna sprang up.

"Cornelius would never think of such criminal—" She darted around the table as though to slap the governor's face. "You imagine—things! You would smear the reputation of Cornelius, you want to become emperor . . ."

Maturus' underlip thrust out challengingly. "As the Christians would say, 'Turn the other cheek.' I am about to be attacked by poor Enna, blue-blooded descendant of the fearless Gracchi tribe, those staunch defenders of justice and liberty and truth."

Her anger ebbed quickly, replaced by a look of dazed and dubious gravity. "Verus, forgive me," she begged. "My mind seems toppling."

He kissed her hands. "As Juvenal the satirist recently wrote, *'lucri bonus est odor.'* The sweet smell of money applies to Classicus. As to you, dear lady, Juvenal also penned, *'mens sana in corpore sano.'* Fear not, you are sound of body and brain."

She was weeping in his arms. "But it's horrible, horrible to think about, Verus. Those men up at the Sil mines. Young Gaius Lacer, the soldiers, the chained slaves . . ."

"Enna, I must place you under protective custody in my legation. Will you work with me to clean up this mess? I need your help. We may both go down, but we will go down with honor, fighting to the last."

She nodded. "I am a criminal myself. I cloaked the defalcations of Classicus. So did Frontinus, but he did it for me. . . . I will help you, Maturus. So will Myron Frontinus. He is coming to Gades soon."

⊓⊓⊓ 97 A.D. ⊔⊔⊓

XXIII

After Enna fled to Gades, Classicus uneasily regretted divorcing her more or less on impulse. He found two paths of reasoning through that morass: Malendi would be committed to war when informed that Governor Verus Maturus had now lured the prominent wife of Classicus out to Gades. Secondly, a curious inversion of love had motivated Classicus to be rid of Enna so that she might not be caught in the catastrophe which could overwhelm him. Now he wondered if he should declare bankruptcy and face the grim consequences. Or (a more traditional course of action) write his last will and testament, pen a full confession of his crimes, then drink poison or open his veins as a defeated Roman should. He was incapable of doing either, and sunshine soon dispersed his black storm of despondency.

The light was Zinga Rutilia, his new infatuation. Her Gallic blood ran hot in love and partisanship. She also avidly desired gold and prestige and would help him push his plan through to triumph. She, too, had fought up out of a miserable childhood, cruel parents, poverty, then marriage—and a second emancipation from an austere and stingy mate who had not lived long enough to file adultery charges against her. She and Classicus belonged together. From now on the empire would pay for having forced her noble Classicus into a financial pit that had threatened to crumble his aristocratic Roman mind. All he must do was marry her and then they both could handle his occasional delusions and hallucinations—Zinga believed that once they were wed, his seizures would cease.

He espoused her in a private ceremony of mutual consent, devoid of priests and pomp. A parchment posted in the New Carthage legation hailed Zinga Rutilia, virtuous widow of Roman Knight C. Aufidius, and great-great-granddaughter of Vercingatorix, Gallic leader of yore, as lady excellency of Hither Spain. She was not exactly a pauper bride and gave the impression of careless wealth.

Zinga brought to her marriage four thousand gold coins, an embossed silver goblet, a limited yet colorful wardrobe, and vast resources of determination. At her behest, Classicus sent her by vessel to Italy as his exotic emissary with a panegyric of congratulations for Emperor Nerva.

During her absence a new feeling of power came over him, and he conducted the complex and burdensome affairs of his province with dignity and unfailing mercy. More and more he heeded the visiting entity that possessed his mind and urged deeds of love and sacrifice. During one such visitation he confiscated fish-hauls and wheat shipments to feed the hungry poor. This not only won plaudits from the starving, but a smile from the goddess *Fortuna*. Money soon arrived from Rome to reimburse disgruntled fishermen and grain importers, and also pay accumulating expenses of the legation. It gave the proconsul a feeling of melancholy martyrdom in making sure that every coin from The City reached rightful hands. His good works were also strengthened when he reflected that he was not alone in facing debt.

Letters from Rome informed him that many a patrician family teetered on fraying tightropes of monetary disaster. Although humane and wise Nerva was emperor, chaos reigned and might force the new Caesar to take radical action. But the aged ruler was constrained by his desire for peace to avoid decrees that might result in bloodshed and undermine his reign.

Yet for a while Classicus clung to the frail hope that Nerva would burn the tax books, expunge all debt, and thus turn over a new leaf of living for every one. No such drastic and lifesaving measures were enacted, but Emperor Nerva at last reluctantly approved a Senate bill declaring a temporary moratorium on debts. Quick disaster was thus averted for Cornelius Classicus. Meanwhile he avoided Frontinus and the treasury wing of the palace as his popularity with other subofficials and legation servants rose to new heights. He also found solace in scrolls from senator friends in Rome.

They wrote that Verus Maturus of Farther Spain was being excoriated as 'the short toga horsefly nipping the tail of the empire,' and was classed by many *Patres Conscripti* with discredited Proconsul Massa of Egypt, who had been imprisoned for plundering his hapless subjects to their loincloths during the reign of Domitian. But another senatorial missive indignantly informed Classicus that buzzing Senator Tacitus and his colleague bumble-bee, Senator

Pliny the Younger, favored enforcement of the investigation law and praised the honesty of Proconsul Verus Maturus. However, their orations had been shouted down by opposition statesmen ridiculing Maturus and all naggers of his ilk with imperial ambitions. So affairs of State dangled in uneasy suspension. Then Zinga returned from Rome late in February, overflowing with bright tidings.

She had wheedled his creditors into reducing his obligations by one tenth, but he must pay the principal and accumulated interest in full after the frozen debt law expired. Zinga bore proof: documents of easement signed by hard-pressed financiers in The Capitol who held Classicus' promises to pay.

The afternoon Zinga's trireme docked, Classicus reclined on the gray velvet couch in Enna's sitting room while on the opposite side of a banquet table the red-haired Zinga lolled seductively on Enna's gold brocade sofa. The balcony doors stood open, for winter hardly touched the Mediterranean coast of Spain. Having heard in detail the encouraging news from Italy, the proconsul bade his bride catch her breath and partake of food.

Finished, she murmured in dulcet tones, *"Carissime,* dear old Nerva is holding you over another year as procurator of this province. His chamberlain also instructed me to relay the emperor's appreciation for your honest and capable administration of Hither Spain."

He basked in the sense of security her presence gave him until he was struck by the idea that Enna hid in the copper heating pipes of the marble floor. She was unseen, but he knew she was there, and she was eavesdropping. He sat up on his couch and stamped the white marble flooring. "I divorced you, you've gone," he muttered. "Begone forever, Enna."

Zinga watched obliquely, her narrowed eyes wary. "Did you have any of those strange spells while I was in Rome?"

"Nothing of consequence, my vulpine love. Pray continue."

She gave him an artful smile. "Maturus, too, is being held over as governor of Farther Spain . . . for the simple reason that no senator, Aedile, praefect or questor wants to go out to the end of the world." She sipped more wine and put down her heavy goblet. "Then I attended a Senate Wives' reception in honor of sweet old Empress Cocceia, who was not there. The eminent lady refuses to leave her farm on the island of Crete."

Classicus laughed. "Nerva and his wife haven't lived together for years. Proceed."

"During that very circumspect gala, many of the distinguished dominas made tart remarks about Proconsul Verus Maturus. Then they turned expectantly to me. I sympathetically observed that Governor Maturus might be bowed down by illness, or losing his wits, and must we not be charitable?" She laughed without a sound. "*Carissime,* you should have seen the looks that passed among those noble wives. The next day various senator husbands of the angry ladies rose up in the Curia and denounced Maturus all over again—and praised *you.*" Zinga Rutilia had imitated aristocratic Roman matrons so long that her speech was generally well-modulated and cultured.

Classicus mused that his fox-of-a-bride had the stealth and courage of a primitive, in contrast to frigid, inbred Enna. He consoled himself that he was well rid of Enna Gracchus. She and old baldy Maturus could mull and debate and throw resounding sentences at each other—but if Enna ever tried to accuse him of tax thefts, he would sue her for slander, and win. And there would be no rooster-squawks from Frontinus, either.

"Adorable old Emperor Nerva is juggling," continued Zinga. "The Praetorian Guards still demand vengeance for the assassination of Emperor Domitian. Before I left The City, our darling Nerva had paid heavy donatives to the Guards. They at last stopped pounding their swords on their shields." Her voice dropped to a rich whisper: "*Carissime* . . . what news from the Sil?"

Classicus ate some jellied lobster and wiped his lips on a white silk napkin. "Commander Rufus Liscus is a wry writing fellow. Of gold and silver there is little—but as substitutes do I want lead, tin, chalk, and a portion or so of copper? He advises that the one or two small goldbricks his slave engineer has already smelted and refined be held until next Spring or Summer, for by that time Tribune Gaius Lacer may bestir himself and make a big strike."

Zinga tilted her head. "My handsome Roman, can you trust Liscus?"

"If Liscus is hoarding a few loaves of gold and silver, let him hoard. Let him dream. His dream will end in—"

"—Nightmare—" breathed Zinga. "And how is the powerful one?"

"A contained conflagration," Classicus said, smilingly. "Thousands of his warriors are snugly in winter camps south of the Sil. Peace-loving blackcloaks. Chieftain Malendi has the right to deploy his troops all over the territory south of the Sil mines, for most of that land belongs to Malendi anyhow. My couriers get through nicely . . . but Maturus' military messengers have to leave their scrolls with blackcloak outposts. Thus, let us wring our hands, Maturus cannot communicate with the men at the Sil, should the notion strike him."

Tensely she murmured, "Why would Maturus write to any man up at the Sil? Has the creature tried?"

"He has," Classicus said, with relish. "The blackcloaks rip off the address tags and Malendi studies them first. Then the chieftain sends the weird missives to me. The ravings of a lunatic. Maturus now goes in for poetry—every line that contains the word 'gold.' He also wrote a rambling letter to Gaius—about gold, a golden horse—I tell you, my foxy charmer, Maturus is digging his own disaster with the point of his pen."

Zinga bit into a ripe olive. "We must consider this: what if Gaius the slave doesn't find gold?"

Indulgently her husband replied: "Gaius the slave will find gold, all right, but not in the Sil basin. Even so, there must be gold in tributaries of the Sil, or in the Cantabrian Mountains. I am gambling that Gaius' experience will soon tempt him to roam afield . . . hunting for flowers of gold."

Zinga let a small laugh escape. "What sort of a man is the famous bridge builder?"

"Not what you'd expect," Classicus said. "An interesting male of exterior rockiness and interior emotion. Even his hair is rebellious. While I was catering to his poetic tastes in this legation last Spring, I noted that he avoided women."

"A deviate who builds fantastic bridges! Interesting. I feel sorry for homosexuals. I saw so many in Rome, artistic people of varied accomplishments."

Classicus laughed. "Gaius is not a two-sexed individual. He thinks he's a rigid idealist. His father was a perfect example of *magnae fortunate pericula,* so all Gaius inherited was slavery and pride in his heritage. To soften the geologist and show him some consideration I loaned him a slavegirl months ago. I expected him to spurn her. But he kept her, to my gratification."

Zinga swore under her breath. "Why didn't you tell me about the girl?"

"My foxy nymph, do not grimace. Tell you about Penelope? I haven't thought of her for months. Have a saffron cake."

She was standing, her purple-blue eyes sparkling. "Every woman is important and that slavegirl may endanger our plans. Think, my Roman love, think. Did you by chance confide anything in that girl before you sent her to Gaius? Let drop anything that might stir her suspicions?"

A worm of apprehension writhed through the proconsul. He clearly remembered his first night with Penelope almost a year ago when he was tantalized by her frantic attempts to save her maidenhood. He had conquered at last, a limp and sobbing Greek girl who still remained cold in spite of his ardor. But wait . . . later had there been a night when he was euphoric with love and wine, and luscious Penelope had unexpectedly become a siren in his embrace and lured him with love and laughing conversation? Through a blur of memories it seemed that he might have babbled something to the Greek temptress. Penelope a menace?

Zinga was standing by his couch. "Does that slave Penelope have any inkling of our plans?"

He explained his vague belief that she might. "But if I did mumble to the girl, what of it? She is my property. She can prove nothing, and she dare not accuse her master."

"Where is Penelope?"

"Up at the Sil with architect Gaius."

Zinga looked sideways, her narrow face fixed in an expression of thoughtfulness. Then she smiled. "Are you sure? Would the builder of the Tagus Bridge keep a girl in a rough mining town? Is he that kind of a man?"

Having a secret and hearty respect for young Gaius, the governor mentally debated whether the slave geologist would want even a luscious woman entwined around his neck while he built a dam, sliced off cliffs and directed gold-washeries. Yet if Gaius had spurned Penelope, she would have been sold at Segovia, therefore he must have kept her. Question: did he take her with him to the goldfields? If not, where was she and who is she with?

"Did your travelling prefect and his troops go north to the Sil to inspect, as we planned, before I left for Rome last December? If so, did they see Penelope?"

Classicus mused, "I didn't instruct them to look for her. I'd forgotten her. But my men did see women—in the custody of their whitecloak sires. Some of the troops hope to wed Roman Celt wives after the mines are closed next year."

Zinga sat down next to him. "Your slavegirl may not be with Gaius. Then where would she be?"

His thoughts roamed back. "Gaius and the expedition were camped in Ioza, a mountain cave village, for some time last year. I sent Penelope to him there. The young brute never even wrote me a note of gratitude for the loan, either."

"Then she may still be there, hidden," Zinga cut in. "Is Penelope beautiful, my Roman?"

"Beautiful, but cold," he said, kissing his Zinga's white shoulders. Once more all was going smoothly, he was protected and watched over tenderly by his woman of the forest.

Zinga kissed him passionately on the lips, then returned to her gold brocade sofa, her red and yellow draperies shimmering in drifts as she reclined again. "I will handle it all. We must reclaim Penelope when we are ready. If she is concealed in Ioza, we must face the prospect that the cave people might bark like coyotes if your troops arrived to take her into custody. She may have protectors in Ioza who would fight with your men, and you cannot afford to lose one soldier, we have so few as it is. We'll bide our time and send two or three men to spy on Ioza . . ."

Classicus had scarcely heard; while dimly aware of Zinga across the table from him, he had been suddenly enfolded in a hallucination of sight and sound. He was lying on white velvet rocks, looking out over the Sil mines and village. The snowy panorama was sharply etched in whites and grays and blacks . . . he heard the squeak and tramp of boots, rasp of chains, clack of horsehooves and distant howling of wolves. Dreamily he examined conic piles of rocks under snowcrust, resembling gigantic teeth upthrust to bite the gray sky. He saw log and clay huts and then stone buildings . . . blue smoke rising . . . flashes of red fire from open-front brick structures . . . he admired soldiers in armor, wearing bearskins and elk hides over their helmets and gear . . . and a huge black dog loping, its paws clacking on crusted snow. Then he heard the voice of Gaius Lacer:

'Yes, commander, a slow and laborious process, one step before the next step. The rock-crushing, the sieve-jigging in water—this settles the minerals to the bottom and leaves the lighter fragments on top. Then we re-crush and re-strain the material, reserving the fifth residue for smelting . . . smelted bars are full of imperfections. So next we use the cementation process . . .'

158

"*Cornelius!*" sounded the harsh voice of Zinga from afar.

He hardly heard, enveloped in the vision. He smelled burning chaff and felt strong blasts of heat on his face and body. '. . . place the smelted bars in bedding of brick dust . . . alum . . . vitriol . . . deep in earthen pots and heated red hot. This melts the silver and lesser metals, but does not soften gold . . . Commander Liscus . . . This process we call cementation—'

Shaken back to reality by Zinga, the proconsul was mildly nettled that she had swept away his visionary world. Was he a mystic, a demigod? The thought appealed, so he took Zinga in his arms and kissed her. "I dreamed I was up at the Sil, listening to Gaius harangue on smelting and refining," he teased. "You should be duly impressed to be the loved vixen of a Roman who can see and hear across distances. I am in excellent spirits. What were we discussing?" Jovially he sent her back to the gold brocade sofa again.

She let out a breath. "Nothing important. But what are we going to do about Frontinus? He was on the wharf when my maids and I came off the trireme today. He had daggers instead of eyes. He is a beast."

"Our scholarly treasurer of cutting optics," Classicus jested. "He has nothing to hone his temper these days. Taxes flow in and flow straight out again for Italy. Auction sales levies, inheritance assessments, imperial tariffs on slave emancipations, levies on bachelors and childless couples. Name the tax and Frontinus will quote the exact quarterly amount squeezed from the people of Hither Spain. The coins clink heavy in the coffers and unclink in Rome. But you and I must economize," he joked. "I mean that, my beautiful foxling. We are not exactly under a Damoclean sword."

Zinga felt her jewelled crown. "We could sell this and those few remaining old baubles of Enna's dower jewels."

Classicus ate some preserved sturgeon and sipped wine.

"They would bring absolutely nothing on the market today. Rich matrons of Rome and other cities are crying for ancient gold ornaments found on one of the sites of Troy, all honor to the ghost of Hector." He gazed at a low centerpiece of red roses and white hyacinths in a silver bowl on the table, trying futilely to evoke again the sights and voices of the Sil camp.

The violet eyes of Zinga glittered. "How can we be sure Gaius Lacer will strike rich gold deposits before the powerful one moves his warriors into the Sil valley next summer?"

"I vow that he will," Classicus answered in a tone of mild reproof.

"A glint of gold, my lover of grapes, always works miracles. And when Malendi is ready to launch the assault on the mines, and I am ready, all I do is write an innocuous but dignified message, something to the effect that the time has come for Malendi to resettle his tribe in more fertile valleys."

The sandarac doors swung open and Frontinus came in. He closed the portals and bolted them.

Zinga stiffened in surprise. Classicus eyed the intruder suavely.

"Dramatic. Melodramatic," smiled the proconsul. "Pray roll up a dining couch and recline. General Myron Frontinus honors the lady excellency and me. Honorary general. Paymaster-general. And if you will allow me a humorous observation, the holder of your delicate Spanish sword does resemble a treasury pen."

"Where are the hall guards?" demanded Zinga, staring in hate at Frontinus.

He looked mildly at her. "Still out there. There was no need for the guards to announce me. I am announcing myself. I have come for a short conference with Classicus."

Then Zinga smiled alluringly, hoping the treasurer would come closer to her couch and the table. He did. She had her heavy silver goblet ready. . . .

He glanced benignly once or twice at her while addressing Classicus: "I did not come to demand the ten thousand you owe me, Classicus; nor the additional ten thousand I placed in the imperial tax coffer last December to replace the funds you filched."

"Ah?" Classicus said, gently. "Myron Frontinus maligns and slanders the imperial procurator of Hither Spain."

Frontinus went to a balcony door and gestured. Soon four husky young men in brown clothes and voluminous cloaks stepped in and stood by the wall. Then the treasurer approached Classicus and Zinga again.

Zinga was sitting on her gold brocade couch. Languidly she glanced at the four freedmen by the wall, but they were looking at their patron, General Frontinus. She next measured the distance between herself and Frontinus, her strong fingers tightening on the silver goblet now to become a missile of death. . . . When the treasurer's eyes were on Classicus, Zinga gracefully lifted the big cup as if to drink. Just as she was ready to throw it at Frontinus, he jerked out his sword, darted to her and nicked her right arm. Down clattered the silver vessel, dragging red roses and white hyacinths to the floor. Zinga made no outcry; coolly she bound her bleeding arm with a white silk napkin.

"You dare attack a helpless woman, my wife, the lady excellency," whispered Classicus. "You'll pay for that, you'll pay for that, you'll pay for . . ."

"The scratch is but skin deep," Frontinus soothed. "Knowledge of vital nerves and blood vessels is essential when one uses the flexible Spanish sword. I trust your apprehensions are allayed."

The governor swung off his couch while Zinga furtively retrieved the goblet from the floor and hid it in the folds of the white damask tablecloth. Apparently the four young men at the wall did not see her, for they were staring at the coffered ceiling.

"Get out, Myron Frontinus," said Classicus, "or my guards will run you through."

Patiently the treasurer replied, "I trust the swift reminder of my weapon teaches the Gallic not to attempt murder with a winecup a second time." His slow smile came and went. "She wears a gemmed chaplet. Inappropriate. That gemmed crown first adorned the head of the virtuous Cornelia, mother of the honorable and heroic Gracchi brothers."

Zinga lost her poise. "Carrion," she spat. "Poisoned face of an oyster! Murderer!"

"My wife has a temper," Classicus smiled, stepping back from the treasurer. "Still on your knees at the shrine of Enna Gracchus, my good treasurer? No doubt she now graces the couch of Maturus as she once bestowed her enticements on you and Gaius Lacer."

The Spanish blade flashed so quickly that Classicus tasted his own blood before fully realizing that the sharp metal had lightly slashed his lower lip.

Zinga cried out hoarsely.

"Wipe your mouth, governor," said Frontinus, softly. "The blood will clot, the cut will heal. But what comes from your tongue . . . there is no healing for that." Another fast thrust, and a slit appeared in the toga of Classicus; a curved Persian Stiletto fell out of the white folds and clanged on the floor.

"The weapon concealed was not concealed enough," said Frontinus, with sympathy. His maimed left hand was at his back while his right idly turned the hilt of the slender sword.

Classicus clapped his hands.

Soldiers appeared outside the open balcony doors. Two marched across the threshold, came to a halt, and saluted with their heavy broadswords.

"Arrest General Myron Frontinus," the proconsul ordered. "Put him in one of the new limestone dungeons."

Frontinus glanced apologetically at the legionaries, and pretended to lunge at an invisible foeman. At length he remarked, "Well, good soldiers? A contest? Can you reach me with your *gladii?*"

"No, general," said the baffled taller guard.

"Arrest him," Classicus commanded.

The two soldiers started across the room while Zinga quickly raised the silver goblet. It jumped out of her hand and the Spanish blade whished past her red curls. She sprang up. "Pack rat!" she screamed. "Dirty yellow bile! Killer jaws of a camel! Toadstool! Fungi!" Then she was in Classicus' arms, one of his hands over her mouth.

"I change my order," said Classicus. "Kill this madman of a General Myron Frontinus."

The four men of Frontinus folded their arms and gazed vacantly while the two guards exchanged looks. Then the taller one advanced and halted. "General Frontinus, honorable combat. No quarter. Sorry, sir, but the governor's orders are the governor's orders."

"As you choose, good soldier," said Frontinus. He sighed. Then he glanced over his shoulder at Zinga. She was mumbling curses. Classicus trying to stop her.

The two combatants faced each other, backed away, and raised swords in salute. Soldiers on the balcony crowded partly in the room to watch.

Broadsword raised, the guard sprang. Frontinus seemed to await a lethal thrust. But before the *gladius* struck his neck or face, he leaped sideways, spun around and drove his narrow blade through the laced thongs of his opponent's leather arm-guard. The counter-attack was so fast, the sword jerked back so swiftly, that the victim was still in motion when his heavy weapon fell from his grasp and clattered on the floor. He came to a halt, staring stupidly at blood spurting from his sword-arm.

"Forgive me, good soldier, for I cut a vital nerve and big blood vessel in your fighting arm," said Frontinus, with honest regret. "Go to the doctors at once. Have them bind a tourniquet on your arm and ligate the ruptured bloodway, or you will bleed to death."

The short guard pulled his bleeding comrade out to the balcony and anxious comrades hustled him away. Others remained staring in admiration at unperturbed Frontinus.

"Soldiers," said the treasurer, "I entered this chamber peaceably and two attempts were made on my life. I am still peaceable. I remind you that I am loyal to Emperor Nerva, the Roman Senate, and the Roman people. Any loyalty below those loyalties is no loyalty."

Not a soldier moved or spoke.

Classicus began chuckling. "Magnificent, my noble Frontinus. Unparalleled. This, soldiers, was our rehearsal. Very realistic. Frontinus, next time we must do a pantomime of Achilles and Hector. You might like the part of the loathsome Achilles, but in our version Hector will not expire." He flourished his hands. "Soldiers, dismissed."

The men marched out on the balcony and tramped away.

"Now," breathed Classicus, holding Zinga behind him, "now you treacherous, murdering, eavesdropping—"

"I did not eavesdrop, nor did my four young freedmen," replied Frontinus. "I am not a murderer. I do not plunder imperial tax coffers. I came not to threaten you or the red-haired domina. Cooler men must deal with you, Classicus. Justice will be dealt you. My four men are my witnesses. They are also deadly swordsmen. I trained them. I have thirty in all. Their Spanish blades are concealed under their cloaks."

Classicus was greatly entertained. "Commendable. More marvellous than the Alexandria Lighthouse. Get out."

Frontinus pushed his bloodstained sword into its scabbard. "I came to present my verbal resignation as provincial treasurer, for I'm afraid you are a . . . collector. I am afraid letters I send by courier never reach my friends, such as General Marcus Trajan. I never hear from Trajan. I am afraid Governor Maturus suffers the same letterless exile."

The proconsul began laughing. "Write to Trajan, do, my good man. Tell him anything you want. Accuse me, ah, there is an excellent idea. Tell him the whole story. Tell him about your cozy little talks with my wife Enna. Tell him how pristine is your own honor. Write to Emperor Nerva. Write—write—write. Spread libel in black ink . . . or crimson. Name my legation as the den of criminals!"

Frontinus stared in contempt. "My thirty freedmen and I now depart this place. I take my money, horses, and other personal property. I now bid you a heart-rending farewell."

Classicus sank down on his couch with Zinga clinging to him. "An accountant in armor," he laughed. "A false accuser tricked out in battle gear, one of the creatures who alienated the affections of my former wife. A model of propriety is my former hero of the abacus! The law is on my side and it is a mighty sword. I can picture the stirring reunion when my mathematical moron joins Enna and Verus Maturus in Gades!"

"*Carissime*," murmured Zinga, "the wretch and his four petty creatures have gone. Let me wipe your lips, my brave Roman. Rest. The monster of a Frontinus will never harm you."

XXIV

Early in February, after suffering false birth-pangs, Penelope realized that her child would enter the world within ten days more or less. At nights her cave bedchamber became an arena where she tried to walk off an army of fears. Dread over the future of Gaius dominated her thoughts. If he were trapped and killed in a gold conspiracy— Separated from him, yearning to be in his arms, and horror that Cornelius Classicus might discover her hiding place; these apprehensions, coupled with her fear that she might not survive the coming ordeal of giving birth, all combined to reduce her at times to despondency. Then the positive side of her mind would rise in outrage.

Gaius was a wary Roman of mind, experience, and physical strength. The All-God of love protected him; her constant thoughts formed a wall around him. They were not apart. It sometimes seemed as if they stood at opposite ends of his Tagus Bridge, signalling each other, meeting in the center with their thoughts. Then the negative part of her thinking would present new reasons for surrender to hopelessness.

For one thing, she was, in contrast to the man she loved, unschooled. If he lived, eventually won his freedom and hers, surely he would be humiliated by a wife unable to move at ease in his sphere of achievement and among men and women of his intellectual class. Proud Roman matrons she would meet would be dominas of distinction, able to quote poetry and philosophy; refer casually to old Emperor Nerva's tolerance, humanity, and lofty character; meet Consuls and Senators without stammering and wanting to hide . . . 'And have you noticed the Greek wife of the famous patrician architect, the great Lacer? Why, in the name of the Divine Diana, did he wed *her*? A former captive, my dears, so be careful what you say, for Lacer is a splendid aristocrat I hope to catch for my daughter. . . .'

Again Penelope's affirmative perceptions would revolt. She, like Gaius, was important. Important in her own way. She served the sick; in a limited way, granted, for she was not a fully qualified physician. But each day the All-God seemed to open new doors of knowledge when she silently despaired over how to handle complicated ailments. And what could prevent her from reading book-scrolls in the future, so Gaius would not be embarrassed? She read and spoke both Latin and Greek. Beryl was right: she was too humble. And had not her first master, the beloved Egyptian avatar, tried to teach her in his mystical way that matching souls loved and grew in life after life? That she would never lose what she loved? That the achievements of love in each existence were leaven to enrich the next incarnation? And even her early life had not been all poverty and pillows drenched with tears at night.

Memories of her childhood usually restored her equanimity. She had been born and reared (haphazardly, by her harsh sculptor-father) in the mountain village of Icaria northeast of Athens. One day in her eighth year she had stopped a dog fight and next calmed furious women haggling over prices at a merchant's stall in the marketplace.

Why did the snarling canines not attack *her* when she pulled them apart? What power had held immovable the upraised arms of angry matrons who turned on shabby Penelope plucking at their robes and begging that they smile and go home in peace? And so had the women, laughing, with their baskets of fish and leeks and beans. One pleased woman had thrown a fish as reward for Penelope the peacemaker.

When she was nine, a Greek librarian from Athens had come to the sculptor's cottage in Icaria and paid the spectacular price of ten *drachmae* for her sire's crude, yet startlingly realistic statue of a ferocious shepherd carrying a lamb. 'This lifesize gray marble is a masterwork,' the impressed purchaser had said, 'because it depicts our country. Rome, our barbaric overlord, carries Greece the helpless lamb. Now observe you your daughter, Penelope, sanding the pots. She is the Achaia our ancestors knew. Marry her off, bury her away, let her be forgotten. Better that than pillage and destruction. Rome and the heartless gods are prodigal wasters of perfection such as your little one!'

At that moment Penelope had silently vowed she would never be wasted or plundered, but would serve. Soon afterward she was helping the aged healer of Icaria. 'And no two childbirths are similar, young Penelope. Observe that in this, the *placenta* emerged first. . . . Yesterday's *multipara* gave a breech presentation we had to correct. Birth is a mystery giving birth to mystery.'

Birth.

She would be a *primipara* (like Beryl) giving birth for the first time. And now, her time almost upon her, she rejoiced even as she feared, that she would bear the child of Gaius, the man she loved.

Beryl had no doubts. Having explained the situation repeatedly to the Most High and the Gods of Rome (on her knees before the white altar table) Beryl had further placated the divinities with gifts of fennel and daily offerings of eight salt cakes, one for each day of the Roman week. Having metaphysical favor firmly on Penelope's side, Beryl waited with subdued excitement for the great event. And would it not be an additional safeguard for Penelope to chew fenugreek seeds in homage to the gods of her native Achaia? One should not offend any deity.

Penelope gently turned aside her friend's earnest suggestions, resolving not to have to drink spirits of wine or an opium concoction during parturition, for she wanted to be conscious when her baby was born. Her health was superb. Then she was possessed by a surge of energy, flying from task to task—

Penelope's first mild labor pains began at twilight four days after the Ides of February. The cave home was clean and all was ready and had been for days. Beryl hurried out and came back with Turdo and his sprightly wife, Eunice, and excited Iozans trying to press inside the cave with gifts of food and wine for their 'Spanish healer.' All save Eunice were packed off, but Turdo and several other men would patrol the ledgepaths and be within call if needed. Oblivious to it all, baby Flavianus slept soundly in the bedroom of Beryl and Flavian.

The delivery was to be in the main room. As the slow hours passed and her pains came with increasing intensity, Penelope walked and walked around the chamber. Often she stopped beside the white altar where Gaius had married her. Then on she would go to the makeshift cubicled cupboard of stacked boxes containing the medical instruments of the deceased Ioza physician, and boxes of herbs, ewers of medicine and jars of salves and balms.

"Let me make partridgeberry tea," Beryl kept urging. "Beverage of poplar? Mandragora? Remember when Flavianus was coming, how frightened I was, and you gave me, what was it?"

"Spirits of wine. Alcohol." Penelope smiled between pains.

"It sent my head spinning and muffled the pain. Why, I was giggling when at last my son was born! Take some?"

"I want to endure if I can." Then a tremendous assault of pain racked her and she cried out in labor.

"After my daughter was born, I forgot the pain," cried Eunice. "My Turdo wants a son this time and I have no fears when my time comes. Think of your gods."

Penelope screamed. She had never realized that the human body could endure such extreme pain. The short periods between attacks gave her strength for the next agony. She cried out again and again, and wondered whose voice she heard, so like an animal's . . .

Two hours before dawn, instinct warned that the time was now. She asked Beryl and Eunice to disrobe her, bathe her with soap and water, and rub her thighs and delta with olive oil. Then they must wipe it all off with clean linen and apply straight spirits of wine and pure alcohol to the areas . . . After her instructions were carried out, Penelope sat down, naked, in the stout horseshoe-shaped seat of the birth chair, its heavy oak legs embedded in bricks. Underneath the open seat lay clean blankets spread with layer after layer of sundried linen. Penelope gripped the arms of the chair.

Beryl massaged Penelope's abdomen. Eunice brought all necessities close, to a scrubbed low table: baskets of washed sponges, clean rolls of washed linen, a wooden spindle of coarse washed linen thread to tie the umbilical cord, and sharp little knives and long steel needles threaded in linen, should Beryl have to perform an *episiotomy* and give the child of Tribune Gaius Lacer more room to emerge from the body of its mother—

Penelope was locked in battle, fighting for strength to endure the next great pain. She tried to stop screaming, while praying desperately that Beryl would understand what to do if a tiny foot, hand, or buttocks came first—would Beryl remember how to cut the *perineum* if she had to? Did Beryl retain the lessons Penelope had taught, as to how to use her clean oiled fingers to reach in, twist and turn the baby, so that the head came. She screamed.

"Courage," called Beryl. "Push, beloved! Push! The Most High gives you His *benedictus,* the All-God—push! Gods of Rome, push!"

"I see the head!" piped Eunice.

"—All by itself it is coming!" said Beryl. "I help you, little head and neck—"

Penelope screamed. She screamed. She screamed.

"Little shoulders and folded arms and hands . . ." said Eunice, in awe.

A rolling agony almost tore Penelope out of the delivery chair. It was killing, it was death, it reached a dreadful climax. She let out a piercing wail.

"The birth cry!" Beryl exulted. "The body! The dear little legs and feet! No, Eunice, not scissors yet, wait for the afterbirth!"

Penelope sagged unconscious. She had died and turned into a Niobe fountain, she was a fountain of tears. Her life was pouring out, squirrels were hopping all about. They were binding her watery cascade of a body, she dimly heard a tiny high wail and a slapping sound. She was being carried and laid down on the Tagus Bridge and they put rocks under her thighs to lift her legs. Then the squirrels covered her with fur. No, it was the gray military cloak of Gaius that she treasured. Not that, but the bloody himation her father had died in the night the Romans stormed Icaria a million years ago.

". . . normal bleeding, use linen packs. . . ." said the voice of Lady Enna.

Governor Classicus bent over her, but was savagely thrown to the floor by Gaius. Her love was a giant smiling down. 'Lambs' wool keeps the hands soft, love,' said Gaius. She tried to kiss his fingers. He disappeared.

'. . . perfect baby,' barked the black mastiff, Mars.

'Blameless young woman,' came the distant voice of Commander Liscus.

Semi-conscious, Penelope dimly realized she was in her own bed and a cup was held to her mouth. She swallowed a stinging draught that sent fire down her throat, a liquid stream, then more. She tried to speak and made no sound. *My baby, a daughter?* Then she was whirled away in a blur of shifting light and sound. At last she slept dreamlessly.

She awoke next afternoon, feeling slightly dizzy. There stood Beryl beside the bed, holding a bundle swaddled in white linen.

Sunlight between the shutter slats flashed off the brass skewers in Beryl's black hair.

"Benedictions. A happy awakening," said Beryl, a catch in her voice. "Would you like to meet Gaia Juliana?"

Penelope cried out in joy and held up her arms.

She was holding the daughter of Gaius Julius Lacer.

Silken wisps of dark brown curls lay on Gaia's head. It was somewhat misshapen but, as Penelope knew, would smooth out to a perfect round in time. Red little sleeping face, feminine miniature of her father's . . . beautifully shaped ears, flat and lovely like her sire's.

"Even so new, so new, she looks like him," Penelope whispered, tears rolling down her cheeks.

"She is her father's daughter," beamed Beryl. "Long of body. Do you know, she moved her head three hours after birth, as proud as you please! Such command! Strength—beauty—high forehead—head of hair! She is perfect, all of her!"

"Daughter of Gaius," murmured Penelope.

"How did you and the tribune do it all?" gasped Beryl. "Both of you knew ahead of time Gaia would be herself and not a son! Honey and eggs for girls, iron water for boys?"

They both laughed and Penelope gazed in wonder at her little one. If Gaius could see his daughter right now—

Beryl took the infant. "Do you want me to rub Gaia with salt?" she asked, doubtfully.

Penelope smiled. "Treat her little body tenderly. Use strained olive oil and very little. Do not touch her eyes yet."

"We swabbed them very carefully with the washed cotton pads dipped in cooled, boiled water," said Beryl. "Then she opened her eyes and looked at us. Blue, of course. Then she went to sleep. Healthy eyes, no infection."

Penelope sighed in contentment.

"No salting," sighed Beryl. "It's an old Hebrew custom," she smiled. "Even though I was female, my mother insisted on salting me, although my Roman sire sternly forbade it. He said it would grow hair on my chest. But mother said that salting me brought Jerusalem to her, so my father, loving her so terribly, gave in. No thatch on my chest either. My father was relieved." Beryl broke into hysterical laughter.

Penelope laughed, too, in a glow of triumphant maternity and luxury of delicious relaxation, her body painless. Already she had forgotten the agony of giving birth; already she was dreamily wondering if the next child of Gaius and herself would be a son or another daughter . . .

"Are you coming into milk?" Beryl inquired.

"I think so," said Penelope.

"You can try nursing her after you eat a mighty banquet," said Beryl. "Ask for anything you want. We have enough food for a legion. Stewed rabbit, boiled rice, roast lamb. Barley bread. Cows' milk, goats' milk. Cheese. Raisins, olives, currants, dates, figs. Chestnuts. Wheat gruel. Strained honey." Beryl suppressed a burst of laughter, as baby Gaia stirred in her arms. "The Iozans are celebrating," she said in a loud whisper. "They hail the arrival of a great-granddaughter to our aged crone of a Spanish healer!" She tiptoed out into the corridor and closed the door soundlessly.

Penelope tried to send a thought-message: 'Dear wonderful up at the Sil. Your strength is mine, my strength is yours. And soon lord Flavian will receive a letter from Beryl.' She even slept lightly until Beryl and Eunice came in with huge trays of food.

XXV

During the winter, outdoor work ceased in the drained channel and embankments of the Sil river. Horizontal shafts in the cliffs, test pits pocking the rockbed, the downgrade wooden sluice troughs— all were abandoned to rain and snow, sleet and ice. Wolves prowled the deepway by night, searching for food. If the moon was full, the arrows and lances of legion sharpshooters slew many of the beasts, thus increasing the mine camp's supply of furs for additional warmth against the cold weather. By day, inquisitive wildfowl coming too close were shot for food, as were occasional antelopes and elks peering out of the pinewoods on the south shore.

On that side were the rock-crusheries, smelters and refineries where Gaius kept the prisoners at work with what he knew to be practically valueless gangue according to imperial standards. Rome wanted gold. Not lead, tin, iron, copper, or non-metallic sulphur. Would the commander want the tribune to direct the reduction of iron-bearing rocks? Commander Liscus would not. Gold came first.

Gaius would salute, and inspect the prisoners working huge leather bellows, clearing the ash-pits in the vaulted cellars under the melting-chamber floors and keeping hot chaff burning in the brick furnaces. Occasionally he glanced at the lonely little clay molds waiting for gold and silver. This would make him smile inwardly. Frequently he had to force out optimistic dreams of *aurum* and concentrate on the clay crucibles and fire-bricks, the flues and chimneys. Clinker must be removed from furnace walls periodically . . . the fire-bars must have a bedding of clay before the crucibles were placed . . . When all was going well in the smelters and refineries he would then inspect the stone and log huts where chained workers in fur pelts and caps ground rocks in mortars and washed the macerated fragments in wire sieves, jigging the mesh baskets in troughs of water. Occasionally beadlets of gold and heavier-than-gold native grains of silver settled to the bottom of the shaken containers. But silver in metallic state was very rare; unlike gold, the glistening white metal was usually combined with other elements. Such precious bits were put aside to be melted.

To obtain gold and silver too finely-mixed with crushed rock to settle to the base of the wire jigs, Gaius had the most promising treated by amalgamation. Crushed to a pulp in water, the ore was then agitated by sticks with quicksilver; this united the gold and silver flecks. Next, running streams of water coalesced the amalgam and extra mercury, the masses falling to pools of mercury in the bottom of stone trenches. After the earthy matter was washed away, the mixtures were shovelled into coarse canvas filter sacks and excess quicksilver squeezed out between wooden paddles. This carried away infinitesimal amounts of dissolved precious metal and left a pasty amalgam in the bags.

These blends were emptied into the clay cauldrons and placed in the enclosed brick furnaces. Air was fed in by pipes, the iron doors closed, and the amalgam heated red. This separated the gold and silver from the mercury, but the latter condensed into vapor gathered into stone bottles for future use. The nearly pure gold and silver remaining was cast into small, plate-like bars. The admixed gold and silver (often brittle) was then taken to the refineries and placed in earthen pots, separately buried in brickdust, common salt and sulphate of iron. Again it was heated red. This melted the silver but did not soften the gold. After beads of silver and unwanted elements oozed out and were absorbed by brickdust, the gold was purified and ready for the ingot molds.

Smelting and refining of lead, zinc, and copper ore went on for a time until Commander Liscus ordered it stopped, as silver was as reluctant as gold to come forth. By the end of March there were two small gold bars and six little oblong wedges of silver locked away in the headquarters cabin of Rufus Liscus. Long before then Gaius had lost interest in it all; by then he was ready to declare war on Beryl.

What was the matter with Domina Beryl? Had she no mercy for Gaius, racking his mind with rising anxiety over Penelope who had surely given birth by now. Flavian's discreet attempts to learn about new births in Ioza went unanswered by his wife. Her communications, to Gaius, were ridiculous.

Aside from the happy task of caring for baby Flavianus, Beryl bore many burdens. She and the village women were stuffing new goathide mattresses with duck feathers, these for adults. Mattresses for infants were easier to make: heavy linen sheaths filled with downy fleece. Beryl also helped the Spanish healer make tonics from iris and lily bulbs, to name but two of the concoctions produced from herbs, roots and plants brought to Ioza by villagers gleaning in the mountain meadows. And would Flavian kindly stop harassing Beryl with questions about babies? His son was sturdy and handsome.

If he found life rigorous at the mines, why not ask for a transfer? Was he not nearing the end of his long service in the legions of Rome? Beryl could use him at home. He could render goose fat. Wash their son's swaddles. Card wool and sing lullabies to Flavianus. It was obvious to Beryl that Flavian had no idea what it was to be a mother . . .

These missives baffled and infuriated Gaius. Of further irritation were the guarded inquiries of Commander Liscus as to the welfare of Penelope. Had her child been born yet? A son or a daughter? As soon as Gaius heard, he would inform the noble commander.

Sitting in his cabin the second day of March, Gaius at last made a silent truce with Beryl. She was protecting Penelope and Penelope's—and his—baby. Probably the most astute procedure, he mused, his thoughts momentarily on Classicus.

The door burst open and Flavian rushed in.

"Congratulations! It's a girl!" Flavian was laughing heartily.

Gaius snatched the latest scroll from Beryl and raced through trivia until his eyes fastened on: 'Babies, babies, from lambs, piglets, goatlets and chicks to humans. The most beautiful—perfection—is the great-granddaughter of our Spanish healer. So strong and gurgly.

I still remember how she yelled when I spanked her little butt right after she was born. She and her mother came through it all superbly, but Eunice and I had to deliver the baby. We dared not trust the infant's great-grandmother. The old one was so overwhelmed, you would have thought that she was giving birth again. We had to put her to bed, get her out of the way . . .'

Gaius sprang up. "I'm a father—my daughter's name is Gaia Juliana! Penelope is safe, my baby is safe—"

"Now you know that feeling, sir," roared Flavian, clapping him on the back.

"—But how old is my daughter—?"

The orderly wisely advised, "When Beryl gets around to it, she may let me know. Or she may not. Maybe better if she doesn't, sir."

Gaius realized the prudence of such a procedure and his mind filled with gratitude for Beryl and regret that he had thought her careless and indifferent. Then his thoughts began to whirl. He must get Flavian out of the cabin before the soldier suspected that Tribune Lacer was excited on two counts. He hustled Flavian to the door.

"Have to test some quartz," Gaius said, boyishly. "Very important. Think it's got goldwire formations. Quartz."

"Ha," grinned Flavian, letting himself be pushed out, "sir, I vow you won't be thinking about gold today." He saluted and marched away.

Bolting the door against any more sudden visitors, Gaius threw pineknots in a flaming brazier near a half open cabin window, then sat down at his table and gave himself over to enthusiastic visions of the future. A future of freedom and prosperity for Penelope, Gaia and himself. Now he had more than a dream. Now he must start to plan and weigh the vital factors. Disclose his secret knowledge of the virgin goldfield he had discovered? Or withold until better times? The last was unequivocally the best and only security against gold-mad conspirators, for Gaius was grimly determined that such men would never find the rich ore territory that his horse Dawn had stumbled into for him that tawny golden day last October . . .

. . . He, Flavian, and two infantrymen had been galloping northeast of the dam for exercise and stopped by a jagged cliff that had split nearly in two, vertically, as if chopped apart by the ax of a giant.

"We'll go through the stone narrows and see what's on the other side," Flavian decided. "Tribune, sir, go first?"

Gaius had reined Dawn through the cleft, which was barely wide enough for the mare's body to penetrate. They emerged in a desolate valley of stunted pines, brambles, rocks and tall, coarse grasses. It was rimmed by mountains. Only the twitterings of unseen birds and dry skitterings of small reptiles through the grass disturbed the brooding silence of the sun-drenched region. Bleached old trees struck dead by lightning littered the dreary terrain.

Suddenly Dawn had slid down on her right foreleg. Gaius dismounted and found his horse's hoof sunk in a hole.

Flavian and his two men got down and all tried to free the mare. The harder they worked the deeper sank her leg. Dawn whickered and snorted, whether in pain or equine disgust, or both, Gaius could not tell. Then she let out a bellow of sound.

"Think her leg's broken, sir?" Flavian asked, tensely. "Is she done for, sir? Going to have to kill her?"

Gaius was agonized. He loved the thoroughbred.

"Sir, here's a dagger," muttered Flavian. "Me and my men'll ride on, give you privacy. Be quick. I know what that mare means to you. We'll bury her for you. Sorry—" He handed Gaius a dagger, then he and his two soldiers mounted their horses and rode away.

Gaius was still on his knees trying to dislodge Dawn's trapped leg. Then furiously he dug a hole around the animal's left foreleg. It sank in; now she bore the downward pulling strain equally on both front legs. She was not struggling.

"Help me, beauty," Gaius pleaded. "Your leg's not broken, and not going to break. Pull, girl, pull. We'll get you out—"

He grasped the fetlock of her right leg and began pulling.

Suddenly the mare tossed her head—and out came the trapped right hoof from the hole. Then she tossed her ivory mane and extricated her left leg without help from Gaius. Snorting in victory, she gave Gaius an affectionate nuzzle and then began curvetting flirtatiously. She was not even lame.

Gaius sighed with relief and began filling the dangerous holes —then he suddenly saw a yellow-red glint in the pit that had almost killed his horse. Reaching down, he pulled out a glistening mass bigger than his fist. Not trusting his eyes, he tested the ore with Flavian's dagger.

"Gold," he whispered, as a tiny green lizard undulated past his knees. "Gold . . . almost solid gold . . ." It was the largest nugget he had ever seen. Then hearing the shouts and approaching hoof-beats of Flavian and his men, Gaius thrust the precious discovery down into the earth and daggered in gravel, sod, and tangled roots. He was tamping both filled holes under his boots when Flavian and his troopers arrived and dismounted. Dawn cantered forward, eager to be stroked.

"Congratulations!" said Flavian. "Sir, how did you get her out? Blistering hades, your golden girl is good as ever!"

"Dawn is a person," said Gaius over the fast beating of his heart. "She worked, I worked. Together we got her free." He talked on, hardly aware of what he was saying. He was thinking: does one huge gold chunk indicate a virgin field? Or had the nugget washed down from the Cantabrian mountains looming around the desolate valley where he stood?

"We'll eat here in Skeleton Forum," chuckled Flavian. "Those whitened tree trunks look like downed wrestlers."

Gaius nearly shouted, *"No!"* Then he sat down on the ground covering the nugget while Flavian's men tethered the horses and got out meat and a wineskin from knapsacks. Trying to eat and drink with his customary good appetite, Gaius surreptitiously studied the earth, rocks, bushes and grass.

At length Flavian said, "Our Roman *Togati* say this general region is haunted, sir. Centuries ago this was a huge mountain, a volcano, they tell me. Then one fine day there's an earthquake and Father Mountain, his belly full of fire and brimstone, lets go. Peace to his shade, eh, tribune?" Flavian tilted the goatskin flab high and let a stream of watered red wine gush down into his mouth. He handed the skin flab to Gaius. He drank and passed the wineskin on to an infantryman. Then Flavian began telling his troopers about one of his battle campaigns.

This gave Gaius time to look around lazily, idly noting mossy rock crests almost buried under bleached tree corpses and thorn bushes. Igneous rocks . . . metamorphic formations, he pondered. Look for ochre stains . . . carefully, or you won't see them . . . so much high grass and overgrowths— Over there? Where parched dead bushes divide slightly? Faint reddish blotches—ochre stains!

The ochre color—yellow oxide of iron—supposedly the best index of gold! One big nugget does not indicate a historic strike—yet how about those oxide of iron signs? He must return and examine the site carefully. Risk? Tremendous—since Flavian and his men might find gold at the same time . . . Yet his orderly still could not tell the difference between gold and iron. And Flavian's infantrymen? Gaius decided to take a chance. . . .

A few days later Gaius suggested to Commander Liscus that styptic earth for metal refining might be found northeast of the dam and was given permission to make a short trip of exploration. Flavian and six of his men went along this time.

At first Gaius put Flavian and his troops to work with spades and shovels outside the rock walls of 'Skeleton Forum.' Then he changed his mind and led the way into the dismal valley. He selected what he hoped was a useless section of stony soil far from the ochre-stained stones he had previously observed. While Flavian and his men exhumed dirt, Gaius gradually moved away until concealed by whitened hulks of dead trees and thorn bushes. Then he saw a nugget the size of his thumb; the mass was remarkably pure gold—Next he nearly stumbled over a tangle of roots partially hiding what looked like a yellow-white clam. It was mixed gold and silver. His body cold with excitement he was soon staring in astonishment at a semi-exposed big quartzhead thickly-interlaced and encrusted with shining gold bands and flakes. He estimated that he saw only the peak of the precious lode imprisoning the gold; its mass, similar to an iceberg, must be deep in the earth. The crystalline mineral matrix head containing the gold had been partway concealed under a cap of cracked rock. Gaius hid the two new nuggets next to the quartz and covered all with dead pine boughs and limestone fragments. He erected a rough cairn of coarse gravel to mark the site. Then he sauntered back to Flavian and the troops, noting with relief that so far the men had dug up only sandy dry earth, tree roots, and small stones.

"This stuff any use to you, sir?" asked Flavian. "I'd say only the armored reptiles love it. Awhile ago I saw a baby armadillo. The thing saw us and rolled into a ball and got away—"

"Gold!" yelled an infantryman. "Tribune, sir, gold!" The excited veteran held out a reddish-brown chunk.

One look and Gaius felt his heartbeats slow down. Gravely he examined the metallic specimen. "Copper," he said, and let it drop.

"Ha, I found myself some silver," said Flavian.

Gaius eyed the glistening sample. "No—mica," he said. He was sure it was silver.

Flavian threw away his find. "Too bad," he groaned. "Gold turns out to be iron and silver is mica." He picked up a gleaming yellow-red ball the size of a cherry. "This, men, is iron," Flavian chaffed.

"See how it glitters?" He threw it into a bush. He had thrown away a gold nugget.

Gaius joined in the groans of defeat while watching two soldiers dig up good-sized gold chunks and promptly bury the precious ore under shovelfuls of dirt.

"Sir, you want to take any of this stuff to the Sil smelters and crusheries?" asked Flavian.

Gaius picked up a handful of reddish earth and studied it. "Hardly worth the trouble. Iron ore if the commander wants it, but very low-grade."

Flavian guffawed. "If you find any more iron, sir, the commander will go stark, raving mad. We'll leave it to the armadillos and lizards. Back to camp for us."

In reveries Gaius had relived his discovery of Gold Valley last warm and colorful October, but his chilled hands at last reminded him that he was in the Sil settlement on a wintry March day—the father of a daughter. What did she look like? She would have fair hair like Penelope, of course. Blue eyes . . .

When—how—and to whom should he disclose the location of the virgin goldfield? To his distant master Apollodorus? How? Not by letter! And now was certainly not the time to announce the great discovery, or men such as Classicus would stampede to the region. Then what was the wise and honest course to pursue? He always reached the same conclusion: wait for the day of rejoicing when Marcus Trajan became emperor.

That day had to come, it would come. He tried to persuade himself that he placed no faith in astrologers' prophecies . . . (but the seers were uncannily prescient). From the humblest soothsayer reading the future in a hoop of sand to distinguished scholars of zodiacal charts—all agreed that Marcus Ulpius Trajan, the soldier of dedicated virtue, the brave Trajan, the patriotic Trajan, the Trajan feared and hated by eastern barbarian armies, would be elevated to the Curule Chair.

When?

The predictors were not in agreement as to the date Trajan would don the Purple Toga. Some claimed it would happen the coming September or October; others solemnly announced that Trajan would not be hailed *Princeps* until the following year.

Gaius stamped around his cabin, adding more faggots to the brazier, and thinking about a mixture of concerns. The blackcloaks were in winter camps south of the mines . . . they were peaceable, however, and mail couriers came and went without any trouble. Another long year to wait and worry over the safety of Penelope and Gaia? Was Liscus a gold conspirator? And was Gaius coming to admire his half-brother? No. Yet . . . ?

Most of all, was he placing the future of his wife and daughter and himself in the hands of Field Marshal Marcus Ulpius Trajan?

"I am," he said to the flaming brazier. "I'm vigilant. I've found virgin gold. Now I have to learn patience. Patience."

XXVI

Balbus, the old trusty who worshipped Tribune Gaius Lacer, had worked for months trying to win the prisoners over to his belief that in time they might be pardoned. At first he was sneeringly muttered down by the men in fetters—but that did not deter Balbus. Patiently he chipped away at the hatred of the shackled workers, telling them over and over that they were adequately fed, warmly clothed, and wore wooden armor and log helmets when they worked in the rock galleries and pits. A few of the men began to listen.

Pressing his advantage, Balbus explained that manacled slaves in the Egyptian and Greek mines were worked and beaten until they died. How different all was here in the Sil mines! Why despair? Admittedly a few workers had died, but from natural causes, not flogging. And who knew—? The magnificent Emperor Nerva might hear of their faithful work in the Sil mines some day. Better, kind old Nerva might pardon their petty felonies and expose wrong accusations of men innocent of any crime, but forced to work in chains at the Sil.

But the unhobbled old trusty actually made little progress until he sagely singled out Zamil. The belligerent young Roman of black hair and whiskers and broken nose was the secret chief of the five thousand prisoners. For months Zamil and his aides chained to each other had planned a mass rebellion with picks, axes and shovels, when warm weather came. They would hack off their gyves, kill the legionaries, and escape into the mountains.

Balbus wisely made no protest and listened respectfully when Zamil insisted that he had been imprisoned for a murder he had not committed; he had never killed or harmed any human being.

He also told Balbus that many of the men were equally blameless of charges of rape, arson, theft and murder. "So hold your tongue, grandfather," Zamil would mutter each time Balbus talked to him.

So affairs stood until late in April when Balbus had an inspiration. He began praising Tribune Gaius Lacer to the men. Who had saved fifty of them from the falling cliff? Tribune Lacer. Who was a slave? Tribune Lacer. Who worked with the fire of hope in his eyes and muscles? Tribune Lacer. If the tribune could hope and work like a freeman, why not Zamil and all the rest of the men in irons? Some day Zamil and many other prisoners might be exonerated and go their free ways. But the tribune, who had saved Zamil, Balbus, and forty-nine other men, might be a bondsman until he died. Therefore, pleaded Balbus, why plot an outbreak that might result in the deaths of the soldiers and that of Tribune Lacer? Kill the Roman who had saved them? Kill the Roman who insisted on humane treatment, fresh drinking-water, wooden gear and fur pelts and stout boots for the laborers? And why endanger Commander Rufus Liscus?

Zamil laughed sarcastically.

Balbus did not give up. He talked on . . .

One day at the end of May, the old trusty was in the stables at the east end of camp, where Zamil and his crew were currying horses and shovelling manure into buckets.

"Zamil," said Balbus, "you and your men are doing a good job."

"We love our work, grandfather," said Zamil. "You have no hobbles. Why not light out for northern Gaul? Swim the Britannicus channel." He stopped to stroke the satiny neck of Dawn. She whickered with pleasure.

"Men," said Balbus, "you mustn't plan to escape. It's wrong."

"Hail the emperor," laughed Zamil. "Our loving Caesar. He sent me a letter the other day. He wants to adopt me. I wrote back, 'So does the King of Parthia and the King of Arabia.' I'm particular about who adopts me, grandfather."

The other prisoners roared with laughter.

"Zamil," said Balbus, "if you give the command, the rest of the men will obey you. Why don't you spread the word that they must work it out, wait it out, not endanger Tribune Gaius and Commander Liscus, and hope for pardons?"

"Grandfather, I am close to tears," grumbled the Roman, but he looked with interest at the old trusty. "So the tribune's a slave and may never be a freedman. So he saved my life. So if I lead the prisoners' revolt, the tribune will probably die."

"So will I," said Balbus. "I'm a Roman. I'll fight with them. I'll have to fight you, Zamil."

Zamil broke into helpless chuckles. "You weigh about as much as that black mastiff. As the commander would say, 'Indeed.' "

Balbus wept. "The legions wouldn't take me when I was a young man. I was too spindly and weak. But if I ever get a chance to fight for Rome, I will. Even now. It's something in me."

"What'd they get you for?" asked Zamil, starting to wipe down the white stallion of Commander Liscus.

"I owed twenty silvers," sighed Balbus. He walked up and down the straw-littered aisle between the stalls, picking his way in and out of the chains linking the waists of the men in Zamil's crew. "To think that some day, if you do the honorable thing, you might go free," Balbus wept. "And then you wouldn't have the deaths of decent Romans like Lacer and Liscus on your consciences. To think what you might be—" He trudged to the open log doorway. "I've lost. I thought I was fighting for the only right cause."

"Wait," barked Zamil. "Who said anything about losing? Balbus, you're a brave man. I'm not going to lead the revolt."

The trusty wheeled around in happy astonishment.

"You've convinced me." The big young Roman was smiling. "Pass the word along. Tell the men that I command them to work it out, wait it out. No hacking off the gyves, for a while, at least."

His mates nodded. "Better the way Balbus wants it," said one man. "Better . . ." The word passed from tongue to tongue.

Balbus joyfully visited the long wooden sheds where another group of prisoners were swabbing cold stone latrine seats with soapy brushes. Shakily he relayed the command of Zamil.

"What Zamil tells us to do, we do," said a shaggy Briton. "I've no complaints. Cleanest open prison yet. Our villa in the wilderness. Soap the latrine seats! Bury the manure! Stone the rats so we won't have a pestilence, and for relaxation, toss gold and silver bars back and forth!"

His crew laughed good-naturedly. All were in sound health and clothed in bearskins, wolfpelts and elkhides.

"Zamil's a brave and honorable Roman," said Balbus.

"The best," sighed a bearded old Jew. "I even ask the Most High to bless the tribune and the commander. I, a Jew, asking benedictions for Romans. Yea, I do."

180

"Let it be so," said a blond Persian, giving the Hebrew a brotherly thump on his bearskin tunic.

Winter had overstayed, Spring had come weeks late, and a chilly white mist beclouded the log huts and cobbled streets of the Sil village early in June. It was morning and Balbus was making his way from the east end latrines and stables to the cookhouse, deepwell shack and supply buildings on higher ground at the west end of the camp. To his right, in a steep fenced pasture near a Roman road pointing north, two other trusties kept watch over expedition mares and their foals. Balbus was in excellent spirits and rather pleased that Tribune Lacer's golden mare had produced an ivory-white colt sired by the stallion of Commander Liscus. A good omen, thought the chief trusty.

Now that the men were united in support of the Imperium that held them in chains, morale was excellent. Having to manufacture work, Balbus often visited the officers' cookhouse to watch the prisoner mess crew unloop long links of red beef sausages from the rafters, cut wedges from huge rounds of coarse white cheese, lift *amphorae* of wine and brined olives from wall-racks and pump leather bellows to keep fires blazing under cauldrons of rice, mutton, and wild boar quarters. Foodstuffs and cattle arrived periodically from Corunna, escorted by whitecloak *Togati* warriors. The arrival of each wagon train and herd of cattle was always hailed by the prisoners. While their food was less varied than that of officers and troops, they got enough meat, wine and bread to sustain health. And next to hoping for pardons, food was of paramount importance to the rock gangs.

On walked Balbus, wearing his thick brown wool cloak like a toga. He sniffed the wet, cold air, and wondered what had happened to Spring. Passing the lean-to huts of the prison compound and the clayed-log bath-house for prisoners, he found another cause to be grateful to Tribune Lacer and Commander Liscus. The prisoners were unchained and bathed once a week . . . Briskly the old man strode past officers' cabins and the steam-bath house where prisoners kept hot rocks ready to drop into plunges when an officer wanted a bath. Stopping to catch his breath and remind himself that he was sixty-four, not twenty-four, Balbus gazed south across the rain-puddled rockway of the Sil.

Most of the prisoners and all the soldiers except Tribune Gaius Lacer and Commander Liscus were over there. Brown smoke and occasional green gobbets of vapor gushed from the tall chimnies of smelters and refineries. Prisoners trudged about, chains dragging, with shovels and buckets of smoking dross to dump in the riverbed. Cavalry guards cantered their horses up and down the vast clearing, and roamed the pinewoods to the south. Then the trusty heard hoof-beats from the north, and turned to see who was coming.

It was a *Togati* astride a saddleless black pony. He looked terrifying. His face peered out from between the agape toothed jaws of a grizzly hide and over the pelt he wore a rainsoaked white toga. As the horseman came close, Balbus saw his drooping blond mustachios and recognized him as a superstitious whitecloak drover for the food wagons from Corunna. He and Balbus had become acquainted months ago. The Roman Celt feared thunder, lightning, lizards, and sundry other visible and invisible, animate and inanimate, signs of the displeasure of the gods.

The friendly warrior slid off his pony and addressed Balbus. "Greetings, Roman *frater,* oh honor age," said the newcomer. "Not good the auspices for me. Evil brews if I dare do what I dare not do."

"Salutations, brother Roman," replied Balbus. "Why the dread, friend?"

"Why my fear?" asked the *Togati.* "The dead eagle in the valley? The whining wind of the mountains? Not good. But greater the evil if I dare approach the god, Gaius Lacer. Where abides he? Where is his shrine?"

Balbus gestured toward a log hut roofed in slate. Chunks of limestone, sandstone, granite, quartz and buckets of loose gravel were piled at each side of the oak-slab door.

"Oh sacred elder, will you do part of my duty for me, for Rome?" asked the Celt. "It is a matter of piety and honor. *Pro Roma!* Will you tell Gaius the god that a fishing vessel docked at Corunna five days ago after battling Father Neptune and the *Atlanticus* for weeks. That the mighty Verus Maturus has received no answers from messages sent by sea to god Gaius? Therefore has the great Maturus continued to send scrolls—such as the one I now give to you." The warrior withdrew a rolled parchment from under his toga and thrust it to Balbus. "By our holy oaths we swear this message has not been opened; nor does the courageous mariner who brought it know its content. Tell the immortal Gaius that other vessels have gone down in the Atlantic which would have brought him earlier tidings. And did our honorable chieftain entrust this invocation to me, the bravest of his six remaining warriors. But great is my fear; I dare not hand the scroll to the deity."

Mystified, old Balbus read the wooden address tag, its heavy cords wound around the parchment and plentifully sealed in wax: URGENT TRIBUNE GAIUS JULIUS LACER. THE SIL MINING CAMP. ROMAN NORTHWEST GALICIA. BY ATLANTIC PASSAGE.

The warrior slapped his black pony on the flanks. *"Avaunt!"* He whipped his horse north on the road as Balbus walked to the tribune's cabin and knocked. The door opened and Gaius looked quizzically at the trusty. Then he smiled in recognition as the old man said, "Noble sir, a message for you." He bobbed a bow and hastened off, feeling uneasy and somewhat superstitious himself . . .

Alone in his cabin, Gaius ripped off the strings and wax, then unrolled the thick parchment. He read:

CONFIDENTIAL TO GAIUS JULIUS LACER AND RUFUS LISCUS FROM MATURUS OF FARTHER SPAIN. IT IS MY FIRM CONVICTION THAT BLACKCLOAKS UNDER MALENDI PLAN TO ATTACK THE SIL MINES AND IF THERE IS GOLD TO CLAIM IT. IT IS ALSO MY PRIVATE INFORMATION THAT CORNELIUS CLASSICUS HAS AN UNDERSTANDING WITH MALENDI AND HAS INFLAMED THE ARVACAN BLACKCLOAK PRINCE AGAINST ROME AND MYSELF. I BELIEVE MALENDI HAS BEEN PERSUADED THAT HIS PEOPLE AND LANDS ARE ENDANGERED BY THE LEGIONS I CONTROL IN FARTHER SPAIN AND BY THE ROMANS MINING IN THE SIL REGION. MALENDI IGNORES MY FRIENDLY MESSAGES BUT IS IN CONSTANT COMMUNICATION WITH CLASSICUS. MY EFFORTS TO OBTAIN MORE LEGIONS FROM ROME HAVE BEEN FUTILE. LADY ENNA, DIVORCED BY HER SPOUSE, RESIDES IN MY GADES LEGATION. SO DOES THE NOBLE FRONTINUS. HAD I ANY AUTHORITY OVER COMMANDER RUFUS LISCUS I WOULD ORDER HIM TO ABANDON THE MINES AND MOVE HIS MEN NORTH UNTIL MALENDI DAMPS HIS WAR FEVER. LADY ENNA BELIEVES THAT CORNELIUS CLASSICUS LOANED RUFUS LISCUS SEVERAL THOUSAND IN

GOLD ON THE STRENGTH OF A NONEXISTENT LEGACY. I DEDUCE THAT LISCUS IS A DUPE. LACER IS A DUPE. MALENDI IS A DUPE. I AM A DUPE. ALL DUPES OF CORNELIUS CLASSICUS. SO ARE ALL THE MEN AT THE SIL MINES. ONE MORE VITAL MATTER: A GLADIATOR, TURDO VISITED ME MONTHS AGO: A LOYAL CHAMPION OF GAIUS LACER. I CANNOT LOCATE HIM. I AM CUT OFF FROM MY THREE LEGIONS SOMEWHERE SOUTH OF YOU. THEIR COMMANDING GENERAL WAS SLAIN BY THE BLACK-CLOAKS IN A RECENT BATTLE NORTH OF THE TAGUS BRIDGE. I PRAY FOR YOU. VIGILANCE. VICTORY. VALE.

Gaius stared at the letter and then at a hollowed rock half-filled with gold dust— When he came to his senses he had the small daggers in his hands. He snatched up the parchment and rushed outside, almost knocking down Flavian who stood talking to Balbus.

Gaius ran along the cobbled street to the large headquarters cabin of the commander. He knocked frantically. Mars began barking inside—

At last the irritated voice of Rufus called, "Who comes?"

"Tribune Lacer! Urgent, urgent!"

"Mars, to your haunches," came the bored response of Liscus. "Enter, Tribune Gaius Julius Lacer. I am overwhelmed and honored—"

Gaius burst in and slammed the door shut. Mars panted at the feet of his master, who sat at a long pine table piled with scrolls and dimly-burning lamps.

"Salute," muttered Liscus.

Moving his right arm mechanically, Gaius thought, here it is at last. If Liscus is a hireling of Classicus—no, I've never really believed that, Penelope is right, but if my brother still hates me—do I believe that? No, never have—

"If the excited tribune wants to have the workers cast iron ingots, the answer is still *non*," observed Rufus. "The gallant tribune will remember that I want gold."

Gaius shot back, "Do you, commander?"

Liscus' bearded face became livid with rage. Then his usual smiling mask took command. "And what is so tremendously urgent— may I ask? If you want to make plumbago crucibles from lead, to vary the monotony of using clay and because—"

"Commander! The blackcloaks are going to attack us!"

Rufus sprang up. Gaius put the letter before him on his table. He snatched it and read silently. His face whitened. Slowly his shocked blue eyes looked at Gaius.

"Listen to me," Gaius bore in. "If I could give you my name, I would. I've known we were brothers for a year, ever since the night you talked to the murdering Classicus. You're no henchman of Classicus. We're brothers! You don't accept bribes. I don't. Perhaps you came to Spain to track me down. I sympathize with your hate. Your mother was a British slave. I'm a slave. Our father—"

Rufus slumped in his chair while Mars began growling.

"You're not going to send Mars at me," Gaius shouted. "I've watched you for months. You're not a killer. You don't hate me any more, Rufus. I don't hate you. You saved Penelope and my daughter— Now we're going to have to fight for our lives. What will we fight for? For our honor, our families." To his astonishment, Rufus looked suffering.

"I thought Classicus was my friend," said Rufus, bitterly. "He loaned me—money. Told me—"

"Told you lies," Gaius broke in. "He slandered me—but that's in the past. Rufus, you have two little daughters. You divorced your wife. Rufus, listen. I'll tell you everything—" Out poured an avalanche of words. Turdo's hidden tunnel in Ioza—the aides to victory—and Gold Valley. All of that, mixed in with Gaius' driving determination to win freedom for Penelope, Gaia, and himself. At last he talked himself out.

Rufus sat like a stone man in a bronze breastplate and scarlet cloak. "My mother was a slave," he said, vacantly. "Consul Julius Lacer sold her to Herennius Liscus when she was carrying me. I thought Herennius was my real father. After he died, I found his old diary. I began to hate—"

"It's all past, we're together," Gaius interrupted. "Penelope was right. From the first she insisted that you were a man of honor! You are, always have been!" He glanced at the quivering mastiff. Mars was growling softly. "Rufus—Classicus thinks he has us trapped. I see his plan now! Malendi's thousands will attack, hope to kill us, and take the gold. Who will get it? Classicus. Who will be blamed? Governor Maturus and the evil left over from the reign of Domitian! Maturus may go down, too, and we who are dead will be labelled absconders and traitors! Do you see it, Rufus? Brother?"

Daringly he moved to the table and touched the clenched hands of Rufus.

Mars let out a gurgling growl but did not move.

"Talk . . . on," whispered Rufus.

Awkwardly Gaius began, "Your treatment of the prisoners. Everything I asked for. Wooden armor and helmets. Sufficient food. Furs to keep the men warm. No flogging— Rufus, a few days ago, the trusty-in-chief told me the prisoners want to work for pardons. Rufus, you're a Roman. A Roman officer. What is Rome's you will fight for—and hold." Gaius sat on the table and looked earnestly into his brother's dazed blue eyes, watched sympathetically as the commander wiped his eyes with his red cloak. Then Gaius laid the aids to victory on the table. Then the dagger Rufus had given him in the night-camp.

Rufus began talking quietly. "Put the aides to victory back in your boots, Gaius. I know nothing about them. So you found a virgin goldfield. Keep it confidential until Trajan . . . *Vero*. You are right. I don't hate my young brother Gaius. Together we will fight the blackcloaks."

"I knew it," Gaius shouted. "Hold the mines and south shore for Rome!"

Rufus' eyes were admiring as he looked at his brother. "Gaius, it would call for a military genius."

"—Which my brother Rufus is," Gaius exulted. "You're already planning it!"

Rufus had a newly excited look as he clasped Gaius' hands. "Could we hold the Sil territory without them?" he meditated. "We might . . . if the prisoners agreed to fight for Rome . . . diversionary tactics on south shore. We are prepared. We divide the blackcloak forces by surprise and reverse counterattack—I do have a plan." He smiled grimly. "But first I will send a stream of messages by Atlantic passage to Maturus and ask him to relay those across Our Sea to Italy. My letters will go to the chief of mines in *Roma*. I will inform him of blackcloak activity and my fears that the mines will be attacked. Therefore, I am sending the gold direct to *Roma*— through blackcloak territory—as a test. I will write exactly how I propose to accomplish that . . . miracle?"

"How?" Gaius was thrilled and admiring.

Rufus got up. "The chief of mines in Rome has sent me several letters recently asking that we return the Archimedes Screws. We realize, now, that Malendi reads all letters going by courier to and from the Sil. Therefore, the Arvacan chieftain realizes that Rome wants its handsome water-lifting machines returned. Now . . . say we conceal gold and silver bars in the helical bronze tubes of the dismantled machines? And ship them by wagon through Malendi's domain . . . that would not excite suspicion, would it?"

Gaius began laughing.

Rufus looked innocently at his brother. "Gaius, are you laughing at me?" Then the commander began to laugh. At last he said, "My young brother, get that chisel and mallet from the corner."

Puzzled, Gaius obeyed.

"Roll up your sleeves," said Rufus. "I will now give you proofs that you can trust me. First I am going to crack off those metal armbands of slavery you wear. If your master, Apollodorus, sues me later, I shall retain the noble Maturus as my defense counsel. Gaius, brace your left arm against the table."

After the commander broke and delicately removed the jagged metals so as not to injure Gaius' arms, he laid the riven circlets on the table and gazed thoughtfully at his mastiff. "Now for the next demonstration that my young brother's trust in me is well-placed." Again he glanced at the black canine. "Mars! Stand!"

The beast got up on all fours.

Rufus put his hand on Gaius and said to the dog, "Mars—obey this man! Obey this man! He is my brother." To the dazzled Gaius, the officer smiled, "Always address our mastiff by his name, then the command. Repeat the order if you want to."

Gaius heard himself saying, "Mars—on your belly."

Instantly the giant dog flattened out.

"Mars—to your haunches," Gaius added.

Up scrambled the beast on his hindquarters. His red tongue lolled out and his white fangs gleamed in the dim light of the thick-walled headquarters cabin.

"Mars," breathed Gaius, "greet me. Greet me."

Up reared the animal and laid his paws on Gaius' shoulder plates.

"Good Mars," said Gaius. "Mars—down."

The mastiff lowered himself to a standing position.

"Mars—salute this man. He is your master. He is my brother." Gaius pointed to Rufus.

Up went the dog's right paw.

"Good dog, brave dog," said Gaius. "Mars—to your haunches."

The mastiff squatted obediently, panting noisily and making soft barks of pleasure.

"Good Mars," said Gaius, with emotion. "You saved my life in the battle of the canyon. Your master sent you to save me. I owe my life to you and your master—my brother."

Rufus spoke shakily. "Mars now replies to Tribune Gaius: 'I, Mars, was saved by the brave tribune from the attack of the black-cloak in the ravine battle.' "

The brothers looked at each other. Gaius could not see clearly. The chisel gleamed dully on Rufus' table, and the ruptured armbands Rufus had struck off blurred. He felt his brother's friendly hands and sensed loyal blue eyes watching. The reconciliation formed a picture in his mind of . . . the Tagus Bridge.

A hearty voice called from outside: "Commander! I heard the tribune shouting. Do you need me, sir? It's Flavian!"

"Enter," Rufus called.

The door wrenched open. Hard-breathing Flavian in battle gear stood on the threshold. At last he saluted.

"Greetings," said Rufus. "This is my brother, Gaius Julius Lacer. We were getting acquainted."

The orderly seemed to shrink in his steel band armor. "Blistering hades," he sighed, "am I glad to hear that, sir. Sirs . . ."

Rufus braced his hands on the table. He was assured and confident. "*Optio,* summon my three cavalry adjutants. Bring your aide. We are holding an immediate military council here. A matter of security and absolute secrecy."

"*Bona,* sir." Flavian saluted and hustled out.

Now Gaius was trembling. "I think we're both feeling like newborns," Rufus smiled.

All Gaius could do was nod.

XXVII

Undetected by Rome and the people of Hither Spain, the province had been administered since middle April by a new governor *sub rosa.* Zinga Rutilia now functioned as the *Legatus Augusti Pro Praetore.* Subofficials, soldiers and servants in the New Carthage legation understood that a change had taken place, but remained faithfully silent. Even though the honorable excellency Cornelius Classicus had been talking and acting queerly of late, he was their genial lord protector under Emperor Nerva.

Hear and forget, see and forget, speak not of the proconsul's odd behavior, for indiscretions might stir up an inquiry from Rome—so went the commands of the high prefect to his aide, the chief decurion, and on down to the humblest slaves working the spits in the kitchen hearths. For it was well known to all that from the beginning the imperium of Nerva Caesar tottered on shaky stilts. Nerva could be overthrown any day by another bloodthirsty Domitian, and a new proconsul sent to Hither Spain in the event that tidings of Classicus' strange conduct reached The City. And what more natural than for the lively, courteous, and dependable Zinga, the lady excellency, to serve as her lord husband's confidential assistant? Had not the divorced Lady Enna (the cold and unapproachable one) likewise acted as chief advisor for the noble Classicus?

As April gave way to May, the fiery Gallic wife realized (and fought) the disturbing conclusion that the sanity of Classicus was in doubt. In daytime he seemed lucid, but the nights were terrors for them both. He would awaken Zinga from sleep she desperately needed, babbling about a giant god of snakes he feared existed somewhere in Spain, and about the skeleton of Publius the architect pursuing him through his sleep world . . . Zinga would spend the rest of the night caressing away his nightmares until each slept at last from utter exhaustion. Then came a succession of nights when he bolted out of their bed, rushed to a gray marble basin in their *lavatum* and soaped his hands over and over while Zinga watched narrowly. One night she awoke and he was not beside her. She sprang up and at last found him trying to pry loose the ponderous washing-font and carry it to bed.

Zinga Rutilia dared not summon physicians.

Some nights he would sleep fitfully, then awaken her with tales of gold coins forming columns in their bedroom. She was ordered to knock down the money pillars and pay tribute to the poor and needy in every *civitas foederata* of eastern Spain. Occasionally he fell asleep early, giving Zinga the boon of a few hours' deep sleep—only to jar her awake with his thick and confused voice mumbling in her ears. Once he extolled Christianity in a sweet voice unlike his own; then in normal tones fretfully ridiculed Emperor Nerva's restoration of humble brick chapels to the sect of the Messiah. Fortunately she was conscious the night he began a much more dangerous manifestation of mental breakdown: writing letters.

He arose and sat down at a lamplit table near their bed. Zinga leaned over his shoulder and watched him pen an account of his crimes, from tax thefts to poisoned wine served Publius after the patrician architect had angrily refused a bribe to share gold from the Sil with Classicus. The governor concluded that account with a grandiose appeal that Publius return from the Land of the Shades and let Classicus wash his feet with melted pearls. Zinga lured her ailing husband back to bed, and after he was sleeping, she tore the incriminating parchment to bits.

Another night, another eerie communication: this one a loving appeal that dead Emperor Tiberius rise from death and rescue the tax-emaciated people of Hither Spain. Trustfully he gave the document to Zinga and then wrote another, a forceful proclamation slashing taxes by three-fourths, the measure to be retroactive for two years with substantial refunds to be distributed among all taxpayers in the province he governed.

Too canny to protest, Zinga always pleaded gently that he let her dispatch the important pronouncements. He always gave them to her. Also, he seemed to have no inclination to put pen to papyrus and parchment unless she stood by his side. In sighing relief he would allow her to lead him back to bed, drink the drugged wine she offered, and go contentedly to sleep. Sometimes the soporific drink controlled him for hours; sometimes not. Each night after she had quieted him, she examined the citronwood and olivewood chests, coffers, and anteroom of their suite. Twice she found letters of confession hidden in old togas. Each accused himself, Classicus, but exonerated Enna, Frontinus, Zinga and all others of complicity.

Sane or insane, she would not abandon him. She even loved him. They were besieged in a woodland lair, two animals of the same breed. Nor did she relinquish her fierce hope that his dementia was temporary, induced by work and worry over debts he could not pay. With the gold from the Sil and a few hundred in gold she had gained from the quiet sale of Enna's ancient jewelry, she would soon be able to spirit her afflicted love far from hate and vengeance.

And had not her cherished Classicus been driven to his deeds by the bestial Emperor Domitian?—the god of Hades curse the phantom of that beast forever. Classicus was not cruel, but Zinga feared the unpredictable reversal of his more familiar avaricious character when he assumed the look and voice of a beneficent god. Some of these seizures were blissfully broken by the savage union of their bodies.

Each sunrise after chaotic nights she would murmur, "Praise the warrior gods of my ancestors." By then the proconsul was deep in poppy-wine slumber and Zinga could lock him in their suite, hastily bathe, dress, conceal the ravages of fear and worry on her face with pink paste and rouge, and be ready for the day.

In the rotunda she would greet respectful officials and slaves with the smiling announcement that His Excellency decreed the auspices of the morning propitious. The governor, however, needed continued rest in bed. He had instructed her, as he always did, how to deal with provincial affairs; and if the chief prefect and his men, the guards and servants, would help in their customary loyal manner, His Excellency would be most grateful.

Sympathetic and wary, the legation staff literally formed a protective cordon around the private rooms and first floor study of Classicus. Apologetic servants fended off visiting busybody officials from inland districts and towns bearing sheaves of lawsuit petitions which must be brought to His Excellency's attention immediately. The noble high prefect would be happy to ponder all appeals and bring such to the governor's attention when he returned from taking the thermal waters at a spa in Gaul . . . or when he came back from an inspection tour . . . Meanwhile Zinga worked behind locked doors in her husband's study.

She stood the strain heroically, but by early June her guardianship of Classicus by night and service as acting governor by day began threatening her own vigorous health. At length she gave in to whispered suggestions from menservants who worshipped the proconsul for his mercy and generosity: let them nurse and guard their beloved governor in daytime while the lady excellency worked or caught up on sleep. The tactful slaves understood how matters were. Jealous gods often scourged the finest and most magnanimous of men in such terrible ways. Reluctantly she acquiesced; she must take the risk or collapse herself.

The male nurses justified her trust and eased her dread. No rumors drifted through the legation and out into New Carthage. Affairs went on as usual. Each day Zinga worked in private with two male scribes whom the governor had freed from prison months before after learning that they had been falsely accused of petty theft.

Panniers of mail were always waiting. Wearily she and her secretaries would skim through reports from municipal prefects and popular assemblies reporting the revival of temple festivals after the death of Domitian; olive oil production; the need for more money to support regional Doles; and was the rumor true that Nerva Caesar was going to divide *Hispania* into three provinces as the land had been under the Sacred Augustus and the splendid Tiberius? And did the glorious excellency realize the efficacy of a pig-bladder worn at the belt to render harmless the power of the Evil Eye?

Personal letters being exchanged between the military and people of high rank were set aside by the scribes for Zinga's private perusal. Censorship was a prerogative of provincial governors and had been rigorously exercised during the imperium of Domitian. A proconsul always had to be on watch for hints of sedition, mutiny in the legions, and plots to assassinate the occupant of the Curule Chair.

After dictating courteous and vague replies to missives from district and town officials, Zinga would dismiss her secretaries and study communications which might threaten Classicus and herself. Of particular interest were letters flowing between Field Marshal Trajan's villa in Colonia Agrippina at the Rhine and the legation of Governor Maturus in Gades.

"Addleheads, all of them," Zinga would whisper as she read Enna's dull nothings and the insipid notes penned by Plotina, domina of the mighty Trajan. The scrolls were nonsense exchanged between two idle women of high rank. Plotina was tired of last year's diamonds; did Enna think that an emerald chaplet would set off the auburn beauty of Plotina's hair? Enna replied primly that emeralds were rather common, and advised Plotina to deck herself in pigeon's blood rubies. Red jewels would soon be in fashion in Spain, wrote Enna.

Zinga re-sealed each vapid epistle and sent it on to its destination, at last able to assure Classicus in his normal periods that there was no menace to him in the written prattle of his former wife. That concern firmly under control, she intercepted occasional terse, but friendly, letters from Field Marshal Trajan to Chieftain Malendi. The army officer had not heard from the Celt leader for a year. Why? Trajan's notes went into a brazier of burning charcoal. Destruction was also the destiny of a dispatch for the guerrilla leader from Senator C. Tacitus in Rome. The statesman was concerned over a rumor that the Arvacan Celt prince was restless and grievously unhappy under the benign reign of Nerva Caesar. If the gallant Prince Malendi would outline his complaints, the government of Nerva would use every resource to ameliorate any ills of the blackcloak nation—

Following a two-hour nap each afternoon on a couch in her husband's study, Zinga braced herself like a wary denizen of the woods and went upstairs to learn how Classicus had spent the day. She need not have worried. The skillful male nurses reported every word and action of the noble governor. Often he sat down at his bedroom table and wrote without pen, ink, or parchment, then went through the pantomime of rolling each epistle and handing it to an invisible messenger at his side. (Zinga had removed ink-wells, pens and parchment nights before.) The work at his writing desk always quieted him, after which he talked placidly to his respectful attendants about the common good of the downtrodden Spanish people and how he would uplift them. One twilight Zinga came in and sat down by his bed while the four nurses stood nearby.

"My dove," Classicus began, "it is love. Love is the torch of time. It lights a river of harmony and a tree of blue diamonds. The nectarous jewels are fruits of brotherhood for the delectation of humankind. All of you must eat the flashing fruits of virtue and bathe in the river of concord. Do this and the base metal of your souls will be refined into pure gold."

"His excellency speaks like a god," whispered an awed servant.

A new fear scorched Zinga, but she waited until her husband slept before beckoning the quartet of nurses to a far archway.

"Does his excellency ever try to dictate letters to any of you good men?" she asked, lightly.

The four shook their heads.

"Never allow him to do so," she warned. "An evil entity of a man executed for murder and gold thefts tries to enter the governor's mind. A dreadful—invasion, good servants."

"The ghost of a wretch trying to possess the moral mind of our master," murmured a sympathetic nurse. "Fear not, domina. We understand. But is it all right for us to leave him in your sitting room for short periods each day? There is no danger he can harm himself. The casements are locked."

Zinga pounced. "Never! You haven't left him alone?"

The nurses had made an exception that day as His Excellency begged for a little privacy. He returned to the bedroom a half hour later and the happy change in him was beyond words. He had looked transfigured. But the attendants would not allow such freedom again.

Sending the four out, Zinga returned to the bed and gently awakened Classicus. Had her beloved lord concealed writing materials in their suite? He had not. He was jovial and debonair. How could he write without pen, ink, and something to write on? Did his fox-love not trust her lord? He adored her. And he was hungry. Supper?

Late that night while he slept heavily after a cupful of poppy wine, Zinga searched the sitting room, anteroom, bedroom, bath and alcove wardrobes. She found no letters that would have doomed them both.

Yet the proconsul had written a full confession of his misdeeds before Zinga removed writing implements and parchment from their rooms. She had failed to awaken one night when Classicus quietly awoke. Here was his chance . . . Carrying writing materials to the lamp-lit anteroom, he sat down and wrote a succinct and full account of his crimes and deliberate involvement of blameless Chieftain Malendi in the gold scheme. Vast relief filled him. Now to hide the scroll where his pathetic Zinga would not think to search.

First he returned the pen, inkwell and remaining parchment to the bedroom table. Then soundlessly he moved with his precious document into the sitting room he still thought of as Enna's. Two night lamps burned cheerfully on a table beside her gold brocade sofa.

Gold . . . the glistening couch seemed to beckon like a friend. He tip-toed to an olivewood chest which still contained hoops of embroidery, scissors, needles and floss that Enna had forgotten when she fled to Gades. Soon he had cut apart a section of a seam and thrust his confession into the soft white fleece stuffing, then re-sewed the gap of the metallic cloth as expertly as a slave needlewoman. No one could detect that it had been slit open, a letter pushed in and the fabric re-stitched.

Back in bed next to the still sleeping Zinga, he tried to separate normal ideas from abnormal obsessions, realizing there was a difference, a line of demarcation his perceptions criss-crossed and which he could not control . . . The only reality was the transparent white entity, the god, the mother, the father, carrying him. He understood its tender commands.

In his mind he answered: 'I will obey, shadowless one. Seize my chance to hide my confession deep in a tax coffer outbound for Rome. When it is on its way I am absolved and can give myself up to the ineffable vision of the tree of blue diamonds, the torch, and the river of the Isles of the Blest.' He slept dreamlessly.

Dubiously encouraged by the apparent recovery of Classicus in June, his Gallic wife dictated cordial letters to senatorial friends in Rome, informing them that His Excellency had been severely indisposed with the flux, but was improving. These dispatches the cooperative high prefect of the legation graciously volunteered to sign and speed on their way by couriers. A few letters had arrived from Malendi. By the innocuous little sketches of crescents she knew that he had fixed the time of the half-moon, July the seventh, as the day he would attack the Sil mines and but awaited a fraternal note from Classicus, to the effect that rehabilitation of the Arvacan nation in more fertile valleys was important. This would be the signal from Classicus for Malendi to launch his savage horsemen against the Romans at the Sil.

The thought of gold obsessed Zinga. She and Classicus were actual paupers, although Rome had unexpectedly sent portions of the proconsul's arrears salary, also funds to pay legation expenses and the patricians and free people of the staff. Such minuscule amounts as arrived for her husband she kept. She burned two letters from money-hungry financiers in Rome again calling the noble Classicus' attention to his debts.

She found yellowed packets of old scrolls far back in the recesses of her husband's sliding-panel wall safe in the study. All but one were letters written by Verus Maturus to the Senate, asking for enforcement of investigation procedures which would empower Maturus to sift both tax and justice affairs in all of Spain. Gleefully she destroyed those. The remaining crumpled papyrus had been written by the slave architect, Gaius, and referred to her lord husband's missing slave girl, Penelope . . . the woman to whom Classicus might have whispered winey babblings about his gold scheme over a year ago. Classicus had forgotten her. Zinga had not. She was positive the Greek captive was hiding in Ioza, and grimly resolved to bring Penelope back to New Carthage in time and sell the girl to someone bound for India or China. Zinga had already planned how to accomplish this. Meanwhile she spent time learning how to imitate the handwriting of Classicus. Then she had to deal with a tiresome baggage situation.

Three days after the Ides of June, two wagonloads of dismantled Archimedes Screws arrived from the Sil mines, bound for Rome. In private Zinga suspiciously scrutinized a laconic dispatch coming with the shipment from Commander Rufus Liscus, and addressed to the *primus procurator* of imperial mines in Rome. Liscus hoped that neither Emperor Nerva nor his commissioner of ores would be irked by the distressing fact that there had been accidental damage to the helix of one of the machines. The hollow spiral cylinder had broken in three places. After several unsuccessful attempts, the chief metallurgist at the emperor's Sil mines had fused the riven parts with bronze patches, which did not impair the efficiency of the hydraulic engine. Uncharacteristically frustrated without knowing why, Zinga re-sealed the document, and next read a fresh communication from Chieftain Malendi. The chieftain extended fraternal greetings, hoped that his brother excellency's health was now on the mend, and supposed that Proconsul Classicus would take care of the matter of speeding the water-lifters on to Rome. A single half-moon drawing at the foot of the page brought a tight smile to Zinga's quivering red lips.

Malendi but waited a letter from Classicus to attack the mines and seize the gold. . . . The date: the Nones of July.

She sent the Archimedes Screws and the letter of Liscus onward toward Rome.

On a sunny morning in July she sat by her husband's bed. Propped against green satin pillows and with the sheer insect-repellent curtains drawn back from the brass poles overhead, he was eating with good appetite. She watched fondly while he consumed cold chicken, figs, barley bread and pale Chian wine and water. Zinga ate lightly, too, and they discussed the new treasurer, Sylvanus.

At length Classicus said, "Sylvanus is a commendable aristocrat, even though, alas, he resembles a rhinoceros. He is that rare being: a moral man. He goes to extreme lengths to make sure not a single tax coin escapes."

"How do you know? You haven't been to the treasury chambers for months!"

"My beautiful animal, of course not. I have been indisposed. I ordered Sylvanus to pay me a visit yesterday afternoon."

"The slaves who tend you told me nothing of that!"

Classicus chided indulgently, "Your voice, your voice. You are the lady excellency, a Gallic Artemis overly-eager to be off and away with bow and arrows. I ordered my faithful four not to worry you—and I refuse to be watched every moment. I sent my considerate servants to the anteroom for a short rest while I conferred briefly with the noble Sylvanus. Then as I am proconsul of this province, I commanded his slaves to bring in the current tax coffer, and Sylvanus and I supplicated Jupiter and Neptune for a safe ocean crossing of Emperor Nerva's money."

Zinga was appalled. "You didn't take any of that money, did you?"

He chuckled. "Every tax coin goes to The City. I am a man of integrity and honor. Ask Sylvanus. I myself closed the lid of the chest and turned the key, while my treasurer observed. Then his men bore out the receptacle. All is well."

". . . All is well . . ." She would talk to the treasurer later.

Classicus yawned and lay down on his bed for sleep. Zinga watched him settle in his pillows and then stole out to the anteroom where the four male nurses were waiting.

For all their loyalty, silence and caution, they had dismissed as unimportant one small action of His Excellency and decided not to burden the exotic Lady Zinga with it: the preceding afternoon the governor had gotten out of bed and insisted on going into the sitting room of the apartment to commune with the gods for a short time. Watching from a doorway, the attendants had seen Classicus pick up the gold brocade sofa cushion and carry it to a curtained alcove. He remained hidden from view for a short while. At last he came out, still carrying the object. Smiling and happy he told his nurses that he was sure Lady Enna had been hiding in the fleece, so he had torn open the fabric—and found that she was not there. His concern was set at rest. And would the men have a legation seamstress sew the seams together again?

Immediately after leaving the menservants guarding Classicus' peaceful slumber, Zinga went to the former office of Frontinus. The elegant pink marble chamber was now dominated by the gross physical presence of Sylvanus, the new treasurer. His heavy face and neck seemed one flesh and his pyramid-shaped body in tunic and toga overflowed the oak armchair he occupied. Yet when he talked, his rich, warm voice and engaging manner lured listeners from staring at his immensity and extreme homeliness. He was happy to give his version of the preceding day's conference with Governor Classicus. It tallied exactly with that given by Classicus—with one exception. His excellency had ordered Sylvanus to kneel and hide his face in his toga while Classicus invoked Jupiter and Neptune for favorable winds and calm seas to bear the tax chest to Italy.

"Kneeling for a man of my weight presents difficulties," continued Sylvanus, drolly. "However, I accomplished it while the proconsul prayed over the open tax coffer. At length he told me to uncover my face and rise. By the hem of Mother Minerva's war-kilt, I almost did not succeed, domina. He then told me to witness him turning the key in the lock of the closed tax chest. My men then bore out the container." The treasurer's small dark eyes, almost buried in fleshy pouches, surveyed tense Zinga kindly. "My dear domina," he continued, "set your mind at rest. Our most excellent Classicus is not a tax thief and never was. But as a precaution against those who would filch, I personally place the counted gold in heavy sacks and seal the drawcords with melted lead before placing each in the revenue chest."

Zinga felt weak with relief and gratitude.

"The tax chest was placed on the revenue bireme last night and, as is my custom, I made sure it was heavily guarded. The vessel sailed with the outgoing tide this morning. Auspices were favorable. The galley slaves had no murderous toil at the oars, Neptune be thanked for that. Fair winds puffed the sails and bore the ship away smoothly."

That afternoon Zinga sat in her husband's study, all doors and windows securely bolted. A mail pouch was waiting. She unlocked it. Out poured the usual flood of letters from city prefects in Hither Spain—and one addressed to Sylvanus. Hastily she read that: a cordial note from Governor Verus Maturus congratulating Sylvanus on his appointment as treasurer of Hither Spain and inviting him to visit Gades at his first opportunity. Maturus would come to New Carthage, only affairs in his province were so grave that he could not leave his legation . . . Zinga tore it up in rage. Then she found a fresh dispatch from the creditors of Classicus in Rome which bluntly informed the most noble Cornelius Classicus that the amnesty on debts would soon expire. Surely his excellency realized that Emperor Nerva and the Senate could not free aristocrats of their obligations merely because they were patricians. Cornelius Classicus must pay in full. Or go to prison and be sold as a slave. Not only that, but any sons and daughters of his would also go into bondage to help liquidate his debts. Zinga tore the letter to bits and ground it under her scarlet kid sandals. When she felt calmer, she got out the correspondence of Malendi and copies of Classicus' innocuous and cordial writings to the blackcloak chieftain. Already skillful in imitating Classicus' flowing cursive script, she practiced some more before she at last was ready. Then she dipped pen in black ink and wrote on a creamy flat of parchment:

CORNELIUS CLASSICUS OF HITHER SPAIN TO CHIEFTAIN LUNA MALENDI. BROTHERLY GREETINGS. AFTER DUE DELIBERATION I BELIEVE THAT WE SHOULD MAKE PLANS TO RESETTLE YOUR WORTHY NATION IN MORE FERTILE MEADOWS. BEAR WITH

ME WHILE I DEAL WITH PLANS WHICH WILL USHER
IN A NEW ERA OF INCREASED PROSPERITY FOR YOU
AND YOUR DESERVING PEOPLE. COMPLIMENTS.
VALE.

She next poured hot melted beeswax at the right side of the page
and pressed down the official bronze intaglio medallion seal. It left
tiny upraised letters in the wax: ULTERIOR HISPANIA LE-
GATUS AUGUSTI PRO PRAETORE. Then she slipped the
rolled parchment into a gray suede case and inserted it in a cedarwood cylinder with a hinged top. Heavy cords attached to the round
lid were then criss-crossed around the wooden case and tied. No
address tag was needed. This would be carried by fast couriers direct
to the blackcloak Celt's headquarters in the far northern mountains.

A half hour later she stood on the breezy balcony overlooking the
courtyard and watched four horsemen of the Theban legion gallop
away, bound north. Now there was no retreat. Now the armies of
Malendi would attack the Sil mines on the Nones of July.

XXVIII

Three days before the Nones of July, the prisoners at the Sil were
staggered when Zamil and twenty other picked men were unchained
and ordered to erect a twenty-foot-high log platform outside the
headquarters cabin of Commander Liscus. Balbus and two other
trusties were put in charge.

"It's a test," Zamil told his amazed crew. "We'll build the best
log tower yet. And expect to be put back in irons afterward. But
once out of chains, even if we go back in, we can hope. No runaway
tries, you hear me?"

His men nodded in agreement, too dazed to notice Balbus and
the other older men who were unhobbled.

Alone of all the prisoners, Balbus knew what was coming. Commander Liscus had sworn him to secrecy. The old trusty bore the
awful burden of knowledge that blackcloak horsemen were going
to attack the mines. As the log structure went up that hot day, Balbus spent most of his time gazing across the parched rockbed of the
Sil to the south. He was praying. In anguish he supplicated god
after god. As a desperate last hope he prayed in his mind to the

Christ. If the untried new divinity, Jesus, could conquer death and the devil—

That night all prisoners were lavishly fed on the hillside mess area near the pastured mares and foals. Zamil and his building crew had willingly submitted to re-chaining after the log platform was finished, but somehow no fetters weighed too heavily. Hope filled the warm night air, hope flared in faces, hope blazed in torches brightening the darkness. Chunks of mutton hot from the spits, flagons of ale, slabs of cheese, warm wheat bread. . . . The five thousand ate heartily, the roar of their talk echoing in all directions. The men even jested now and then, shared their meat, and talked about families and homes. And was the noble commander going to shut down the mines? Have you heard the rumor that the brave Liscus is going to write to Emperor Nerva requesting pardons for all of us? *Evoe!* Praise the mercy of Ahura-Mazda, the one true god who guards Persia . . . the Most High . . . my god is Mithra, the deity of soldiers . . . the Most High . . . who else but Jupiter?—The Most High—of the Christians. There is no God. Every man his own god . . . Who cares? I won't argue with you, friend. Any god you want . . . Give me Bacchus, eh, comrades? . . . never win. They claim we are all sinners. I'm no sinner, those Christians woo death like I courted my wife— Be sure you answer roll call tonight . . . Did you see that falling star just then? The gods have fallen, there's hope for us.

In the blazing sunrise next morning the prisoners were massed around the log platform. On the top stood Commander Liscus and his adjutants; Tribune Gaius Lacer and Flavian the *optio*. Troops stood rigidly here and there among the tense and expectant men in gyves.

"Attention!" said Liscus through a brass megaphone. "Attention!"

The rattle and grating of chains ceased as the workers stiffened to listen.

"Men," said Liscus, "we are facing life and death."

The masses stared without comprehension.

Liscus spoke slowly through the brass amplifier so that every prisoner could hear and understand. "Men—the blackcloaks camped thirty miles south of us are going to attack these mines of Emperor Nerva."

A murmuring in the sea of shackled creatures.

"Men," continued Rufus Liscus, "a few nights ago, my scouts overheard enemy scouts talking in the pine forest to the south about plans of Chieftain Malendi to launch a surprise cavalry assault tomorrow, the day before the Nones. Tomorrow, this will be an area of battle." The prisoners stared up at him.

"I am bound by my holy oath of allegiance to Nerva, the Senate, and the Roman people, to defend Roman territory—or die in the attempt. We have no choice. We are on Roman soil." Again he paused. "We are cut off from the three legions to the west and far to the south. North are a few loyal *Togati* and Roman colonists and the Emperor's seaport city of Corunna. Our allies to the north are not strong enough to come to our aid. They rely on *us* to save *them*."

In the prisoner ranks, Zamil and his mates chained together started to move forward towards the log tower. Balbus, tears streaming down his wrinkled face, led the group.

"Men," Liscus went on, "you men in chains. How do I, with less than one hundred and fifty soldiers, hold sacred Roman ground against thousands of blackcloak warriors? I and my military council have mapped a surprise defense. It is not enough. I need men to fight for Rome."

The prisoners were craning their necks to watch Zamil and his fellows at last reach base of the high log structure. A hum of whispers rippled through the orderly ranks of men in irons.

"Commander, I am Zamil, leader of the prisoners!" called the black-haired Roman of broken nose. "Commander—if your troops will unshackle me again, I ask that you let me beseech the workers!"

The massed thousands stared transfixed.

"Strike off Zamil's bonds," shouted Liscus. "Let him come up and stand beside me."

The prisoners yelled vociferously while troops removed the waist and ankle irons of Zamil and hoisted him up the ladder where Liscus and his soldiers stood.

Zamil dominated all as he gazed down on his fellow bondsmen. Liscus handed him the megaphone and Zamil put it to his mouth.

"Men! We're alive today because of Tribune Lacer and Commander Liscus!" said Zamil.

"LACER! LISCUS! LACER! LISCUS!" The prisoners blasted. When the thunder from human throats subsided, Zamil called through the megaphone: "Men, we all have to die. But we live until we die. And while we live we hope. Do you want to die without hope?—in chains?"

"THE COMMANDER! THE TRIBUNE! LACER! LISCUS!"

Zamil stretched out his arms for attention. "I volunteer to fight for Rome! By my sacred oath I will not escape. I will live or die as a soldier for *Roma*. Men—what do you say?" His final words were almost lost in roars from the massed thousands:

"WE'LL FIGHT FOR ROME! FOR ROME!"

"*PRO ROMA! PRO ROMA!* WE'LL FIGHT!"

"*ROMA!* THE EMPEROR! FOR ROME!"

Two prisoners had Balbus on their shoulders and were trying to hoist him up the log scaffold. Gaius leaned down and helped the weeping trusty ascend the last rungs of the ladder to the top.

After the noise died down, Commander Liscus took the megaphone. "I believe your leader, Zamil. I believe all of you will fight loyally for Rome. Now. You will proceed in your groups to the vacant land behind the cookhouse, storage buildings and well-shack. My troops will strike your irons. You will be armed with what weapons as are available. Meat-knives. Saws. Chisels. Shovels. Mallets. Hammers. You will then march slowly, in small groups, to various designated points in this mining town. You will put on your wooden breastplates and log helmets. You will then be divided into war training squads by Acting Centurion Flavian and his aides. That is all. *Pro Roma!*"

"*PRO ROMA! PRO ROMA!*

"*IO TRIUMPHE! IO TRIUMPHE!*"

All day long while a few Roman cavalrymen patrolled the south shore from the dam northeast past the mine buildings and on west, Flavian and his few infantrymen converted the unshackled prisoners into the equivalent of *roararii*, or lightly-weaponed troops. There were no riots or breakaways. Once freed of fetters, each man squared his shoulders and became a legionary. Zamil was everywhere. He relayed the orders of Liscus and his adjutants, ran errands for Flavian, and slapped the newly sworn-in troops on their backs.

The new fighters helped each other strap on oak or pine cuirasses and leg-greaves, and stuff their shaggy hair up under the rims of hollowed beach and oak log helmets. Eager white hands, dark hands, yellow hands and brown hands grasped the horn handles of knives; iron files; mallets and lead pipes of force pumps. Hands for

Rome tested the heft of spades, shovels, chisels and hammers. Balbus, master of artillery, watched proudly as his cohort stacked choice specimens of granite and limestone in rough pyramids near the well-shack. During all of this, intense defense preparations were going on across the Sil and down the embankment of the rockbed. Hours before, cavalry scouts of Liscus, camouflaged with leafy branches tied to helmets and armor, had melted away to the south to spy on blackcloak scouts and gain any possible information as to enemy strength and time of attack.

At noon that day of punishing July heat, Gaius found Flavian behind the wellhouse, watching two of his infantry troops teach the volunteers how to lunge and parry with their emergency weapons.

"Flavian, our new fighters are soldiers," said Gaius.

The orderly saluted. "Sir, they are. No bustaways and I don't think there will be any. Great spirit." He lifted a wooden dipper of water from a barrel and sloshed it over his perspiring face. "Any new reports from our guerrilla friends?"

Gaius threw a handful of water over his face. "Malendi has twenty thousand cavalry warriors. Ten thousand more at the rear. To the rear of the rear, we'll have to guess."

"Ah," breathed Flavian. "I'm used to slaughter according to the rules of warfare. No rules for this. We won't have slingers, archers, skirmishers and heavily-armed infantry to launch a counterattack. No cavalry to support the flanks. Well, I never think of losing. I never say, 'This is my last battle, because as of tomorrow I'm a time-expired veteran.' If I made that statement I might die before that lady fate, Atropos, was ready to cut my life's thread." Two British volunteers marched up and saluted. Flavian gestured to the water barrel and both drank gratefully, saluted, and rushed back to their mock conflicts. Pulling a dagger, Flavian ran an experienced thumb along the honed blade. "The gods be praised for you, Governor Maturus, and your brother," muttered Flavian. "Because of you, Tribune, the commander's got fighting men to back up us few veterans." He hitched up the flexible steel bands of his shoulder armor and tested their straps and buckles fastened to his leather tunic above metal strips encircling his thorax and abdomen.

"Flavian," said Gaius, "when does forgetfulness start? How long will people remember Hesiod, Homer, Vergil? Plato, Lucretius, Aristotle, Pythagoras? Cornelia Gracchus, Horace, Sappho, Cleopatra? Alexander the Great, Hannibal, Julius Caesar? Scipio Africanus,

Empress Livia and Augustus? Cicero, Tiberius, Vespasian, Nero, Caligula? And—Trajan. Perhaps true death comes when the last man who remembers thinks the last thought about those moral or immoral personages?"

The aide brushed away a green fly buzzing around his perspiring face. "Nobody'll think of me," he said, drily. "But I rather think, sir, that your name will be remembered."

Gaius became embarrassed until deciding that his aide had jested to ease the strain of coming battle. "Undoubtedly," he joked. "The great Lacer, slave."

"The great Lacer built the Tagus Bridge."

His bridge. He had not thought about it for days. . . . In the landscape of his mind the gray granite columns and arches formed and again he stood in centerbridge and then he was wrenching the whip away from Ferox Piso. Slowly he responded, "Flavian, I first saw the Tagus spans in my mind. Then I drew the plans on parchment. But I didn't build the bridge. Hundreds of men built it, stone by stone. Men died so that the bridge could live." Thoughtfully, he concluded, "Once I desperately wanted recognition and fame—not any more."

"That is a profound thought," said Flavian, his face becoming sad as he too thought about immortality, and life and death—and his wife and child. "Some day we'll all be forgotten—"

Gaius turned away. A man could not afford deep thought before battle, but again his mind turned to his Tagus Bridge, and the smiling face of Syphax, the crinkled blue eyes of Cifgli, the scarred visage of Quadratus the legionary and the calm face of valiant Pomponius triumphant in death. . . .

And what is it like to be a woman? he wondered, permitting himself for only a brief moment to think of Penelope.

Tomorrow we fight.

XXIX

Before sunset three mild earthquake temblors rumbled upchannel to the east around the dam which held back an enormous impounded lake. The earth shudders were felt in the camp and diggings, causing no damage, but its menace to the soldiers of the Sil was genuine and it was ominous.

204

Trying to formulate fresh plans in case of a new emergency, Gaius galloped into the settlement at twilight after a hasty ride to inspect the threatened dam. He had kept to himself signs of impending catastrophe, and hoped the cavalrymen of Rufus had not seen the rivulets trickling out of the precipitous west wall of the earth-barrier that reared up three miles east of the mine village. While still retaining its truncated triangular outer shape, Gaius realized that the inner core wall must now be fractured and dislocated in all dimensions.

Two cavalry inspectors of the earthwork were leaving as Gaius rushed into headquarters where Flavian leaned over a table studying maps for defense and offense. Mars, in his canine armor, crouched at the polished black boots of his master. Rufus glanced up, his blue eyes haunted. "Well, brother, what is your report?"

"Sir," said Gaius, "damage is minimal."

A strained silence gathered.

"My cavalry troops do not agree with you, Gaius," replied Rufus. "They, too, examined the works. As a result, Flavian and I are revising the strategy."

Gaius moved to the officer. "Commander, brother, your men are not experts. I am."

Rufus stared at Flavian. "Acting centurion," said the commander, "do you think my brother Gaius might tell a lie in order to render patriotic service to Rome?"

Hastily Gaius said, "The earth-shocks did minor harm. Two narrow fissures in the walkway, a fairly long crack in the clay and log facing of the western escarpment. But the floodgates are water-tight and still hold."

"Hold—for how long?" Rufus demanded. "My cavalrymen aren't engineers, architects and geologists, but they reported the dam seemed to quiver underfoot. They said the lake was slopping over."

"The melting snows from the mountains, then the heavy rains—the tributary streams have built a huge lake, granted. And remember, we didn't boom off in April or May—thank the gods we didn't." To deflect the talk, he asked, "Brother, why didn't you let me order a boom-off? I wanted to."

Rufus picked up a clay lamp and gazed at the flame. "Instinct," he mused. "A curious sense of coming disaster. My brother's dam seemed a friend, shall I say. As long as your dam stood, my young brother. But now the pile is doomed."

"But sir," said Gaius, "a thick earthwork of that type can sustain settling and such and not disintegrate. Brother—do not change plans."

The commander turned to Flavian. "Acting centurion—would you order Tribune Lacer out on that dam tomorrow if the blackcloaks attack?"

The somber aide looked from brother to brother. "Commander . . . duty is duty . . ."

"—And what if the dam should collapse?" asked Gaius, reasonably. "It'll be a slow crackup. Plenty of time to get back to the north shore, commander." He glanced at Flavian's haggard face and sad dark eyes.

Thoughts of the huge parapet built by the toil of men, caused Gaius to listen for the muffled roar that would signal the death of the dam. There was no fearsome, dull, and distant thunder—yet. But his quick inspection an hour ago had shown him that the barrier holding back the lake could not last forever and might be breaking under right now. Imagination supplied the sounds and sight of the final agony of the dam . . . And if the cofferdam foundations had been dislodged and broken by the earthquakes, when the floodgates went up (if they went up) the sudden wild outpush of water would let loose the entire lake and destroy the dam. Would it hold long enough—and serve obediently when ordered—to save the soldiers of the Sil? Gaius still believed that it might.

"Commander," said Flavian, "any chance that some *Togati* warriors will volunteer?"

Rufus put down the lamp and picked up another. "None. The peaceful few whitecloaks north of us dread committing their few remaining fighters to a conflict such as this. They are farmers and cattlemen. They fear for the safety of their wives and daughters. They want no war with Malendi. They depend on Rome to protect them. As for our *Togati* allies far to the west, the Asturians, their cohorts are helping the legions fight small-scale blackcloak attacks in that sector. The only allies I could count on are the Lusonian *Togati*. But their lands are a peninsula, like a tongue of land jutting from central Spain northwest, between Malendi's northern and southern boundaries. The hordes of Malendi are between us and the Lusonians." Rufus sat in his armchair and laid down the second lamp. "However, Gaius, your *Togati* warrior who brought the message from Maturus, is camping with a few comrades on the mountainside north of this village. They expect you to demonstrate your godly power again tomorrow and annihilate the blackcloak thousands."

"Which we will, sir," said Gaius instantly.

"Perhaps the outcome is already decided against us," said Rufus, quietly. "Since the emperor and senate don't know, or don't care what's happening in Spain, I'm beginning to consider my decision to fight as a senseless sacrifice of life and a senseless dedication to death." Abruptly he said, "Gaius, I'm not going to send you out on that dam if the blackcloaks attack tomorrow." His grave blue eyes looked with love at Gaius.

This is what men fight for, live for, die for, thought Gaius. He bent over the commander. "Rufus—now I will tell you the whole truth. The dam *may* crumble and crack apart any time. But if it still stands tomorrow and the enemy attacks, the success of your plans depend on me and ten men walking out on the works and opening the floodgates. Those plans must be carried out. We'll start the cranes and pulleys, not raise the gates all the way."

"My cavalrymen said the spillways are jammed."

"All the better," Gaius lied. "I think the dam will go in big chunks, once the gates rise. The pressure of water will do the rest. There should be time for the troops and me to save ourselves. If some of us can't get back to the north cliffs, we can rush to the south embankments."

Bitterly the commander observed, "Indeed, my dear young brother, right into the custody of blackcloaks riding along the south shore toward this camp."

"Making so much dust and thunder that they won't see any of us reach the cover of willows and blueberry bushes at the southern terminus of the dam," Gaius retorted. "You'll all be wiped out unless I do my part as planned. Rufus . . . call it faith, vision, what you will . . . but your men and I will get off the dam before it breaks apart."

Mars let out a soft whine and settled his broad head on his paws. Rufus slumped in his chair. Flavian trudged to a grindstone and began honing a sharp dagger. Losing interest, he thrust the weapon under his belt. He moved around the cabin, inspecting bracket lamps and glancing occasionally at maps on the commander's table. From outside came the far-off whinnies of horses in emergency pastures up the mountainside. Nearly all the animals of the expedition had been removed from the camp stables that afternoon.

Except for the blazing lamps in Rufus' headquarters, the entire town and buildings across on the south shore looked dark and deserted. Not deserted. Nearly five thousand prisoner-fighters commanded by infantry and cavalry troops were posted in the cookhouse, storage buildings and wellshack at the west end of town, and in the long stables and latrine sheds at the east end. On the south shore, Zamil, Balbus, and ninety-eight volunteers were at their stations. Ten miles farther south, Roman scouts and their fast horses, concealed in thickets, watched the blazing campfires of blackcloak thousands. The enemy was spread out for miles, east to west, a scant two miles south of lookout posts where Roman eyes observed.

A sarcastic laugh from Rufus broke the brooding tension in the cabin. "And the gold for Rome reached Rome. To think that the chief of imperial mines criticized me for using the helix of one of his beloved Archimedes Screws to ship the gold. And the silver. His indignant letter to Maturus must have been a masterpiece."

Gaius smiled. "Maturus isn't angry. He is overjoyed. The gods be praised for biremes plying the Atlantic between Gades and Corunna."

Time crawled. Sand slid smoothly through the girdle of the hourglass. Gaius tried to eat meat and bread. He gave up. The gray of false dawn filtered in through half-open shutters, then black night settled down again. Rufus sat in his armchair, staring fixedly at Gaius.

He was too tense to sit. He got up and began marching around the table, conscious of his brother's eyes following him. Seeing the dam in mind, Gaius mentally began the hazardous operation of raising the highset floodgates. Would the great doors jam? Always that terrible possibility . . . solve that if it existed when he and his men reached the south watergate. Chop the south door loose if they had to, partially raise it if it would go up . . . Then he and his assistants would rush for the north floodgate while he signalled the troops there to start lifting that one when Gaius and his men ran abreast. Up it would go, a third or halfway—then off the dam to the north shore with all of them.

The cabin door burst open and a cavalry scout rushed in.

"Celt horsemen approaching from south!" shouted the trooper. "Distance, six miles! Ten thousand first attack wave! Ten thousand second! Battle charge formation, a horde of howling barbarians!"

"Any indication the enemy will split forces?" Rufus shouted. "Attempt crossover between here and the dam?"

"No, sir," panted the scout. "If present advance holds, enemy cavalry will race past dam a half mile to the south of it. Looks like an all-out smash at this town and the buildings on south shore, sir!"

Slowly Rufus looked at Gaius. Moments melted away. The last of the sand had fallen in the glass. Mechanically Rufus upturned the timepiece. At last he spoke thickly:

"My brother Gaius, you and your ten men will ride to the dam. If the Celt enemy tries to cross over near your position, open the floodgates without delay. If not, watch north shore for red flags of attack. When you see red semaphores—" Rufus bowed his head— "when you see red flags . . . follow orders . . ."

Gaius saluted. "To be done, sir."

He looked reassuringly at the bowed head of Rufus and tried to glance with hope at Flavian. The acting centurion averted his face.

Gaius wheeled about and marched out.

XXX

High on the forested cliff above the mortared stone north terminus of the dam, Gaius and his ten men tethered their horses deep in a beech grove, then clambered down a natural rock ramp and out on the roadway of the earthwork. To their left a turbulence of water spread out north, south and east, twelve miles at its widest and fed by a confluence of three rivers flowing in to the far eastern end of the artificial lake. To the right, the west flank of the dam reared out of the rockbed which angled southwest for three hundred feet before elbowing into the Sil channel. Three miles downchannel to the west lay the camp. Yellow gray clouds floated across the murky sunrise and there was a smell of rain in the hot and humid air.

After briefing six men at the north water outlet, Gaius and four other legionaries rushed to the south floodgate, where, even as he placed his men in position, Gaius saw fresh evidence that the dam was doomed.

Waves slapped over the walkway through the split log fences and streamed down the almost vertical west side. Since Gaius' inspection the previous afternoon, new cracks separated the stones and cement of the truncated top. Runnels had formed in the clay and log facing of the once dry west face of the construction. How much longer would the works hold?

"Guerrillas!" called a soldier. "Celts galloping up from east and southeast!" His warning was almost unheard in the rumble of approaching hooves and the groans of the straining dam.

Gaius looked over green willow trees on the south cliffs and saw the flashing swords and casque helmets of the blackcloak Celts caught by the morning sun, an army of ponies and riders rocketing west a half mile from the south banks of the Sil rockbed.

"Watch north shore for red flags!" Gaius shouted, his eyes on the enemy horsemen, as the fierce cries of the raiders reverberated off the cliffs and out of the Sil channel. It seemed that he watched a long time while water sucked at his bootsoles and splashed his ankles.

An aide shrieked, "How many so far?"

"About ten thousand. There goes the second line—ten thousand more!"

"Heading for the camp!" yelled a soldier.

No guerrilla warriors clattered down the south banks into the deepway of the drained Sil; the blackcloak thousands were streaking on west, the town and mine buildings their obvious target— Gaius cupped his hands around his mouth:

"Attention! I repeat orders. We at this south gate raise it first. You at the north outlet watch for my signal and wait my command. Then start your gate up—and run for your lives. Every man for himself!"

"Red flags!" a cavalryman hailed. "Red flags on north shore, sir!"

Gaius and his four were already raising their ponderous barrier. A growl of water burst through the aperture as the door slowly began to ascend. Then it jammed and it was inevitable that the pressure against the gate would rip it apart and the dam would disintegrate.

"Run! Run!" Gaius shouted to his four aides.

They stared north, turned back to help him, but he furiously waved them on. "Run! Run!" If he tried once more, he might raise the south barrier.

The six soldiers at the north gate, now joined by the other four, waited by the pulley-wheels and hoisting tackles.

"Start it up!" shrieked Gaius, raising his arm—and at that moment the south gate shook as if struck by a titanic fist. Gaius started running north towards his troops. He saw all ten scramble off the walkway and start up the rock ramp—then a tremendous surge of water burst the north log door, not the south, spuming up a tangle of ropes, metal, and logs.

His escape to the north cut off, Gaius spun around and ran south, past the other gate which still remained partly raised in its thick log frame. On he ran, on, on . . . his speed reduced by water swirling around his knees and beginning to push against his thighs. Then the walkway began to move and crumble under his boots.

A gaping abyss split the walkway ahead and Gaius barely managed to leap a four-foot chasm and land on the walkway remaining. Only fifty feet more to fight his way to the south shore—forty—going slower, water heavy on my thighs—keep going—

The concrete underfoot began to buckle and sink. He slid down into the comparative safety of the lake, his armor and helmet scraping against the slanting waterside concrete—and now he was only thirty feet from the beckoning green willows of the south banks.

"Penelope! Penelope!" he screamed. Then, as water washed over his head, he held his breath and grasped the first object he felt: a log protruding from the diagonal wall behind him.

On the south shore the advance ranks of raiders galloped through the pine forest into the vast clearing around the smelters and refineries. Fifty blackcloaks sprang off their horses while screaming hundreds urged their beasts down into the Sil channel. Behind them yelling comrades kept arriving.

"Roman traitors!"

"Land robbers! Dogs of Rome!"

"Gold stealers!"

Sudden accidents began disorganizing the first long line of Celt horsemen plunging down into the rockbed. Ponies stumbled, bucked, and a few turned somersaults. The agile animals all landed safely on their hooves, but a few guerrillas were thrown screaming in pain or lay silent in sudden death. They were hauled out by dismounted comrades while other warriors discovered the cause of the trouble.

"Copper wires! The Roman scum stretched wires!"

Dirks and swords hacked away the almost invisible metal strands and savage brown hands carried bundles of fine wires up on the south banks. That danger conquered, the attackers walked their mounts down into the deepway of the Sil. Five thousand reached

211

midchannel, spread in a long line from east to west—when a roar split the air and the earth shook from concussion. A tribal captain signalled his riders to a halt.

"Again the earth shakes!" he keened. "The Black God is wroth against the Roman traitors!"

"The auspices favor our immortal chieftain!" shouted a nearby Celt.

But the puzzled Celt officer eyed the vacant streets of the Sil settlement with mounting suspicion—until he heard terrified screams from his troops. He saw a gigantic tidal wave booming west in the Sil channel toward him—a fury of water tossing boulders, logs, jagged hunks of cement and whole young trees in its titanic surf. The sight so stunned him and his fighters that they sat transfixed.

But the Celt ponies sensed disaster and stampeded for the nearest high ground. Hundreds bolted, threw their riders, and clambered up the north bank and the south. Scores of horses bore their riders to safety up the south banks, passing hundreds more galloping their mounts down into the channel of coming disaster. Four thousand maddened Celt ponies bore their masters up the stony bank of the north terrain, reaching high ground one half mile away from the eastern end of the river basin.

Then the leviathan of water struck three thousand milling guerrillas and horses trapped in the rockbed.

And now the Sil, for many months a dry, deep gorge, foamed with the roar of a flood sweeping everything before it. Celts, ponies, rocks, bricks, mortar, saplings, fish, logs, bushes, birds' nests—all were pounded, tossed up and thrust forward by the chaotic tides thundering west.

The Celts stormed the rock-crushery sheds on the south shore. Finding no gold or silver bars, the raiders poured into the smelters and refineries. These were no longer open at one side. Each now had four brick walls with oak doors invitingly open. Inside were ordinary brick hearths with blazing fires under suspended crucibles of molten grayish ore.

"Silver!" the Celts exulted. When each building was filled with gloating Celts, hails of rock suddenly roared down from overhead, slamming the oak doors shut. Up on the roofs, Roman volunteers in concealed brick eyries around the chimneys pulled bearhides over the chimney vents. Soon the buildings below began to fill with corrosive silver gas.

The trapped guerrillas wheezed and coughed and tried to hack through the oak doors and tumbled rocks. The few holes they managed to gouge merely let in enough air to stoke the fires under the cauldrons of crude silver ore. The rank gas eddied out and choked the enemy imprisoned in each smelter and refinery.

In the open ground around the buildings, Zamil and his men (except Balbus, who waited in the forest) had won their delaying action rolling down rocks to block the shut doors and plugging the chimneys of the silver gas death chambers. Fortune favored the Romans, helped both by their stealth in sliding down off the roofs and by the thundering flood in the channel that held the glazed-eyed attention of guerrillas massed on the south shore watching the destruction of their comrades down in the raging water. But thousands of blackcloak reserve horsemen now broke into the clearing and saw Zamil and his troops making a swift and light-footed retreat to the west and south, bound for new combat stations in the pine forest.

"Romans in the pines!" shrieked the new Celt riders. "Romans in the forest! Kill!"

A confused battle began among the trees. Roman volunteers attacked the enemy from behind with a barrage of rocks, rusty chains, and lethal flying meat-knives and chisels. The Celts launched slingshot lead bullets, threw stone maces, and heaved short lances. Romans and Celts began going down, but the bulk of Zamil's men disappeared into the western wilderness of pines. Old Balbus had been ordered by Zamil to stay out of danger, but the fighting trusty wanted to fight for Rome.

Zamil saw the old trusty stumble and fall, struck by a Celt mace in his left shoulder. Rushing to the old man, Zamil swung an ax and killed a guerrilla ready to decapitate the aged Roman trusty. Standing astride Balbus, Zamil stabbed three more blackcloak attackers. Then, his weapons gone, he strangled another.

"Fire! Fire!" screamed Celt voices. "The Roman fiends set fire to the pines!"

Flames burst out of the forest and swept toward the smelters and refineries and the Celt horsemen swarming the south shore.

Snatching up Balbus, Zamil ran west to rejoin his troops, but safety was cut off by scorching blasts of fire and smoke.

"*Pro Roma! Pro Roma!*" voices hailed from beyond the fiery pines.

Suddenly a net of braided rushes shot out and settled about Zamil and the old man in his arms. The more he thrashed to break loose, the tighter gripped the meshes until Zamil, shielding Balbus in his embrace, went down.

"Aye, and you are a brave warrior," said a guttural voice from the haze of yellow smoke. "We will take you and the soldier in your arms to our immortal chieftain, oh Roman in wooden armor."

Billows of smoke poured out of the burning forest over hordes of guerrillas tearing down the smelters and refineries. Waves of deadly silver ore gas rose from the wreckage, driving back the troops of Chieftain Malendi, the deadly green vapor of the molten ore mingling with the heat and smoke of the blazing pines. At last somewhere in the choking fog a horn blasted and a stentorian voice shouted:

"Brave comrades, to horse! To horse! Away from this cursed place of Romans! Back to our immortal chieftain and our holy land!"

The retreat was disciplined. Celt cavalry swiftly re-formed, un-wounded tribesmen carrying wounded and dead blackcloaks. Zamil was roped stomach-down on a horse's back, but Balbus was carried by a grinning guerrilla. Away they galloped along the south shore of the roaring Sil river, out of the pall of fire and smoke.

On the north shore, four thousand guerrillas whose horses had saved them from the engulfing waters raging in the Sil channel, cantered unopposed to jump their ponies over stone and earth breastworks into the east end of the mining town. The settlement looked abandoned. Wary Celt eyes flashed from building to building, at the closed doors of stables and long sheds at the east end of the camp. On went the Celts, trotting along the main cob-bled street of the Roman village.

Then Flavian and eighteen infantrymen suddenly emerged from the wellhouse at the far west end. At the same time two thousand volunteers poured out of the cookhouse, storage sheds and wellshack and fell in behind Flavian and his thin line of troops in metal armor. Flavian's helmet bore a white plume.

The Celt commander halted his hordes three hundred feet from the massed Romans on foot.

"Roman coward, you call that an army?" jeered the guerrilla officer. "I count your Roman jackals in armor! Nineteen! Holy high nameless god, and you want to fight!"

Flavian and his infantrymen drew their broadswords.

"Roman traitors, surrender!" bawled the Celt. "Beg mercy of our sacred Chieftain Malendi! Forever renounce your plan to drive us from our sacred land! Get out of Spain! Give up the gold you plan to keep! Surrender—or die!"

Flavian and his infantry began marching forward in swinging cadence, long shields up, swords ready. Behind swarmed the slaves with shovels, picks, and files raised.

Suddenly the piercing voice of Rufus Liscus rang out from the buildings at the far east end of the town behind the enemy:

"PRO ROMA! ATTACK!"

The commander and hundreds of volunteers rushed out of the stables and began slashing into the rear of the foe. Flavian bellowed:

"PRO ROMA! ATTACK!" He leaped forward, beheaded the nearest Celt with a savage swing of his *gladius* and slashed off the nose of another guerrilla in the return arc of his blade. His infantry fought with veteran ferocity, pushing the spearhead of the frontal assault into the heart of the blackcloak forces.

Into the bloody gap hacked by Flavian and his troops rushed the volunteers. Spreading out, they swung mallets, hammers, iron files and shovels. Celt slingshot bullets took toll of Romans, Celt stone maces smashed down Romans. Roman javelins pinned Celts together. Roman hammers cracked Celt skulls. Roman rocks thundered into dismounted guerrillas forming a vast circle to try and trap the soldiers of the Sil. Celt ponies by the hundreds threw their riders and snorted madly up the mountainside to freedom.

Now it was a hand-to-hand fight.

In the center of the combat, Flavian and his infantry formed a traditional Roman square with shields interlocked and red swords held horizontal. Volunteers pushed howling Celts towards the square. Dead guerrillas began to pile up in mounds of bloody flesh. But the Celts had re-formed and were attacking from the west and north.

Now the Romans led by Rufus were close.

"Get them in pockets!" Rufus kept yelling. "Mars—attack, kill! Get them in pockets! Mars—attack—kill!"

Rufus and Mars were themselves pocketed by Celts, but the commander signalled a cavalry adjutant and the aide blew a shrieking blast on a whistle.

"RESERVES!" shouted Rufus, as Mars lunged at the neck of the nearest blackcloak menacing his master.

Out of the prisoner stockade, officers' cabins and bath houses of the village sprang scores more of *roararii,* and the division of the raiders into groups became swift.

But Rufus had fallen under his shield and a tangle of Celts. An enemy dirk cut his forehead while another gouged his right leg.

"Mars—attack—kill!" It was the roar of Flavian's voice close by.

Abruptly the weight of sweating guerrillas lifted and Rufus tried to get up, but his wounded leg would not bear his weight.

"Mars—attack—kill!" yelled Flavian.

Strong hands lifted Rufus. He could hardly see, the blood from his forehead dripping down into his eyes.

"Fight's about over, sir," crackled the voice of Flavian over the roar of battle. "Got the foe in pockets, volunteers finishing them off— Here's Mars. Good dog. Mars—heel. Mars—heel. We'll take your master to headquarters cabin . . ."

Commanded by cavalry adjutants, the Roman defenders now had the Celts hemmed around into eight segments, the volunteers killing the blackcloaks in diabolic ways with ladles, lead pipes, saws, pickaxes and the foe's own rock maces and short spears. The encircled masses began singing paeans of victory and slaying each other before the soldiers of the Sil roped the defeated into immovable packs. Over the carnage drifted the odor of burning pines from across the raging river; on the south shore the enemy horsemen were already streaking east in retreat. Rain began falling.

An hour after the battle of the Sil began, it ended in an overwhelming Roman triumph. Disarmed blackcloaks, hands tied behind them and roped waist to waist, were marched to the east end of camp. The still bloodthirsty *roararii* would have slain every Celt prisoner, but Liscus ordered the killing stopped and the enemy prisoners held for possible exchange of Roman hostages. Then came the aftermath of the victory of the Roman Eagles.

Volunteers carried Roman wounded to the officer's steam bath house. They carried the dead to the prisoner's compound, and laid the stiffening bodies on blankets to await identification. All the Roman slain were volunteers.

Above the pastured Roman horses the *Togati* bearer of the message from Governor Maturus had watched the conflict with two elderly whitecloaks. When all was calm below, the mustachioed Roman Celt smiled at his aged comrades.

"Aye, sacred elder warriors," he remarked, "'twas a day the god Gaius triumphed again. Even so did I prophesy it. What will be his next victory? May he meet and destroy the evil black god of the blackcloaks!"

An elder remarked, "Young warrior, the black god is only a legend. Fear you not."

"Think you so?" mused the whitecloak messenger. "My soul whispers that the black one lives. Holy comrades, let us carry the glad tidings of our victory to our sacred chieftain and the Romans in Corunna. *Pro Roma!*"

By sundown the Sil current had slowed, but the waters were freighted with bushes and marigolds, dead frogs and muskrats, rats, beavers and mudfish. Rain was falling heavily, thunder rumbled in the mountains and tridents of blue lightning forked the gray sky. In headquarters cabin a silent group watched Rufus.

He sat with his bandaged right leg on a slab of limestone. A red scab drew a diagonal line across his forehead. Flavian stood at attention and Mars, still in armor, crouched by his master's boots.

"Reports from south shore," said Rufus in a monotone.

A cavalry aide saluted. "Sir, we got over and back on rafts. Buildings destroyed. Forest fire smoldering out. Five volunteers slain; bodies brought back. Zamil and his aide, old Balbus, missing, presumably captured by the enemy. Ninety-three volunteers holding that sector. Heavily armed with Celt weapons. Swore fresh oaths of loyalty. Await your orders, sir."

Another cavalry scout reported. He and three others had swam their horses across the river and followed the retreating invaders. The blackcloak hordes had already passed their camp sites of the night before, with no indication of halting to re-form for a second assault on the mines. The four scouts agreed that all tokens pointed to a general evacuation of territory south of the Sil by Malendi's armies. On their return trip the Roman scouts had searched the willow groves and blueberry bushes on the south banks next to the site of the vanished dam. They reported the muddy shores in the trees thick with hoof imprints and had also found a Roman helmet half buried in mud. It bore a bedraggled white horsehair crest. Silently the trooper handed it to Rufus.

He stared at it.

"Sir, it's the tribune's helmet," said Flavian, hoarsely.

"The ten men who were with my brother, Tribune Lacer, one of you tell me what happened," said Rufus, mechanically.

A cavalryman saluted. "Sir, the tribune was the last man off the dam. We followed his orders. We saw him running towards us. Then the north gate burst and big waves spumed up. The tribune turned and ran south. The dam began to go. We saw the tribune jump over a break in the walkway and start running again. He was close to the south shore. The paving gave way under him. He fell, or he dove, into the lake. Then we saw bushes and boughs pile up and pin him against the dam. Sir, I thought he had drowned—then I saw his white crest. Far away, sir, but I saw it. Then the center-dam burst, and I didn't see him any more."

"Did any of you see my brother reach the south shore?"

Another of the ten men who had been with Gaius saluted. "Sir, I think a few feet of the waterwall near the south terminus of the dam still stood after the rest of the works collapsed—but I'm not sure. All of us kept looking for that white crest. We all prayed to the gods . . . We think we saw a log bobbing close to the south shore, might have been his head. Then the rest of the dam heaved up, the water boomed up." He bowed his head. "We watched a long time, sir. Saw nothing but those drooping willows on the south banks."

Another member of the ten spoke. "The tribune's golden mare, sir—I heard her screaming like a woman when the tribune was in the lake. Then at last she stopped crying. When we went to get our horses, Dawn stood calmly, nodding, as if she was relieved. No trouble leading her back to camp, sir. I felt better. I think Dawn knows her master reached the shore even if we don't. I have a lot of faith in the brains of a good horse, commander. I know them."

The cabin door crashed open and a cavalryman burst in. "Reinforcements! Advance couriers of the VII Gemina just swam their horses to this side! Three hundred cavalry and six thousand infantry due at sunrise to relieve you sir, commanded by General Glaucus! Men of the Gemina report all blackcloak attacks have ceased in west and southwest; guerrillas in general retreat to the east, sir!"

Rufus absently fondled Mars' head. The dog whined softly and licked his master's hand. At last Rufus said to the room in general:

"My mastiff is a mixed breed. He can stalk by scent. Also, he seems to possess a mysterious sense of knowing when a particular individual is near . . . Flavian, go to my brother's cabin. Get his other boots, uniforms, anything he has worn next to his skin."

"Right, sir!" Flavian tore out of the cabin.

XXXI

In the lake, Gaius clung to the log and stroked savagely with his free hand to avoid being swept into the roaring cataract. The short reprieve helped conserve his strength—then a new menace bore down. It was a mass of gnawed birch-boughs, mud and stones. Crouched in the branches was a trapped beaver, squealing in terror as his watery home circled crazily in a whirlpool. The nest thudded against Gaius.

He tried to kick it away, but the submerged twigs and stones of the beaver lodge pressed his legs against the remains of the dam at his back. Unless he fought free of the animal lair he would go with it over the mammoth waterfall. Debris began piling up behind the beaver prison: sagebrush, furze, yellow daisies, bluebells, purple heather and a single wild rose with a dead bee drowned in its limp petals. Another section of the dam collapsed, catapulting tons of water in a crashing surge through the tremendous gap in mid-dam. Gaius felt the log he clung to shaking. Suddenly the lashing current around him reversed itself.

Was it pushing him and the beaver ashore, deflecting them from the deafening plummet of water? The log he grasped broke loose and his fingers tightened around a slippery birch-bough pressed against his body armor. A strong undertow dragged him and the beaver lodge out—back—out—back— Then a stupendous roar deafened him.

Gravel, sand, concrete and logs flew high and the rest of the dam seemed to collapse. The explosion back-lashed, pushing him and the entrapped animal towards shore. Then the water began dragging him and the birch-cage out again.

Now it was swim for his life.

Gaius inhaled through his mouth, buried his head in water and began crawl-stroking, but the weight of his armor and finally his exhaustion was so overpowering that he sank.

Underwater was blue-green, an Elysian world of repose, a soothing universe of bubbling whispers and a lilt of lulling water. Peace . . . rest. How easy to stretch out, deep down, go to sleep and dream. Give up. Die . . .

Penelope! his mind cried as he began exhaling air.

Gaius, I am with you! My strength is yours! Up to the surface!
Up! Up!

Did he actually see his wife's white arms stretching down to him?
Had he heard Penelope's voice?

He broke surface under a mass of bushes; then treading water, he
tried to breathe slowly and gain energy for the fight to shore thirty
feet away. He began crawl-stroking, spending every ounce of
strength.

He became dimly conscious of crawling under a burden of bushes
and twigs through the muddy shallows . . . slowly dragging himself
by his elbows. Drooping, long green fronds of willows brushed his
face. Vaguely he saw a bloody-whiskered beaver hammering its scaly
spatulate tail in the ruin of its lodge . . .

Beaver—lost—his dam. Beaver—build—new—one. Dully Gaius
realized he had lost his helmet. Then he sank into unconsciousness.

In his sleep world he was carried in a hammock of water slung
between two hippopotami. Something hard pressed his lips and he
was swallowing a spicy sweet liquid that burned his throat and
warmed his body . . . He tried to move, to awaken, but slimy reeds
and eel grass coiled tightly around his arms and legs. There was a
roaring in his ears, but he heard other noises, too. Clattering
hooves. Harsh voices. He was bumped and tossed and pain tramped
over his body. Sleep. He dreamed he heard the ghost voice of
Flavian:

Blistering hades! We'll give you a gold mine in exchange!

A phantom dog was barking.

He was forced to drink more of the cloying liquid. He was blindfolded. He slept.

Something slapped his face.

"Wake up, Roman!" croaked a guttural voice. "Wake up!"

But Gaius was dreaming about astronomy. Solstices, equinoxes,
and the earth's circumference . . . distance between earth and
moon? He was mining chalk in Gaul. Chalk used to make plaster
. . . The ancient Greeks believed the planet Venus to be inhabited
by a superior race of mankind—

"Roman—wake up!"

His sluggish consciousness began to stir and dispel the dreams.
The band over his eyes had been removed. Slowly he opened his
eyes to see a spinning circle which gave way to clear images of men

220

in a circle leaning over him. Seven men in long black tunics and sheepskin mantles.

Guerrillas! Arvacan blackcloaks!

"Is our dozing hostage awake at last?" inquired a dulcet voice.

"Aye, chieftain. The Roman who swims in armor is awake."

A commanding guerrilla bent over Gaius as the seven tribesmen bowed and stepped back. The resplendent newcomer wore a silver cuirass, gold helmet adorned with two curved ibex horns, and a yellow chamois cloak. His healthy brown face triangled from a bulging brow and thick bridged nose to a jutting, pointed chin. Lustrous black hair rippled to his shoulders. He made a mocking little obeisance.

"May I introduce myself, Roman?" inquired the Celt. "I am Prince Chieftain Malendi. Your admiring servant." His Latin was exquisite.

Gaius blinked and tried to focus his eyes and mind more clearly.

"Aye, your servitor am I," said Malendi, graciously. "Educated in my earlier years in Rome, re-educated to simple virtues and honor in the plateaus and mountains of my native *Hispania*." He swept another disdainful bow. Then he pulled sheepskins from Gaius and lifted his bound body upright.

"We allowed you a long sleep," said Malendi. "Prolonged with our potent *somnus* wine, Roman. We relieved you of your armor, kilts, tunic and daggers, but you still wear your *brachae*—in the interests of modesty. And your waterlogged boots which are cemented with mud to your noble feet." His white teeth gleamed.

Vision and mind now clear, Gaius seized on one word: *boots*. Coolly he glanced down: he still wore his boots! The aids to victory? He flexed his toes and felt the pressure of the tiny weapons against his ankles.

"Our Roman guests usually spit out defiance and threaten us with the wrath of Jupiter," remarked the Celt general, with a show of false horror. "Your name, oh Roman?"

Gaius, dizzy—no doubt from the drugged wine administered to him—looked around at the large square tent of camel hair-cloth, the earth floor covered with orange and black felt carpets. Long, high-backed settles lined each wall, the seats piled with sheepskins and black tunics. He saw incongruities: a shining cypress table and arm-chair inlaid with silver and gold arabesques, and suspended on a swinging bracket from the ridgepole hung a magnificent big silver lamp shaped like a bireme with silver oars protruding from the two tiers. Flames burned from wicks in the silver rigging and miniature deckhouse of the ship.

"You are no doubt surprised to find us Arvacans to be clean, courteous and civilized," observed Malendi. "And may I inquire, Roman: did our wine paralyze your tongue? We forced you to imbibe copiously, as some of your legion comrades attempted to pay us a social visit, miles from here. For a while they tried to parley for prisoner exchanges."

At last Gaius spoke. "Comrades, noble chieftain?"

Malendi inclined his head sardonically. "We were on a high ridge and the Romans came galloping up below, led by a splendid black mastiff baying its voice to the heavens. One fighter had a northwind voice and spat a strange oath: *blistering hades*. Quaint. The leader of the delegation was a creature of yellow beard who wore a green crested helmet and scarlet cloak. Alas, he had a bandaged leg. I beat my breast in grief. Your friends offered to give me a goldfield if I would relinquish you." The idea amused Malendi. "Gold? Another falsehood, say I. We held you up so they could see you, Roman, fast asleep, your head against the shoulders of my warriors. In a way I regret not coming to terms with your frantic comrades. I would like to have had that riderless golden mare and the black dog in armor. The mastiff almost crawled out of its skin and armor trying to climb the steep ridge up to us, Roman. But dogs are not mountain goats. And—woe—we at last had to toss down a few rocks to persuade your friends to disperse. Virgin goldfield." Malendi laughed.

Gaius was overjoyed and kept his expression grim. Rufus, Flavian and Mars were alive! Trying to rescue him. Then his brother must have won the battle of the Sil.

"You Romans are unpredictable," continued Malendi, with an ostentatious yawn. "You have adopted new and unique fighting tactics. Bursting dams. Forest fires. Copper wires. The suffocating, deadly breath of molten metal. Roman, what is your name?"

Be deferential, grovel if you must, flatter him, gain time . . . "My name, honorable Prince Malendi, is Gaius Julius Lacer. I am an architect. I am also a slave. A special legion officer without pay."

The Celt turned away and whirled around. "The builder of the Tagus Bridge lies. The legions do not allow slaves to serve!"

"I was inducted as a special temporary officer on recommendation of Field Marshal Marcus Trajan," Gaius flashed back. But he read murder in the swarthy faces of the guerrilla warriors.

Malendi whispered to a fighter. The warrior bounded out of the tent and soon returned, dragging a roped and gagged prisoner by the arm-pits. The bound man was black-haired and bearded, and wore a loincloth and battered Roman boots.

Recognizing Zamil, Gaius signalled a look of encouragement. "Chieftain, I know this brave man," he said.

"You do not speak with the profanity of this ferocious blackbeard Zamil," said the Celt leader. He signalled a nearby guerrilla. "Go, now, bring the old one hither."

"You olive-oil decadents," mused the Celt prince, eyeing Gaius with weary contempt. "Yearn you now for a couch and a woman? Alabaster flasks of lily oil to anoint your hair and superb body?" He laughed in derision. "Rome. The City of white temples and golden roofs—and starving slaves. City of glory, bloody history, and human despair—and debauched Vestal Virgins, whores or lesbians, in vile Domitian's reign. Roman, you are a slave? I see no welts on your body. Roman! Do I reek of violets or the perfume of slain roses?"

Humor might help . . . Daringly Gaius replied, "No, honorable Malendi. You smell of fragrant pines and buttermilk."

A glint of amusement seemed to show in Malendi's black eyes for a moment.

Good . . . any gain of time was gain . . . Gaius moved his ankles and toes, and felt the blessed pressure of the knives in his boots.

A warrior entered carrying Balbus. The old man's left shoulder was neatly bandaged. He wore a black tunic and his wrists were tied together with ropes of braided rushes. Seeing Gaius, the valiant trusty smiled happily.

"Old Roman brave one, do you recognize this Roman who claims to be the builder of the Tagus Bridge?" inquired Malendi.

"I *am* the builder," Gaius snapped, folding his arms.

Guerrillas lifted hands over Gaius, but Malendi waved them back. Balbus was seated on the other side of the chieftain and the Celt leader bowed in respect to the old man. This was not lost on Gaius. He would use every device to gain the trust of Malendi.—Now you have to fight with truth. . . . Make him listen. How? If he is the sworn friend of Classicus—

"Merciful chieftain," Balbus faltered. "This brave Roman is Tribune Gaius Julius Lacer. The architect. He saved me and fifty men a year ago when we were in the channel and an earthquake began toppling a cliff."

Malendi laughed melodiously. "Aye. So he is who he claims to be. The empire must be decaying if it uses slaves as officers and pays them not. 'Tis a paradox. A puzzle. Mayhap a supernatural conundrum. We of the Arvacan nation admire magic in any manifestation. Mayhap this Roman Gaius is in touch with Olympus?"

"Chieftain," said Gaius, "I challenge your strongest warrior to combat. I will kill him. By magic."

Malendi was startled. So were his warriors.

"In the legions they call me 'Steel fingernails,'" Gaius pressed on. He held out his mud-caked hands.

"Liar," muttered Malendi. "Roman traitors, you are going to die."

"Not traitors," Gaius shouted. "If you kill me and my two friends, we will be avenged by the bravest and best Roman—Marcus Trajan!"

Malendi looked pleasantly pained. "You creatures of treachery. Your emperor, the Nerva, of roving big nose and underpulled rabbit jaw. Do you beasts think you can annihilate my people and drive us off our lands? Not so long ago, Trajan and I sat in this tent in amity. But now does the once noble Trajan ever answer my letters? Nay—"

Gaius arose from the settle. "Chieftain, did your scrolls to General Trajan ever get to him in Germany? Has he written to you and his letters never arrived? Think, gallant Malendi. Who has mail censorship powers in Hither Spain? Where do couriers stop first with mail from the eastern provinces for Hither and Farther Spain? Where? They stop in New Carthage! Do all the letters that arrive from the east continue on to Governor Maturus in Gades and up here to your realm? Where do outgoing couriers, bound from the east, stop before travelling the road system into Gaul and on? *They stop in New Carthage.* Who can read every letter? Destroy those he does not want to continue to their destination? Who? Cornelius Classicus!"

"Beware how you malign Classicus," said Malendi softly. And blackcloak fighters, their dirks pointed at Gaius' naked chest, forced him down on the bench.

"Chieftain," shouted Gaius, "Cornelius Classicus is your enemy. Not your friend. Classicus stole twenty-five thousand in gold from the tax coffers of Hither Spain last year. Classicus is a thief, who would sacrifice every warrior, woman, and child of your tribe if by so doing he could lay his hands on gold that is not his!"

"Roman, you are rash," said the Celt. "Why do I waste time letting a prisoner slander my friend, when even now enemies are preparing to attack us—enemies paid by Maturus from gold mined at the Sil!"

"No, chieftain," Gaius interrupted. "Sir—listen! I was chief engineer of the Sil mines. We found very little gold and silver. It was safely received in Rome." Gaius dared smile. "It was transported by magic, honorable Malendi." Had he gone too far? He was fighting for his life—

"And how was the miracle accomplished?" asked Malendi.

"Through your helpful cooperation, chieftain. My brave brother, Commander Rufus Liscus, sent the precious metal in the helix of an Archimedes Screw—through your territory. For by then we had been warned by Maturus that you were going to attack us and seize the gold for Classicus. The gold reached Rome." Gaius rushed on, "The gold is where it belongs—in the custody of its rightful owner, Emperor Nerva."

Malendi looked at Gaius and his long brown hands made delicate chopping motions. But he only remarked, "Fear is the father of frantic falsehoods, Roman scoundrel."

"Not falsehoods," Gaius said. "The truth. How did Governor Maturus warn us? You ignored all his messages. But ships do sail the Atlantic, chieftain. They dock at Corunna. That is how the warning from Maturus reached us at the Sil. That is how we later learned from the chief of mines that the Archimedes Screws—and the gold and silver—had reached Rome!" He was standing again and no Celt warrior tried to make him sit this time. He must press his advantage, talk while there was yet time. "Chieftain! Many of your brave warriors died at the battle of the Sil. For what? Because you were betrayed by Classicus. I advise you, sir, to make peace quickly with Rome. Expose Classicus for what he is, Classicus slandered me, chieftain. He slandered my brother, Commander Rufus Liscus. He expected us to be killed, your brave warriors to claim the gold . . . is that what he planned, chieftain?"

Malendi arose. "I and my valiants are not impressed by the fantastic outpourings of Roman Gaius," said the chieftain. Yet he was frowning. "I must put this bold Roman to the test. My noble prisoner, will you swear by the Black God that everything you have said is the truth?"

Keening cries of terror swelled from the Celt tribesmen in the tent. They fell to their knees and hid their faces.

"I will," said Gaius, recklessly. Black God? A hideous stone image spouting flames? Ebony statue? Or—a *living* thing? A five-hundred-pound mountain gorilla?

"You know not by what you so recklessly swear," said Malendi, slowly, almost with regret. "But vowed have you. Accept do I. Therefore, doomed Roman, say I this to you: if the sacred Black God judges you a man of truthful tongue, the terrible divinity will allow you and your two friends to pass his sanctuary unharmed and with his heavenly blessing. You Romans bow to the decrees of your emperors. We Arvacans hold the decrees of our Black God to be the final judgment. But you swear by the arcane and unknown, so pity is in my heart for you. And since this is your last night on earth, you and your doomed comrades will be my guests of honor. We shall feast and discuss, say, immortality?"

Gaius had lost his courage but managed to give the impression of an unconquerable Roman. "Chieftain, your black deity will rule in my favor."

" 'Tis madness or death to gaze at the dark immortal," Malendi sighed. "You and your two brother Romans must try to walk past the shrine of the unspeakable Black God, the dreadful one, the high and horribly-beautiful one. Aye. I salute your insane courage. But we must needs sup and talk of religion? Or mundane affairs?"

A distant trumpet blasted in the distance outside the tent and a blackcloak rushed in:

"Chieftain! *Togati* night raiders coming up from southwest! Lusonians!"

Malendi dashed out of the tent, followed by his warriors.

Gaius jerked the tent flaps shut, then he was sawing apart the ropes binding Zamil, using his aides to victory. The tiny blades were dry and sharp. "Zamil! Take sheepskins, cloaks, stand behind me—" He quickly freed Balbus of the ropes binding his wrists. Then they heard screams from outside and the thin and defiant hails of the whitecloaks:

"*Pro Roma!* Vengeance!

"Death to Malendi!

"*Pro Roma!*"

Gaius furtively pulled aside the flaps and peered out, hoping to see Rufus and Flavian. But the sudden battle between whitecloak horsemen and blackcloaks on foot was thundering in the middle of a vast clearing rimmed with domed huts. By the uncertain light of the campfires Gaius could see only a rushing mass of dark warriors and an occasional Roman Celt, white robe over his metal breast-plate, hacking with sword. Was this an independent grudge attack of the whitecloaks against their traditional blackcloak enemy? Or retaliation for battles fought in the west between the legions and *Togati* allies and the allies of Malendi? Now—how to escape with Zamil and Balbus? He felt a sheepskin thrust over his bare shoulders.

"Your orders, sir," said Zamil.

"Ready." Boldly Gaius led his two friends out into the black shadows, then they began hurrying towards the last row of thatched huts near a vast pony corral. Celt women had rushed out to fight side by side with their blackcloak men and their habitations seemed empty. Yet terrified children poked their heads out from under cowhide curtains serving as doors. Gaius and Zamil pulled out child after child, even two infants in woven wicker cradles, thrusting them for safety back into stands of evergreens, for some of the huts were on fire. The last cabin next to the excited ponies in the big pasture was empty.

A dimly-burning clay lamp showed the round hut to be a combined arsenal-kitchen.

"Zamil—those two goathide sacks," Gaius ordered. "Fill them—anything. Dirks, ropes, food, anything—" He lifted the cowhide portal and looked out.

Bonfires and burning huts cast eerie light on the fighting in the great cleared area of Malendi's fortified plateau camp. Far to the right the Celt chieftain was fearlessly directing his counterattack against *Togati* on fast brown horses. The whitecloaks seemed outnumbered at least fifteen to one. They can't win, thought Gaius, watching in fascination a few more moments as the roar of conflict surged first one way, then another. Slingshot bullets whizzed into human targets, lances flashed, Celt women screamed, and then Gaius saw Malendi's tightly-packed warriors start an inexorable forward push and the gallant whitecloaks began galloping away.

Now was the time for Gaius to launch his own offensive. He overturned an oil lamp to set the hut on fire, then he and his companions rushed out to the pony enclosure. Zamil lugged two goatskin bags bulging with supplies, while Gaius picked up Balbus.

There were no sentries guarding the horses, but the animals were so maddened by the sudden war that Gaius realized it would be dangerous to try and capture any to aid their own escape. "No ponies—we'll have to walk," he told his friends. He dragged open the log gates and yelled,

"Pro Roma! Charge!"

The blackcloak steeds clattered out and thundered towards the warriors of Malendi.

Safe for the moment, he studied his position. Trying to flee through the blackcloak settlement would be suicidal, despite his sense of direction telling him it was the only route to the valley. His swift looks around had shown the Celt prince's stronghold to be on a high plateau surrounded on three sides by mountains. At last he decided: we can't go down, so we'll go up. Up the mountains.

With Balbus in his embrace and Zamil carrying the loaded sacks on his shoulders, they started a slow climb through a dark forest. Gaius' eyes soon adjusted to the blackness and strange white-dark of the clear and starry sky. He set their course by the stars, heading in a general southeasterly direction. At last they stumbled onto a worn path leading that way.

Disturbed birds were chattering and invisible woodland creatures skittered and scurried. Then they heard a gravelly snarl and saw two green glowing eyes in the dense blackness ahead.

"Zamil, halt," Gaius said in undertones. "Give me something hard from your sacks." Gaius put Balbus to his feet.

"Here, tribune," whispered the husky volunteer leader. "Crock of Celt butter. Have to save our dirks, sir."

Gaius took aim and threw the heavy dish. He heard it strike something and with it a roar of animal rage. The green glowing orbs disappeared. They heard the creature thrash away into the forest.

"Butter for the bobcat," chuckled Zamil. "Wonderful strike, tribune, sir."

Up, ever up. The air became cold as they climbed over fantastic stone pinnacles and fields of petrified lava. Now the forests were below and they were helped by the arc of the moon and the clear brilliance of the night sky. They could see into dangerous crevasses, move around or take big strides over to safety.

Before sunrise Gaius found the ideal hideout: a wooded waterfall glen, its narrow entry half-concealed by scrub pines, broom and furze. Sending Balbus and Zamil in, Gaius destroyed their bootprints leading up to the slender rock corridor giving egress to the peaceful glade and its tumbling cascade. Backing in, he piled stones and branches to barricade the entrance to their hideaway. He watched the sun come up and felt the chill air begin to warm. From back in the hidden retreat came the cries of bluejays and buzz-saw drumming of woodpecker beaks at work. Today would be hot.

When Gaius joined his comrades, Balbus lay asleep on sheepskins, covered with black tunics. Close by a tumble of water splashed down from a mass of limestone. Dense stands of pines, firs and stunted junipers edged the small clearing, the cold green shade cast by the trees already becoming tempered by the warmth of the rising sun.

Zamil snapped a fine salute. "Breakfast, sir," he said, with a grin. "Sorry, sir, you threw the bowl of butter at the cougar or whatever it was. No butter for your acorn bread. I washed the dirt off the olives. That corked jug is full of buttermilk. The other one contains cider. That hard hunk must be dried codfish, tribune. Tell by the smell. The other is dried venison. Think we have bearmeat, too, in the sacks. Will the tribune recline? Or sit?"

Gaius joined in the spirit of banter. He felt like yelling over the joy of escape. "Dirt on the olives, Zamil? I shall have to report that to the emperor. Negligence such as that? Where is my velvet couch? Do you think I am accustomed to sitting on pine needles while I eat? What sort of an orderly are you?"

Zamil doubled up with laughter. He and Gaius ate heartily. A man could march for miles after eating the tough acorn bread, and, sour as it was, they even relished the buttermilk.

"Zamil," said Gaius. "I'm climbing the waterfall summit to try and gauge where we are. Guard the entry to this glade. Let Balbus sleep."

Sixty feet above the glen, he stood on a stone platform that to his experienced vision seemed to have been chipped and crudely smoothed by human hands using flint tools. Thrusting the thought away, he looked north into the rocky coniferous land sprawling down into a far valley. The fortress camp of Malendi must lie down there somewhere, hidden by the forest, but Gaius could not see it. After a careful examination of that panorama, he looked southeast into a verdant valley.

Tiny puffs of dust were rising far below, meaning men on the move, for Gaius recognized the wide sweep of greenland as the territory of Lusonian Whitecloaks. Had they won the raid last night against Malendi's fortified rocky plateau camp? Probably not, but with good fortune the conflict might have ended in a stalemate. Suddenly he wondered: did the *Togati* attack on orders of Rufus to try and rescue me? Now he remembered that two of the Roman Celt horsemen had dashed through the melee towards Malendi's tent.

Yet after they reached the valley of the Roman Celt tribe, Gaius dared not run any hasty risks, because Celt loyalties now might be uncertain. Worse, if the *Togati* saw Gaius and his party in black tunics and sheepskin cloaks . . . how obtain ordinary brown or gray clothes? Travel furtively through Lusonian land *by night,* hiding by day in forests of ash, lime, birch, oak . . . Press steadily southeast under the stars towards the arid interior of Spain. Somewhere they would come to Roman farms or waylay a Roman shepherd; even the dry plateaus were not entirely wasteland. There were still rich stretches of cork and holm oaks to cover their progress.

And avoid Roman legion patrols; such might be under the orders of Cornelius Classicus. Go home—home to Ioza. Home to Penelope and Gaia Juliana . . .

Surveying the sheer rock dropoffs shouldering down into Lusonian territory, he saw a long serpentine green ribbon far below, and after a careful inspection of the landscape he at last knew where he was. The stream was a headwater of the Tagus; that straight gray thread across the land near the river was the roadway used by the gold expedition last year. The Sil mines must lie sixty to seventy miles northwest, and Malendi's domain would be between, so it was hopeless, then, to try and return to the Sil. His first instinctive decision had been right: go home to Penelope and his baby daughter. Now the perils of getting down to the Lusonian valley. His first thoughts on that were weapons and food.

Zamil's sacks were stuffed with round loaves of the acorn bread. A pot of brown honey. Quantities of green olives. Slabs of sharp white cheese. Dried codfish, bearmeat, antelope and venison. Jugs of buttermilk and cider. They could fill empty earthen bottles with pure cold water from the cascade. The precious goatskin sacks also contained several sharp dirks and coils of rush ropes. And once in the valley, even in blazing, humid July, when most rivers were trickles, Gaius knew how to track down rushing brooks protected in gulleys by overbending trees and bushes where trout could be caught with frayed rope strands, worms or dragonflies or beetles for bait. Eat the fish raw; fires might attract hostile eyes. Find mushrooms, even truffles. Long ago he had learned the difference between lethal toadstools and edible puffball food of the forest. Knowledge, priceless knowledge . . . the lore of the wilderness he had learned while building bridges and roads. All was now more valuable than gold. He next considered how to descend to the tempting green vale of the Lusonian *Togati*.

He stood on the highest of five peaks at an elevation of approximately four to five thousand feet. Westward, natural solid stone temples and weird watch-tower formations loomed out of lower levels of green forests and the perilous rocky region they had covered during the night to reach their present haven. Retrace that route, branching south at some point to reach the green lowlands? Too hazardous.

Malendi's warriors might be searching that area right now . . . Gaius turned north, seeing that his crag and four other mountains formed a huge horseshoe, a rough arc. Beginning with the height he stood on, the other mountains to the west, northwest, and north formed an enormous crescent looping east, surrounding a great forested gorge. The adjacent mountain west had a flattened, jagged top which he recognized to be an extinct volcano, but his eyes searched this carefully.

Extinct? With the early morning mist evaporating, he began to make out faint clouds of vapor rising from the crater, and glimpsed a sparkling blue-green gem in the maw. Warm lake in the rocky cone? Very possible. He stared—had he seen a tiny dark mass appear and disappear in the blue? Could there be a lake and trees inside the dead volcano?

He eyed the fissured lava declivities and the lower rough folds where grew a few warped pines, green cacti, gray smoke bushes and encrustations of lichen and moss, and he observed the volcano's eastern flank where a corded lava formation from the cone down resembled giant stairs, ending in a sheer drop of about three thousand feet. But that stair-lava with a few pines and bushes for gripholds, could be crossed . . .

With increasing hope he followed the rim of the tremendous chasm around to the north where a narrow stone ledge descended west to east . . . down . . . down . . . down to the Lusonian valley! But the escapeway could not be more than two or three feet wide. One crumbling rock, one wrong step . . .

There was no other way, Gaius saw, once more examining the vast panorama of peaks, forest, and volcanic cone, for a less precarious descent. Then they must cross the lava terraces, move out on the granite projection across the dangerous big gap and—perhaps—thus get down to the Lusonian valley.

Down in the cool green glade he found Balbus had eaten codfish and acorn bread and washed it down with handfuls of water from the cascade.

"Balbus, how is your wounded shoulder?"

The trusty smiled gratefully. "Tribune, sir, before the blackcloaks attacked the mines, I prayed to every known god. Then I prayed to the Christ Jesus of the fisherfolk sect. I am not religious, but it seems that the god of Christians has taken my sore shoulder on his back."

Zamil tore in from his sentry post at the entry to the glen.

"—Blackcloaks coming up from west," he panted. "They just emerged from trees about three hundred feet below us. Think Malendi's leading them—saw a flash of gold. His helmet?"

XXXII

At the entry to the waterfall glade, Gaius and Zamil lay on flat boulders and warily peered through piled pine branches. Now two hundred feet below, pacing their horses, came twenty-five Arvacan blackcloaks led by Malendi on a dappled gray stallion. The chieftain's silver breastplate and gold helmet glittered in the sunlight. The Celts were following the route taken by the fugitives.

"Zamil," whispered Gaius, "go over the rocks to our right, to the west slope of that volcano to the north. Start a stone fall—draw their attention past this place!"

The volunteer was already on his way before Gaius stopped speaking. While he watched the inexorable ascent of the guerrillas Gaius assembled a pile of rocks . . . He began to sweat. He piled more stones, fist-size chunks that could crush a skull. The advantage was his, he could hold off an army from his high nest. At last a familiar musical voice rang out from below:

"Roman Gaius! Rash fool! You are up in the waterfall glade, for where else could you be?"

A rash fool . . . ? After a pulsing silence Gaius called, "Good morning. *Saluto.* The rocks are loose up here. The view is inspiring."

"Madman!" screamed Malendi. "Disturb not the Black God! *He lives!* Do not trespass, challenge not the ageless one!"

Rocks began hurtling down from the western flank of the extinct volcano, and then came the reverberating cry of Zamil: *"Pro Roma! Pro Roma!"*

When the thunder and echoes died away, the blackcloaks were crying in horror.

"Blasphemers!" bellowed Malendi. "Defilers of the Black God's holy shrine!"

Gaius shouted, "The black deity and I had a conversation at sunrise, Celt murderer. The sable dark divinity and I formed a pact of mutual aid!"

"Liar! You have seen not the dark leviathian or you would be insane or dead! Go not across the lava to the granite ledge! I have come to save you!"

"Liar!" Gaius replied, furiously. "Treacherous Celt! Gold thief of a blackcloak! Stay where you are, my ignoble host!"

Zamil crawled up from behind and sank down beside Gaius. "What's the black devil yelling about, sir?"

"Roman, I will kill you for your insults!" shouted Malendi. "I come in mercy, and you—"

"Celt, I will kill you," Gaius flung back. "I know rocks, my cowardly Celt. The bridge builder knows rocks. Do you want death from rocks?"

There was silence from below.

Gaius felt slightly uneasy. "Zamil, they must have a wild beast up there in the volcanic lake. Did you see anything, any signs, on the western slope of that cone?"

The younger man shook his shaggy thatch of black hair. "Slippery stuff at the base of the slope, tribune. Patches of rain, I think. Before I pulled the rocks loose, thought I heard a kind of whistling sound from high up by the lava top. Perhaps the wind."

"I offer you a clean, swift death!" shrieked Malendi. "Come down, come down, reckless Roman!"

Gaius replied with slow emphasis, "Malendi, last night you promised to leave the decision to the Black God. Your black deity was to judge whether I told the truth—or not. Deny that!"

"Come down—come down—" pleaded Malendi.

What kind of a beast or beasts lurked in the volcanic crater? Now Gaius was sure the warm lake in the volcano contained some mystery. But once the Celt lured Gaius and his comrades down by fear, they would be captured again, and sure of dying.

"Start your horses down, Celt," Gaius roared, "or you'll be killed by rocks. Start!" He flung a few.

At last Malendi's delegation reined their restless ponies around and began descending. Gaius watched the retreating guerrillas until he saw them reappear five hundred feet below and finally vanish in a stand of pines. After a long wait Gaius and Zamil agreed that the threatening Arvacans had all departed.

"Zamil—load the sacks. Get out dirks and ropes. We're crossing the eastern lava reefs to a stone shelf at the north down to the Lusonian valley."

Before leaving, they drank from the crystal cold water of the small stream, then Gaius roped them all together, allowing twelve feet of slack cord between each. He looped the length hanging from the waist of Balbus around his right arm and picked up the aged trusty, as Zamil, behind them, pulled the supply bags over the pine-needled rocky ground.

Pines, junipers and wind-bent scrub oaks sheltered them until they reached the first wide rough step of pink-gray lava rock. There Gaius called a halt behind a screen of smoke bushes resembling twisted tentacles of paralyzed vapor.

He knew why he had stopped. He was afraid. It was not the sudden shock of dread when he had seen the *turbo* rumbling out of the sky towards the Tagus Bridge, nor was it the icy chill that gripped him when he had stood on his log platform in the rockway of the Sil and seen the cliff begin to thunder after the earth tremor. This fear was different. It made his body clammy and hot, seemed to pull like quicksand, dragging him down. If he gave way to the alien horror his very soul would die. They must go on— He saw an eagle soar overhead, dip slightly over the cone, and then with a scream of fright, veer off to the east . . . What had frightened the eagle, symbol of Roman courage? He watched the big winged being vanish far away—

Balbus let out a choked gasp and at the same time Zamil cried hoarsely,

"Holy . . . god . . . of . . . hell . . ."

Gaius was the last to look west and up, and see what the others had already seen: the monster high on the lava, far up, yet hideously there. And alive.

Alive!

"The—black—god—" Gaius spoke almost with reverence.

He stared in frozen disbelief at an enormous serpent spread out in triple S-shape at the jagged lip of the lava orifice. Mottled with coral and sulphurish streaks, the gray-black leviathan moved its wedge snout languidly. Then the horrible head froze as if discovering the three puny humans crouching behind the ghost bushes below it.

"Has he seen us?" Zamil's teeth were chattering. "How long is it?"

". . . Lord Jesus, maker of all creatures . . ." faltered Balbus.

"Thirty feet—forty?" muttered Gaius. "Python? Anaconda? Marine monster? In this altitude? Lives in hot lake and trees in the crater? Tropical snake in northern Spain?" Talking helped him keep body and spirit together, brought back a faint thread of courage. "Ancestors of that titan brought to Spain centuries ago by the Phoenicians? Stand perfectly still! Don't go demented and jump into the gorge."

The behemoth viper's head swung upward as the loathsome creature began writhing down the corded lava of the northeast volcano flank. When the lateral undulations ceased, the serpent lay between the humans and the granite escape ledge, gazing at them across the lava stepway. Gaius imagined he could see the horror's gummy and lidless eyes—eyes that belonged to a life form that must have fought the gods when the world was young, back beyond time . . . Gaius' dread was so overwhelming that it had given way to a curious and peaceful detachment. Did the serpent have vestigial legs or flippers, and were there knobs on its head? Was it a true snake?

Then one section of the scaly monster humped up its thick cylindrical length and moved its head back and forth with a dry hissing and ghostly ululation. An eerie idea seized Gaius: the Black God was *benevolent!* He began considering the serpent without horror and revulsion, but as a marvel he had never seen before.

"Gods! Can the black monster be starting back up to the crater?" Zamil gasped.

The miracle was happening. The serpent turned and began oozing upward in rhythmic contractions, and after a long time of death-filled waiting the head vanished into the cone of the volcano. Then followed black and coral and yellow-streaked sections of the forty-foot long body. Soon there was no sign of the mammoth reptile.

They heard a dull splash from the crater lake.

The Black God had spared them and returned to its watery lair. The rockslide Zamil had started must have disturbed the snake king of the crater lake . . . Gaius wondered if serpents *heard* or *sensed* vibrations, such as clattering rocks. He did not know. One thing he did know: his unsuperstitious mind now accepted as fact the legend of the god Apollo slaying the Python. For a taut few moments he was a child of six, standing with his master Apollodorus in the marble Baths of Titus in Rome, gazing up at the frightening statuary group of Laocoon and his sons being squeezed to death in the coils of huge snakes.

"Let us return to the waterfall glade," sighed Balbus, shaking like an aspen in Gaius' hard hold. "Many names has god and over all is— I am not afraid to die."

"No." Gaius was measuring with his eyes the distance to the granite projection. "Eighty feet to go on the lava. The snake moves slow, we can get across before— Zamil, walk with care, don't slip on that viscous exudation left by the Black God. Forget the sacks."

"Better drag them. Sir, I'm rear guard, I'll keep eyes up on the lava, let's go."

It seemed as if Gaius walked for years on the rough hard lava, moving like an automaton with Balbus tightly in his arms, the rope binding both to Zamil pulling steadily from behind. Hotly the sun beat down, but Gaius was a man of stone flesh and bones walking a treadmill, actually standing still.

Then suddenly all three stood on the rocky shelf leading down to the valley.

Old Balbus moved slowly ahead while Gaius helped Zamil drag the goatskin sacks . . . Boughs and leaves of overhanging oaks shielded them from the sun as they moved carefully along the narrow rock path that ended in a precipitous drop close at their right. Had the Black God ever writhed down the ledge to the Lusonian valley? Would it follow and destroy, or force its maddened human prey to jump into the salvation of the forested chasm? The strain was too much. Sour hot liquid gushed up in Gaius' throat. He vomited. Zamil held his shoulders until the convulsions stopped.

"Steady, sir," said Zamil, gently. "Watch out, Balbus, you're too close to the edge. Hang on to the oak boughs as you go."

They plodded on. After they had put nearly a mile between themselves and the volcano of the snake, Gaius looked back. There was no sign of the scaly monstrosity that should have been fossilized and entombed eons ago.

Their progress now was easier and safer than Gaius had dared expect. Normal animal life appeared: a red fox darted out ahead as the ledge widened into a small meadow, then sprang back into the woods after seeing the approaching travellers. Brown squirrels frisked and chattered. Birds caroled in the forested heights to their left. The sun was in the west. The deep green gulf of trees on their right was now only five hundred feet below the ledge. The sun blazed at their backs.

Rounding a huge granite boulder, they saw a rocky, wooded meadow and a squat apple tree bent down with yellow fruits. A dry stream bed and gaunt gray rocks flanked the welcoming green retreat at the north. To the east, the life-saving stone walkway disappeared under trees to the valley floor. Gratefully they sprawled under the apple tree, drinking water from a Celt flask and eating the mellow-sweet *pomum*. Gaius soon sent Zamil to explore the dried-out watercourse where blackcloaks might lie in wait, while he went out on the ledge to look back again at the now distant and misty volcano. A shout from Zamil brought him back in panic. "—Malendi—?" he asked.

"No! Gold and silver!" Zamil exclaimed. "I found this in the gravel back there, tribune!" He thrust out a gleaming rock sparkling red, dull blue and gray.

Even before testing the specimen with a knife, Gaius knew the metallic elements of Zamil's find were iron pyrites and copper. But protruding from the mixed mass was a hard, serpentinous mass of blue green. Partially embedded in it was a grayish formation resembling two small pyramids joined base to base, the whole the size of a small apple. The mass was colorless, brilliant of luster and felt greasy to his touch. He was incredulous, unwilling to believe the evidence his eyes and hands recognized.

He had to convince himself by trying to gouge the mineral with an aid to victory.

Anxiously Zamil asked, "What's wrong, tribune? Did I find gold for you?"

"No." Gaius smiled. "You didn't find gold. You've found a *diamond*."

Balbus and Zamil stared as Gaius finally pried the precious gem out of the blue-green hard ground holding it. "My blade can't scratch it."

"Try and bite it!" cried Zamil.

"Break my teeth," Gaius chuckled. "If my knowledge is correct, this is not quartz or white sapphire, either. Sapphire has a different *feel*. This prize has one of the individual crystal forms, adamantine fire, and impervious hardness of diamond, the hardest substance on earth." He handed the stone to Balbus.

"Holy gods," whispered Zamil.

"It feels slippery," piped Balbus, giving the jewel to Zamil.

"Another indication that it is a true diamond, the most imperishable creation in the world," said Gaius, dazzled by the discovery made by Zamil.

Zamil pushed it into his hand. "It's yours, tribune. Keep it! I'd give you the empire if I could!"

Gaius was tempted. He held possible emancipation for Penelope and sure freedom for himself in his palm. Rich Romans or wealthy lapidarists would pay from thirty to fifty thousand goldworth for the raw diamond . . . buy Zamil's pardon, and pardon for Balbus, use the rest of the money to help Rufus pay back the despicable Classicus. Yet there were mineral laws governing rights to precious stones and ores, and personal laws of morality he tried to live by. At last he said to Zamil,

"Keep the diamond. Conceal it until you can turn it over to Governor Verus Maturus of Farther Spain. That is the lawful procedure. Maturus may decide you to be the rightful owner. Or he may rule that the stone belongs to Emperor Nerva."

"No Caesar gets his claws on this," growled Zamil. "It belongs to you, tribune. *You*." The young volunteer bit into another sweet apple and ate it furiously.

Balbus interceded sweetly. "Zamil, so like a son to me, would you want misfortune to overtake Tribune Lacer? Would you want him to break the laws?"

"No," agreed Zamil. He stalked back and forth, the diamond clenched in one hand. "The laws! Yet I want to be right and do what's right. I want to work for a pardon for Balbus and then myself. All right. I'll give this diamond to Governor Maturus the first chance I get. All right."

The jewel was a glistening augur of future good fortune, and even Zamil became cheerful as they set out again for the Lusonian valley.

An hour before sunset they reached a densely-wooded bluff fifty feet from the valley lowlands. Concealed among ancient oaks, cedars and beeches was a squat, truncated pyramid building of weathered granite and loaf-shaped interlocking roof tiles. An air of vast antiquity emanated around the structure and Gaius was again enthralled in the awe of trying to decide the true essence of *time*. The weird old building was remarkably preserved and so thickly surrounded by trees that the sunlight barely penetrated into dusky green shade. It was apparent that no human being—or snake—had invaded the wooded bluff for years. Perhaps centuries.

"I think it's an ancient shrine," he told Zamil and Balbus. "I'll see what's inside . . ."

He saw dim carvings in a huge granite slab within the walls. Inscribed in the rock were faint outlines of incised monstrous forms holding men in their giant jaws . . . a dinosaur . . . a fiendishly-grinning tyrannosaurus . . . and a flying reptile . . . There were a few almost-obliterated hieroglyphics which he could not decipher. Carved by men? Or man-like beasts? All the time of the world's living seemed to be pressing around him, begging to tell him the story of the past. The top of the carved stone was deeply-hollowed. Altar . . . ? Human or animal sacrifices of ages gone? Sacrifices for what? He summoned his friends.

Hastily he and Zamil cleared out dead leaves, spiders, and clacking black beetles while Balbus clumsily spread sheepskins and blackcloaks on the mossy green slab floor for beds. A gaping hole in one wall was plugged with an enormous grapevine spreading over the roof outside. Gaius and Zamil blocked the narrow doorway with bundles of oak boughs interwoven with woodbine and Celt ropes. When they finished, they were secure from invasion by man, beast, or giant snake. Surely the hideous king of the crater never went far from its warm lake; Balbus insisted on staying awake, on guard.

After a meal of acorn bread, bearmeat and cider, they stretched out on sheepskins and wrapped themselves in black cloaks. Balbus soon arose and sat against a wall.

"Sleep," the old man said. "You let me sleep this morning. I am wide awake. There is no fear."

Gaius was fighting sleep. Chill night and darkness came suddenly and with it a silence that seemed to whisper in forgotten language the forgotten sagas of forgotten centuries.

They rested next day in the temple and that night set out again, reaching the valley undetected, and making their furtive way at the bottom of a deep and wooded ravine. During the dark hours they heard horsemen—Celts—in the vicinity, but were not discovered.

They had to take one enormous risk before dawn—cross a small stone bridge spanning the headwater stream of the Tagus. No one saw them reach the shelter of a cork oak grove on the other side. Had they crossed the Lusonian valley and reached Roman farm land? Then Zamil stumbled and tore the ligaments of his right leg. Leaving the volunteer leader with Balbus among the trees, Gaius stripped off his black tunic and sheepskin, and wearing only his loincloth, stole on towards a low sandstone wall and small farmhouse and sheds. Concealed by bushes he watched a man limp from the farmstead and move to a barn. Soon the man emerged, cursing:

"Vesuvius take that bastard of a weasel! Six chickens gone! Feathers everywhere—and for this I served in the legions, lived through Vesuvius spouting—"

The farmer was Quadratus, the soldier! Gaius was sure of it when the ex-legionary came nearer and he saw the man's scarred face.

"Greetings, Quadratus!" Gaius called. "Remember me? Lacer the architect? Remember the Tagus Bridge? The tornado?"

The astonished agriculturist gaped, then hobbled to the wall. His smile made his face even more hideous.

"The bridge builder!" said Quadratus. "Gods—welcome! Where are your clothes?"

"The last I heard, you had gone to Malta," Gaius exclaimed, as the two embraced over the wall. "Pensioned because of wounds, friend?"

"Wounds? Me? Except for my face, architect, I'm sound. Never a scratch until I land on that island of Malta. I fell down a well. Gods! What a heroic end to my years in the army! Climb the wall, Lacer—my home is yours!"

They embraced again.

XXXIII

When *Togati* horsemen galloped into Ioza before dawn on the day before the Nones, with news that thousands of Malendi's warriors were in battle formation close to the Sil mines, Beryl became hysterical and had to be put to bed. Penelope forced her to drink strong spirits of wine until she sank into a mumbling half-sleep. Sitting by the bedside, Penelope prayed soundlessly:

"All-God of love and strength, save Gaius, Flavian, all the men at the Sil . . . All-God, pure love, save them . . ."

240

Somehow she worked through the day, diagnosing and prescribing for the ailments of sick Iozans. She plucked slivers from sunburned hands and feet. Wrapped cleansed cuts with wine-soaked bandages. Smoothed calamine ointment on the sore eyelids of a senile Spanish woman. Each healing was saving for Gaius, saving for Gaius. "This decoction of iris root should ease your cough . . . Upset stomach, little boy? Shall we try dandelion water, little soldier? . . . We will try this decoction of anemone leaves for that headcold, domina . . . A love philtre? I cannot be of help there, do forgive me."

Early that afternoon while Beryl slept on, Eunice bustled in with heartening news. Turdo and several other men had gone north by horseback with *Togati* warriors to try and learn what was happening at the Sil mines. Penelope must not give way to grief, her Roman aristocrat was strong and wary, all would go well. Penelope nodded, and fed a wooden spoonful of crocus medicine to a Spanish wife suffering from a headache. Then without warning, real hope surged through her. Gaius and the men at the Sil had been forewarned!

She and Beryl had misinterpreted Flavian's last epistle from the mines. It *had* been a strange letter. He had harped about Beryl's black hair. He wanted her to dye it red or bleach it yellow. He was tired of all that black. To Flavian his domina's dark tresses reminded him of the nights at the Sil mines. Those sudden nights could catch a man of no experience, but not a campaigner like Flavian. '*You build a night-camp wall before night hits,*' he had written.

Penelope was jubilant. What Flavian had actually written to Beryl was: '*The blackcloaks are going to attack. We're ready.*'

All Beryl did, when awakened and told, was weep and moan. Penelope became stern.

"Stop this weeping," she told Beryl. "Our husbands were forewarned! They are great fighters! I saw them fight in the battle of the canyon. They were outnumbered, but they triumphed. Flavian lives —he loves you! He is brave and canny—don't you understand?"

Beryl cried against Penelope's shoulder. "I want my baby," she sobbed.

Smiling, Penelope soothed, "Flavianus is sleeping. So is Gaia. Eunice is taking care of them. Now, we'll re-read that letter from your husband again . . ."

At last Beryl began to smile faintly. Then she said, "I'm dizzy."

"I know," Penelope agreed, muffling a laugh. "Alcohol does that, dear friend. I had to put you to sleep."

Women of Ioza whose husbands were with legions on the eastern front where the Dacian barbarians threatened, arrived and sat disconsolately in the various chambers of the cave habitation. The atmosphere of the home became funereal. Wearily Penelope took the babies' cradles to an unused bedchamber and prepared them for the night. Both children were restless, but at last she got them to sleep.

In the main room she glanced at Spanish wives sitting in solemn grief. Eunice alone seemed cheerful as she soaped and sanded medical instruments, put used compresses and dressings into a cauldron of boiling water on the brazier and tidied the makeshift cupboard of herbs and remedies.

"Eunice—I am tired. I am going outdoors for fresh air," said Penelope. She wanted to find a private place and pray for Gaius.

Eunice turned. "Our Spanish healer will stay within. Remember what Turdo ordered. No one outside Ioza must ever see your face or golden hair. More so now than ever. Forebodings fill me. Tonight you sleep in my cave or in the tunnel. Turdo would command it. My man Turdo is not here. So *I* command it."

The other Spanish women nodded and again returned to thoughts of their legionary spouses.

"There is no danger," said Penelope. She wrapped a blue cloak around her white smock and gray skirt and pulled the cowl over her forehead to conceal her bright braids. "The mountain meadow above is safe. You and Turdo often take me there on moonlight nights, remember?"

"It is still daylight and my husband is not here," Eunice retorted. She dropped forceps and metal probes into the bubbling potful of soiled bandages and sponges. "No flockmen up in the highlands either, to keep watch over you and their sheep. Our shepherds have driven the animals east to better pastures." She pulled Penelope to the cupboard of medicinals. "What is in that jar?" Eunice demanded.

"Poplar gum to be used for eyewashing," said Penelope.

"What do you give when people pass too much water?" It was clear that Eunice intended asking questions all night if she had to and so detain Penelope.

"Medicine of madder is one," Penelope replied, with a glance at the blue door giving access to the ledge path. Somewhere outside she would sense the presence of Gaius. . . .

"I shake all over," mourned Eunice, holding Penelope by her arm. "Give me something to send away the trembles."

Penelope's patience ended. "Eunice, you are as healthy as an oak. You do not need rosemary distillation or any other decoction to quiet you. You do not have dizzy spells or weakness, so you do not need iron water. You are carrying your unborn second child perfectly and I cannot forsee any complications."

"Do I nestle a son or a daughter inside?" Eunice asked, briskly. "Will you give me narcissus medicine if I need it when my child is born?"

"If you need the *narka,* you will have it." Penelope removed Eunice's restraining hand gently but firmly.

"Stay within," warned a Spanish woman sitting near the flaming brazier. "Obey Turdo and Eunice."

"My back is starting to ache," cried Eunice as Penelope reached the door. "Oh, my back! Such agony!"

Penelope opened the blue door and went outside.

The lower tiers of cave homes were already in green and lavender dusk as Penelope moved along the ledge path. Down by the rushing stream men swore at donkeys and goats, women shrilled at their children and black pigs grunted at barking dogs. None of the villagers saw Penelope hasten up a steep rough stair cut in the rocks near Beryl's cave.

At the top she emerged on a flatland of rough grass nibbled to the earth and surrounded by tall sweet chestnut trees and huge boulders. Remote mountains glistened white and gold in the westerly sun. Here was a woodland sanctuary of the All-God, her place of meeting with Gaius.

Penelope's blue cloak dropped to the ground. Which way was north? West? Which way was Gaius? She heard the rustle of leaves, not the voice of her love. She heard only the wind grieving among the chestnut trees.

She stretched out her arms. "All-God of love, I heard Gaius this morning. He called my name. You gave me power to help him. Give him more aid! Help my Gaius. He lives, he lives, he is unharmed."

An indignant voice from the stone stairs called, "Penelope! *Penelope!*" Beryl's head appeared above the top rock tread. "What are you doing alone up here? I did not believe it when Eunice— Songs of the sainted King David, come down at once! *Aie,* may Jehovah forgive your rashness! May the fighting gods of Rome and Greece—" The wife of Flavian darted to Penelope, picked up the fallen cloak and wrapped it around her. Scolding in undertones Beryl forced her friend down the stairs and both disappeared.

They had been seen by a watcher in the woods.

The witness was a soldier of the Rapax Legion cavalry wing that had arrived recently in New Carthage from Mauretania in western Africa, bound for an outpost in northern Gaul. Temporarily the Rapax horsemen were substituting for Governor Classicus' riders of the Theban Legion who had been sent upcoast to Valentia to aid that city's municipal guards put down an uprising of taxpayers in that coast city of Hither Spain. Spying on a cave village was hardly to his taste, yet his respect for Cornelius Classicus began to rise. No wonder His Excellency yearned to recover his lost Greek captive—there was a girl worth owning. Too bad she had not ventured close to his rocky lookout where he had been whittling to pass the dull hours while waiting for something to happen. Well, his two-day observation of Ioza had borne successful fruit at last. The girl sought privately by His Excellency was here in the cave settlement, as the exotic Zinga had suspected. And the legionary and his two comrades had followed orders . . .

Do not be seen by the Spanish settlers. Remain concealed. Try and learn if a Greek girl of surpassing beauty, golden hair, blue eyes, and named Penelope, is in the town. She is a slave of Governor Classicus' and must be returned. If you see her there, return at once to New Carthage . . . her re-capture will take place later.

A short time later the trooper and his companions were riding fast horses back to New Carthage.

The next morning villagers spread word that a cavalry contingent and carriage were approaching Ioza from the Mediterranean. When the coach and horsemen stopped by the stream, polite peasants swarmed around curiously. The sole occupant of the open vehicle aside from a veteran soldier driving the two sleek white horses was an Egyptian with a look of secrecy. He wore blue livery, a gray mantle fastened with gold braid frogs and held a blue parasol. He had come on a confidential mission from Governor Verus Maturus of Farther Spain. He introduced himself as Phrones, confidential aide to the noble Maturus. He had come to claim a lady named Penelope.

Since his cautious orders drew no response from the puzzled Iozans, he repeated his command in Latin. Then in Greek. He tried two dialects of Egypt. Next, Hebrew. And at last, Aramaic. Since none of the villagers had ever seen an Egyptian before, their apparent blank uncomprehension aided them in protecting Penelope and her baby, both hidden in Turdo's cavern. The natives silently appointed Beryl as spokeswoman.

She was frightened and did not believe Phrones to have come from Maturus. The Egyptian looked crafty and he was certainly out of place as chief of a body of troops.

"His most clement excellency, Maturus, thinks that a lady by name of Penelope, may be living here," said Phrones to Beryl. "I cannot disclose any further information. If the lady is brought at once, she will ride in comfort in this carriage. I will loan her my umbrella if rains come," he added, with a narrow smile.

The courtesy of the Egyptian and his enigmatic smile raised Beryl's suspicions and convinced her that Phrones was a spy sent by Classicus—not by Maturus. Rapidly searching her memory, she recalled that Turdo, after his secret journey to Gades and secret return to Ioza, had made no mention of an Egyptian scribe of Governor Maturus. Proud of the thought that she thought and acted emotionally most of the time (and was right most of the time) she at length said,

"The lady named Penelope was here. She went long ago. She went north. She has gone."

A look of horror overspread the wedge face of Phrones—and Beryl misread it to be anger. Now she was sure the man of the Nile had been sent by the orders of Classicus.

"And why do you look around at us, noble sir?" she demanded, folding her arms. "I tell the truth. The Greek girl is not here."

"I pray to Isis that she is," said Phrones, firmly. "I regret that I must order my troops to search this village."

Beryl drew herself up proudly. They would never find Penelope. "Then do!" she said, sharply.

But first the Egyptian tried diplomacy. He had come to escort Penelope to Gades. If the noble villagers would trust him—and he was worthy of that—all would be well. He understood their desire to shield the Greek lady. As these appeals only solidified Beryl's suspicions, Phrones and his soldiers questioned the children.

All acted their roles to perfection. They remembered the Greek lady of golden hair and were sorry she had gone away so long ago.

Then they romped away to play with their dogs and wade in the stream.

The soldiers of Phrones did not find Penelope.

They failed to discover the tunnel leading out of Turdo's cave home. The entry to it was hidden under an outspread lion pelt and fierce, black-maned beast head. It looked to be nailed to a wall in the habitation; actually the lower section could be lifted, showing a small door that led into the chilly marble tunnel.

Conceding defeat, Phrones repeatedly told the Iozans that if Penelope still was concealed in the village, she must come forth and have the Iozans take her to Gades—quickly. If there existed any misunderstanding, Phrones tried to make it clear that grave trouble might threaten the Greek lady if she failed to obey His Excellency Maturus.

Eunice had joined the throngs around Phrones while his soldiers searched every level of homes in the mountains. "Penelope has gone, noble Nile sir," said Eunice, over and over. She was grimly committed to the shielding of Turdo, for her gladiator spouse had fiercely cautioned her never to mention his trip to Gades. Turdo would do anything to help Gaius and Penelope, but at the same time he must never get caught himself by Classicus.

Phrones and the villagers were at tragic cross-purposes. He had asked several times if a gladiator named Turdo lived in the settlement, only to be met with blank looks and head-shakes from the townsfolk. The Egyptian scribe made the error of being overly cautious—but he was committed to the protection of Governor Maturus and, to a degree, Lady Enna. It was she who had at last reasoned that Penelope had not gone north with Gaius, but might have been left for safety in Ioza. And since she might be an important witness against Classicus, Governor Maturus had dispatched Phrones on this journey.

His face expressionless, Phrones at last got in his carriage that afternoon. As a light rain had started to fall, he opened his blue umbrella and departed in dignity, his forty cavalrymen thundering behind.

Four days after the Nones, armed couriers and escorts clattered through Ioza from the north, and tossed a scroll on the road as they sped through without stopping. Beryl was washing the babies' swaddles in the stream and knew the message must be for her.

246

Not looking at the address tag, she shakily ripped it open while women gathered around:

Confidential to Domina Beryl, wife of Acting Centurion Flavian from Rufus Liscus, Acting Legatus of the Sil imperial mines. War launched by Malendi's blackcloaks the day before the Nones resulted in overwhelming victory for our forces. Your husband survived without a wound and is on his way to New Carthage to be mustered out of the legions. He will not go through Ioza. My beloved brother Gaius Julius Lacer was captured by blackcloaks after performing incredibly heroic service for the emperor. We saw him alive after the battle and tried to bargain for prisoner exchange. We failed. To my joy I later learned from Lusonian Togati warriors who later made an independent night raid on Malendi's main camp that a man answering my brother's description was seen there and escaped into the mountains with two other Roman prisoners of Malendi during the indecisive night battle between our whitecloaks and Malendi's tribesmen. I trust my brother in every way and most of all I place faith in his caution. I now start in haste for Gades. The mines are held by General Glaucus and the VII Gemina. Burn this epistle. Vale.

Beryl hurried up the mountain paths to her home where Penelope was setting a child's broken leg in the main room.

"The All-God be praised, great is his mercy!" cried Beryl. "Gods of Rome be praised! Every god be praised!"

Penelope finished binding leather straps around boards holding the little girl's fractured right leg before she spoke.

"They are safe," murmured Penelope, giving her patient over to the anxious parents. Then her control gave way and she began crying. She was taken to her room by Beryl and Eunice. She read Rufus' letter so many times that the words seemed written in her mind.

"Gaius is coming home," she breathed. "He is nearer every hour. He is coming home to me and Gaia. I feel it. Great is love. He and his brother. Great is love."

But Turdo had not returned on the morning of ill omen: the Ides of July, the ninth day after the battle of the Sil. It was a bright and sunny morning. Penelope and Beryl had just finished bathing and swaddling their babies when Eunice bustled in, bubbling with laughter.

"A carriage and troop of horsemen are coming this way from the Mediterranean," she said. "It seems like that man of the Nile is going to pay us another visit. Come you, Penelope—into the tunnel. I'll bring Gaia. Hurry!"

Two lamps burned dimly in the dank marble cavern while Penelope peered out of the crevices and down at the stream. Women knelt by the waterside, pounding red and black and white garments with porous rocks and slabs of brown soap. Children raced back and forth, dogs barked, chickens and ducks clucked and honked and goats were being milked. A mule stood on the roadway while his eloquent Spanish master pleaded graciously that the noble four-foot earn his fodder by moving a few hoofsteps. Then mounted soldiers clattered into the village.

They were everywhere. They were off their horses, they were roping the women and men into terrified groups— They were lashing the screaming children together—

Penelope watched in stunned inertia.

"Orders are orders!" came the voice of an officer in a black crested helmet. "A slave named Penelope is in this settlement! Surrender her at once in the name of Governor Classicus! The slave named Penelope is the property of the noble proconsul Classicus!"

"She is not here, she has gone—" Beryl screamed.

"Liar!" shouted the officer. "The golden-haired girl named Penelope was seen up in that mountain meadow the afternoon of the day before the Nones. A black-haired woman of this town called her by name: Penelope. You are guilty of harboring an escaped slave unless you surrender her at once to her lawful master, the most noble excellency Classicus. If the girl is not found, or does not give herself up, every tenth one of you will die!"

The dazed villagers stared mutely. A few women screamed. Children cried in terror and tried to break loose from the ropes binding them in tight clusters. Dogs barked and snapped at the soldiers until two troopers slashed their broadswords and slew the frantic canines . . .

Like a somnabulist, Penelope carried Gaia out into Turdo's cave home. She laid her child on Eunice's bed and wrapped the sleeping baby snugly in a gray blanket.

"My little wonderful," she crooned to the sleeping infant. "The

All-God watch over you, child of Gaius, love of our love." She dared not kiss her baby.

Penelope moved out on the ledge path in full view. "I am Penelope," she called. "I will do as you say."

The officer in the black-crested helmet started coming up to meet her.

"I give myself up," she called, "but only on condition that no person in Ioza is harmed. Do you understand?"

"Orders are orders," the officer hailed. "No one dies now. Have no fear, domina. Your good master Classicus wants you at his side again. You will ride in state back to New Carthage."

She stared unseeingly as the polite officer helped her into the cushioned carriage. She hardly heard the wails of Beryl, the cries and protests of the other villagers. She had saved Gaia, saved Gaia, saved Gaia. Gaius and his daughter would go on. Gaius . . .

But she turned back as the vehicle started rolling out of Ioza. The officer was true to his promise: his troops were hacking the ropes binding her friends together. She caught a glimpse of Beryl trying to run after the carriage, and then Eunice stopped her and led her up to a ledgepath.

At noon Turdo arrived alone on horseback from the north. Within minutes the enraged German was in a wagon drawn by two dependable brown horses and on his way in pursuit. He had sworn to wrest Penelope from her captors; the villagers were to leave her rescue to him. Now the Big Lion of the arena would become the Tiger-Stalker. He would save Penelope.

Before sunset a bearded traveller in brown homespun and a wide brimmed black felt hat climbed down the rock stairs from the mountain meadow. Gaius had come home to Penelope and his daughter.

Beryl threw herself in the arms of Gaius and gasped out the dreadful story. He listened dumbly.

"—And she gave herself up to save us," Beryl sobbed. "Oh, God—God—God— They would have killed every tenth one of us . . ."

Eunice's pretty face was drenched with tears. "Noble sir, brave patrician, here is your daughter." Mutely she held out Gaia Juliana.

Awkwardly Gaius held his child; he was looking in a daze at the lovely baby face, the dark brown curls. He seemed to be looking at a small version of his own face. His trembling lips touched Gaia's forehead. He was crying. Then he gave his daughter to Eunice.

He turned and stared at men of the village crowded into the main cave room. They understood.

"Two fastest horses in the village, lord sir," said one. "One to ride, one on lead rein. Yours."

"He'll need money."

"Food."

"Come with us, lord tribune."

As the full moon glowed in the tranquil evening sky, Gaius was on his way. He did not run his horse to death. Make better progress if he allowed both animals to canter, then gallop, then slow them down . . . mustn't kill my horses . . . I'm coming, Penelope, I'm coming. I'm coming. Full moon, the Ides, ride all night, I'm coming. Daggers in my belt, aids in my boots, I'm coming— Red sparks showered from the horses' hooves.

XXXIV

Gaius lifted an arm across his head and tried to shut out the mournful cries that dinned in his ears, while his other hand groped for Penelope. A blur of alarm stirred in his dulled consciousness as his fingers touched moisture and stones. Had his wife slipped away to let him sleep off his exhaustion? Then the distant weird sounds struck his eardrums so forcefully that he came fully aware to the worst of the dreadful truth. He was not with Penelope.

He was in prison.

Prison.

Keeping his eyes shut he tried to remember—what? It was coming to him. He had made a desperate effort to rescue her . . . Then the knockdown, gag, hood of rough sacking pulled over his head, blindfolds, ropes . . . a jolting journey in a wagon . . .

He lay quietly, giving mind and body time to regain full consciousness and energy and at last cautiously opened his eyes. A resin torch in a thick sconce flared outside an iron-barred door. Cries from somewhere outside thrummed and drilled in his ears. Birds? He recalled the aviary of the New Carthage legation. Was he in a dungeon of Classicus' palace? He must be. Where was Penelope? He strove to recall the sequence of events from the night he had arrived in Ioza on the Ides of July. At last he was reliving it again.

He recalled bits of his furious pursuit of Penelope . . . The faithful strides of his two brown horses, ridden alternately. . . . If he had only been astride Dawn of the flying hooves—a thunderstorm, market towns sleeping under the half moon. Black cattle grazing behind pink walls in daylight . . . forced stops he resented for rest and food, and to water, feed and wipe down his reliable but not too fast horses. Then into the saddle again, cutting the distance between himself and Penelope.

Clearly he remembered the afternoon of the third day out of Ioza, galloping up a rise on a short cut he had taken through a forest of dwarf palm trees. There below, the jewel-blue Mediterranean, the New Carthage legation a white marble mass several miles away. And close below, a carriage and cavalry detachment! Concealed in a pomegranate grove on a low cliff, he watched the troops dig a ditch and erect a low palisade of wood stakes. His horses becoming restless, he hastily led them back into the woods and tethered them. At his observation post once more, he peered through evergreen shrubs until he saw Penelope emerge from a tent and stand talking with pleading dignity to a commander in black crested helmet. Then she went back in her shelter and closed the flaps. The heartbreaking view of her had so wrenched him that he forgot to be on guard, and he was suddenly hurled to the ground from behind.

He lashed out futilely against hard hands, until getting a glimpse of his antagonist's face.

"Turdo," he gasped, "I'm Gaius Lacer—tribune—grown beard."

The German pulled his hands away. "Bad, bad, down there. I just come back up cliff from spying. Soldiers in camp are desert and mountain fighters from Africa. Famous sword fighters, the eyes of Argus. No quarter asked or given. Turdo knows when to fight, when to wait. We wait." Then a warm smile banished his satanic one. "We tiger-stalk. I have cart and horses back in forest. You will ride in my wagon. I go to New Carthage to get quarry tools. I get into legation grounds, nobody say Nay to Turdo, killer of Thrysa the Terrible. We watch where golden goddess is taken in legation. Then we get her out, put her in wagon with sledgehammers and you—and then away. You be reckless, go down the cliff and try to rescue her alone, and she die. We do it my way or I sit on you all night."

Gaius had promised so convincingly that the gladiator finally went back in the forest to see to his horses and those of Gaius. Once sure the German was out of earshot, Gaius crawled head first down the cliff, under cover of oleander bushes and evergreen shelter. When he reached low ground, he saw the moon shining brightly over the camp. The troops were busy with trenchers of skewered hot mutton and flagons of wine. Keeping to the shadows Gaius maneuvered undetected through sentry lines, at last reaching the wooden palisade wall. Clawing the soft earth, he burrowed under three stakes and sank down behind a carriage in the encampment. Penelope's tent was at the opposite end of the area. To reach it Gaius moved on his elbows under the shrubs next to the wall. During his noiseless advance he saw the cavalry commander in a black crested helmet seated in the open by a campfire, drinking.

The cavalry leader got up and began strolling towards Penelope's tent. Gaius kept in advance of the probably ardent officer, and at last dropped prone between the rear of Penelope's tent and the camp wall of sharp boughs. Now he must risk all to save her.

"Penelope," he said, distinctly, "I have come. It's Gaius." He reached under the bottom of the canvas between two pegs.

He heard her gasp of delight, felt her soft lips on his hand. "Dear wonderful, dear wonderful—go back. Go! I love you!"

He thrust a dagger into her hand. "The cavalry officer is coming to this tent—"

"Go," she whispered, sharply. "They know nothing about you— Gaia is safe in Ioza—"

"I saw my daughter; I kissed her."

"Go," Penelope begged. "Don't let them capture you! Go quickly!"

Gaius remembered turning to watch the cavalry commander; the officer had stopped to talk to one of his troopers. Gaius used the time to try and punch the heavy tent fabric with a dagger, but the thick cloth was waxed to make it waterproof and his blade slipped. Frantically he thrust it aside and pulled out his aides to victory. The needle-like blades gouged holes that he widened into a narrow slit, giving a partial view of Penelope's taut face and fearful blue eyes. Then he heard quick bootsteps and saw a sentry enter her tent.

"Commander's compliments," chuckled the guard. "How is the lady's would-be rescuer? So he even gave you a poniard! I'll take it, Greek beauty— There. Gods—he's even ripped a gap in the tent! Commander—we've got him!"

Gaius jumped up and stormed around and into the tent. His knuckles cracked the guard's jaws, sent him sprawling, then protecting Penelope at his back, he rushed her out to a clump of shrubs beside the palisades.

Troops converged from all sides.

Lunging at the nearest legionary, Gaius's fist missed as the soldier nimbly side-stepped. Another soldier picked up Penelope and carried her screaming back into the tent.

"Spare him," she cried. "Spare him! Spare him!"

The man in the black plumed helmet strode forward, but kept his distance from Gaius.

"You are guilty of attacking soldiers," shouted the officer. "The penalty is death. Do you want immediate death? Or do you want to be taken to New Carthage and turned over to His Excellency the noble Classicus?"

"I'll take Classicus!" Before he could leap on the officer, he was knocked down from behind, gagged, tied, a sack pulled over his head—

And now he was a prisoner. His sole garment was a dirty brown tunic belted in twine. Where was Penelope? But his daggers—the aids to victory—all were gone.

He was doomed to rot in a dungeon of thirst and starvation, using his failing strength to fight off tarantulas, ants, scorpions, rodents . . . His coarse tunic and limp twine girdle: garb of the condemned. He sank face down on the cobbles, his right cheek in a tiny pool of water.

He wept.

Wept for Penelope, himself, his baby daughter and the end of his fight for liberty. Oddly, tears gave him a curious refreshment, slight consolation, and the feeble urge to get up and fight again. He leaned against a cell wall and in lethargic despair suddenly thought about his father, Consul Julius Lacer, the man he had never known and hated for years. His loathing had lessened after Domina Plotina told him about the Consul's frenzied attempts to re-purchase infant Gaius from Apollodorus—only to fire up again after learning that Consul Julius Lacer had cast off the mother of Rufus. But now . . .

Did despair breed understanding that reached back through the years to the penitent, dying man his sire had been? Suddenly he pitied his father, the man slain by luxury and idleness. He wept for his father, as well as for himself.

Courage flowed in. He began studying his cell.

The three walls were fitted stones and the fourth was the wide iron-barred door of the dungeon. All were fitfully illuminated by the flaming brand out in the passage. How thick were the walls? As if his father were beside him urging him on, he grasped two oiled shafts of the one narrow window slot to the outdoors. Grimly he pulled himself up and got a good look at the outdoor night. It was lighted by distant iron fire baskets and close by he saw a white marble section of the Staircase of Fountains. He estimated the wall thickness: four feet of solid limestone.

On the cobbles again he began glancing to his left and right at the other two walls. What kind of stone?

His skilled fingers, ears, and acute vision agreed that both dry cell walls were dolomite rock, a gray magnesium limestone he had used in small bridges and steppingstones. And both were dry. Desert dry. Instinct nudged his attention to his bare feet.

He stood in a small puddle in a depression of two cobbles. It was fed by a tiny current seeping out of the base of the limestone wall below the barred window space. On hands and knees he traced the stream to its source. The rivulet was oozing out of a minuscule fissure of the window wall where it joined the cobbled floor of the dungeon. And did that wall look grayer, feel slightly damp to this fingers?

Was this wall, too, dolomitic? Softer limestones in their natural habitats often showed weathering—runnels left by rain. Rain . . . water . . . Water trickling out of a stone wall.

He knelt and thrust a finger into the water outlet, and touched a moist, prickly substance. Not hard dolomite! Not stone! He identified the gritty rough matter his finger felt.

The window wall was constructed of imperfectly-dried *mud bricks* coated with mortar and artfully scored to simulate the other two solid limestone walls. Not the most durable cement of volcanic ash and lime, either, held the softened brickwork, but a cheap, sandy mixture. He clawed out a sticky mass of clay and bits of straw, his heart pumping so fast he could hardly breathe. Enlarging the hole, he pulled out a chunk of sandy cement and part of a wet mud brick. If he only had a sharp blade he could cut through the imitation limestone wall. He could hack it out with emergency bits of sharp mortar, but it would be slow work. And where was the water coming from? Defective pipe in the mud brick wall? Down trickled the slow drip.

Hearing footsteps out in the passage, Gaius hastily pushed the dislodged wet clay and cement flush with the wall, noting with relief that it was in fairly dark shadows. Then he moved to the barred portal. A guard approached, the raffish soldier armed with daggers and carrying a bowl and flagon.

"Awake at last, big boy?" asked the bearded legionary, his belly protruded under his metal-tabbed leather lappets. Gaius glanced obliquely at the guard's three daggers thrust under his belt.

"*Verbero!* You need a bath," yawned the soldier. "Who are you, big boy? Sad to say, you're being crucified at sunrise. You and an escaped Greek woman slave of His Excellency."

"Not without a trial," Gaius said, quickly. The soldier was too far from the door or Gaius would reach through, snatch a dagger—lure him closer. . . .

"Governor Classicus is not able to try anyone," said the guard. "But he gave orders through his domina, the Lady Excellency Zinga, that you and the Greek female be nailed up."

"Where is the Greek girl?"

"Her? Gods, in the legation somewhere. She was ranting so much Lady Zinga couldn't question her. So the Greek woman was taken away and put in a room and tied to a chair, I guess. She's not down here in your regal hades, fellow. Too bad. You like Greek women? Here's food. Your banquet. Thick meat soup with beans and mushrooms and the best Falernian from the kitchen. Wish I could wish you an easy death tomorrow." The guard held out the flagon and big bowl of steaming soup.

"I can't reach it, come closer," said Gaius.

"Take your hands off the bars of the door and I will."

Gaius pretended to drop his hands weakly. But the guard had become wary and turned away.

"Wait." Gaius hit on a new subject to detain the soldier. "Brave one," he said, "are you satisfied with your legion pay? Wife happy? Do you have a country villa at the Naples shore? Plenty of slave maids for your domina and daughters? Tutors for your sons?"

The bemused guard let out a snort of laughter. "Are you crazy, big boy?"

"Comrade," Gaius breathed, "would you like to have a virgin goldfield all your own? Would you like to have a map of the hidden ore land, soldier? For you alone?"

The bemused guard stared in a daze and drew close to the barred door. "Gold . . ." he whispered.

Instantly Gaius reached between the iron shafts and snatched a dagger from the soldier. He backed away while the stunned legionary dropped the bowl of soup and winecup.

"You bastard of a stinking—I'm coming in to get my dagger."

"Welcome," said Gaius. "Can you wrestle, friend? Do you want to take my bet? I wager one million in gold that you can't get this pretty little throat-slitter from me. Besides, I have the right to commit suicide."

Scowling, the soldier stared, at last saying, "All right with me if you want to slash your wrists, but you'll be nailed up dead or alive in the morning, big boy. I gave you a present of one of my blades. Too bad you're going to bloody this fine clean cell. It was repaired a year ago." The disgusted soldier spat into the dungeon. "I now bid you *vale*. It breaks my heart. Big dice game going on in the barracks. Pleasant nightmares." He clumped off down the corridor.

As soon as he was convinced that he was alone, Gaius first picked up what broken crockery of the soup bowl he could reach and wedged the sharp bits into the keyhole to jam the lock. Then he went to work with the dagger. He pried out the mud and mortar he had pressed flat to the wall. Then he thrust the sharp blade into the cavity and carved loose a larger chunk of waterlogged mud bricks and flaky cement. He began excavating at an angle that should open into the leafy ditch he had seen in his hasty look at the fire baskets and staircase of fountains. Tunneling steadily, he finally struck a tile pipe, the joinings so loose that water flowed out in a thin stream. Detouring around it, he toiled with care, for the difference between life and death rested in the weapon he had. And now he raced time.

It was night, but what hour of the watch? And was he doomed in spite of his work? Would the dagger strike an impenetrable blockade of kiln-fired bricks or limestone as the last barrier blocking his updig to freedom? Stubbornly he worked, widening the steep angled hollow in the wall, debris piling up on the cell cobbles. Occasionally he stopped to listen. No sounds came from the prison corridor and from outside only the squawks and shrieks of captive birds and the far, melodic music of nightingales. He seemed to dig for hours until his blade grated against a hard surface.

In the blackness of the dank and slippery tunnel he could not see the obstruction, but he could feel it: a hard, kiln-fired brick. . . . His despair became so acute that he considered death objectively. Gaius Julius Lacer, architect, has disappeared. Never found.

Ah, but he was . . . he was immolated in a dungeon wall in New Carthage . . . gods, what a way to die . . . they walled him up.

He lay in his burrow, a trapped and sweating animal, hands mechanically prying loose more soft mudwork exposing more fired bricks. He was Prometheus fighting a losing battle against Zeus; the high deity was cruel and vengeful. *'The All-God is love, Gaius,'* murmured the voice of Penelope in his mind. Love?

Again he thought of his father, Consul Lacer, now as a pure and kindly entity sustaining him, and who never despaired and never lost.

'Love finds the cleft in the rock and breaks it,' sounded the voiceless voice of his father.

. . . Cleft in the rock . . . ?

It seemed as if his father's strong hands guided his to a hard brick with a vertical groove. Again Gaius remembered the first stone he had split years ago. Fixed a wood wedge into an incised line, struck it with a mallet—

Fixing the blade of the dagger into the cleft of the kiln-fired brick, Gaius used his right fist as a mallet on the horn handle of the weapon, striking gently but firmly, gradually increasing the strength of the blows when the blade did not break.

The fired brick broke apart.

Its frame of hard volcanic ash cement fell away—

Weak and gasping, he was looking through a breach left by the broken substance, he was seeing a glimpse of the staircase of fountains! Now the dagger moved without his conscious volition, carefully prying loose the cement around an adjoining brick . . . then another . . . another . . . and he was pushing freed bricks out into the ditch.

It took him only a moment to make the hole shoulder-wide, then to writhe out and lay panting in a bed of leaves, looking up at the starry blackness. He lay motionless, his energy returning, listening for the hails of sentries. All had quieted; even the birds in the legation gardens were temporarily silenced.

Gaius fitted the bricks back into place as well as he could in the darkness, and piled leaves against the site of his escape from the dungeon. Crawling up out of his refuge he bent low and stole to a white marble flight of the staircase of fountains, keeping to the shadowed side. He crept up the marble steps. At last he pulled off his dirty prison shirt and twine belt and boldly stepped under a spray of tepid, carnation-scented water showering down from a huge marble shell upheld by a gigantic statue of Venus. The gushing curtain not only screened him but washed the foulness from his body and hair. The cataract seemed both hot and cold, soothing and invigorating him. Fully revived and cleansed, he climbed out of the basin of the beneficent goddess and donned his filthy garment and rope belt. He dodged down the treads to a wide terrace where another staircase gave access to green turf.

Avoiding tripod iron fire-baskets, he darted through white marble pergolas and arcades, along avenues of sculptured boxwood, between lanes of flowering almond trees. Finally he crouched behind hedges of rose bushes, close to the first floor of the legation, where he could see the glimmer of lamplight through the windows. Which chamber held Penelope? Was she still imprisoned in the palace or had they killed her already?

Trying to get a better view, he got up and moved a few steps sideways—and struck something solid.

It was a soldier in armor and white plumed helmet.

There was no time to escape. With superhuman strength Gaius locked his hands in the legionary's thick neck, but huge hands were choking him. His antagonist was a Hercules, too strong, far stronger. At last Gaius thrust with his knees against the guard's thigh and his assailant reeled backward.

"Blistering hades!" muttered the man.

"Flavian," whispered Gaius. "Flavian . . . ?"

They embraced hilariously.

"Holy everything, we might have killed each other," muttered Flavian. "How did you get out of that cell? I was going to get you out or die trying. I've got your jailer drunk over in barracks! It's about two hours until day. Turdo's waiting near the courtyard in his wagon, he sold your two horses. Now we go for Penelope, stow you both in Turdo's cart and you're on your way!"

"Do you know where my wife is?"

"Second floor of legation, slave women's quarters, room at far east end. I've got a plan."

"So have I. I'll get into that room, but I'll need armor and trappings. I don't want you involved, Flavian."

"What's your plan?" Flavian was hurrying Gaius along through aisles of carved yew.

"Impersonate an officer," said Gaius. "You don't know anything about it, Flavian."

"Sure, sure," whispered the former *optio*. "I'm an officer myself, now. Re-enlisted. Junior centurion, lowest grade. Seems I've got to take instruction in how to heave a javelin and lead an attack—ha. Being transferred to Gades tomorrow. Tried to see Classicus when I first got here a few days ago, but I hear from the household guards here that the proconsul is soft in the brain. I hear, too, that his new wife, Zinga Rutilia, is a lady to watch. I heard Penelope had been taken and a madman of a man tried to rescue her and he was thrown into a dungeon, then I met Turdo and he told me, so I knew it was you down under." Flavian stopped for breath and continued,

"There's an officers' armory next to the room in the barracks where I've got a dice game going like a hurricane. Everybody's winning but me. Most of the lazy troops of the legation are playing—all lucky. I'll put my chair in front of the door leading into the armory. You watch your chance and get into that room through a window—two or three are open."

By now they were concealed in a small circular temple near the looming barracks in the courtyard. A sentry marched past, not too steadily. When he had gone on, Flavian rapped instructions:

"Tribune, don't take an emblemed shield. New regulation, no time to explain, but cover your shield somehow or the sentries may challenge you. Better dress it heroic—plenty of good conduct badges, medals for gallantry in action, figure out some legion you belong to, you're on leave—now's your chance! Crawl through that window!"

In the armory Gaius hastily set to work by the flames of two iron lanterns suspended from rods in the stone wall. He put on a leather tunic, green wool kilts and black leather halfboots. Next, an apron of iron-tipped leather lappets and then a breast protector of flexible banded steel that he locked with clasps under his left arm. Shoulder armor like narrow metal shutters went on next, hugging his neck, back and shoulders like a steel shawl and fastening to his leather shirt with straps to buckles in his tunic. Leather armguards next, then leather greaves for his legs. He put on a harness of cross-straps and belt and thrust three daggers under the girdle. He decided against a pike and unhooked the scabbard of his belt. Finding a battered combat helmet with a small gray crest, he put it on and buckled the strap under his chin. Draping a red-bordered gray cloak around himself, he quickly pinned a centurion's bronze *C* on the left of the collar; below it a small copper torch of good conduct —then two brass oakleafs signifying gallantry in combat. Picking up a small round shield with the embossed head of a snaky hydra, he remembered Flavian's admonition. His buckler must be covered—

A goatskin pelt on a table would serve. He wrapped it around the shield and fastened it in back with a bronze fibula. Ready at last, he looked at his reflection in a polished phengite stone mirror propped at an angle on a table. His warlike appearance was a reassuring shock. Metal cheekguards gleamed against his black mustache and beard. Nobody would recognize him; he did not recognize himself. Stealing to the open window through which he had entered, Gaius slunk back behind hanging cloaks as a sentry tramped past outside.

Meanwhile voices boomed in from the adjoining roomful of dice players. Every so often Gaius heard Flavian roar in hurt surprise when his throws failed to come up with the sacred seven or divine twelve. He vowed by the gods Mithra, Hercules, and Mercury to win some of his silver coins back—and proceeded to lose more. At last, with a great deal of noise, he came into the armory to get some more money, as he told his gaming comrades.

In the room he whistled dolefully, strolled to a window, then gestured furiously for Gaius to leave.

"I'll be stationed under the balcony of the room where they've got Penelope," he whispered. "Work fast . . ."

In the yellow rotunda of the legation, Gaius swaggered past the white marble Fountain of Ceres, attracting sighs of admiration from women slaves in black scrubbing the red and green mosaic floor. Lamps burned dimly in wall niches. Sauntering on, Gaius tried to remember which of many halls opening out of the great domed chamber led to the white colonnade where he had first seen Penelope long ago. Then he saw a shapely woman in brown homespun and cowled cloak enter from a corridor and stare at him in sharp surprise. Her red hair was parted in the middle and hung in tight curls at each side of her wary face.

Gaius halted, for the oncoming woman had an air of authority. When she drew close he saw a black beauty patch on her whitened skin and felt the impact of her animal magnetism . . .

"Who are you?" Her violet eyes met his interested gaze boldly.

At last he remembered Flavian warning him about the second wife of Classicus. He answered, "Beauteous domina, one sight of you and I forget my identity."

"Are you a courier?" she demanded.

He grinned rakishly, blew a kiss, and nodded.

"Where is the message?" Zinga urged.

He pretended to be swept away by her charms. Now to try and lead her—and with her the detestable Classicus—into a trap. "Noble domina," he murmured, "in western Spain we do not see women such as you. Celt girls, while willing—"

Her violet eyes gleamed. "I am Zinga, the Lady Excellency! Where is the scroll? Do you have intelligence from the north?"

Quickly he assembled a tale he hoped would convince her. But first a little necessary delay or she might suspect. . . . "Glorious lady, I am Brutus Sempronius," he said in a conspiratorial whisper. "A man of action. A man of many conquests." His gaze swept her neck and rounded figure. "The lady must forgive me for losing the message on my way from a powerful friend of His Excellency . . . but its contents were confided in me. I heard there was a guerrilla uprising not long ago—"

Zinga's thin rouged lips tightened. "Noble centurion, the governor has heard rumors of war, too. He has not been well and I conduct matters under his orders. The message?"

Pretending to be half drunk, Gaius swept her into his arms, murmuring his wild desire to possess beauty such as he had never seen before. Would the lovely Lady Excellency allow Brutus Sempronius to console her during the lamentable illness of her lordly proconsul spouse?

Zinga relaxed like a limp coil of steel in his arms and for a few seconds Gaius feared she might invite him to her bed. Kissing her cheeks roughly, he looked quickly around the rotunda, catching interested glances of women swabbing the floor. Which passageway led to Penelope? *Which one?* Time was flying!

Pulling out of his caressing arms, Zinga smiled in triumph, but there was anger and fear in her violet blue eyes.

"Quickly—the message," she whispered.

"I would pay gold to have you," Gaius replied, watching her closely.

Gold lights seemed to glint in her splendid eyes.

He must finish this quickly . . . "Most gracious domina," he crooned, "I want a woman. If not you, then a slavegirl? I heard that His Excellency keeps women on the second floor . . . ?"

"The message first," Zinga retorted, letting Gaius lift her chin and kiss her lips roughly.

"The lady toys with me," Gaius smiled. "Tell me where the slave-girls are kept and how to get there. That comes first."

An enormous eunuch in toga entered on light feet from another hall and approached.

"Domina," he said, "is it wise to start on a journey before dawn? Surely another day or two until Governor Classicus feels more able to travel?"

"We must leave soon," murmured Zinga, while Gaius felt the benign dark eyes of the newcomer resting on him.

"The noble Sylvanus need not concern himself," said Zinga. "Kindly return to your bed, great Sylvanus. I am grateful for your kindness. My husband is grateful."

It was obvious to Gaius that Zinga wanted to rid the rotunda of the huge aristocrat. At last Sylvanus nodded and left the yellow marble chamber.

"Now—" Zinga's eyes were flashing with frustrated rage, "the noble centurion will deliver the message!"

Gaius stared as if infatuated.

Impatiently she gestured to a far corridor flanked by two yellow Corinthian columns. "That hall leads to a white loggia and pink statue of Diana," she whispered, jerkily. "There is a staircase to the east wing of women."

Gaius pulled her into his embrace again and then let her break free. "The message," he murmured, "is strictly confidential for His Excellency. It is from Chieftain Malendi."

Zinga resembled a huntress who had suddenly seen her prey.

"I do not know the details," whispered Gaius. "I and my men heard of a war up north, but we were not involved. It seems that Malendi is claiming victory. While I was in his stronghold on a goodwill visit, he entrusted me with a communication for Governor Classicus and told me its contents. The noble chieftain has found a virgin gold-peak in his land and wants to report it to the proconsul."

Zinga had heard enough. She turned to go, but Gaius clasped her in his arms.

"The excellent blackcloak king invites Proconsul Classicus to come north as soon as possible," Gaius told her. "He is anxious to confer with the governor as to the proper method of notifying Rome as to the magnificent new gold territory."

Suddenly she spat, "Snake—take your arms away from me! You

262

reek of carnation perfume, you are drunk, you dare try to make love to me, the lady excellency!"

Gaius leaned her back against his fur-draped shield and savagely kissed her to silence.

"A little love will quiet the lovely one," he said. "Beware how you slander Brutus Sempronius the undefeated. Beware lest Brutus go north and find the virgin gold!" He let her writhe away.

She looked frightened for a few moments, then darted through a hallway.

Gaius blew kisses after her, to the envious sighs of women washing the floor. Then he strolled into the corridor Zinga had indicated. Once out of sight of the servants in the rotunda, he walked rapidly. He passed no guards. He broke into a run—and at last entered the white colonnaded space with the peach alabaster statue of Diana in its niche. He rushed up the white marble staircase—

On the second floor he saw approaching a dapper tribune in spotless gray tunic, lappeted kilt, and gray cloak with two bands of scarlet. The officer was not in armor and gave the languid impression of a man weighed down by centuries of noble ancestors.

Gaius snapped a salute and marched past.

"Halt," ordered the tribune.

Gaius wheeled about, clicked his heels together and saluted again.

Glacially the tribune's sharp gray eyes inspected Gaius from helmet to boots. "Name? Legion, cohort, maniple and commanding general?" inquired the suave interrogator.

Already knowing his antagonist to be slighter of muscle and body than himself, Gaius replied, "Sir: I am Brutus Sempronius, commander of the Python century of *Legio Primus*."

"I am charmed," came the icy response. "There is not a First Legion or Python hundred! You are inebriated and insubordinate! Worse—you are impersonating an officer. Far worse, your blasphemous exhibition is defiance of Jupiter! Or is that Jovian aegis of immortality on your shield the infantry's idea of a practical jest? The sacred goatskin of Jupiter and his mighty daughter, Minerva, degraded thus. A sin against the gods and the sacred authority of Emperor Nerva! You will die at sunrise with two other felons!"

Gaius glanced swiftly around the hall of mottled green marble columns and panels. It was deserted. Suddenly he struck the tribune's jaw, caught the unconscious man and dragged him behind a white marble statue of Eros and Psyche. Then Gaius sauntered on, tossing kisses to women who began peering out from doors ajar. They lured and swayed, but on he went. He turned a corner into the east wing. At the far end stood two guards beside a white pilastered portal barred on the outside. Gaius quickened his swinging gait.

"Jubeo te salvere, young comrades!" said Gaius, heartily, in cordial greeting. "I came to get my property—a girl named Penelope. A Greek."

The youthful soldiers thrust out spears in salute. Then the taller one said, "My regrets, sir, but the Greek woman is to be flogged and crucified at sunrise. His excellency's orders, sir, brought by Zinga herself, the lady excellency."

Gaius cocked his head. "Somebody trying to cheat me? I paid good gold for a girl named Penelope—and she's behind those doors, lads." He glowered menacingly.

"That is correct, sir," piped the smaller guard. "The men dice for anything in the barracks, sir. Sorry, sir. Will another slave suit the brave centurion?"

"I want what's mine," snapped Gaius. He hunched over the puzzled guards. "Are they taking them younger than sixteen in the legions? Things change fast. Listen, comrades: I haven't sliced a man apart since I saw action against the Parthians last year. I'm a peaceful fellow. Less than an hour ago I paid a lot to get a girl named Penelope. I'm here to claim what's mine." He had noticed that the lances of the guards were cheap shafts with brittle ornamental spearheads of copper . . . not hard wrought-iron . . . not steel. Carelessly he took the weapons from the two dumfounded guards and with strength that seemed not his own, he bent the metal tips down like withered petals. Then he returned the lances to the frightened young legionaries.

"I like to help my friends," Gaius grinned. "Now you can't hurt yourselves, comrades. Bolt this portal after me. Penelope and I are going to bed-wrestle and I won't have any embarrassing interruptions!"

The astounded guards bobbed their heads. Gaius unbolted the door and entered a dusky room.

Inside, he heard the soldiers shoot the bolts back into place. Then he found a bolt on the interior side and he shot that. Wheeling about he at last saw a drooping figure of a woman in an armchair near a table.

She was blindfolded, gagged, and half-naked in a soiled brown tunic. Her disheveled braids hung loosely down the white linen band over her eyes.

He reached her in three long steps.

"Penelope, Penelope, love, love," he whispered, a dagger already at work on the ropes binding her. "It's Gaius—"

He had her free at last and in his arms.

Never had she looked so beautiful, her speaking blue eyes filling with hope, weak hands trying to stroke his cheeks. Her lips were parched and cracked, and tenderly he kissed them and cradled her in his cloak. Then he made her sit down and drink water. He jerked a green velvet cover from the table, poured the rest of the water on it and gave her a hasty sponge bath. He ripped off his scarlet-bordered gray cloak and wrapped it around her. She watched in tender amazement, too emotionally spent to say a word. But her eyes talked to him as he led her to a balcony door hidden behind thick lace draperies of green and yellow. Hiding her in the folds of netting he noiselessly opened the portal and stepped out.

He was on a long balcony. It was still night, but he soon saw that the balustraded ledge ended against a wall a few feet to the left; opposite the shelf stretched like a narrow granite road fenced in filigree stonework interlaced with scarlet hibiscus and green leaves and vines. From the distance came the raucous calls of tropical birds—

"Have you got her?" came a sharp voice from the dusk below. "It's me—the junior centurion! Remember me?"

"I've got her," said Gaius, trying to see Flavian.

"Let her overside, I'll catch her," ordered Flavian. "Then you drop. The only way! Sentries thick at the staircase end of this balcony. Lots of heavy hedges, dwarf trees down here. Fast!"

Drop his cherished Penelope over the balustrade? Flavian was a Hercules, but was he strong enough? If the fall killed Penelope—

"Hurry," came the frantic whisper of Flavian. "Sunrise is almost here! False dawn came and went already."

"I'll hurry," Gaius replied.

Inside he had to waste a few moments trying to tie a rope around Penelope's waist, but his dagger had hacked the cords that confined her into useless short lengths. He peered out to be sure no sentry was coming, then carried Penelope to the balustrade and lowered her into the darkness. At the last his hands froze to hers.

"I can almost touch her sandals—drop her!" called Flavian in desperation.

At last Gaius let go and stood in agony—

"Safe!" came the grunt of Flavian. "Penelope—over in those bushes. You up there! Sentry's coming!"

Gaius re-entered the room and shut the door. He tore the goat-skin off his shield and lay the buckler on the floor. At the door he waited until he heard the sentry's measured pace come near, pass, then re-pass again. When all was silent he went out, closed the door, and straddled the railing. He lowered himself into a network of vines and flowers, hands clutching the stout granite spokes of the balustrade.

The voice of Flavian reached him: "I've got a mattress of boughs and bushes down here. Drop! Let your muscles loose! Not far to fall! Quick!"

Something tugged at his boots—

"Feel me touching your shoes?" grunted Flavian. "Let go! Fall!"

Gaius let go—he plunged—

Then he was sprawled in a springy matwork of broken evergreen bushes and dwarf cypress branches. He was pulled upright by Flavian. He was not hurt.

Flavian hustled them across a circular dell rimmed by white marble emblems of the Signs of the Zodiac, then through a narrow lane bowered in pink oleanders.

They cautiously emerged almost into the rear wheels of a big wagon harnessed to a team of powerful brown horses. A tarpaulin canopy covered the top and high sides of the conveyance. The tail gate stood open. A huge figure in a cowled cloak sat holding the reins.

"Sssst," Flavian hissed.

"Watchword," replied a sibilant voice from the driver's seat.

"Ioza," muttered Flavian.

"Get in," rumbled Turdo. "Straw and blankets. Water cask. Two loaves. I have sledgehammers up with me. Stay quiet. I talk us past guards at courtyard gates."

When Penelope and Gaius were in the van, Flavian bolted the tailgate from the outside and pulled down a canvas flap to conceal it, fastening that by heavy cords to hooks.

"The gods protect you," Gaius said through the canopy. "Flavian —be careful."

"I haven't left the barracks," came Flavian's soft response. "I'm in the armory trying to find some more *sestercii* to keep my friends winning a while longer. They're all soused to their skulls. The gods go with you. See you later, in Gades or before. Turdo—get going!"

The cart joggled into motion, iron-hooped wheels grinding on the cobblestones of the legation courtyard.

In the shadowy darkness, Gaius wrapped blankets around Penelope, then took her in his arms and kissed her again and again. Her tears were on his cheeks. His were on hers. Each was thinking of the courage of the other, and to Gaius it seemed as if his father rode with them, nodding paternally, and that soon Rufus would join them and the Lacer family would be complete, triumphant again and for all time. For the love of the father was lavished on all his children. Rufus, too, was in that mighty circle of love.

Then Gaius and Penelope became tense, for the wagon had halted.

"Ho, Turdo at sunrise—there's a sight to strike terror," shouted a strange voice outside. "Big Lion, you promised to tell me how you got Thrysa the Terrible long ago in Rome, people still talk about that one. How did you do it, champion?"

The German replied good-naturedly. "The people all bet on Thrysa. I never was a sword fighter. Thrysa, he was mighty with the blade. What chance had Turdo from Germany? None. I was dead before they sent me out on the sand. The dead can do anything. So I plot to live. Thrysa salutes me, I salute him but I can't hold my sword. It starts to slip out of my right hand. The crowds jeer. Then I switch blade from right to left. Thrysa, he hasn't expected that, and his eyes go to my left hand. I was waiting for that—up goes my right fist, up goes my clumsy left hand with the sword. All over fast. Thrysa goes down, dead, my blade in his neck. Yah. Too bad. A beautiful Thracian was Thrysa the Terrible."

Gates clanged open.

"Watch that road to Gades when you cross into Farther Spain," called a man's voice. "Wild country out there. Thick with thieves, champion."

"Yah, I know. *Vale,*" called Turdo.

The wagon moved out of the legation grounds and the iron gates grated shut behind.

While the cart rumbled west on the Mediterranean coastal road, Gaius fought exhaustion while Penelope slept. He tried to think unemotionally. His battle now was no longer a fight for freedom, but a fight for lives. Lives. Penelope's. Baby Gaia's. His own. He had knocked down soldiers, but his tired mind refused to consider the grave consequences of such actions. How was he to buy his freedom from Apollodorus? Had he escaped with his wife only to enter a final prison? Could he escape again? Escape?

"There is none," he told himself.

Then what to do?

Go to Gades. Place your family and yourself under the jurisdiction of Governor Verus Maturus, with full cognizance of the legal rights of your master, Apollodorus. Surely he would not be summarily executed because he had fought for the life of his wife—and saved himself, too. Surely there must be justice that would save him . . . surely he had rendered useful service to Rome, the gold had reached Rome . . . His mind was slipping into sleep, but he must think on. The problems of the world were greater than those of the individual . . . Will Maturus place statutes first and gratitude second . . . Was he to be like the Oedipus of Sophocles, a man doomed by his own acts? The closing lines of Sophocles' great drama ebbed through Gaius' half-conscious thoughts:

'Mark him now dismayed, degraded, tossed on seas of wildest woes; think on this, short-sighted mortal, and, till life's deciding close, dare not to pronounce thy fellow truly happy, truly blest, till, the bounds of life passed over, still unharmed he sinks to rest.'

Still unharmed . . . faithful friend driving the horses . . . home was this wagon with Penelope in his arms, fragrant straw and blankets for a bed. . . .

Gaius slept.

He and Penelope awoke to the sounds of sudden fierce conflict outside the motionless wagon. Turdo was yelling murderously, men were screaming in challenge—

"Two!" bellowed the gladiator. "Three! You like sledgehammer, bandit? Four!"

The wagon began to jolt and Gaius jerked out daggers from his belt and began trying to pry open the tailgate that Flavian had bolted from the outside.

"Five!—Six!" blasted Turdo. "Yah, the skinny thief—"

"Turdo, I'm coming," Gaius shouted. Now he was trying to slit the tarpaulin of the canopy, but the weapon slipped from his hand. Precious moments fled while he and Penelope groped in the straw for other weapons, but the interior of the cart was almost as dark as night.

"Seven!" shouted Turdo. "You like my stranglehold, bandit? Eight and nine, I crunch your skulls together!"

Over the screams and clash of battle, Gaius began hearing the oncoming harsh bay of a dog and fast hoofbeats approaching, and with both, the fresh challenging cries of men—

Then the voice of the dog again, a deep, snarling warcry—

"Mars—attack—kill!"

It was the voice of Rufus outside!

"Ten!" Turdo blasted. "Yah, the black dog commander and his men! We finish off bandits together! More over in the woods!"

"Rufus!" Gaius called. "Open the tailgate, open the tailgate!"

Nobody heard him.

Then Penelope had him in her arms, the useless daggers lost in the straw again. "Gaius, the All-God sent your brother. Rest, dear wonderful. Your brother has come."

They clung together passionately in the dark wagon until the conflict ended. At last all outside was quiet.

Then the tailgate was wrenched open. Weak sunlight filtered in. Gently Penelope parted from Gaius as Rufus, in armor, looked in. General Myron Frontinus looked in. Freedmen fighters of Frontinus pressed close to peer in.

"Gaius, my brother," said Rufus, hoarsely, "Mars found you again."

Then the brothers were embracing on the road.

A brown horse galloped up and Flavian gingerly let himself down from the saddle.

"Blistering hades! Another fight and I missed it! Lost money last night and too late for a road battle today!"

The reunion began all over again. They all talked at once; Penelope had to remain seated in the wagon while General Frontinus served her bread and wine and told her that she would soon be under the care of his wife, Lady Enna, in Gades.

XXXV

At the eastern European frontier late in June, new duties and new honors had been the lot of General Marcus Trajan. Dispatches arriving from Emperor Nerva appointed Trajan governor of both

Upper and Lower Germany; promoted him to the highest military rank of a Marshal of the Empire; and commanded him to inspect empire boundaries from the *Mare Germanicum,* or North Sea, to the *Pontus Euxinus,* the Black Sea. And he was to hold the Eagle Standards firmly against barbarian armies across the Danube. At the *Mare Germanicum* the legions also occupied an anchor wedge of territory east of the Rhine in the land of the Frisii barbarians, who made no moves against Trajan. All was peaceful among the Romanized Germanic tribes and Latin colonists west and south of the Rhine. No defense problems of any consequence threatened imperial forts between the Rhine and the Danube; east of that region the Hermunduri and Marcomanni barbarians were at present inactive. Along the upper Danube the Quadi savages were quiescent. But a state of sporadic and indecisive warfare existed along the middle and lower Danube where the legions fought off periodic attacks from the armies of the King of Dacia, the most powerful challenger of Roman supremacy.

Inspired by dedicated zeal to smash Dacia, and now commanding all fourteen legions and their auxiliaries manning the eastern European boundary, Marcus Trajan faced the Danube front in Roman Moesia, a province, bound on the east by the Black Sea and on the north by the Danube. On the opposite banks of the winding blue waters were massed the maniacal hordes of King Decebalus of Dacia.

That monarch's primitive flotillas always rowed across to Roman territory at night, ramming ashore in Roman lands where the Danube was narrowest. The foe concentrated its offensives in a one hundred mile stretch. Within that disputed region the Dacian hosts hammered most frequently along a fifty mile area and usually launched several attacks simultaneously.

To blunt these assaults and also maintain imperial lines from the *Mare Germanicum* to the *Pontus Euxinus,* General Trajan's total armed might was two hundred thousand troops. The fourteen legions of six thousand each comprised eighty-four thousand seasoned fighters; the greater majority of men aiding the legions were provincial auxiliaries serving in all divisions of the legions, and bringing the total to two hundred thousand.

The King of Dacia commanded more than a million warriors.

But the men of the Eagles excelled in patriotism—strategy—weapons—and combat tactics. Their united and passionate determination to exterminate every last Dacian soared higher the third week in July when Trajan and his command staff (and Plotina) arrived in the hub of the lower Danube sector most often periled by Dacian invasions.

Along the four hundred and fifty mile Danube boundary of Moesia, forty-two thousand veteran legionaries were supplemented by fifty thousand auxiliaries. Ninety-two thousand in all. They were the troops of the XXX Ulpia Victrix; the I Minervia; the VIII Augusta and the XXII Primigenia; the recently reactivated Alaudae Legion (founded long ago by the Sacred Julius Caesar); the XIV Gemina and the VII Claudia.

Ninety-two thousand Romans confronted over one million Dacians.

Within the fifty mile salient the barbarians evidently considered a weak point of the Roman Empire, were stationed the steady fighters of the XXX Ulpia Victrix, who seemed omniscient in sensing impending attacks; the brilliant and daring VIII Augusta; and the ferocious mop-up fighters of the Alaudae. Constant communication by couriers and semaphore signals was maintained with brother legions up- and down-river. On sunny days brass heliographs flashed coded intelligence of activity seen in the green forests of the Dacians across the Danube. At night the legions shot flameballs if the enemy attacked their sectors.

All was unnaturally quiet for several days when Trajan arrived at his headquarters. Then one morning towards the end of July when he entered his log house command post, he was pleased and surprised to find waiting for him Licinius Sura, a Marshal of the Empire and commander of the eight Roman legions in Asia Minor against the Parthians, a strong Oriental nation with conquest-of-Rome ambitions. General Sura wore a flashing gold helmet crested in white, glinting breastplate of silver, spotless gray kilt and scarlet cloak and gleaming boots. He resembled a canny and contented satyr with a left-sided smile. After he and Trajan embraced, Sura removed his splendid headgear and laid it on an oak table, revealing thin hair the color of ice.

"Marcus, where is your gold and silver regalia?" Sura chaffed. "Ask not, ask not! You look more a centurion than commander of over half our armed forces. Remember the Parthian awe of our sparkle and dash, old friend?"

Trajan nodded. "As a captain during the Judean War years ago I was a vision. Later as a tribune on the Parthian front, my head was compressed in a gold-embossed silver helmet."

"One way of having to think hard," Sura bantered. "Keep the

thoughts confined—eh? How about the Dacian foe? Does brilliant gear frighten them?"

"No, sir." Trajan became dryly humorous. "Truthfully, gold and silver armor seems to infuriate the Dacians into fresh attacks."

Sura groaned. "Thunder of Jove and Mars Repulsor! Off with my dazzle and on with field grays and bronze like yours. Marcus—do not address me as 'sir.' You now out-rank me. Thank all gods that you do."

"Only in the number of legions I command, sir." Trajan smiled admiringly at Sura.

"As you choose. Marcus, will you remove your helmet? Let me really see you? It's been over four years." His dark eyes under thatchy white brows squinted cordially as Trajan laid his steel headgear next to Sura's golden magnificence on the table.

"Marcus, your face is the same," Sura judged. "Serene. Dedicated. The look of the eagle, the look of the future. But long have I considered you as my son. It comes as a stark reminder of my years that your hair is no longer black."

They sat down on a bench near the table while aides of Trajan marched in with maps. Trajan arose and conferred quietly with two of his officers before dismissing them and then returned to sit with General Sura.

"My hair, sir?" Trajan resumed. "Plotina used to call it black stormcloud." He smiled briefly. "Now she calls it gray avalanche."

Sura did not smile. "Marcus, are you discouraged?"

"No. Too much to do." He mixed red wine with water and filled two small and battered wood flagons, handing one to his guest. They sipped reflectively.

"Never think destiny will pass you by," said Sura, firmly. "You are still on the eastern side of fifty." He gave Trajan an approving thump on his backplates. "How well I recall your parents, your distinguished sire and estimable *mater*. Good parents—good son."

The wary black eyes of Trajan beamed. "My wife resembles my mother in character and personality."

"How is Plotina? Your gracious widowed sister? Your charming niece and lovely grand-nieces? And your nephew, Hadrian?"

"When the girls all talk at once they remind me of nightingales," Trajan chuckled. "They are at home in my Colonnia villa. They spin and weave and boat on the Rhine. I transferred my nephew from the Second to the IV Flavia. For a youth of twenty-two,

Hadrian is doing fairly well as a tribune." His sunburned face brightened. "Plotina is here with me."

Sura's angular smile came and went. "Of course! She is always with you . . . but is it safe for her to be in this combat sector, Marcus?"

Trajan sipped the watered wine. "She is my best soldier," he said, simply. "Plotina is an outstanding military tactician—although she denies that. Calls it womanly intuition. She has helped me and my staff plan several land-traps for the Dacians. We have a new one ready. The next time they roar over the Danube, we hope to inflict a smashing defeat—Jove willing." Trajan got up and motioned towards a log portal. "Sir, in the next room you will find uniforms and gear. Then I suggest that we confer in the cool of the forest."

In a stand of hemlocks on the edge of a cliff, they sat on boulders gazing across the sunlit blue-green Danube towards the low forested shores of the Dacians. On the Roman side not a soldier was in view; the two generals might have been taking their comradely ease alone in the wilderness. Sharp eyesight was needed to detect the tree-bunkers and earth breastworks hidden in boughs and bushes. Glancing around in approval, Sura said,

"Marcus, I have much to tell you in confidence. Where to begin?"

"As you choose, Sura."

Sura examined the cinnamon red bark of the nearest tall hemlock and turned to Trajan.

"Marcus," said Sura, "we are loyal to Emperor Nerva."

"*Semper,*" said Trajan at once. "*In aeternum.*"

"Always and forever," Sura duplicated his younger comrade's quick affirmation. "Marcus, I came not to talk treason, so candor is my guide." General Sura chose his words with care. "I arrived in Rome recently to report to Emperor Nerva on the military situation in the Middle East. During our conference, the Emperor asked me to evaluate the characters of outstanding military and civilian leaders. You were one of those." He looked in keen appraisal at Trajan. "Nerva also gave me permission to visit you before I return to my command in Asia Minor."

Trajan still watched the enemy lowlands across the Danube. "Sir, I have not yet had the honor of meeting Emperor Nerva. He orders me to hold this front."

Frowning, the visiting general replied, "Marcus, the Caesar and his Senate advisors are conducting a confidential search for a strong man to recommend as Nerva's successor. After the death of Emperor Domitian, you and many other legion chiefs had every reason to hope that the *Patres Conscripti* would hail you. Instead?"

"Sir—I am loyal to the Imperator, whoever he is. Nerva is our Chief of State."

Sura's whole body seemed to nod reluctantly. "I know, Marcus. From what I hear, the temper of many of your troops is not as equable as yours."

They looked out over the Danube and a cool breeze touched their faces. A gray squirrel darted along a path in the forest, stopped, peered at the two officers, and disappeared.

Trajan at last said, "I have difficulty restraining my men from hoisting me up on the shields. I am not a revolutionist. Who will be our next emperor? Astrologers to the contrary, sir, I think the Senate will pass me by again. My family is Roman and ancient, but of a Spanish agricultural tribe. Not truly patrician. Not by inheritance."

Those restrained observations seemed to Licinius Sura worthy of a light reply. "Marcus, I am one of your long-lineage aristocrats. Let me whisper a dreadful secret: ten, twelve generations ago, the founder of my family helped build the masonry of the *Cloaca Maxima*. We grant that The City could not survive without the Big Sewer—yet we have now disposed of the question of what constitutes a patrician, eh? My boy, your great father, the first Marcus Trajan, advanced from foot soldier to general and then to Consul under one of our greatest emperors: Vespasian. You march the same path taken by your sire. And you were a Consul under Emperor Domitian."

Trajan examined his sunburned hands and wiped sweat off his forehead. He watched a brown-crested lapwing blunder past in convulsive flight and vanish in the green arches of the woods. "I was a Consul, but Domitian kept me out of Rome. Far from Rome. Too far. Strictly without authority, sir."

Sura leaned forward in order to see more of Trajan's face than his profile. "Emperor Marcus Cocceius Nerva is a provincial like you, Marcus. For generations the tribe of Nerva lived in Crete. It is my belief that our Chief of State privately favors a colonial soldier from Spain to succeed him."

Arising from his boulder, Trajan remarked, "Frankly, as you know, I am more at home in camp than in court."

"So was Emperor Vespasian." Sura was standing. "Marcus, you underrate yourself. While in Rome I read some of your battle dispatches from this Danube sector—terse and accurate reports of so many thousands of Dacians thrown back across the river; meticulous lists of our dead and wounded, and lists of Dacian captives taken. Yet a bit of embroidery as to your own superlative victory tactics would not have offended the emperor or the senators."

Trajan grinned wryly. "I report facts. Embroidery is for the ladies."

This drew a humorous shrug from General Sura. He fell into step with Trajan and they strolled between ranks of evergreen trees, the drooping branches thick with pendulous cones.

Sura drew a deep breath. "Marcus, here it is. Nerva told me his government is tottering. He seeks a strong new man to be his Caesar and partner in government—and his successor. When your name came up, I told Nerva that Marcus Ulpius Trajan needed no impassioned panegyric. Later I told the two Consuls and the Senate in private emergency session the same. I stood on the rostrum in the Curia and hurled this at them: 'Who keeps the Dacians at bay? Who hurls them back across—or into—the Danube? Who maintains friendly relations with the northern Germanic tribes, and do German peasants revere as a strong and kindly Roman father-protector? Who inspires highest respect and affection as much by his character as by the legions he commands? Who inspires terror and hatred in the heart of King Decebalus of Dacia and his vast army? Who is the strength of Rome while far from Rome? The name, my noble Consuls and Fathers, is a name you well know: Marcus Ulpius Trajan.' "

They were standing at the brink of the stony cliff, again surveying the Danube and the green shores of the enemy.

Trajan looked tense. He was tense. "Sir—I have been away from Rome a long time. Too long. Your own name, General, stands at the head of the list in my mind."

"Too old," smiled the visiting officer, laying a friendly hand on Trajan's shoulder-plates. "As my cherished sire said to me before his peaceful death, '*I yield my dying lesser sun to you, my son.*' "

"The *vale* of a brave man, sir." Trajan looked up-river and gestured that Sura do so. They saw on-and-off flashes of blazing light in the green cliffs of the Roman banks of the river. When the heliograph signals stopped, Trajan said, "We can expect an attack upriver tonight. We are ready."

Sura nodded. "Marcus Trajan is always ready. Marcus, our next sovereign must be a soldier-emperor who will command not only the fealty of the Legions and Praetorian Guards, but a man who will expose and punish the corruption rampant during the reign of Domitian. Nerva has, I grant you, made a start by imprisoning a few notorious false informers and one or two vicious former proconsuls; the ex-governors of Egypt and Syria, to be exact. But our emperor lacks the force and thrust to investigate all the provinces. He has to spend much time pacifying the Praetorian Guards and preventing riots in Rome. And there still remains the stench of crimes against the people perpetrated during Domitian's principate not only in Egypt and Syria—but in Judea. Belgica. Armenia Minor. Northern Gaul." He paused thoughtfully. "May I ask: what is your opinion of Proconsul Versus Maturus of Farther Spain—your native Spain, my boy?"

When they again sat on their boulders, Trajan replied, "I have all but lost touch with both Spanish provinces for over a year. I heard rumors that Chieftain Malendi's tribe was becoming restless. I wrote six letters to Malendi, urging him to ask Classicus or Maturus for flocks and seeds. Famine is a sinister threat to many blackcloak tribes. No answers from Malendi. Of course, fist-size Celt wars are not new. Even the *Togati* seem to live but to fight." His expressive wide lips became ruefully humorous. "Years ago my sire was commanding general of the VII Gemina at Legio in northwest Spain. One morning in the month of July, my father received a message from a blackcloak tribe that a state of war would begin two days later. The reason? The tribesmen had seen my sire and two tribunes strolling the twilight before. All they were doing was admiring the magnificent mountains. But to the suspicious guerrillas, the sight of a Roman general on foot smacked of treachery; generals of the Eagles always rode plunging chargers." Trajan was chuckling warmly. "My father was able to avert the impending war by sending a courteous message to the blackcloak leader that the reason for his walking was that he was recovering from carbuncles on his rump."

Sura broke into laughter.

"After that," Trajan continued, "my father never left his garrison except preceded by heralds blasting trumpets and himself astride a thundering gray stallion."

"And your father was never very good at trying to sit a horse!" Sura clapped Trajan on the shoulders. "I trust he never was thrown."

"His stallion was a Roman, too, sir." Trajan said proudly. Then his expression became grave as he again looked out on the blue river.

Sura picked up a hemlock cone. "Do you ever hear from Verus Maturus?"

"Once. He referred vaguely to other letters he had sent by couriers. Those I never received. The one I did came two months ago by ocean transport to Italy, asking me to use my influence with the Emperor and Senate to send at least three more legions to western Spain. I realize that province has long been classed as a disorderly one due to guerrilla quarrels—but I need at least six additional legions *here*. I need much more. I want a large navy. I want ships decked in lead plates. Flame-throwers. Grapples. Catapults. Troop barges by the thousands—to ram the shores of Dacia. Influence? I cannot obtain these things for myself to cut out the festering sore that is Dacia!"

They discussed Dacian belligerency during Domitian's reign. Ten years ago the hordes from across the Danube had invaded with an army of one hundred thousand, surprising and killing the Roman proconsul of Moesia, his household guards, family and servants. Hundreds of peasants in the region were also slain. Rushing to avenge came the I Italica, the V Macedonia, the XI Claudia, the II Adiutrix, and the X Gemina—without auxiliary support. Thirty thousand enraged soldiers of Rome encircled the invaders already celebrating the fall of Rome, cut half the enemy to pieces and drove the fleeing remainder back across the Danube.

"Negligence—corrupt carelessness," muttered Trajan. "Then Domitian retaliated by sending General Fuscus and his four legions into Dacia—a disastrous defeat for us and the loss of an outstandingly gallant and obedient general and many of his men. Too few troops, too few of everything, attack too premature," he said, tersely. "Our sacred Standards embedded in Dacian pig sties. And still the lesson not learned."

Pleased to have stirred Trajan into brisk talk, Sura inquired, "You would have used force and only force?"

"What other way, sir? When former allies turn hostile and hammer our walls, will diplomacy and gifts establish peace? Domitian's negotiations finally established what he hailed as a victorious peace for Rome—actually a truce disgraceful to Rome." Trajan's anger was rising. "Domitian sent the Dacians some of our trained military engineers! Paid the King of Dacia annual gold subsidies! They will never bow to Rome. They plan to destroy us. Do we submit? Every day that passes—Submit? I say no."

Both were standing.

At length Sura said, "The gold tributes to Dacia stopped after Domitian was assassinated. And your solution, Marcus, if you were emperor?"

"My solution?" Trajan began pacing. "Invade. Invade—*when we are ready*. Invade in force. Enormous reserves at our rear. Conquer Dacia. Annex it as a province. Colonize heavily with all classes of Romans. Convert the resources of Dacia—including their gold mines—to our uses: the uses of civilization." He marched back and forth, striking his *gladius* at stones and bushes. "Wars solve many problems. Peace is built on power—not pleading."

Sura nodded gravely.

"Frightful as conflict is," Trajan went on, "it will continue until the *Pax Romana* of the Sacred Augustus is reality. There must be only one master of the world: Rome. Roman armed might, laws, roads, bridges, sanitation, education, trade. The Roman way is the strong and peaceful way. The gods favor the Roman way. Let us never at our peril fall out of favor with the invisibles." He returned to his rocky seat and unstrapped his helmet, taking it off. His close cut hair was the color of a stormy sky.

Sura slowly sat down on his boulder. "Marcus, I wish the Emperor and Senate could have heard what you just said. How I wish."

"Conquest is the only way," Trajan resumed. "If you had a minimum of three more legions, you could smash the Parthians. Instead you must hold truce banquets, fight with subtle harangues, impress the wily Orientals with gold and silver gear. Like I, you must constantly redeploy your troops and so give the impression of the arrival of limitless new legions. We have cut off gold tributes to the Dacians, but now you, under orders from Nerva and the Senate, must pay in gold to buy peace with Parthia."

General Sura nodded. "The tapestry of military-political-economic threads forms one fabric and one design. My boy, we need a new man at the shuttle. New hands at the loom. Hands about fifty years of age, I say."

"A weaver who will not waver," said Trajan, practically.

Sura looked at the younger general with pleased awe.

A feminine voice called from a grove of pines and hemlocks: "Ah, Marcus, may I join you and General Sura?" Plotina strolled from the stand of trees. She wore a bronze breast-plate over her gray linen dress. A steel helmet dangled on its thick strap from one freckled wrist.

Both men arose and raised their right hands in courtesy salutes.

"Plotina," said General Sura, "this is the first time I have seen you in military garb! You would do credit to Minerva."

"Plotina, put on your helmet," Trajan ordered. "I told you to wear your gear at all times. Where is your shield? Your honor guard? This zone is the edge of disaster."

Smiling and frowning she came to them. Her green eyes were guileless as a child's and her silvery auburn hair was pulled back severely in a flattened ball low at the nape of her neck.

"My dear husband, I had to remove my helmet; I was suffocating." She and Trajan sat down on his boulder and Sura returned to his stony seat. "Now Marcus will stop talking," said Plotina, ruefully.

"Why?" Sura was interested and amused.

"The female presence, General Sura."

They laughed and turned to look eastward across the river. The sun was overhead in the pale blue sky.

Trajan turned to his wife. "Plotina, do you smell danger? Danger for tonight?"

"I, too, saw the heliograph signals upriver," she replied. "My distaff intuition says the enemy will launch a big attack tonight."

"How many Dacians are apt to cross in one offensive?" Sura asked Trajan. "Difficult to estimate?"

"Varies," said Trajan. "Sometimes two, three or more diversionary assaults, from five hundred to five thousand warriors in each. Then a big smash at a point we are not supposed to be guarding too heavily. Chess game, sir."

Plotina looked bland and relaxed. "Marcus, I have an omen for tonight." She smiled and frowned. "This morning I saw a black bear cub preparing to thrust its long tongue in a beehive."

"Who won?" Sura chuckled.

"Either the mother bear was careless, or the bees held a war council before the female and her young approached the buzzing stronghold. The honey is safe." She glanced fondly and maternally at Trajan.

He looked at her dotingly. "We should add a bee to our empire Eagles."

Plotina's slow attention ebbed to General Sura. "Sir," she said, "your escorts at the command post told me you had just arrived from Rome. I wonder . . . while in The City, did you hear anything about conditions in Spain?"

Sura lost his aplomb. An uneasy silence held for a few moments. "A majority of the senators are incensed over Verus Maturus' demand that the investigation law be enforced in both Spanish provinces. Furthermore, the *Patres* suspect Maturas of imperial ambitions because he wants more legions in Farther Spain. Contrarily, dispatches from the noble Classicus in Hither Spain state that no more troops are needed to cope with periodic guerrilla unrest."

Plotina seemed to be watching a golden oriole in low flight through the forest. At last she inquired, "General Sura, would you care to give me your opinion of Maturus?"

Sura and Trajan exchanged a glance or two. "Maturus impresses me as an acid absolutist, perhaps unfortunately tending to injure the innocent in his—how to say it—every stand of turf has a few weeds. I gained the impression in Rome that Maturus wants Spain to be a perfect green peninsula of silken green grass. Frankly, the noble Proconsul Maturus is violently detested in the Capitol. Yet he possesses the great virtue of revering Marcus Trajan." Sura glanced admiringly at the thoughtful, sunburned face of Trajan.

"I wonder," Plotina mused, "perhaps an innocent man gathers soot from another man's fire."

"Our good friend Classicus is certainly suffering from indirect blasts of Maturus." Sura shook his head. "If the fire of Maturus' eloquent demands could scorch, Classicus would be singed and sooted. Does Plotina agree?"

She was turning a hemlock cone between her fingers. "I concur with the theory of the deathless Epicurus that a beneficent person is a fountain watering the earth, and therefore it is more delightful to give than to receive."

Sura was relieved. "Classicus is honest, just, and generous. Popular among the senators and highly regarded by the emperor. He works without cease to help the poor classes of Hither Spain; he remembers his own childhood in very straightened circumstances.

The few times I met Classicus in Rome several years ago, I was also impressed by the man's mysticism."

Plotina idly inquired, "Did you know that he divorced his wife, Enna Gracchus?"

General Sura shrugged. "I had heard. An estimable domina. Rather aloof."

"Enna is my closest friend," said Plotina, evenly. "Her letters to me used to be feasts for the intellect. Many of her formulas for honest and humane government agree with Marcus' ideas."

Trajan nodded, but was more absorbed in gazing over the Danube.

Plotina frowned deeply. "Since Enna went to Gades months ago, her letters seem to indicate mental or physical decay—or both. I, too, write magnificent examples of minutiae to Enna. We regale each other with comments about wigs and fish. Jewels and climate. Anti-freckle pastes. How hot tongs should be before the hair is curled."

Sura was amused. "Momentous topics."

"*Ad extremum*," said Plotina, promptly, to the surprise of Sura. "Enna and I communicate a great deal to each other, General Sura, for we deliberately send our scrolls by couriers . . . through New Carthage." She turned to watch her husband. He had risen and now stood again at the edge of the high bank, hands shielding his eyes as he stared over at the Dacian side of the Danube. He turned and said, "General Sura, we must eat. You will want to study our defense plans for tonight. Plotina, you must take a nap. Soldiers!"

Cordons of guards suddenly materialized out of the forest. They marched forward, halted and came to salute. Then they divided into three groups of twelve each.

Before sunset that day the clearing around Trajan's command post was filled with officers and couriers arriving and departing. Trajan listened to his aides and read dispatches. Plotina stood near him. She was in armor and helmet and carried a small oval shield. General Sura stood with Trajan.

A handsome, bearded, Roman-Jewish commander saluted Trajan. "My general: artillery is emplaced, maniples on heights, rafts ready, in Zones G and H."

"Excellent." Trajan gave his earnest informant a quick smile. The officer gazed in worship, saluted, and marched away.

"Sir," a Roman centurion reported, "General Acilius reports enemy rafts rowing out fifteen miles upriver, off Zone D. He estimates fifteen to twenty thousand oncoming Dacians. He and his *Alaudae* are ready."

Trajan nodded. "Acilius and his lethal Skylarks—some of our best and none fiercer."

Another officer saluted. "Sir: relay couriers of General Norbanus report indications of massive enemy attack tonight in Zone K. He and the VIII Augusta are ready and have alerted the I Minervia outside the fifty mile zone downriver."

Trajan glanced at Sura. "The enemy is spreading his attacks widely tonight."

Trajan next heard that flameball signals, relayed by closer legions, warned that Dacian flotillas in vast numbers were starting across the river two hundred miles up channel, opposite the position held by the XXII Primigenia. Heavy support from the XIV Gemina and auxiliaries was waiting to augment the Primigenia, if needed.

At last Trajan summoned an orderly. "Get the horses," he ordered. "General Sura, Plotina, if our cordial invitation and trap works tonight, we shall see action in Zones G and H."

When the rounded glowing moon rose, rafts made of sealed empty casks lashed to plank decking pushed out from Roman shores in G and H zones, each float carrying ten legionaries and four rowers. They poled away from tiny islets and stony peninsulas thick with willows. There were long stretches of water off shore where nothing grew. Behind that region of quiet river the land widened into a vast, natural amphitheater enclosed on its remaining three sides by steep wooded hills. The grassland of the huge meadow and its rocky, wooded heights were in darkness, but shore bonfires and torches embedded in rock cairns near the Danube lighted two miles of river land on the Roman side. In the distance up and down the waterway far away flames illuminated battles already being fought between barbarian invaders and Roman defenders.

In the lookout station on a high crag, General Trajan stood watch with General Sura and Plotina behind log and clay breastworks. The almost full moon and shore fires made visibility easy. The air was fresh and balmy and smelled of evergreens. At last Trajan said, "Our troops have reached midstream. Listen."

From out on the river came the piercing hails of Trajan's raft troops:

"General Trajan invites you to a peace council!"

"Do you hear us, troops of the King of Dacia? Come to our side! Follow my advice! Come to our side and confer with General Trajan!"

"Remind King Decebalus," boomed a lusty Roman voice, "that he agreed not to wage war against Rome! Send peace emissaries! Come over to our side!"

Distant shouts began blasting from enemy shores.

Trajan glanced at Sura and Plotina. "The enemy prefers war to peace. The Dacians heard my men clearly; they are using megaphones."

Plotina looked stern. "So are the Dacians. Listen to them."

Amplified voices of the Latin-speaking barbarians penetrated to the lookout post on the crag:

"Scum of Caesars! Looters!"

"Killers of children!"

"Garbage in stolen gold and silver!"

"Your women have beards!"

"Too brave to fight! Pirates!"

"Statue stealers!"

"Roman monsters of mass murder!"

"Death to Rome! Kill Trajan! Kill Trajan!"

"Death to Nerva the unnatural one!"

"Death to Rome!"

When the roars of defiance subsided, General Sura said, "Our Parthian enemies clothe their hates in more diplomatic terms."

"The Dacians go wild on hashish wine before invading," Trajan remarked, matter-of-factly.

Officers arrived with progress dispatches for Trajan. In the uncertain dusk of twilight, a surprise force of two thousand Dacians had reached Roman shores five miles upriver. This position was held by the first cohort, 600 men, of Trajan's own command *legio*, the Ulpia Victrix. The 600 legionaries allowed the raiders a firm foothold, then surrounded and slew the entire horde. On the left flank of the Victrix, the tenth, ninth and eighth cohorts of the *Alaudae* were held in reserve to be used, if needed, to support the other seven cohorts and auxiliaries of General Acilius against twenty thousand Dacians now swarming ashore to engage the ferocious *Alaudae* Legion. There was no report so far of the conflict raging two hundred miles away between the XXII Primigenia and barbarian invaders, except for relayed fire signals: *"All going well."*

Twenty miles downchannel, towards the coast of the Black Sea, fifteen thousand invaders were being methodically thrown back into the Danube by the Ethiopian archers and armored cavalry of General Norbanus' VIII Augusta. In reserve to aid the men of the Augusta were the troops of the I Minervia, occupying the first fifty mile Danube salient of the river from the Black Sea.

Trajan passed the documents to General Sura. He read them by the light of a resin torch and gave the reports to Plotina. She nodded gravely. "Tonight will be crucial," she said quietly.

Watching the moonlit and torchlit river, Trajan said, "Here they come. Longboats. Inflated animal skins. Ox bladders. Driftwood. Anything that floats. Last winter I hear that they tried iceberg navies. Upchannel, not here. This fifty mile zone they have not attacked so far. All the better for Rome."

"Marcus, do they ever swim over on horses?" asked Sura.

Trajan smiled grimly. "Certainly." He tested the strap of his helmet. "Dacian horses make excellent mounts for our cavalry."

"Marcus," said Plotina, "this looks like the largest single assault force the enemy has ever sent over."

"It is. This is their big strike—at this point. You can hardly see the river for the foe."

Plotina thoughtfully observed, "Marcus, your plan is going to work—as you hoped it would."

"Our plan," he smiled. "May the gods give us victory."

Hundreds of Dacian boats, rafts, and swimming warriors supported by ox bladders swarmed ashore. The Romans on rafts had all returned safely and disappeared into bastions on rocky crags jutting up from the land. Screaming hatred of Rome and cries of triumph, the savage warriors began snatching flaming pitch torches embedded in the shore and lifted the brands high to light their advance into the vast meadow surrounded on three sides by steep, dark hills.

Far back in the natural amphitheater, Roman voices, magnified through funnels, hurled the challenge to victory at the oncoming enemy hordes. Shrieking fanatically, the Dacians pounded through shallows to wet sand and earth. Many stumbled and went down, while comrades surged forward in fresh landings. The main body of

invaders accidentally trod tributaries of hard land through treacherous bogs.

Fifty thousand Dacians stormed into the meadow.

But back along the shoreline, the troops of Trajan's Ulpia Victrix
had a secret ally:

Quicksand.

It sucked and pulled, sucked and pulled . . .

Hundreds of barbarians heaved up out of the deadly morass and
reached solid ground.

"Kill Trajan! Kill Trajan!" The enemy cry blasted.

Those saving themselves from the engulfing sand spread out and
began racing east and west—only to run into ambushes of Roman
swords and spears held horizontally. Not a Dacian escaping the
deadly marshes escaped the Roman blades.

Out on the river, an enormous, mile-long new invasion flotilla
was approaching. It did not ram ashore. After watching hundreds of
their comrades floundering and trapped in quicksand to their
thighs, the enemy admiral shouted commands and the thousands
of yelling Dacians reversed their flimsy vessels and returned to their
home shores.

In the lookout post, Trajan said, "Now for our artillery offensive.
The watchword is *Fulgor*." His lean, dark face was sad.

"Lightning," said General Sura, with approval.

An aide of Trajan held a long, straight brass trumpet to his lips.
He blew a series of piercing blasts.

Far down in the fertile grassland of the huge meadow, the fifty
thousand barbarians had divided into cohorts and spread out to
find passes through the high hills into the rolling rich lands of
Moesia, a heartland of southeastern Roman Europe.

Enemy cries echoed up to the watchers in the lookout post:

"On to Rome! Burn Rome! Raze Rome!"

"Kill old Nerva! Kill the senator swine!"

"Trajan! Stuff him with straw, take him to Rome!"

"On to Rome!"

"Conquer for our sacred king!"

Somewhere high in the hills encircling three sides of the meadow,
a far voice bellowed through a megaphone:

"FULGOR!"

Stones began thundering down on the fifty thousand Dacians.

The unexpected crashing rock barrage killed scores. Other warriors had time to raise metal shields over their heads and stave off succeeding avalanches of rocks. Then heavier stones began catapulting down, some colliding in mid-air and plummeting into the now disorganized enemy.

"FULGOR!"

"FULGOR!"

"FULGOR!"

Artillery rocks from other emplacements began hurtling down while companion batteries reloaded their *ballistae*. Many of the missiles scored direct hits on clusters of enemy fighters trying to escape the terrible hail.

Again the Roman watchword rang out—and a sinister new counter-offensive showered down: flame balls of tar and resin. Enemy wool cloaks and uniforms were set ablaze and in trying to rip off their burning clothes, many of the foe set fire to wounded comrades prone on the ground. Scores of the enemy blazed up as human torches and died horribly. Meadow grass caught fire and added to the panic.

Hundreds of barbarians tried to flee up the hillsides and were coolly run through by infantry swordsmen of the Ulpia Victrix. Again and again the 'wild ass' *ballistae* went into annihilating action with rocks and fireballs. These fresh onslaughts killed many and disabled hundreds. Then the bulk of the fifty thousand began retreating out of the meadow of sudden death to the shore—only to meet hundreds of flaming arrows launched by Victrix sharpshooters stationed on river banks and driving the foe back into the burning meadow again.

"FULGOR!"

"FULGOR!"

"FULGOR!"

The green-white round of moon bloomed serenely and birds flew shrieking away from their nests to escape the tumult.

The quicksand claimed victim after victim.

Behind shore parapets, men of the Victrix systematically shot mercy arrows into the heads of Dacians engulfed in quicksand to their necks and begging for swift death. The few who managed to struggle free and reach firm ground were prodded by Roman lances, and shackled in wooden neck-and-hand collars and led to the rear.

But twenty thousand Dacians broke through the flaming arrow fire and floundered out into the Danube to their longboats riding at anchor. And suddenly, enemy biremes appeared from the Dacian shore and started firing catapult rocks up into the Roman crags and hills. Two of the missiles passed perilously close over the helmeted head of Trajan. Sura thrust Plotina under his shield and remained standing by Trajan.

The next stage of the conflict began.

Roman storied towers on hard, flat shore a thousand feet upriver were already being rolled downriver. Hundreds of Victrix infantry on the tiers of the great structures began firing flaming arrows into the enemy biremes while others operating small *ballistae* on the top of each tower catapulted fireballs into the siege engines on the Dacian decks. Then three hundred cavalry of the Victrix swept out of tree cover on the right flank and began mopping up enemy warriors trying to re-form on hard ground. The foe was disorganized and most were killed. The rest swam out into the Danube.

The Dacian war vessels were blazing. No more rocks catapulted from the enemy ships. The vessels were veering and trying to return to Dacian shores.

Roman batteries that had meanwhile been moved up to heights close to the river now launched a general flame-ball attack on enemy swimmers, longboats and retreating biremes. The siege vessels escaped, their sails smoking. Back in the meadow, stones still thundered down.

Roman rocks and fire still took toll of the retreating foe until the hordes had passed midstream. Gradually the fire and fury of battle began to ebb.

Plotina had pushed aside Sura's shield and stood valiantly next to her husband, Marcus Trajan.

When dawn pearled the overcast sky, troops of the Ulpia Victrix marched into the battle meadow. It reeked of burnt flesh and hair and charred wool cloaks and uniforms. Dead animals and birds lay conglomerately mixed with ten thousand dead barbarians. Twenty thousand wounded savages were groaning and helpless.

To each fallen living enemy, a Roman asked,

"Death? Surrender?"

The surrendered were chained.

The defiant were slain.

By the end of that day, Trajan learned that Rome had won smashing victories all up- and down-river. Altogether the defending legions had defeated over one hundred thousand Dacians, taking many prisoners. Before sunset, three emissaries in flashing gold and silver armor and hoisting white flags had been rowed across the river and landed in General Norbanus' zone twenty miles down the channel from Trajan's men of the Victrix. The holy Majesty, King Decebalus of Dacia, wanted the Romans to know that if they did not inflame his warriors again, he would not launch new attacks on Roman territory and hoped that gold tributes would soon render future warfare unnecessary. General Norbanus listened stoically and sent the enemy ambassadors back to their own side.

Trajan smiled when he read Norbanus' report of his parley with representatives of King Decebalus.

"The vanquished demand gold of the victors," he told Sura and Plotina. "My future tributes to the enemy will be iron. Rocks. And fire."

The next morning he, Plotina, and the command staff bade cordial *vales* to General Licinius Sura, returning with his escort troops of the IV Scythia (Syria) and the X Fretensis (Jerusalem) to Rome and then on to his Asia Minor headquarters.

XXXVI

Four days after the Ides of October, legion horsemen and a brown wooden carriage moved north on a German road bordering the Rhine. Cavalry outriders escorted the vehicle and fifty troopers clattered behind. Far in advance of the cavalcade rode heralds holding aloft the *Signa Militaria*. Each tall standard bore a small gold Eagle emblem and campaign victory plaques fused to the staff below the golden bird of Roman supremacy. The leading ensign in scarlet and purple held a standard displaying the gilded bronze winged figure of *Bona Fortuna* poised on a gleaming gold ball over the bronze medallion likeness of Emperor Nerva.

When the coach rolled past Germans working in fields of barley and rye above the river, the Teutons called joyful salutations, which the two people in the conveyance acknowledged by waving or saluting.

In the carriage Trajan told his wife, "Great people, the Germans. Some of our best Romans are Germans." He looked over his shoulder and then told his driver to stop the coach. Back on the road stood a blonde girl in brown and a pink shawl, holding the elbow of a tall and emaciated old man in a patched gray field uniform.

Trajan walked back to the pair. "Young domina?" he inquired, saluting her courteously.

She gazed in agitated and tremulous worship. "Great Trajan, dear Governor," she stammered in accented Latin, "this is my—my beloved, brave sire. He cannot hear very well—" She gasped, "He is blind."

"Who speaks?" asked the old legionary, harshly. "Daughter, they say he will pass this way. I would salute him before I go to the Divine Shades."

Trajan moved closer. "Comrade, whom do you wish to salute?"

"I hear a man's voice," said the old veteran, gnarled hands groping to Trajan's short gray cape. "Are you a soldier of Trajan, man? Know you him, sir? Be you one of his brave ones?"

The soldier's daughter looked tearfully at Trajan. "Beloved governor," she murmured, "my father served with the V Macedonia in lower Moesia. General Trajan—sir—if my father could know you —touch your hand—he would die content."

Trajan took the veteran's bony hands. "Comrade," said Trajan, loudly, "hear me. I stand beside you. I am Trajan."

The sightless gray eyes of the aged fighter filled with tears. "You are Trajan? Your brave hands touch mine . . . ?"

"Comrade, your valor touches my heart."

A wondering smile lighted the raddled features of the ancient defender of Rome. "The gods bless you, General Trajan." Freeing his hands from those of Trajan, he stepped back and snapped a magnificent salute. For a few moments he was a young recruit again.

Trajan returned the salute humbly. Then he removed his gray cloak and draped it around the old legionary's sunken shoulders. "Comrade," Trajan called, "you are Rome triumphant. Do me the honor of wearing my cloak, sir." He embraced the old man, stepped back, and offered another salute.

Back in the carriage he said to Plotina, "The gods give many gifts. That great old soldier."

Plotina's green eyes were tender. At last she commented, "I see our watch tower and pink walls of home there in the distance. Home to Colonnia at the Rhine."

"Imagination," he said, fondly. "You are so eager to arrive you are already there. Mapping the home campaign already. Anxious to see my sister and nieces—and learn if young Hadrian has exploded Apollodorus' temper yet."

After a smile and a frown, she acknowledged, "How well you read me, Marcus. My husband, Hadrian is unusual. Erudite. A good soldier and well liked, too, because he is your nephew. He tries to emulate you."

"I recognize his talents, my legal ward," responded Trajan, "but Hadrian reveres architraves more than offensives."

Plotina laughed contentedly. "So does our great friend Apollodorus! Hadrian is the same as a young son to me. Come, try and smile? All is secure on the Moesian front." As there was no response from him, she asked, "Marcus, have you lost heart?"

He leaned out the open window to salute a German girl holding a swaddled infant happily aloft for him to see. Turning back in, he replied, "I am a soldier."

"Marcus—it could be you," she said, slowly.

He waved to more Germans lining both sides of the road. One stout German peasant held up a squealing pig for Trajan's inspection as the coach bumped past. The sight amused and touched Plotina.

Abruptly he remarked, "It's four days after the Ides."

She studied his handsome profile. "There must be a good reason for the couriers' delay. I know that General Sura's letter said all provincial governors and legion chiefs would receive official letters of Nerva's new partner and successor before the Ides, but surely—"

"Accept the fact the emperor and senate did not choose me."

"I cannot accept it," she said, instantly.

"My thought is that they elevated Senator Julius Severianus."

"And why, Marcus?"

"Why not? Our most distinguished senator. Vast experience in military and civil affairs. Patriot. Popular."

"—And nearly seventy," she said.

Then pursing her lips severely, she asked, "Marcus, what do you think will be the most important tasks of Nerva's partner and successor?"

"Burn the tax books. Restore confiscated property. Abolish arbitrary seizure of people and their possessions. Expose and punish corrupt people who grew rich during the imperium of Domitian. Build vast new public works all over the empire. I want a canal from the Nile to the Red Sea. I want many more bridges, roads, harbors. Libraries and schools for all. Encourage births among the plebs and farm populations. Enforce the investigation law. Install honest provincial governors throughout the State. Conquer Dacia.

Conquer Parthia. Push on to the steppes of Sarmatia. Annex that, too."

Her green eyes narrowed, she said, casually, "Regarding men of integrity for proconsular positions . . . you are thinking of Spain . . . ?"

He glanced in some irritation. "Plotina, you don't bother to hide your distrust of Cornelius Classicus, yet remember, men in his position are natural targets for slander. I cannot believe those rumors. Classicus is a man of honor."

Plotina remarked: "Marcus, you trust everybody who appears trustworthy on the surface. You want goodwill, you need people more than you should."

"Would you have me become suspicious? A tyrant? I do need people. I expect a great deal of people." He eyed her sharply.

"But Marcus, that is both your weakness and your strength. People of integrity want and try to conduct themselves like you and like old Nerva. But the secretly dishonest—"

An outrider shouted through a coach window space:

"Sir! Praetorian Guard couriers approaching from rear!"

"Stop the carriage," called Trajan.

Soon they stood on the road, surrounded by dismounted cavalrymen and curious German farm people. They watched the oncoming horsemen loom larger until four riders in red uniforms cantered up and halted.

"General Trajan," said the chief dispatch rider, a young aristocrat of classic good looks. "The emperor and the senate profusely apologize for almost neglecting to start us off with these imperial letters." He leaned down and handed two scrolls in ordinary gray canvas to Trajan. Wooden plaques tied around the canvas cylinders bore wax seals with upraised legends. One legend read:

NERVA AUGUSTUS.

The other wax bore the reading:

SENATE ROMANUS.

Holding the communications unopened, Trajan inquired of the chief Praetorian courier,

"Whom did Nerva and the Fathers choose?"

"Sir, we are not sure, but the noble Severianus was stopping riots in The City when we set out." The messenger's bored dark eyes had wandered to a pretty German girl kneeling on the road.

Marcus Trajan felt a mixture of emotions. Resignation. Relief. The quick death of his ambition . . . and a soldier's immediate readiness to swear obedience to Severianus Caesar . . . He glanced at his nearest cavalrymen, troops with prayers on their faces, men who would follow him to the death. And Plotina?

He led her into a stand of hemlocks to the right of the road. Cavalry guards followed and spread out around the husband and wife. To Trajan the people, soldiers, carriage and black horses, the glittering Praetorians holding their spirited white horses in check —all formed a colorful frieze, an entablature outlined against the terraced green hills above the Rhine. He looked up and saw a flock of snow geese whirring high in the cloudless sky. Why this indecision? Read the scrolls.

"The one from Nerva—first—" whispered Plotina.

He handed her the senate dispatch. She held it limply in her right hand while Trajan calmly removed Nerva's dispatch from its heavy cloth case and unrolled it. His black eyes scanned right to left, right to left, right to left down the page. Then he thrust the page to Plotina and stood staring in a daze.

Quickly she read:

MARCUS COCCEIUS NERVA, First Citizen, Augustus, to MARCUS ULPIUS TRAJAN, Defender of Rome, a Marshal of the Empire. May the gods look on you with divine favor. Heeding the dictates of my heart and conscience, and the recommendations of the Senate and many of your military comrades, and the cries of the people, I have adopted you as my son and successor; to take from my tired hands the burdens of State which my ill health and years no longer allow me to carry. My son and Heir, you are the rock of civilization. You, my son and Caesar, are the embodiment of clear eyed vigilance and justice. Your military prowess is matched by your high moral character, unbiased judgment and solemn reverence for lawful government. You are youthful and vigorous. You command and deserve the loyalty of all legions, and the burning faith and love of the people. My paternal love and trust is yours. Deliberately the Fathers and I sent our messages to you late, thus giving your loyal aide, the noble Severianus, time to restore order in Rome and disperse many rebellious cohorts of Praetorian Guards who tried to force us to choose an officer of their corps. They have been led to believe that Severi-

anus will make such a choice. This strategem was necessary to save Rome from another civil war. When you read this, my Heir, two legions from Gaul will be in control of The City and your elevation will be publicly proclaimed. You are Trajan Germanicus Caesar; my full partner in government; and when you read these words, the actual emperor. I have but one more command to give my Caesar: maintain your headquarters at the Limes Germanicus until you decide our eastern boundaries are impregnable and Dacian invasions no longer menacing. My son, we may never meet. I say not farewell. I say Hail! Ave Nerva Trajan Germanicus Caesar, son of Nerva Augustus. Hail Nerva Trajan, First Soldier, First Citizen, Tribunician of the People, High Pontiff, Father of the Country, Emperor of the Romans.

The scroll dropped from Plotina's trembling hands. Gently she took Trajan in her arms. His sunburned cheeks were wet.

Cavalrymen dashed forward. One picked up the letter from Nerva. He would not have been human had he not stolen a few glances at the imperial communication. Skimming it completely, he at last yelled:

"*Io Triumphe! Io Triumphe!* Trajan Caesar! Adopted son and successor to Nerva!"

Pandemonium shattered the air. Troops of Trajan clashed swords on shields. Horses neighed and reared up. Deliriously happy German men and women joined hands and began folk-dancing on the roadway. Harvesters from the lowest terraced vineyard above the Rhine scrambled down with baskets of silvery dark blue grapes— victory gifts for the Emperor-elect and his *Augusta*. All were too joyful to notice the astonished Praetorian couriers. After the first shock of learning that Trajan had been elevated, the four men from Rome jumped off their white horses and thrust clenched hands high in salute to the new Chief of Empire.

Trajan led Plotina into a glen partially screened by moist ferns. When they were somewhat removed from the roar of celebration out by the road, he said, unsteadily,

"Plotina—my Empress and my conscience—help me find a place to pray."

⊓⊔⊓⊔ 98 A.D. ⊔⊓⊔⊓

XXXVII

Emperor Nerva died suddenly in Rome on the night of January twenty-fifth, whether from poison secretly administered by unknown enemies in his household, advanced age (or both) was not known and never would be. His reign of less than a year and a half had halted the widespread persecutions of his predecessor, Domitian, but at the same time unwittingly established another evil. Nerva's feeble campaign against corruption had opened the doors to private vengeance against the innocent. Many people of moral character and fortune had been imprisoned, awaiting trials, after being accused by envious enemies (with forged evidence) of crimes against the State. Grudgingly the people had found his general policies of fair treatment for all worthy of mild praise, yet what fitful popular acclaim he had won by charitable acts was criticized by the rich and hailed by a special class of the poor.

Under the *Lex Agraria* he had combined his own private fortune with funds from the imperial treasury and purchased enormous land acreage which was granted with low-interest loans to impoverished citizens, the new farms serving as security. While paying the interest the new rural class also won imperial aid for their dependent children. Yet united feeling was, on the whole, against Nerva for his tolerance of the secret society of seditionists who called themselves Christians, and because he drastically reduced Games and chariot races, all but abolishing the spectacles.

The public expected Games and hailed their popular heroes, the charioteers. Of no importance to the masses was empire defense, government solvency, and reduction of inheritance taxes. Too soon had the majority forgotten the horrors of Domitian's reign. Only the thoughtful appreciated and revered the greatness and mercy of Emperor Nerva.

So passed to his gods Marcus Cocceius Nerva.

The Senate accorded him divine honors and his ashes were ceremoniously interred in the Sepulchre of Augustus.

Men and women were already shouting:

"Trajan! *Optimus Princeps!*"

"Bread and circuses!"

"Emperor Trajan!"

"Emperor Trajan!"

The acclaim roared as thunder from Rome to the provinces.

On a stormy day late in March, Gaius and Penelope walked on a loggia of the Gades legation promenade above the seawall. They had not spoken since coming outside. He drew Penelope's cloak more snugly about her as a shield against fine rain driving in from the sea and then he led her to a less exposed section of the pillared walk open to the elements.

Gaius wondered if the verdict in his case would be death. Or would Emperor Trajan bestow mercy on him? A new Princeps could use his absolute power magnanimously. He could empty prisons, halt executions, extend limited or general amnesty. Or render justice to evil-doers.

Am I a criminal? Gaius pondered. He had attacked legionaries. Snatched a dagger from a prison guard. Broken out of a dungeon. Stolen a uniform and armor and masqueraded as an army officer. He had knocked down a tribune, bent the spearpoints of two guards and wrested Penelope away. He and his wife had escaped crucifixion and escaped. Escaped.

Mitigating factors? The discovery of Gold Valley? His action in the triumphant battle of the Sil by Roman defenders? His denunciation of Classicus to Malendi? The fact that the contested few bars of gold and silver had reached Rome? His record as an architect? The sensational disclosure in Rome, the news reaching Governor Maturus at last, that Classicus had hidden a confession of his deeds in a tax coffer that arrived in Rome? The unexpected, baffling and heartening discretion of Sylvanus, the obese Acting Governor of Hither Spain? That kindly official had no knowledge of where Classicus and Zinga Rutilia had gone—or, if he did, he was convincingly bewildered by it all. Nor did his records show that Gaius Lacer had been incarcerated in a dungeon of the New Carthage legation. He had admitted when Maturus visited him in the eastern Spanish city that a slavegirl had been condemned to death last July, ostensibly on orders of Classicus, and that she had vanished under peculiar circumstances.

Sylvanus had tried to untangle the accusation of a senior tribune that he had been assaulted by a creature in the guise of a legion officer, but had gotten nowhere. The criminal could not be found. As to the guards whose spears had been rendered useless by the mysterious man with the goatskin-draped shield, they had started a cult of worshipping the lance-bender. Surely he was a demigod, the son of Hercules. To ward off wrath from a deity, the subdued officer had joined the cult of guards and servants who offered libations to the goatskin demigod each morning in the rotunda.

Thinking of this did not make Gaius less anxious. His impersonation had already been described in letter after letter he had sent to his master, Apollodorus—and also, his wedding of Penelope and determination to keep her. He had also dared mention he was the father of a daughter.

"Gaius," said Penelope with love, "try and stop thinking about it. There will be dispatches from Emperor Trajan in time. Surely there is a good reason for the delay."

"Good reason? Only one imperial letter so far from Trajan to Maturus—pardons for prisoners who fought at the Sil! Small pensions for families of the prison force who died in the fight. But no exoneration for me yet."

"You forgot the emperor's letter unofficially commending Balbus and Zamil, and approving Zamil's adoption by Governor Maturus. There is a good augur for you, my dearest. Dear man, you are not in hiding. Since we came here last July, you have been building roads in Farther Spain. You come and go from Gades. You are not under surveillance, and you just finished the white marble Victory Arch for Trajan at the main road gate of this city."

"But what next? More work on the sewers of Gades, I suppose. Maybe I overlooked a fissured arch. Keep busy, work, work. If I have nothing else to do, race Dawn across the salt flats. Return at sunset to you and Gaia. Try and be a civilized, unsurly husband and father."

"I love you uncivilized," she said, with a smile, "I love your black moods and your sudden kisses."

He kissed her quickly. He rocked Penelope back and forth in his arms, protecting her face from the dampness with the collar of his cloak. He was achingly aware of their secret: she was going to bear their second child in six more months.

"So here you are," declared Governor Maturus, stamping up, muffled to his sharp nose in a gray mantle.

"Sir, mail couriers?" Gaius demanded.

"Nothing about you, Gaius, or your case, if you can be called one. All being peaceful all over Spain these days, people of this province flood me with the customary scrolls: petitions, affidavits, appeals, litigation . . . enough. I came to present you a ray of hope. Two rays. First: a complicated performance of battle tactics exist in legal continuances. Should an order for your arrest come from Rome, I will seek a way out. Before your freedom of movement is restricted, I must marshal witnesses and testimony. The noble Sylvanus does not know you; that gallant gentleman suffers from weak eyes, and were I to produce the bearded Brutus Sempronius, the estimable Sylvanus would never be able to identify him, as many legionaries are now wearing beards . . . Gaius, I know you have written a confession of your deeds to Apollodorus. He is in Germany with the Emperor and Empress. I pray he remains there a long time. Meanwhile, to return to where I started: should The City order your arrest, I shall unearth people who will swear they can identify the demigod who knocked down a tribune. I also anticipate sinister augurs from the higher gods and dire warnings from the *Lares* and *Penates*." His dark eyes glinted with humor.

"Be it known that divine displeasure halts all proceedings and forces a jurist to begin all over again. In addition, there are one hundred and fifty-two days annually when courts cannot function; to do so would be sacrilege. So before your freedom of movement could be restricted, time would flee and keep on fleeing, young man. Do you follow me?"

"I do, sir," he said. "But you cannot do so much to try and save me, governor."

"All power to the gods," said Maturus, giving Penelope a look of judicial approval. "Gaius, have you ever been in the Balearic islands?"

"I have not, sir."

Maturus faced the rainy wind and watched the waves battling the base of the seawall. "Do you hold any religious tenets as to a future life?"

"Sir, every man to his own belief in his own hereafter. I do what I ought to do, according to what I am and what I feel. I try to obey a higher power, morality, or what. Why do you mention the Balearics, sir?" Yet Gaius knew why, and his emotions were in conflict. Here it was again: *escape.*

Trying to lure a fluttering seagull to his hands, the proconsul of Farther Spain said, "Several mornings ago I interrogated an old couple accused of stealing a wheat loaf. They had paid for the bread, as I shortly learned, for my guards found the copper that had slipped between the boards of the surprised baker's counter. However, during my informal questioning of the old husband and wife, I ordered them to burn incense before the medallion likeness of Emperor Trajan. They sweetly refused and confessed to being Christian. This as you know immediately changed the situation radically. Emperor Nerva was not only lenient with fisherfolk sect, but actually helped them in minor ways. And even the bloody Domitian, oddly, never attacked the *Messias* people as a group because of their religion. In truth, Domitian even commended the Christians and seemed fearful of their displeasure, if a Christian could ever show disapproval. But Emperor Trajan's firm new policy is realistic. He orders his governors not to search out Christians; to repudiate anonymous information as to men and women who belong to that strange superstition. The Princeps further commands, however, that if Christians are hailed before provincial tribunals on civil and criminal charges and refuse to burn incense to the Gods of Rome, and revile their false god, they are to be punished."

The governor continued:

"And how does one punish a Christian? Wide latitude is allowed the proconsul. If a male confessing to be a Christian refuses to serve in the legions and defend our empire, the obvious sentence must be imposed. Yet our splendid Trajan wants unity of all Romans, not disunity. He wants no war among Romans. The only wars Trajan will fight are wars of conquest against the Dacians and Parthians. Yet in the considered opinion of our emperor, the Redeemer sect, which is growing, may threaten the strength of Rome."

Gaius had listened with slight interest. "Sir, what was your judgment of the old couple who did not steal a loaf?"

"I liked them," said Maturus. "The old man had fought bravely in the legions for twenty years. He was certainly not an anarchist, nor was his charming old wife. Before my astonished eyes they knelt and asked their Christ Jesus to bless and inspire and protect Emperor Trajan. They called Trajan the highest and best of God's children; they praised the divine soul of Trajan. They gave thanks for the divine soul of Nerva and told me it was their joy to pray the soul of Nerva into Paradise—whatever that is. The old man also insisted that Trajan and Nerva were both Christians and did not know it—but God knew it and had them safely in his almighty arms. And so on. I was rather impressed," said Maturus, slowly. "The aged man and woman did not revile the deities of Rome. The simplicity and serenity of both was touching. Separately each told me that whatever deity a moral human being worshipped, by whatever name, was their God, whose ways were mysterious in harvesting human souls."

"So you exiled them to a Balearic isle, sir?" asked Penelope, gravely.

"We will call it an isle in that group," muttered the governor. "I gave them seeds, some milking goats, an obstreperous he-goat named Vulcan, and whatever else might ease their existence in their new island home. Their voices came back to me: *'God bless you, divine Governor.'*

"Why cannot all people comprehend that Trajan does not want to be worshipped, but insists on absolute obedience which must take the form of worship?" proclaimed the governor. "The empire would collapse if people placed their invisible gods above our rulers. Our emperors—our virtuous emperors—are gods in a sense. Perhaps our Emperor Trajan, one of the noblest men of all time, is a god and we know it not." The proconsul looked at Penelope. "Young woman, could you and your husband and daughter be happy on an island?"

"Dear governor, I will not, I can not escape," she replied, her blue eyes tender and brave. "I have no fear. I am sure that Emperor Trajan will vindicate my husband."

"Young woman," said the proconsul, irascibly, "after brave old Balbus expired in your arms, you told me he had acknowledged the *Christos* and babbled about invisible baptism of salvation. You also avowed that you were convinced that Christianity was the one, true, supernatural reality."

"Penelope—" Gaius gasped. *"Penelope!!"* Here was a menace that could doom them all. Undoubtedly she had been reading too many scrolls on philosophy lately, thinking too deeply, trying to make herself into a woman of learning, as if his adored woman needed more knowledge and wisdom. She was a constant marvel, a woman of many moods, a woman of healing.

"Governor, I will never join any Christian congregation," Penelope remarked, reflectively. "I will never refuse to hold Emperor

Trajan in any but the highest reverence, worthy of earthly worship. He is our soldier-emperor, the finest, the best. Gladly will I burn incense pellets of obedience before his likeness."

"All that is required," Maturus said. "Trajan himself is a man of piety. What does he worship? Every moral human being worships something over him. Yet why do you think that the Christ is the answer to this enigma of life?"

Gaius had her in his protective embrace.

"Because," she said, "I am a healer. Jesus the Christ was a physician. He healed. He cast out devils, and He taught '*Love ye one another.*' That I believe. They say He will come again. That I do not believe. I think He comes constantly in every act of charity we perform. His physical appearance is not necessary. Can we see our own consciences?"

Maturus was smiling. "Ask me legal questions I can answer, young woman. Do not ask me to argue with a rainbow; order the tides of *Mare Nostrum* or the Atlantic to obey the laws of Rome."

Gaius even laughed, feeling light of heart.

They heard a brisk barking. Mars loped forward and behind came Rufus. Wearing no helmet, Rufus' whitening hair and beard were rumpled by the seawind.

Penelope inquired, with gentle tact, "Rufus, any tidings yet?"

He nodded. "I was afraid to open Domina Lucilla's letter for an hour. At last I did. She wants to be by my side again, to face with me whatever comes. She and our daughters will arrive in Gades—" Rufus looked anguished. "Why does she do this for me? I divorced her, she re-married, then her noble husband was killed in battle— why is she so merciful?"

Penelope nodded. Gaius wondered if disaster might sweep over his brother and the woman he would re-marry—the courageous woman who had been his wife and would again be his wife.

Maturus remarked, "Commander, have I at last convinced you that you face no danger of court-martial for arming prisoners at the Sil?"

"I hope, sir, you are right," Rufus replied to the governor.

When he was alone with Penelope again, Gaius felt despondent and trapped. What decree would Trajan hand down in the case of Gaius Lacer? Trajan the magnificent, yet Trajan who revered the laws? His mind roved back through the months since the battle with bandits on the Gades road, the survival of himself, Penelope,

Turdo, Rufus, General Frontinus and the freedmen fighters of Frontinus and their safe arrival in Gades . . . and then the departure of Flavian for a new assignment in Britain . . . and at last Gaius' letters to Apollodorus in Germany. Letters of revelation, concealing nothing from his architect-master.

And the astringent replies from Apollodorus, each in substance a repetition of the others: *"Gaius, my bondsman you are an architect, not a literary man. Your flood of letters never stop. Your high adventures stir me to various emotions. I know not whether to curse the gods or your own rash actions. I turn over all your missives to Empress Plotina. Stop harassing me. I am building border forts. I can read. So can you. I am mildly pleased that you at last appreciate the education I gave you and have learned a degree of humility. As to the girl you claim you wed, and the offspring of that union, I make no comment. I commend your heroism which others have written about to our emperor while at the same time I mutter imprecations over the labyrinth of law-breaking you have drawn yourself into and from which there may be no exit. Your fate is in the hands of Emperor Trajan. I have made and will make no appeals on your behalf to our imperial majesty. Remain under the orders of the noble and great Maturus until Trajan and his counsellors reach your case and decide your future—if you are to have one. Meanwhile, is it necessary for me to order you to stop writing letters and resume building roads or whatever Maturus needs in the line of architecture? Vale."*

Gaius paced on, holding Penelope's elbow, while the rain flicked their faces and the ocean boomed below. Have hope, his instinct advised. Hope, always hope. Maturus has sent dispatch after dispatch to Trajan. Rufus has sent two masterpieces to Trajan. Frontinus and Lady Enna have written full confessions of their misguided efforts to shield the tax-thefts of Classicus . . . even Turdo dictated a letter to Trajan, signing it with his X. Flavian had sent letters to Trajan . . .

"Gaius, love," asked Penelope, "do you think Governor Classicus and Zinga Rutilia—if they went to Malendi, do you think he . . . killed them?"

Irritably he said, "Is that any concern of mine?"

Penelope's eyes were troubled. "My dearest, please stop hating."

"Penelope, do you feel any pity for Classicus?"

"I do," she said, thoughtfully. "From things—odd things—that I witnessed when I belonged to Classicus, I think his sanity was weakening then. And the confession he wrote that came to light in Rome, admitting to the murder of poor Publius and the plan to incite a guerrilla war with the help of Malendi. I keep remembering that Classicus confessed he would *not* incite any war—and that he exonerated Lady Enna and Frontinus, you and Rufus, and his new wife, Zinga."

"Then who did order the black hordes to attack us at the Sil? What malevolence dictated *that?* What if Rufus and I, Flavian, all the *roararii*—what if we had been surprised and wiped out? Would you still pity Cornelius Classicus?"

Her eyes blurred. "Dearest, I honestly believe, that in time I would still have pitied Classicus."

"Woman, you are a mystery," he snapped, but his loathing of Classicus was swept away as if the Atlantic had washed over him, and a tide of love for Penelope filled him.

Then they saw Phrones hurrying forward, trying to shield his neat blue livery under a red linen umbrella. The grave Egyptian scribe was drenched and unperturbed.

"Noble sir and domina," said the secretary, "there is sudden confusion within. I am not on duty today and was in my apartment praying to Isis, when one of my aides came in haste to summon me to the library of His Excellency Maturus. There had been an explosive exchange between the worshipful Maturus and a very, very, unexpected visitor. Never have I been more frightened."

Gaius' apprehension shot up. "Who is it? Who made the proconsul angry?"

Phrones turned his parasol full against the driving wind. "Sir, the newcomer wants to talk to you . . . in the red marble chamber. I am praying."

"Who wants to talk to me, good Phrones? Someone from Rome —come to arrest me?"

The wind suddenly ripped Phrones' umbrella out of his trembling clasp and away it flew out over the Atlantic. The Egyptian's green eyes watched the flight of his property dully.

"Noble Lacer," said the Nile man, shakily, "the fearsome individual awaiting you in the red marble chamber is Chieftain Luna Malendi."

Gaius' jaw tightened. "Phrones," he said, sharply, "kindly escort my domina to our apartment. Penelope, bar all doors and windows. I love you," he murmured. "I love you."

XXXVIII

Gaius strode into the red marble room. The Celt general stood at some distance from the doors with his back to the mahogany portals, staring out a closed casement window. Chieftain Malendi was vividly black against the rose stone pillars in his black sleeved tunic, belt, trousers and boots.

"Has the bridge builder entered?" The guerrilla leader did not turn around. "Perhaps he has a blade or two ready to drive between my shoulder blades?"

"Did you kill that murdering Classicus? And his woman?"

"Remain where you stand, architect," came the measured response. "I have much to impart before I meet your enraged eyes. First, I am honored that Emperor Trajan has graciously accepted my written oath of allegiance. The infuriated and honest Maturus has likewise accepted my written and oral vow of fealty to our Caesar. Unfortunately, the brave Maturus refuses to accept a decision of mine based on the religious traditions and customs of my people."

Gaius stared at the chieftain's back and dark mane of hair. "Something about the Black God—perhaps?" he asked, almost shouting. "If you fed Classicus—dead or alive—to the mammoth reptile, I would feel some concern. Why desecrate the stomach of a terrible yet benevolent snake with a poisonous viper such as Cornelius Classicus? Did you know that Rome is roaring over the disclosures of Classicus' written confession? Did you know that he admitted murdering Publius, a distinguished, moral and patrician architect—because that noble refused to be bribed by Classicus the bankrupt? Did you know that Classicus in his written confession admitted duping you because he wanted you to throw your army against us at the Sil? What did you do with Classicus?"

Patiently the guerrilla prince answered, "If the architect will bear with me, I will answer his questions. Giant reptiles have lived in the crater lake for how long? How many centuries? No one knows. From whence did they come, or did they begin there? No one knows. To my knowledge no human being has ever entered the volcanic cone and explored the forest and serpent lake. It is another world within the world we men call our world. I think it may be a link with past eons, to remind us of the Omniscience that created all living things. Is the world of the Black God a terrible warning to man? Who can answer that? Can the architect?"

Gaius smiled sarcastically. "I did not come here to answer conundrums. Proceed, chieftain. Without riddles." The Celt did not turn around and Gaius had to stare in contempt at Malendi's flowing dark hair and back.

"The first of my distant ancestors to see the giant reptiles by accident went insane," continued the chieftain, meditatively. "That same fate has befallen men in modern times."

"I saw the Black God. I wait for Malendi to continue his dissertation," said Gaius.

Malendi suddenly turned around. There were no daggers in his belt, no sword, and his long brown hands hung limply at his sides. The Celt was unarmed.

"I entreat you, let the hate depart," said Malendi. "Architect, I watched you and your friends progress unharmed across the lava. The Black God approved of you. The giant harmed you not. Never does the holy titan depart the lava and wreak havoc among men. It comes out to sun itself only in the hot months. Never has it, to my knowledge, slain a human being. It seems to appreciate gifts of slain wild beasts and bundles of leaves, all blessed by my tribal priests and taken by my bravest warriors to the lower lava reaches and left with prayers and gratitude for the dark divinity. In return the Black God seems to protect the Arvacan nation from famine and wars that in past centuries have threatened us with extinction. And is there but one great serpent in the crater?" He paused meditatively and continued, "Three of my valiant warriors told me that they think they have seen a Black Goddess snake in the cone, being fed by her fearsome mate. A mirage? If true, are the sacred creations so old they no longer spawn young? I myself have seen only the one we call the Black God. And frightful though he is to behold, who is man to loathe that which is incomprehensible?"

The flow of words left Gaius speechless.

"Methinks puny man may be repulsive to the Black God," mused the guerrilla prince. "Think on that. Love shows itself in many forms. The Black God could destroy, yet he in greater wisdom and tolerance unknown to us witholds judgment and destruction of man, the destroyer."

Malendi advanced a few steps. "Architect, on our way south to extend greetings to Maturus, I and my warrior escorts rode across your Tagus Bridge." He came closer and at last stood face to face with Gaius.

"My bridge," said Gaius, seeing it in his mind.

"Aye. Lusitanians and Celts and Romans walking on its footways. Horsemen, wagons, donkeys, burros and mules moving across the center roadway. I and my warriors halted on centerbridge to pay silent homage to your granite miracle. The voices of the people and animals, the low murmur of the Tagus, the brisk wind from the green hills and far mountains, and never so blue a sky." He sighed. "I found three links of rusted chain on the paving of the great halfmoon arch that triumphantly leaps the river. I have those mute mementos for you, architect."

Gaius bowed his head.

"As to Cornelius Classicus," the chieftain murmured, "his flesh is unmarred. His transition was glorious. Surely there is no better way for a man to leave this mortal existence. His handmaid, Zinga Rutilia, is adapting. She begged me to kill her. I refused. We pray and hope she is adjusting to some degree of serenity. Does the passing of Classicus slake your thirst for vengeance, friend?"

Gaius answered: "Cease calling me 'friend'! Stop shaming me!"

Malendi smiled warmly. "Maturus told me your precarious situation, friend. Let me help you if I can. The governor forced me to accept a huge rough diamond discovered by his adopted son, the brave Roman by name of Zamil."

"I do not want or need help," said Gaius, decisively. "Keep your diamond!" Yet his hope was rising.

The Celt bowed respectfully. "You go to meet your destiny as an honorable Roman always does. Architect, henceforth Roman am I, as Roman as you. Despite your protest, I will do all in my power to aid you and those you love."

Now Gaius' thoughts were in turmoil. The blackcloak prince was indirectly offering safety for him—Penelope—Gaia—Rufus—Lucilla, the former wife of Rufus and soon to be re-wed to him—Primula and Sophronia, the little daughters of Rufus—safety in blackcloak land. Protected by the warriors of Malendi. Safe . . . at last. No. No. It would be another halfway escape, a staving off, a repudiation of all he had fought for so long. He shook his head and said, "Chieftain, I have no words to try and thank you."

The dark eyes of Malendi glowed with understanding.

Then Zamil rushed in, daggers in each hand, his black eyes murderous.

"Stay back, Zamil," Gaius warned. "I am with a friend. Stay back."

"*Friend?*" shouted the younger Roman, in amazement, but he came to a halt. "I've been reading my eyes out, tribune, trying to find a way through the statutes to save you! The laws!"

Gaius felt his confidence rising. "I'm still alive, Zamil," he said. "And you can't substitute daggers for laws. Remember, as Maturus keeps telling you, you want to be a lawyer." Gaius began seeing humor in the rage of his young champion. He was not alone. He had many champions.

Then the chieftain spoke. "Methinks this crucial time calls for something of a ridiculous nature. Friends, the morning after you escaped my camp, my warriors found a dead lynx in the woods. It was a huge and ferocious beast that had slain two children of my tribe and maimed one of our women. Long had the creature evaded the traps and arrows of my huntsmen. And marvel did we when we found the lynx carcass whole and unmarred—yet dead it lay in the forest." Malendi was heaving with soft laughter. "Perhaps the architect could tell me about that?"

Zamil sputtered, "The tribune can do anything! He threw a bowl of butter at some snarling thing the night we got out of your camp!"

The white teeth of the Celt shone as he laughed heartily. Soon his words came, "Aye? Another marvel. Ponder, brother Romans: The predacious lynx died not from wounds—but from suffocation! Its nostrils and throat were plugged with butter!"

Gaius began trembling and first thought he was going to be sick. Then he knew he was shaking with laughter. It poured out—the first release from strain he had felt in months. Zamil broke into laughter, too. All three men began clapping each other on the back.

"Butter," gasped Zamil. "Holy gods!"

The doors opened again and in came Maturus, his short toga flapping defiantly. Behind came Rufus in armor and helmet, with Mars on the leash. Lastly came Phrones like a lean phantom in blue to stand in dignified anguish close by Maturus. At a murmured command from Rufus, the mastiff sank to his haunches.

"And what cause is there for merriment?" boomed Maturus. He sat down at a rose marble table and thumped its gleaming surface.

"The honest Maturus still steams with ire," laughed Malendi, "but we wiser Romans have found temporary unity in levity."

"Chieftain, our spectacular half hour conference in my library clarified nothing," announced Maturus. "I intend no disrespect, but your curious claim to sovereign tribal rights as superseding Roman justice only befogs the complex issue."

"My friend Maturus is in error," responded Malendi. "Unwillingly do I bow, however, to another decree friend Maturus dispensed regarding the enormous rough diamond. You have forced it upon me, friend Maturus, insisting it is mine, according to mineral rights laws. It is a tribute to your character, Maturus, that you made infuriatingly clear that the valuable gemstone is in no way to be construed as a bribe for the exchange of Cornelius Classicus. In the diamond matter you acted in accordance with the high and noble tradition of the disinterested and unbiased Roman magistrate."

Gaius was thunderstruck. "But you told me Classicus was dead!"

"Nay, architect. I told you the flesh of Classicus was unmarred and that his transition was glorious . . . and there was no better way for a man to leave this mortal existence. The evil that *was* Classicus has gone. A god now inhabits the body of Classicus."

"A god . . ." Gaius stared at his brother. Rufus, too, was staring in disbelief at Malendi.

Governor Maturus arose and confronted the Celt. "Noble chieftain," said the proconsul, "let me elaborate a few of the statements I hurled at you during our talk an hour gone. Last Fall I spent a month in New Carthage, working with Acting Governor Sylvanus. We found all evidence gone that Cornelius Classicus had censored mailscrolls or destroyed such. His archives and secret wall coffer were bare of any except ordinary documents having to do with arrival and departure of troops, ship schedules, tax reports. Everyone queried by the honorable Sylvanus and myself—from the legation chief prefect on down to servants and slaves—all were indignant that their humanitarian lord, Classicus, was suspected to be anything except an honest and hard-pressed *legatus* who had protected them during the odious reign of Domitian. They mourn his sudden departure last mid July. Where is he, they asked me. Friend Malendi, can you surmise my anger and the benign bewilderment of Sylvanus, a man whose integrity is as vast as his flesh?"

The Celt nodded in sympathy. His friendly glance rested a while on Phrones, busy with tablet and stylus by the door. He next looked admiringly at Gaius and finally his interested gaze settled on Mars. The mastiff squatted like a beast carved of black obsidian.

After a long silence, Malendi announced, "Maturus, I will clear away some of the fog. The pathetic handmaid of the god, the forest-faced woman of red hair, confessed on her knees that she had used the Great Seal of Hither Spain and forged the handwriting of Classicus to an order that committed me to war against the men at the Sill"

It was now Maturus who was dumbfounded—and triumphant. Gaius could not analyze his sensations. He simply looked and listened, seeing in his mind the feral, yet strangely appealing face of Zinga Rutilia, the second wife of Classicus . . .

"The second domina of Classicus is a criminal," said Maturus, after regaining composure. "And we now know that Classicus was not only an inveterate writer of letters, but demented—I repeat—*demented* prior to his disappearance, bound for your territory last July."

"Not demented," Malendi interrupted, softly. "There be many gods. We Arvacans believe gods sometimes inhabit the bodies of beasts and men." He looked at Gaius as if hoping for confirmation of his remarks. To his surprise, Gaius nodded.

"Sir, I have not yet told you this," said Maturus. "After the Ides of last July, a tax chest arrived in Rome from New Carthage. It contained more than money and a tax report signed by the estimable Sylvanus. It contained *another* scroll! Who had penned that document, that confession?"

"Governor," Gaius interrupted, "I have told the chieftain something of that matter."

"Aye," murmured the Celt prince. "So Classicus wrote a full statement of his crimes, secreted it in a tax coffer, while he was in his godly identity—"

"Identity!" Maturus bored in. "That scroll did not come to light for months! A slave of the subquestor found that document and—loathing his cruel master—secretly turned in the confession to the High Questor. And so did the senators and Rome learn the true corrupt nature of Cornelius Classicus!"

Gaius came to the aid of Maturus. "And so, chieftain," he began, "Rome found out how Cornelius Classicus had planned to obtain gold through a guerrilla attack on imperial mines. Rome learned how Classicus had artfully led you to believe that Proconsul Verus Victrix Maturus planned to wipe out your tribe, conquer Spain, and go on to conquer the empire and declare himself Princeps." He was talking easily, as if to a friend, and, strangely, Gaius felt at peace with himself. "The document also included a confession of the murder, by poison, of Publius the architect. It exonerated Lady

Enna, his first wife; the noble General Myron Frontinus, former treasurer of Farther Spain; myself and my gallant brother there by the portals, Commander Rufus Liscus."

"The confession of Classicus even exonerated the Gallic woman, Zinga Rutilia," Maturus thrust in. "A paradox. The she-felon turned into a lily. The vicious female who incited the war and caused the deaths of many of your gallant warriors—and gallant defenders of the Sil mines! Think on all of this, chieftain. But let me tell you what else Classicus put in that amazing document. His admittance of crimes was lucid and written by a man in sound mental health. But the last half of his letter dwelt on a torch of time, a blue tree of diamond fruits, and a shadowless entity of eternal verity! And other incomprehensible statements that could only have been written by a mind bereft of sanity!

"Cornelius Classicus is guilty of heinous crimes! And hear me, friend Prince Malendi: the keystone of Roman justice is this: an accused is guilty until proven innocent!"

"So be it," reflected Malendi. "Yet methinks it is impossible to bring to justice a man already dead."

"Classicus the criminal lives," said Maturus. "Zinga Rutilia, criminal and—undoubtedly—co-conspirator of Classicus—lives. You harbor them in your domain. Prince Malendi, I know the laws. Rome will not accuse *you*. You will not be imprisoned and put on trial!"

"The body of Classicus lives," said Malendi. "But what dwells within? A god. And sacred to us, too, is the god's handmaid, Zinga Rutilia, now cleansed of sin and devoting herself to the care of Classicus the god."

Gaius inquired, "Chieftain, surely you do not propose to defy Emperor Trajan?"

The Celt placed friendly hands on Gaius' shoulders. "Not defiance, architect. In my dispatches to the virtuous Trajan I have explained all vital matters in full and placed myself and my tribe under his jurisdiction. Our glorious emperor's brief, yet prompt replies assure me that my appeal for the custody of Classicus the god will be respectfully considered and fair judgment reached; and too, does Trajan solemnly write that the religious traditions of the Arvacan nation under Roman dominion will be fully protected."

"But chieftain," said Gaius, "what if Trajan orders Classicus and Zinga turned over for trial? What if he orders both executed?"

Malendi became melancholy. "If such is the judgment of our

emperor, I, as monarch of the Arvacan nation, must then take my own life. My oldest son will become chieftain; there is no other way.

"Not too long ago my ancestors worshipped the mistletoe and oak trees. My priests still intone prayers whose meaning is now lost to us. Many of my warriors revere the moon and think she is inhabited by a goddess. And when the moon disappears a few nights monthly, my fighters prostrate themselves and confess their transgressions. Yet since the deity, Classicus, has come to bless my realm, have my tribesmen found themselves united in reverence of all they do not understand."

"Classicus is not a god," Maturus objected.

"I respectfully disagree," responded the blackcloak. "The valiant Maturus still fails to recognize the subtle difference between a wicked past identity and godly immortality residing in a human body. That divinity has been the protector of my tribe since he and his handmaid arrived in a haycart late last July. My warriors met them at my dominion boundaries and the god's sweet benediction and marvellous flow of words enthralled my fighters. In awe did they escort him and his maid and the holy cart to my stronghold."

"I am impressed," grumbled Maturus. "Classicus riding in hay! Kindly proceed, friend chieftain."

"—And how did I, Malendi, know a deity had arrived? Because they drove in, drawn by two draft horses—"

"Which the Gallic wild woman undoubtedly stole," said the governor, acidly.

"So arrived Classicus, the supernatural being—during a violent storm," Malendi resumed. "And when the god got down from the vehicle, needing no help from my warriors or his weeping handmaid, a spear of lightning struck the earth behind him. He feared it not—yet I and my people were terrified. And when the roar of Jove followed the lance of heavenly fire, the god Classicus smiled and stretched his arms upward. The rain stopped. The black clouds fled. The moon shone down on him."

"*Magni Dei datum,*" came the sarcastic retort of Maturus.

"We knelt at the god's feet," said the Celt. "His handmaid swooned and two of my wives bore her reverently to my tent. She slept for two days. And the god? He walked among us, murmuring in alien tongues, yet we understood and our souls were exalted. We have built him a stone sanctuary roofed with silver ore. His handmaid tends him, feeds him a little milk and bread. He eats no other food. She robes him in white garments each dawn before he walks among us. The god sleeps most of the time. But when he honors us we kneel. We listen. Sometimes his exhortations are not clear, yet the beauty of his face and voice gives meaning. We know he speaks of love and that love is limitless."

Maturus shouted, "This is monstrous! A travesty of justice!"

"Governor!" Gaius urged. "Sir—let us hear all of it!"

"When the god speaks in Latin or Greek, he discourses of fair beings winging over green leas," continued Malendi, "and flying peacefully across the azure heights of heaven. He talks of bodies that die not; of atoms of deathless power that reside within each human house. Oft does he describe and we Celts see it clearly, a blue tree of diamonds. We seem to taste the honeyed gems as the god plucks them from the invisible tree and graciously distributes them to us."

Arising, the governor said, hoarsely, "Insanity—not divinity!"

"That is the judgment of Maturus," replied the Celt leader. "Does any other friend in this chamber care to comment?"

Mars let out a friendly whine. Malendi smiled at the dog and then his gaze went from man to man, coming to rest on Gaius.

Gaius oddly now felt all hate, and dread of the future, abating. It was a going away, a slow tide withdrawing from his mind, carrying its flotsam and jetsam as sickness at last recedes from a body building new health. He tried to speak, as Malendi waited, but no words came. Then he remembered wisdom—not his own—and replied, "Chieftain, the genius Aristotle reasoned that all men's souls are immortal, but only the souls of the righteous are both immortal and divine."

"The brave architect has built another triumph," murmured the chieftain.

"Now we walk on air, we fly like birds," said Governor Maturus. "Some of our soft-brained astrologers even prophesy that men will fly some day. I deal with reality! Noble Prince Malendi, the insanity of Cornelius Classicus and his past record as a just *propraetore* until the commencement of his crimes would mitigate his punishment. The magistrates in Rome would put forth superhuman efforts to be sure he was given a fair trial. And the same for the Gallic woman. Both would have three defense advocates. I strongly doubt if Zinga the Gaul could escape execution, but Classicus might. If damages were paid to relatives of Publius the architect, and in view of the insanity of Classicus . . ."

The Celt's expression was that of an indulgent father heeding the outbursts of an immature son. "Maturus, what is insanity?"

"What is sleep? What is death? And what is divinity?" proclaimed the proconsul.

Gaius had to speak, give words to the thought filling his mind: "When an evil consciousness departs a human body, and is replaced by one as pure as an infant's . . . like my daughter, Gaia's . . . is that not divinity?" He could not answer his own question. Had he solved partially the search of philosophers through recorded time for the answer to the enigma of man's being, doing, and becoming?

"Gentlemen," boomed Maturus, "you have heard the judgment of our friend, Prince Chieftain Luna Malendi, loyal Roman. I challenge him no longer. I invite him and his warriors to be my guests for as long as they care to stay in this legation. I will debate no more with him. I trust we can talk of felicitous subjects in the scant hours I can take away from studying the laws to try and find a way to safety for Gaius Lacer; for Lady Enna Gracchus; for General Myron Frontinus; and for Commander Rufus Liscus and his family." Maturus marched out with Zamil and the Egyptian scribe.

Malendi took Gaius by the arm and drew close to Rufus.

"Commander, may I stroke your noble mastiff?" asked the Celt.

"Do so, sir," replied Rufus. His blue eyes were friendly.

Mars panted happily while the blackcloak's fingers patted the broad head of the canine. Then the mastiff began licking the Celt's hands. Malendi smiled. "Does the noble Mars have a mate?"

"He will, soon, chieftain," said Rufus. "Governor Maturus has sent to northern Gaul for a thoroughbred female of somewhat the same breed. If you want one of the puppies, I will be honored to give you one."

Malendi turned away and began pacing. Mars followed, sniffing the boots of the blackcloak leader in pleasure.

"Friends," said Malendi, "you do not fear the future. I do not fear it on your behalf. I trust in the mercy of Trajan. The fate of all of us now rests in the hands of our emperor."

Gaius nodded. He felt renewed. Unafraid. He read the same thought in his brother's eyes. He thought of Penelope's faith that he would be vindicated. He began feeling that he would be. . . .

XXXIX

For almost a year Gaius Lacer waited to learn his fate. At the beginning, uplifted and optimistic over having won the friendship of Chieftain Malendi, he was patient, but as weeks and months passed racking fears and doubts settled down again. The triumphant and splendid new Imperium of Marcus Ulpius Trajan seemed to ignore the existence of the builder of the Tagus Bridge, or if not that, allowed him to live on sufferance. For a long time his pride had revolted at writing a letter to the Emperor, the ruler who revered the laws. Would the great Imperator remember the architect he had dined with years before and advised: *'Always hold yourself in high regard'*? And how could Gaius justify his attacks on army men and impersonation of an officer? Yet at last he was driven to writing a missive to the Princeps.

It was a respectful and thoughtful recounting of his life since the building of the Tagus arches to the present. He was humbly happy to have discovered Gold Valley and hoped that the emperor's prospectors were finding the site rich with gold ore to help the prosperity of the State. He described his desperate actions which had resulted in the saving of his life and that of his wife. He did not plead for mercy. Two pages extolled his domina, Penelope of Icaria, whose heroic medical aid to wounded troops in the battle of the canyon had saved soldiers of Rome. Admitting he had inadvertently fallen into defiance of his master, Apollodorus, and espoused Penelope, and had children by her. But never would he submit his blameless wife and children to slavery and possible execution because of his misdeeds. He asked mercy for his family. He requested imperial clemency for his brother, Commander Rufus Liscus, and the family of Rufus. . . .

Gaius and Penelope were now the parents of a son, Gaius *Secundus,* born late the preceding September. Healthy and lively, the flaxen-haired baby was considered by his sister, Gaia Juliana, to have been created for her delight and motherly care. The precocious little girl, going on two years old, regarded young Gaius as her property, and as the new year came, Gaia's devotion to her brother gave constant joy to Gaius and Penelope.

There was no reply to Gaius from Emperor Trajan. But an acrimonious communication had come from another quarter.

Apollodorus, first architect of the empire, had written a peevish letter to Governor Maturus, accompanied by a legal document formally filing suit against Commander Rufus Liscus for having struck off the armbands of slavery from Gaius Lacer and aiding Lacer the bondsman in illegally wedding a slavegirl and having offspring by her. Now in Rome supervising the new Forum of Trajan and magnificent Ulpia Basilica Hall of Judgment, the older architect demanded two hundred thousand sesterces as damages, plus a public apology from Rufus on the steps of the Temple of Peace. Rufus Liscus must stand trial by *consilium* (jury) for aiding and abetting the illicit sexual acts of Gaius Julius Lacer, half-brother of Rufus Liscus.

Proconsul Verus Maturus reacted to the challenge with characteristic vigor. Helped by Zamil and two freedmen apprentice lawyers, the governor laid obstruction after obstruction in the projected litigation of Apollodorus. The estimable Apollodorus was misinformed and laboring under a dangerous misapprehension on the charge that Commander Liscus had helped his brother espouse a Greek woman captive of Cornelius Classicus. And as a patrician citizen and legion officer of heroic record, Rufus Liscus was under the absolute jurisdiction of Emperor Trajan. Then the proconsul assembled a mass of quotations and precedents going back to the original Laws of the Twelve Tables, bolstered by the annual interpretations of imperial praetors for the past two hundred years. The resulting lengthy-paged document was so impressive and baffling that Maturus himself was unable to understand his legal gymnastics when the bulky papers at last went off by courier post to Apollodorus in Rome.

The result was to silence Apollodorus.

Eventually, however, cordial scrolls came to Maturus from Senator Pliny the Younger and Senator Cornelius Tacitus. The advocate for Apollodorus had given up his client's cause and the papers concerning the defense of Rufus Liscus were now in the hands of the famous two Conscript Fathers high in the councils of Trajan (still at his headquarters on the eastern frontier). Impressed by the legal erudition of Maturus, the renowned legislators would require months to dissect, interpret, and equate his many counterclaims. Eventually, the gods giving clear reasoning to Pliny and Tacitus, they would arrange a hearing for Rufus Liscus. Each communication contained witty and solemn allusions to the slow movement of justice and extended warm personal greetings to Maturus the magistrate and his client, the noble commander.

The reprieve heartened Rufus and Gaius. But their friends, Lady Enna Gracchus and General Myron Frontinus, were in a precarious position. Those two had moved to Segovia at the onset of Trajan's principate the previous January. They had resigned themselves to death for their protection of Cornelius Classicus, and had decided to end their lives together when the order of execution arrived. But Maturus independently became their defender in a long letter to Emperor Trajan. Elaborating the point of Classicus' insanity, the governor pounded away on the point that the Imperium had suffered no loss of revenue due to the deeds of Enna Gracchus and Myron Frontinus in covering the tax defalcations of Cornelius Classicus.

This document seemed to vanish into a void somewhere in Germany and elicited no answer from the Princeps.

Nor had there been any messages from Chieftain Malendi for months. All was quiet over Spain.

Two of the three legions had been sent to the Danube front, leaving the VII Gemina to maintain order in both provinces of Spain. The troops had little to do but ride patrol, pay goodwill visits to *Togati* and blackcloak settlements, and watch bull-conflicts. The legionaries were always welcomed in Malendi's main encampment, hospitably entertained, and allowed quick glimpses of Classicus the god walking in the forest and raising his hands in blessing of pine trees presumably bowed down with diamonds. Zinga, redhaired and in sackcloth, with retinues of blackcloak warriors, always attended the demented ex-Governor of Hither Spain. Two of the Gemina officers, first fortifying themselves with oblations to Jupiter, God Almighty, had daringly ascended the lava and peered through a fissure in the cone and seen the Black God—and its consort, the smaller Black Goddess—swimming languidly in the waters of the sacred serpent lake. More, the awed soldiers reported having seen two snakes about ten feet long on the shore of the body of water.

Gaius further learned that the Gemina had visited Gold Valley and found the Rapax Legion from northern Gaul mining under the direction of two imperial geologists dispatched by Emperor Trajan. According to the enthusiastic troops of the Rapax, Gold Valley was competing nobly with the output of the Egyptian mines. Wagonloads of rough glittering yellow ore and whole nuggets went to Rome for smelting and refining. More auspicious still, the imperial geologists had discovered a sluggish river northeast of Gold Valley that promised to be even richer in *aurum*.

Trajan himself was burning the tax books and ruthlessly rooting out waste and inefficient workers in all departments of government. He was installing a graded civil service and rewarding efficient and loyal men with promotions, better pay and more responsibility. It was now a capital offense to launch false accusations or lodge anonymous information against law-abiding men and women who might be Christian. Nor did burdensome new taxation cloud the brilliant sun of Trajan's rule. To the dismay of the rich (and economists, too) he was wiping out monopolies which had brought huge revenue to the Treasury. But by the end of his first year in power, free trade was flourishing and money beginning to fill the depleted coffers of the *Fiscus*. This gave the emperor financial power to plan and begin extensive public works: buildings, bridges, aqueducts, harbors—and to intensify his defense preparations against the Dacians and Parthians.

Delegations from both hostile nations had visited Marcus Trajan at his Rhine headquarters, suggesting mutual disarmament as balm for world problems. Trajan received the ambassadors courteously, listened to their presentations, then tersely replied that he was levying twenty new legions. His troops made sure that the discomfited barbarians and Orientals returned safely to their lands.

Trials were proceeding in Rome before the Court of the Hundred Judges against former governors and other officials accused of crimes against provincial peoples during the reign of Emperor Domitian. People innocent of crimes, but imprisoned on charges of false accusers during the imperiums of Domitian and Nerva were being released and financial redress made by the imperial *Fiscus*. Men whose money and property had been arbitrarily confiscated by Domitian were promised eventual restitution.

"Let every just man, woman and child be safe at home, on the streets and in the fields," came the order of Trajan.

Gaius kept informed of Trajan's reforms by perusal of papyrus editions of the *Acta Diurna* arriving in Gades from Rome. He wondered what, if anything, special judiciary commissions could do to pay the debts of bankrupts such as Cornelius Classicus. Philosophically he concluded that Gold Valley would remove that burden from the shoulders of Emperor Trajan. As for himself, the forgotten discoverer of Gold Valley and architect of the Tagus Bridge, better to be consigned to forgetfulness than executed. His conscience was in excellent working condition and so were his mind, hands, and muscles. The love and faith of Penelope was his strength, the wonders of his son and daughter his inspiration. No brothers could be closer than he and Rufus, who now served as unofficial military advisor to Governor Maturus.

Gaius and his freedmen crews demolished shaky old buildings and cottages built in former ages of wood bricks in Gades, and replaced them with sound structures of fired brick or stone. In his free hours he built clay models of bridges and canals, which Gaia and Rufus' daughters converted into dolls and cradles. Then in February came an epistle from a freedman of Emperor Trajan.

Gaius Julius Lacer, bondsman of Apollodorus, was to supply the name and all pertinent facts about an aged Egyptian who had purchased Penelope, resident of the destroyed village of Icaria in Greece, transported her by sea to New Carthage and sold her to Cornelius Classicus. In perplexity, Gaius turned to Penelope. She still did not know the *praenomen* or *cognomen* of her benefactor from the Nile, but supplied all other information, including a description of the Egyptian avatar and his vessel, and the fact that the ancient had died and been buried at sea. After his reply was sent by courier post, Gaius and Penelope puzzled over the affair and could find no logical explanation for it. They endured. They waited. They laughed over letters from Flavian and Beryl in Londinium. The former orderly of Gaius had been assigned to a desk position as a tax collector and the noble Lacer could imagine what thoughts passed through a soldier's mind. Of equal grief to Flavian was that he and his Juda-Rose and young Flavianus lived in a luxurious house in Londinium and, with no exercise, the erstwhile *optio* was building a pot-belly. . . . Hail Trajan!

On the Kalends of March, an imperial dispatch arrived for Governor Maturus. He read it, scowled fiercely, showed it to Zamil, and then summoned Gaius, Rufus, and Penelope to his library. When they stood by his table, he abruptly read aloud:

LICINIUS SURA, CHIEF COUNSELLOR TO TRAJAN IMPERATOR. TO VERUS VICTRIX MATURUS, IMPERIAL LEGATUS OF FARTHER SPAIN. GREETINGS FROM NERVA TRAJAN GERMANICUS, TRIBUNICIAN OF THE PEOPLE, AUGUSTUS, CONSUL IN HIS SECOND YEAR. THE FOLLOWING PEOPLE NOW UNDER YOUR JURISDICTION ARE TO COME TO ROME AND PRESENT THEMSELVES AT THE ROUND TEMPLE OF HERCULES CUSTOS HARD BY THE CURIA OF POMPEY AND TEMPLE OF MINERVA CHALCHIDICA. THEY ARE TO IDENTIFY THEMSELVES TO OFFICERS OF THE TRAJANA LEGION IN THAT DESIGNATED SANCTUARY. THESE PEOPLE ARE GAIUS JULIUS LACER, BONDSMAN OF APOLLODORUS: RUFUS LISCUS, LEGION COMMANDER NOW ON DETACHED SERVICE AS MILITARY AIDE TO THE NOBLE MATURUS; AND PENELOPE, FORMER BONDSWOMAN OF CORNELIUS CLASSICUS AND NOW AN IMPERIAL SLAVE. VALE. WRITTEN AT COLONIA IN GERMANY.

Gaius was benumbed and speechless. His wife a slave of the *emperor?* At that moment he finally gave up all hope.

"Courage, dear wonderful," said Penelope, tenderly. She took him in her arms and his despairing eyes saw only the silvery white streak in her golden braids—

Maturus growled, "The children of the honorable Lacer brothers and the Domina of Commander Liscus are safe in my custody, and I defy all the Praetors of Rome to try and wrench them out of my grasp! I immediately appoint myself their guardian, *Pro Tem.*"

Rufus, in green kilt and peacetime cuirass of leather, at length commented, "The emperor never announces his decrees in advance. Penelope must be right."

"I shall also claim temporary ownership of Mars, his mate, Cham-Cham, and her litter of four puppies! Commander, tell your mastiff to obey me while you are in Rome!" said Maturus.

Rufus tried to smile. He nodded.

The proconsul grumbled, "I have met the great Licinius Sura and he approves of me not. Once he told me I talked too much and pursued gnats. I will now pursue the offspring of gnats!" Calming down, he continued, "I will have a century of the Gemina escort you to Rome. A cushioned carriage with all comforts for Penelope.

Overnight stops at inns along the route through eastern Spain, southern Gaul, the *Alps Maritimae* pass, and so down Italy and into Rome by the Aurelian Way. If the flamens of weather are not dozing, they will make sure you are not blockaded by snows in the Alps!"

Gaius was so despondent that he could not even smile.

⊓⊓⊓ ROME ⊔⊓⊔⊓

XL

G aius Julius Lacer looked at Rome.
He had not seen it for half his life, having left the Capitol at fifteen. Sitting in the lumbering wooden carriage with Penelope, he held her rigid hands in his more relaxed clasp. Rufus rode his white stallion outside at their right; ahead and behind clattered horsemen escorts of the VII Gemina. They were entering the city three days after the Ides of March.

Rome.

Rome, the heart and mother of the empire's ninety million people. And she *is* female, thought Gaius. Woman at her best and worst. She could praise and reward a man, sweeping him into the embrace of her many white-columned temple arms. Or condemn him to death in a subterranean dungeon. He wondered if what he saw was real . . . the towering white edifices, sacred green groves, a stork or two flying over nests in the glittering gilded tile roof of the Temple of Concord.

As they crossed the Aemilian bridge, he turned to Penelope. "We are entering Ward XI of Rome," he said. "That long mass over to our right is the Circus Maximus and near it is the Forum Boarium, or cattle market. That great hill of white villas and gardens left of the Circus is the Palatine. The Palatine is Ward X. To the left of that is the Capitoline, or Ward VII. Continuing left, you see Ward IX . . . the Campus Martius at the far end and many temples, baths and theatres between the military section and us." Then he pointed to the river at their left. "See that midstream temple shaped like a boat with its prow towards us? That is the Temple of Aesculapius, my dearest."

Penelope gazed tenderly at the Island of Healing, the great white and gray temple shining with gilded glints in the morning sun.

Her serenity filled him. He was relieved that he felt calm, had the courage to face whatever was coming. His wife was a slave of Emperor Trajan . . . she would be well-treated . . . as for himself he felt a tremulous sense of coming victory which he tried to consider with detachment. . . .

They left the carriage and two brown horses at a public stable and refreshed themselves in unexpectedly clean and quiet rooms over a harness shop that Rufus paid for. Every person they met went to great lengths in showing courtesy to Commander Rufus Liscus, his brother and sister-in-law, and the Gemina cavalry escorts. The bulk of the troopers departed for the barracks in the Campus Martius, leaving eight to aid the litters of the brothers and Penelope up to Capitoline Hill. By the second hour of day Gaius and Penelope sat in a portable chair, Rufus seated behind, and all were hoisted up by cheerful Nubian slaves.

Rome the Mother was indulgent towards her children today. They shouted and laughed, screamed and pushed and quarreled, yet over and under all, Gaius sensed good will and contentment. Rich or poor, slave or free, men and women were going about their affairs purposefully and without any real animosity. He witnessed men in fierce argument cease debating to help crippled beggars with coins or assist aged people across the cobbles, then resume talk on trivial subjects. Women carrying baskets, or balancing brown water jars on their heads and also trying to keep eyes on darting children were gallantly aided by important passing strangers with retinues of slaves. He observed a prosperous bearded Jew in green talking in apparent amiability to a bearded Arab in white turban and spotless blue robe . . . two men of races historically hating each other.

"The unifying power of Trajan," Gaius said to himself.

Up went Gaius and Penelope and his brother, with their eight horsemen, bound for the *Fori Imperiali* on important duties and then destined to be taken to the Temple of Hercules *Custos*, The Guardian, and identify themselves to officers of the new Trajana Legion.

At the Rostra in the Forum Romanum, a polite censor's aide inspected their road-pass certificates proffered by Rufus and witnessed them place incense pills on a bronze tripod wafting fragrant blue smoke up before a medallion likeness of Trajan.

They were carried westward on the Capitoline towards the Tiber. Gaius began breathing fast, his hands hard knots, while Penelope tried to cheer him.

"Gaius," said Penelope, "I know what you are thinking, but you must not. You must not. We are safe—do you understand?"

He stared at her. She met his eyes with determination. Then he was in her arms, hiding his face against her breast.

He did not remember getting out of the litter, but here he was with Penelope before the tiny round Temple of Hercules *Custos,* its brickwork encircled by fluted gray Ionic pillars. Adjacent was the *Curia of Pompeius Magnus* where Julius Caesar had been assassinated one hundred and forty-three years ago . . . history, Gaius had studied it along with architecture, poetry. Then he was staring at the right of the Hercules shrine, at a Temple of Minerva of gray antiquity and severe Doric columns. Rufus was presenting their credentials to a centurion of the Trajana Legion at the open bronze portals of the Hercules shrine.

Gaius looked away. Did he know anything about pigeons? They were everywhere around him and Penelope, swooping up and down on creaking pinions. Purple flyers of silvery undertints. Silver . . . gold. Gold for the Caesars. Pigeons in purple, people hurrying past in brown and gray and black, donkeys carrying panniers of tallow candles, a woman with a goiter the size of a melon—

Then Rufus approached with the dashing officer in field green and bronze gear. Gaius stared at the soldier's sleeve blazons: large black felt shields in which gold thread depicted an eagle, a bee, and a bear. The bird was disemboweling the beast while the insect stung the animal. Gaius could understand the eagle as a symbol of the new Trajana Legion, but as for the grizzly and honey-buzzer . . . ?

"Commander Liscus, you will report to the officers' house at the Praetorian Barracks with your remaining eight horsemen of the Gemina," said the Trajana centurion. "The Greek captive, Penelope, who is claimed by Gaius Lacer as his wife, and the mother of his two children, will be transported to a villa of imperial female slaves on the Palatine. As for you, Lacer the architect, where will you stay tonight?"

Caught by surprise, Gaius replied, "Sir, I thought I was to go to the villa of my master, the noble Apollodorus, on Aventine Hill."

"I have no orders about that."

"Sir," said Gaius, "my brother, Commander Liscus, paid for rooms over a harness shop near the Emporium pier and the marble import wharf."

"Stay there tonight," ordered the centurion. "You arrived in good time from Spain. Your hearing has been set for the day after your arrival. Commander Liscus, Lacer the architect, present yourselves at the far west nave of the Ulpia Basilica on Capitoline before the third hour tomorrow. The Imperator is in Rome for a few weeks. He may preside tomorrow. Hail Trajan!"

Four infantrymen of the Trajana came up with a curtained litter. Briskly they helped Penelope in, lifted the poled seat to their shoulders and marched away.

Gaius watched her go out of his life, watched her white hands fluttering for him until her portable chair disappeared behind a bronze equestrian statue. He stared at the metal horseman whose journey was never started or finished, until Rufus jarred him to reality.

"Gaius, *vale* until tomorrow at the third hour." Then Rufus was in his litter and being borne away, followed by the eight Gemina troopers. The centurion had gone into the Temple of Hercules.

Gaius was alone except for his Nubian polemen. They had heard it all. They knew he, too, was a slave.

"*Quo vadis,* patrician?" asked one bearer, sympathetically.

Where was he going? Aristocrats did not go around in brown tunics and cloaks and legion boots scuffed from granite and shale and limestone. But he weighed the simple query as his hands weighed the small leather sack of silvers and coppers Rufus had given him that morning. "Take me to the Egyptian Quarter. I want to look at the white marble colossus of Serapis and its reflecting pool. Is it still there? The monument erected years back by Emperor Vespasian, a duplicate of the original in Alexandria?" He had to talk to someone.

"It is," said another husky Nubian. "The statue of Isis, too. Rome has almost as many gods as people, patrician." Lowering his voice the poleman whispered, "You are an aristocrat of good soul and great deeds. Peace to you."

"Silence," said another swarthy bearer, with a look of quick fear.

Another one said, "No silence for me. I am a Christian."

Gaius looked at all four with vague interest. What they believed in was not important. "I wish you well," he said. "Your secret is safe with me."

Slumped on the hard seat he wondered why he was going to the Egyptian Quarter of the city. Egypt, land of many gods. Rome, the home of many more gods. Yet why this sudden need to visit the *Serapeum* and *Isaeum*? Then he had the answer: an aged Egyptian avatar had brought Penelope to Spain—to Gaius, her lover. Egypt had given him his love. He would try to repay in the only way he could—with prayer.

Stand before Serapis, God of the Nether World. Serapis in marble loin cloth, giant hands flat at lean marble thighs, Serapis wearing the tall, tubular, corn-measure Crown of Upper Egypt. Serapis, the wise, compassionate Judge of the Dead. The benevolent idol would understand, know without Gaius having to say a word. He would talk with his soul, address the image Serapis and every other name of every other divinity decent men revered and lived by. Confide in the marble man until exhausted. Then back to the harness-shop lodgings, ask the courteous proprietor to awaken him at dawn. If it was to be his last sunrise, Gaius would have cleansed his soul first.

In sleep that night he swam in the pool reflecting the empty pedestal of the Serapis idol. The god was a living man of strong and beautiful face and walked with tame lions and crowds of people at the rim of the pool. They talked in a strange language Gaius did not understand, but he belonged with them, while separated from them. Then he heard a few words that sank into his brain: '*Byati remembered. Remember Byati. Remember Byati. Byati the Bee-man. Byati the Bee-man . . .*' The mysterious words were consolation and lulled him into deep and peaceful sleep.

XLI

Next morning Gaius was pleased to see his four Nubians of yesterday waiting outside the harness shop.

"Our Christian master asks no fee today, friend," whispered a dark poleman. "We prayed for you, your fair wife, your children and your brother last night. A vigil of prayer we offered for all of you. *Pax vobiscum.*"

"Amen," murmured each of the other three.

The strange word, '*Amen*' was oddly comforting and Gaius smiled his thanks. His spirits rose and he wondered how Penelope had spent the night. And Rufus? Out in western Spain it was still night, but he saw Gaia Juliana asleep in her high-sided bed near the cots of her two Armenian nurses. And in the next cubicle, baby Gaius the Second slept on his fleece mattress in a barrel-shaped oak crib. His children were safe—

A voice seemed to say in his mind, 'Byati' and he remembered his last night's strange dream. *'Byati the Bee-man.'* Throngs pressing upward to Capitoline Hill all seemed to be muttering *Byati the Bee-man, Byati the Bee-man.* Over and over sounded the syllables in his mind.

Gaius had considered himself immune to the splendors of Rome's buildings, villas, arches and fountains, seeing them as so many architectural problems solved in marbles, granites, limestones, brick and stucco. He raised a hand in ironic salute as his Nubians bore him past the Temple of Saturn; there was a beautiful structure, its underground vaults filled with public treasure, Senate laws and decrees and Legion Standards. He had twelve silvers of the money Rufus had given him yesterday. A very rich man was riding past the Saturn shrine, the Temple of Vespasian and the Temple of Concord, and Gaius was sure the deities in residence inclined their Olympian heads as he was carried past in triumph . . . Gaius Lacer, insignificant architect, on his way to be judged. . . .

He was unprepared for the beauty of the Ulpia Basilica going up next to the tremendous new Forum of Trajan. The great Apse with its rounded roof seemed completed and his experienced eyes estimated the structure to exceed six hundred feet in length, close to two hundred in width (when all the naves were finished) and about one hundred and forty feet in height. Workmen swarmed wooden scaffolds of the naves, and Gaius silently placed his Tagus Bridge against the Ulpia Basilica being built by his master, the renowned Apollodorus.

A smile drew down his lips. The Tagus Bridge was *longer* than the Ulpia Basilica. It no longer mattered. Apollodorus would claim credit for having built the spans over the river in western Spain—

As he was carried closer with a solid mass of other litters and people on foot, he saw workmen sliding down ropes from the timber framework. He heard soldiers shouting:

"DOWN FROM THE HEIGHTS, DOWN FROM THE HEIGHTS. WORK WILL RESUME AFTER THE IMPERATOR DECREES JUDGMENTS AT TODAY'S AUDIENCE. . . . DOWN FROM THE HEIGHTS . . ."

Judgments. So the Emperor would be in the Basilica today. Emperor Trajan. *'Sir, I build honest bridges.'* —*'The only kind worth building.'* It flooded his mind, that talk with Trajan in the New Carthage legation, how many years ago?

Then he had bade his anxious and cordial Nubians farewell and was swept in a stream of humanity converging from all directions on the majestic Basilica. He and other unknowns had to give way to senators in white, attended by important freedmen carrying porfolios. On went a number of Conscript Fathers, aided by alert scribes whispering *cognomens* of important men coming from other directions. A senator never forgot a name.

Gaius trembled with suppressed laughter over the legislative method of keeping the memory honed. He might as well laugh, he had lost his way, he had no idea how to reach the far west nave of the Basilica. He did not even know in which direction he was going. People were disappearing in archways towards marble stairways leading up to galleries of the vast *auditorium*. The splendor of the building impressed Gaius more and more as he was shoved and pushed and elbowed—

"So we meet again, Gaius—and you bound the wrong way," said a voice of Olympian authority.

He had almost bumped heads with his master, Apollodorus.

The architect *primus* wore a spotless toga embellished with diagonal purple stripes and seemed to wear his fame as he wore his garments—with shattering distinction. Ribbons of white hair intersticed his bushy gray, and his profile was that of a conqueror. He was sunburned and his big hands were as callused as those of Gaius.

"Greetings, master," said Gaius, with no emotional response. Lamely he added, "Sir, the sun is coming out from the clouds. A good breeze, sir."

Young men in brown clothes like his own peered curiously from behind the great architect, and Gaius knew they were staring in admiration at *him*. Apprentice architects? he wondered . . .

"I approve of the white hair above your ears, Lacer, young tiger. How fares the Lacer pride these days? Dare I ask?" Apollodorus drew himself up to his Jovian height and peered sharply into Gaius' eyes.

"Sir . . ." Gaius wanted to try and state some important conclusions in simple terms. "Master, *you* taught me how to build the Tagus Bridge. Your knowledge, patience, generosity— If I live, I am obligated to earn a great deal of money for you. That will be my duty and privilege. I owe everything to you. Everything."

"Oh, suffering gods," the great man whispered. He took Gaius by the arm and at once the throngs opened a pathway. In they walked to grandeur such as Gaius had never seen before. He had no time to form even a hasty impression of the glorious vistas, for Apollodorus sat him down on a cushioned marble bench in a sequestered bay between two coral-hued marble columns, and stood in front of him.

"I have six apprentices working on this Basilica," said Apollodorus, in sour good humor. "One is an acoustical expert. His ideas may be feasible. Tubes in the pillars coming out in the friezes. An attempt to spread audibility, and if we conquer the echoes, we will celebrate—" He stopped. "My boy, listen to me: if a pupil cannot excel his teacher, then the instructor is an imbecile! Gaius, I have had several talks with the Emperor about you. I know not what his intentions are, but I do not think he plans to—" Apollodorus looked genuinely concerned— "Gaius, you are brave. Face whatever is coming as a Lacer would. And keep in mind: a genius built the Tagus Bridge. An architect is building this Basilica."

Gaius bowed his head and felt his master's rough fingers stroking his hair. Gratefully he kissed the hands of Apollodorus. Then he began hearing voices, tiny voices, but clear and distinct, coming from distances in the great Apse. One feminine voice from far across the immensity said, "But if my husband's awful relatives come from Belgica to live with us, we will have to put away all the silver-plate!"

Apollodorus let out a rollicking laugh and Gaius found that he, too, could laugh. Laughter, like love, healed and strengthened. "Come," said Apollodorus, "we have reserved places a few hundred feet away."

In an armchair next to Apollodorus in a shadowed space between two majestic columns of gray marble, Gaius could see the Dais and opposite high gallery without being seen. Somewhere flutes were playing and cymbals were clashing rhythmically. Again the words sounded in his mind: 'Byati the Bee-man' . . . People were everywhere and the soft chuff of sandals, bits of conversation ebbing and flowing, senators in white taking marble armchairs on each side of the purple-carpeted rostrum, a woman in red with a pet monkey being ushered to a chair up in the balcony.

The bronze Curule Chair stood in the center of the platform.

Soldiers of the Trajana behind the Seat of the Caesars, lances held straight in front. . . . a long, curved filigree ivory screen to the right of the Chair. . . . And embracing all and over all, the spectacular Apse itself, the Hall of Judgment. He turned to Apollo-dorus.

"Great master, your Basilica is a victorious song—a *carmen trium-phale.*"

"You should try your skills at poetry," smiled the elder. "Some of the wretched hexameters I have listened to this month—the Greeks said it all long ago and said it better. This auditorium is far from completed. The gilded bronze beams supporting the roof are permanent as are the first and second orders of columns, and the entablatures. The total length is six hundred and seven feet. Width, with the five naves, when finished, to be one hundred ninety-six feet, ten inches. Height, one hundred thirty-seven feet and ten inches. It will serve as a place of justice; for emancipation of slaves; and an exchange for merchants, my boy." He looked with proud affection at Gaius. He added, "What is your opinion of Verus Maturus?"

Instantly Gaius answered, "Sir, he is one of the truest and bravest of men. One of the best friends I, my wife, and Rufus will ever have."

"So I concluded," remarked Apollodorus. "Maturus frightened the career out of an experienced advocate who urged me to file suit against your brother, Commander Liscus. My erstwhile lawyer has retired to his farm to raise figs and pomegranates." He fathered a family of chuckles. "I trust your noble brother will not hold that ill-advised legal affair against me, Gaius?"

"Never, sir, never!" Gaius had answered as if a future loomed ahead for him and his brother.

Then a roar boomed from the galleries—and Gaius saw Turdo in a lionskin tunic and cross-laced black boots mount the rostrum and stand near the Curule Chair! The German waved to the bal-conies, he grinned, he flexed his muscles—

"Trajan's new personal bodyguard," explained Apollodorus. "Over too many cups the other evening, one of the Senators pro-posed the gladiator for membership in that high body. Occasionally a sound and original idea emanates from that source."

A blast of trumpets brought everyone on the main floor to his feet. People stood in the balconies.

A voice that seemed to come from the air over Gaius, announced: "The sword of Justice."

A soldier in plain field greens and steel armor and white-plumed helmet marched in slowly from the right, holding a glistening blade upright. He went up on the podium and stood behind the Curule Chair.

"The Most Honorable Excellency, Licinius Sura, Chief Counsellor to the Imperator."

In marched a dazzling figure in gold helmet crested with white, silver breastplate, gray kilt and scarlet cloak bordered with purple. On the platform he saluted the Curule Chair, then moved to the right and sat down in a cypress armchair. Sura smiled and then his angular face became soberly reflective.

Again the disembodied voice seemed to enfold Gaius and he heard:

"Plotina, the *Augusta*."

Gaius felt his pulses begin to pound as Empress Plotina moved in slowly from the left. Behind her came twenty-four ladies vivid in pinks, greens, yellows and amethystines. The imperial consort and her court of attendants swept deep curtsies to the Curule Chair and disappeared to take chairs behind the cutwork ivory screen at the right of the sacred Chair of the Caesars.

The pageantry was so colorful and impressive, that Gaius could not absorb it all. He heard the Priests of Jupiter announced, vaguely listened to a low voice performing a religious *formula* in Greek, and tried to watch eleven attending flamens as they paced the graceful measures of a slow dance around a tall bronze tripod of burning, fragrant oleoresins. He did not see a figure in purple on hands and knees, almost completely-hidden by a tall flamen with upraised arms, his flowing white garments spread around the man bent low before him.

Gaius looked away to try and assimilate his sensations, to find a root of meaning. When he turned towards the Dais again, the priests and human being in purple had gone.

An expectant hush settled down.

"*Senatus Populus Que Romanus!*" hailed the voice. "S. P. Q. R. The Roman Senate and the Roman People!"

Cheers and applause reverberated. When all sounds ceased the voice of the invisible announcer rose exultantly:

"NERVA TRAJAN IMPERATOR SEMPER AUGUSTUS! FIRST SOLDIER! FIRST CITIZEN! TRIBUNICIAN OF THE PEOPLE!"

The Basilica became a vast marble and granite shell of tumultuous screams and applause.

Gaius dropped down on one knee, accidentally stubbing the black kidskin encased toes of Apollodorus, who remained standing.

"Genius, you have iron bones," groaned his master, lifting him up. "Oh gods—all of this and bunions, too!"

Marcus Ulpius Trajan entered alone from the right.

He wore a purple toga, the hem ornamented with gold palm trees, maple leaves, oak leaves and pine cones. A narrow chaplet of fresh green laurel circled his short gray hair.

He was barefooted.

He bowed to the Senators, who were clapping in abandon, crying, "*Salve! Salve!* Hail, Roman! Hail, leader! *Ave! Ave!* Up to the Dais!"

On the platform, the Emperor knelt and kissed the Sword of Justice held horizontally by the soldier. Watching the rite closely, Turdo assisted his imperial master up, then stepped back to keep his eyes on the legionary with the sacred blade.

Trajan sat down in the Curule Chair.

At his back the Sword was raised vertically and flashed white-gold in light from the high clerestory windows.

After the acclaim ebbed into a low murmur, military bailiffs in side aisles pounded the red and yellow marble floor to assure complete silence.

At length Emperor Trajan began speaking in measured, full tones that Gaius heard clearly:

"We, Marcus Trajan, your leader, have solemnly sworn to use the Sword with justice—or have it used against us."

Behind him troops of the Trajana Legion thrust their lances forward and then to their right sides.

The great Apse became tensely silent.

Gaius lost all sense of reality. He was a phantom, he stood beside the strong and tender ghost of his father, Consul Julius Lacer. What was the shade of his sire whispering? Those enigmatic words he had heard in his dream last night: '*Byati the Bee-man*.' Irked at his mind's persistence, Gaius decided he had blended the bees on the blazons of the Trajana centurion with the image of Serapis and his sleeping consciousness had produced the mixed result which signified nothing. Then he looked at the Dais.

Lady Enna Gracchus and her husband, General Myron Frontinus, stood with bowed heads before the man in the Curule Chair. Both wore purple-hemmed white garments.

Gaius heard Trajan sternly admonish Enna and Frontinus for having shielded the tax thefts of Cornelius Classicus. The fact that the Imperium of Domitian had not suffered financial loss was not a point in their favor. The facts that both had written full confessions, awaited imperial judgment, and also aided Governor Verus Maturus unearth the looming Celt war in Spain, were points definitely in favor of complete exoneration, as was, also, the confiscation by Emperor Domitian, of Enna's fortune. But dishonesty, even well-intentioned, was dishonesty, and the Senate had decreed that Enna and Frontinus be punished.

The decree was exile for two years to their villa in Segovia, Spain, and loss of the freedom of Rome for that period. During that interval they could come and go freely in Segovia, write and receive letters, and control their properties. Nor were any people in Segovia to display at any time contempt of Enna and Frontinus. At the end of the two years they were to return to Rome and be fully pardoned by the Senate and Emperor.

Enna sagged in her husband's arms, her eyes turned towards the ivory screen concealing Empress Plotina. Then Enna and Frontinus bowed low to the Curule Chair and backed out of the Basilica.

Then Chieftain Luna Malendi marched in, wearing his ibex-horned gold helmet. He came to a halt before the Dais, and raised both hands in a blackcloak salute to Trajan.

A murmur swept the Apse and died away as Trajan spoke: "Noble Malendi, Prince and Commander-in-Chief of the military forces of the Arvacan nation under the Eagles, during our brief conference yesterday morning we clarified vital matters having to do with the causes for the war of your tribe against Romans at the imperial mines in the Sil basin. Further did we understand that correspondence between us, and mailscrolls intended for you from other individuals, was never delivered to your headquarters. There remains but one grave matter. Our special Senate commission, after careful study of your claim concur unanimously with us in that: you are awarded the custody of an individual you hold venerated as a god, and his handmaid. Know you this, too: Cornelius Classicus is now declared *civiliter mortuus*. The freedom of Rome is yours, gallant Chieftain. When you return to Spain, do so with our fatherly good wishes."

Malendi knelt. He removed his gold helmet and laid it on the gleaming floor below the Dais. Then he retrieved his headgear and backed across the floor and vanished in an archway. The galleries hummed with puzzlement, ladies languidly waved ostrich fans and whispered.

Gaius next was swept into drama intimately affecting him, watching with brotherly pride as Rufus stood before the platform and snapped a salute to Emperor Trajan. He was courteously greeted by the Princeps, and then by imperial mandate offered the legal right to the name of Julius Lacer, as eldest son of the deceased Consul Julius Lacer. This Rufus at once refused.

"Imperator, Sire," said Rufus, "I could never take from my brother the name which is his and to which he has brought great honor by his heroism and durable works for the State and his discovery of goldfields for the Imperium. Freely do I choose to keep the name bestowed on me by my adoptive father. I am Rufus Liscus."

Gaius was deeply affected by Rufus' statements.

"When this audience is over, I pray all of us can go to my Aventine villa and enjoy a repast," murmured Apollodorus. "Hold to courage, Gaius. The ways of Trajan are as unpredictable as they are just and magnificent. My bunions have gone to sleep; such is always a sign of impending good tidings for my household—and you, my boy, are of my *domus*."

"Father, I regret stepping on your feet," whispered Gaius, impulsively.

The older architect grimaced pleasantly.

Following came honor for Rufus: the Emperor walked down to face Rufus and ordered him to kneel.

"Citation," announced Trajan, reading from a scroll held by one of two soldiers attending him: " 'In recognition of your inspired defense of imperial goldfields in the Sil valley; in admiration of your unflagging devotion of your soldier's oath to defend Roman soil; with cognizance that, to accomplish your purpose you were forced to use any available fighters; and, in gratitude for a victory that could only have been won by a Roman, you are awarded the *Corona Ovalis*.' "

A legionary handed the Emperor a wreath of myrtle leaves which imperial hands placed on the bowed head of Rufus.

"The *Corona Ovalis*, Romans," said the ruler to the Hall of Judgment, "is awarded in special cases to commanding officers victorious in undeclared wars waged by aggressors not considered by the government to be actual enemies." Leaning over, Trajan kissed the forehead of Rufus and helped him stand again. Then the Emperor and his aides saluted. Rufus returned the gesture well, but his right arm shook slightly. And more recognition was coming.

"Rufus Liscus, eldest son of the demised Consul Julius Lacer, you are relieved of your rank of commander," continued Trajan. "You are promoted to the rank of General. You are assigned command of the VII Gemina Legion, with headquarters at *Legio* in northwest Spain." Smilingly the leader of the Romans took a gold fibula from an aide and pinned the brooch on the green cloak of General Rufus Liscus.

Gaius began clapping even as his brother saluted, wheeled about, and marched away to the opposite side of the room. Applause followed; attentive ladies asked who the handsome bearded General was, and how long had *he* been in Rome.

After a short interval Gaius suddenly saw Penelope emerge from under the long gallery and advance towards the platform. He wanted to spring out and be with her, but was restrained by the hard grasp of Apollodorus.

Penelope caused a sensation among the Senators. Her fresh beauty and simple apparel, in contrast to patrician dominas, wearing purple and green and orange wigs and loaded with jewels, caused several elderly *Patres* to raise flat smooth rounds of crystals to their failing eyes, thus bringing the fair Grecian girl into clear and magnified focus. Younger statesmen of acute vision and rapid blood inspected Penelope with frank appreciation.

Seeing it all, Gaius felt no loathing of the lawmakers. He would have despised them had they failed to admire his Penelope, for they were indicating approval of a woman of morality as well as beauty. Proudly he watched her sweep a low bow before the Curule Chair. Again came the clearly-audible voice of the Emperor, as if from over Gaius' head:

"Penelope, three years ago a small freedom fund was collected by soldiers on your behalf in New Carthage of Hither Spain. That money was safeguarded by the noble Myron Frontinus. When my Principate began after the death of my Sire, the Divine Nerva, those coins, with a report, arrived at the Treasury. With the consent of the Senate, we deposited the money in a fund to feed abandoned babies and young children, and had our Public Criers invite all Romans of generous hearts to add to that fund. There was and will be no coercion. We are glad to tell you that the fund has grown to great proportions. Many infants and small children are now fed and clothed because of it. What say you to that, Penelope?"

She looked delighted, blue eyes sparkling. "Sire—the money that heals," she replied, clearly.

The Emperor looked rather puzzled. "Money heals?"

Gravely she answered, "Great emperor, father, defender, the wailing innocents gathered up, borne to safety, warmth and ewers of milk—" her voice caught on the words as she labored on—"what greater healing than the lifesaving good of money, Sire?"

Thoughtfully the head with the green laurel wreath nodded. Then followed the remarkable statements of the Emperor that astounded Gaius:

"Penelope," continued Trajan, in a fatherly manner, "when you were taken captive in Greece several years ago, you were first sold to an aged Egyptian who was known among mariners and merchants as '*The Nameless One.*' Four trusted slaves to whom he gave ample incomes in his lifetime signed their names to all his business documents. Only those four knew the secret name of their benevolent master. It was '*Byati the Bee-man.*' "

Gaius heard himself gasp. His dream of last night. The beautiful Basilica seemed to move and sway before his eyes in rippling tints of coral and gray and yellow and red.

"The name, *Byati,* and its pictograph signifies 'Bee-man,' " continued the Emperor. "In Ancient Egypt it signified not only that but betokened Kings of Upper and Lower Egypt. Byati the Beeman claimed descent from Egypt's most splendid dynasties, predating the last Ptolemies and Cleopatra; before the land of the Nile was conquered by the Sacred Augustus. The aged Egyptian who purchased you was revered as both secret King of all Egypt and as an Avatar, by his devoted slave scribes."

A vast hush held the Hall of Judgment, every ear straining to catch the slow, audible voice of the Emperor. Penelope looked uplifted, hands crossed over her bodice. By now Gaius could follow the revelation with more poise, but Apollodorus kept a firm arm around his waist.

"Emperor, father, I never knew his name," said Penelope at last. "And so did my husband, Gaius, write to your noble freedman."

"This is a mystery," continued Trajan, solemnly. "Reports spread that Byati had died and been buried at sea. The financial officers of the prince, my predecessor, Domitian, at once tried to seize the property of 'The Nameless One.' Great was their terror when Byati himself greeted them and vowed by the most frightening oaths of ancient Egypt to shrivel their souls if they tried to confiscate his fortune. He asserted himself to be a man of two worlds. Moreover, he was seen by merchants and sailors in eastern ports until after we, Marcus Trajan, lawfully assumed the Principate."

An unearthly and peaceful enchantment held Gaius, and the grandeur of the Basilica appeared to fade and he was standing on a high mountain far above the griefs and hatreds and fears of humankind. He listened in rapture as the voice of the Emperor resumed:

"After we had become the First Soldier and First Citizen, a scroll arrived at our villa in Colonnia, Germany, signed by the four scribes of Byati the Beeman. His last will and testament was waiting to be ratified by us. Byati, so wrote his friends, had made his 'transition' to another plane of life three years previously. The rumors had been correct. All that remained now was for a Grecian captive girl to be located."

Trajan's serene black eyes rested on Penelope.

"And so, Penelope, one of my freedmen concluded you might be the Grecian girl, from descriptions of some of your experiences in letters from Gaius Julius Lacer to his patron, the great Apollodorus." He smiled. "The Empress as you may know, read all such scrolls and was aided by my freedmen, while I concentrated on empire defense."

Trajan came down from the Dais. Penelope sank to her knees. The Imperator lifted her up.

"Penelope, the Egyptian known as Byati the Bee-man willed you his fortune. Two cotton fields in Egypt. Two biremes. Necklaces of gold, jasper, carnelian and colored glass. Gold, silver and ivory statuettes of Egyptian divinities. Carved furniture inlaid with gold. A splendid collection of blue faience scarabs. Yellowed scrolls in ancient Koptic dealing with the mysteries of man's soul and its 'graduation' from life to life. A small and perfect villa outside Alexandria, exquisitely ornamented with gold lotus bas-reliefs, which Byati called 'The House of Transformation.' "

Gaius found himself staring at his master. Apollodorus was looking in astonishment at Penelope, and now the elder architect needed the help of his bondsman's arms to remain upright. Low hums of excited talk swept the vast Hall of Judgment until Emperor Trajan began speaking again.

"Penelope, the valuation of Byati's estate comes to fifty thousand goldworth. A sizeable fortune. Yet . . . the debts of your former master, Cornelius Classicus, precisely equal that amount."

Penelope was nodding. "Emperor, great Father, that, too, is good and just. You will use the estate of Byati the Avatar to pay the creditors of Governor Classicus?"

Trajan looked sadly at her. He nodded.

Then Chieftain Malendi came forward and knelt before the ruler. "You wish to speak, friend Malendi?"

"Aye, Imperator, father, leader. I have in reserve to aid my friend, Lacer the architect, fifty thousand goldworth. That I realized from the sale of a huge rough diamond which was found by Zamil, adopted son of the honorable Maturus. Yet had it not been for the presence of Lacer the architect when the gemstone was found, the honorable Zamil might have cast it aside as worthless. Yet, advised by Lacer, did Zamil turn in the valuable stone to Maturus of Farther Spain. That estimable dignitary insisted that the diamond was mine, according to mineral rights laws. Therefore, peerless Emperor, gladly do I offer the money from the sale of the stone to pay the debts of the deceased Cornelius Classicus."

Gaius leaned against Apollodorus. Fortunately the booted feet of Gaius did not assault his master's bunions again.

The senators had risen and were applauding.

Trajan nodded assent to the Chieftain's offer and embraced the blackcloak prince. Yet the weathered face of the Imperator still looked troubled. He continued to Penelope:

"We commend you for healing services rendered to troops in Spain during and after a battle in a canyon three years ago. And now our Consort, Plotina the *Augusta*, has words for you."

Whispers ebbed throughout the *auditorium* as stately Plotina, robed in plain white, attended by two patrician ladies in rich blue and scarlet, came from behind the ivory screen. One lady-in-waiting carried a white silk *palla* cloak. The Emperor stepped aside to watch as Plotina stood facing Penelope.

Penelope bowed deeply to the Empress.

"I, Plotina, place my hands on the shoulders of Penelope, my bondswoman." The *Augusta* smiled and frowned. "Penelope, you will kneel."

She went to her knees and her head was bowed.

Plotina lifted her up and turned her so that she faced the far distant end of the Basilica.

"Libera est!" declared the Empress. She guided Penelope around again to her original position. "Penelope, you are a citizen."

A lady-in-waiting draped the white silk cloak around Penelope.

"Penelope," said Plotina, "you are a patrician."

The spectators went wild with applause. Again senatorial crystal magnifiers were raised for old eyes to survey Penelope, the patrician and heiress. In the bay between two pillars, Apollodorus muttered, "Oh blameless gods, oh blameless gods. Gaius, help me to that bench, my son. I would sit for a while . . ."

Gaius was reviving his master with a goblet of chilled wine and water when a bailiff tapped his shoulder:

"Gaius Julius Lacer, come to the Dais."

It seemed he walked for miles across gleaming expanses of red and yellow marble, great forests of gray and coral, white and yellow columns towering on each side of him in the distance.

He stopped before the purple carpeted platform, his world constricted to a man of black eyes wearing a green laurel crown, a man in purple and gold seated on the Curule Chair. Behind the figure robed in the purple of absolute authority, a shining sword pointed to the high gilded bronze beams of the Basilica ceiling. Gaius' boots were raw and scuffed from rocks and sand and clay, his brown tunic and cloak were clean, but out of place in splendor such as this.

Awkwardly he bowed to the Emperor; he did not know what to do with his hands . . . his fingers had lives of their own and were clawing his cloak . . .

"Gaius Julius Lacer," said Trajan.

His mouth dry, no response came. He nodded.

Trajan arose and bowed to the senatorial ranks on each side of the imperial rostrum. "Will one of my wise advisors, Senator Pliny, of the special *jurisconsultant* commission on the complex affairs of Hither and Farther Spain present the considered decisions of that body?"

A man of slight frame, in a meticulously-draped toga, arose. Pliny began unrolling a long scroll, but did not read aloud from it. After scanning most of the parchment, he spoke informally:

"Sire, we of your commission unanimously recommend mercy for Gaius Julius Lacer, notwithstanding that he committed crimes against soldiers and masqueraded as an officer. He has admitted in writing to such felonies. Technically he should be executed. However . . ." Pliny smiled . . . "the noble Maturus brought to our attention an imperial rescript of the Sacred Augustus which establishes a precedent. During the reign of the Divine Augustus, a man was brought to trial for attacking legionaries in order to save the life of his father who was under villa arrest, yet against whom no charge had yet been made. The house catching on fire, the devoted son knocked four soldiers unconscious, rushed in and saved his sire. The son made no attempt to escape the consequences of his act, nor did his father defy the authority of Augustus. Later the father was vindicated of the charge laid against him by a false accuser.

"The Sacred Augustus Caesar was impressed by the son's devotion and did decree that, since the son's acts had not imperiled the State, nor been committed for the purpose of illicit gain of money or property, he should be publicly exonerated and all charges against him dropped. We of your special investigation commission, therefore, *communi consensus,* respectfully submit that charges against Gaius Julius Lacer on similar counts be dropped—with one exception. It being an offense of extreme gravity to attack a soldier for any reason—" Pliny coughed politely and went on— "we see no way to clear Lacer the architect fully unless he pays damages to those loyal troops he assaulted in saving his life and that of the lady he claims as his wife. If one-half the fortune of Penelope the patrician heiress be divided among the soldiers assaulted by Lacer the architect, we feel the purposes of Justice will be fulfilled." Pliny bobbed a bow to Trajan, carefully adjusted the folds of his toga and sat down while his colleagues applauded.

"Let it be so," said the Fathers, in unison. "Let it be so."

"We concur," said Trajan. "The grave matter of life or death for Gaius Julius Lacer now having been happily settled in favor of life, we come to another matter: the amount he owes to his patron, the great Apollodorus. Our foremost architect owes debts which he is struggling to pay. We do not feel that Gaius Julius Lacer should be freed of that obligation to our noble Apollodorus."

Gaius stood abjectly . . . Penelope's money, which was hers, was floating away in a golden tide, being taken from her, to pay for his life, pay for his debt to Apollodorus. *You fool!* his conscience objected. *You can earn money later! As long as you have your brain and eyes and strength, you can build more bridges, earn, give to Penelope what you earn—once you are free, you can earn money for her! Life and love is the wealth!* He began to smile, met the sympathetic eyes of Emperor Trajan in gratitude.

At last the Emperor spoke: "I do therefore decree that the fortune of Penelope, patrician, be lawfully confiscated to pay, one, damages to soldiers due to the actions of Lacer the architect; and, two, the balance of twenty-five thousand to go to his master, Apollodorus. Further do I decree that after such financial claims are paid that all charges against Lacer be dropped and expunged from the records." Trajan came down from the Dais and faced Gaius.

"We, Marcus Trajan, First Citizen, place our hands on your shoulders," said the ruler to Gaius. "You will now kneel."

Gaius sank down and was immediately raised by Trajan and turned to face the far end of the Basilica. Then the strong hands on his shoulders reversed his position so that he faced the Dais.

"Libero est!" proclaimed Emperor Trajan. "Gaius Julius Lacer, you are free. Gaius Julius Lacer, you are a citizen." He held out his hands and Rufus gave him a toga. Trajan wrapped the spotless white garment around Gaius and then said: "Gaius Julius Lacer, you are a patrician."

The deafening applause reminded Gaius of a tremendous waterfall plunging from a rocky height. Penelope at his right and Rufus at his left held his elbows. He looked down . . .

"Look up, man," said Trajan, simply. "Always hold yourself in high regard."

Gaius looked up.

"Gaius Julius Lacer," continued the Princeps, "we pronounce the marriage solemnized between you and Penelope of Icaria, to have been legal since the night it was solemnized in the cave village of Ioza. Therefore do we pronounce the son and daughter of that union to be the freeborn children of their noble parents."

To Gaius it was bright death, death the golden door that opened to a new beginning. Then Penelope's soft lips kissed his right cheek, Rufus kissed his left, Malendi pressed forward to grip him by the shoulders and step back. Apollodorus swept him into his hard embrace and turned away.

"There is more," Trajan resumed, his thin wide lips widening in a warm smile. "Gaius Julius Lacer, architect; builder; geologist; aristocrat: we extend our heartfelt gratitude and that of the Senate and People and the *Augusta* to you for the discovery of Gold Valley in northern Spain. We praise your reasons for witholding that knowledge until the times were propitious. Gold Valley and nearby territory is rich in precious gold ore, silver, and other needed metals. Too much gold has gone out of the Empire in past Imperiums. The wealth of Gold Valley will replace part of those depleted resources."

Loud applause burst out again. The senators arose in a body and clapped.

"Lacer, noble Roman, hear you this," the Emperor continued. "According to law patricians must own property of fixed minimum value. But many deserving and afflicted older patricians are ahead of you—the sick, the maimed, the starving surviving sons of honorable patricians of wealth slain by one of my predecessors. We must heal their wounds first, as best we can. We must give grave thought to the welfare of all classes of people, the free and the enslaved. We therefore ask that you be patient until the *Fiscus* can award you and your lady your just due of property valued at thirty thousand goldworth."

Gaius felt more composed. "Sire, Father," he said, "patience, too, is wealth."

"Wisdom," smiled the ruler. "Meanwhile the Treasury will supply you a reasonable monthly allowance and in addition you will receive allotments of grain, meat, oil, clothing and such other necessities for yourself and family." He beamed paternally. "And yet more to come, noble friend. We, your Emperor, need your great skills.

"We ask," said Emperor Trajan. "We do not command. We ask: will you resume your work on projects we have in mind?"

New work! Gaius was thrilled. Another bridge? Aqueduct? A temple? Roads? Triumphal Arch?

"Sire," he replied, "command me!" He felt the firm and cordial grasp of imperial hands on his arms—and in that exalted moment he and Emperor Marcus Ulpius Trajan were brothers, united not by the accidental kinship of blood but in the dedicated and greater bond of two men, each working in his way, for the security and prosperity of the empire. Gaius looked into the steadfast black eyes of the sovereign and realized (as if for the first time) that the high morality, bravery, unselfishness and vigilance of the man in purple formed true human greatness. He was looking at greatness, and felt it touching him.

Then he was talking eagerly to Trajan:

"Sire—the men and I—we built—even before we sank the first pier, I knew we were building the Tagus Bridge for you. It is still not finished, Sire. Let me build a Triumphal Arch in centerbridge for you? No adornment. Simple and soaring. Firm and victorious." Encouraged by a gracious smile from the Emperor, he pressed on,

"And some day, Sire, permit me to build a small temple at my expense, a shrine to the gods of Rome, on a hill overlooking your Tagus Bridge?"

The voices of the senators chorused: "Let it be so! Let it be done! Let noble Lacer finish the Tagus Bridge in honor of our leader, Trajan!"

Cascades of applause and shouts of approval dinned from the floor and galleries of the Basilica until at last military bailiffs pounded their oak staves for silence.

Then the Emperor said, "Noble Roman, builder, friend, know this: the inscription for the Tagus Bridge shall read: THIS BRIDGE GREAT LACER BUILT WITH WONDROUS ART TO STAND UNMOVED THROUGH ALL ETERNITY."

Gaius bowed his head. He felt tears in his eyes.

"Look up, man," said Trajan. "Always look up."

He nodded and again gazed into the serene and watchful eyes of Trajan.

"Before you finish the Tagus Bridge, friend," said the ruler, "we hope that you will plan and start construction on a canal between the Nile and the Red Sea. Old waterways are filled with silt and hardly navigable."

"A canal . . ." Gaius turned and caught a wise and approving smile from Apollodorus who was standing near by. "A canal—" Already he was planning it, surveying the terrain, seeing men at work— A canal to be born. If he had elephants—the noble big beasts to do the work animals could easily do, men performing work men could do.

"Sire," said Gaius, "if I had elephants . . . ?"

"Elephants, friend? How many do you wish?"

Gaius decided to ask for two—at the most, four—of the splendid pachyderms to haul the drag-carts of excavated rocks and soil . . . better to request a few and succeed, than petition for a whole herd and be regretfully refused. Building was going on all over the empire— Then to his embarrassment he felt himself grinning.

"Share the jest, friend?" Trajan invited.

"Sire," said Gaius, "when I needed elephants for heavy work at the Tagus site, I couldn't obtain them. Later, at the Sil mines, I decided to try and get the big beasts by writing specifically that I did not need them. That was how matters went in those days, sir."

"And did my predecessor send you the massive animals after all?"

"No, sir. I didn't get them that time, either. But I did receive two Archimedes machines, Sire."

The Emperor laughed. "Two left boots," he said.

The galleries applauded loudly.

Gaius looked up. Through a clerestory window Olympian sunlight sloped downward, encircling him in an aura of gold.

THE END

About the Author

Florence Augusta Seward is a descendant of the Secretary of State in Abraham Lincoln's Cabinet, William Henry Seward. This relationship inspired her first story, which has since appeared in three anthologies and in textbooks for children. She has also written other adventure tales for children, has been a newspaper feature writer and reporter, radio script author, and advertising copy writer.